"[Roberts] is pe...
sprawl of...
—*Pub...*

Praise for the novels of John Maddox Roberts

THE SEVEN HILLS

"Mastering the details of later republican Roman life, Roberts builds a very convincing alternate Rome, full of intriguing characters who pose readers the fun of figuring out their real-life counterparts."   —*Booklist*

HANNIBAL'S CHILDREN

"What would have happened if Hannibal had received the reinforcements necessary for him to topple the Roman Empire? That fascinating 'what if' is the central premise of Roberts's latest historical novel . . . first-rate . . . intriguing."   —*Publishers Weekly*

"Exciting, provocative, and entertaining . . . This is far and away the best book I've read by Roberts."
          —*Science Fiction Chronicle*

"John Maddox Roberts, the author of the historical series SPQR, has written a fascinating alternate history novel in which the exiled Romans conquer the land around the Danube River. The reader is immersed in the culture of Rome as seen through the eyes of Tribune commander Marcus Scipio."   —*Midwest Book Review*

continued . . .

"A well-researched and vivid alternate history of the rivalry between Rome and Carthage."   —*Library Journal*

"Endlessly fascinating."   —*Locus*

THE SPQR NOVELS

"Wonderful . . . All the wild imaginative stimulation of the best detective fiction."
            —Marion Zimmer Bradley, author of *The Mists of Avalon*

"Roberts deftly re-creates his ancient world, constantly reminding the reader that it was a cruel and violent place where people thought and acted a lot differently from us. A double-edged solution perfectly caps a highly entertaining story."   —*Publishers Weekly*

THE SEVEN HILLS

JOHN MADDOX ROBERTS

ACE BOOKS, NEW YORK

THE BERKLEY PUBLISHING GROUP
Published by the Penguin Group
Penguin Group (USA) Inc.
375 Hudson Street, New York, New York 10014, USA
Penguin Group (Canada), 90 Eglinton Avenue East, Suite 700, Toronto, Ontario M4P 2Y3, Canada
(a division of Pearson Penguin Canada Inc.)
Penguin Books Ltd., 80 Strand, London WC2R 0RL, England
Penguin Group Ireland, 25 St. Stephen's Green, Dublin 2, Ireland (a division of Penguin Books Ltd.)
Penguin Group (Australia), 250 Camberwell Road, Camberwell, Victoria 3124, Australia
(a division of Pearson Australia Group Pty. Ltd.)
Penguin Books India Pvt. Ltd., 11 Community Centre, Panchsheel Park, New Delhi—110 017, India
Penguin Group (NZ), Cnr. Airborne and Rosedale Roads, Albany, Auckland 1310, New Zealand
(a division of Pearson New Zealand Ltd.)
Penguin Books (South Africa) (Pty.) Ltd., 24 Sturdee Avenue, Rosebank, Johannesburg 2196,
South Africa

Penguin Books Ltd., Registered Offices: 80 Strand, London WC2R 0RL, England

This is a work of fiction. Names, characters, places, and incidents either are the product of the author's imagination or are used fictitiously, and any resemblance to actual persons, living or dead, business establishments, events, or locales is entirely coincidental. The publisher does not have any control over and does not assume any responsibility for author or third-party websites or their content.

THE SEVEN HILLS

An Ace Book / published by arrangement with the author

PRINTING HISTORY
Ace hardcover edition / March 2005
Ace mass market edition / February 2006

Copyright © 2005 by John Maddox Roberts.
Cover art by Scott Grimando.
Cover design by Rita Frangie.
Interior text design by Kristin del Rosario.

ISBN: 0-441-01380-5

ACE
Ace Books are published by The Berkley Publishing Group,
a division of Penguin Group (USA) Inc.,
375 Hudson Street, New York, New York 10014.
ACE and the "A" design are trademarks belonging to Penguin Group (USA) Inc.

PRINTED IN THE UNITED STATES OF AMERICA

10 9 8 7 6 5 4 3 2 1

CHAPTER ONE

"NOTHING LIKE IT HAS EVER HAPPENED BEFORE," Zeno said. He drew in a deep breath, savoring the smell of fertile land. That was Italy over there, long a Carthaginian tributary and now—now it was something else.

"Nothing like what?" Izates wanted to know.

Zeno smiled. His friend was a Cynic and practiced contrariness for its own sake. "You know very well. Never before has a nation vanished, only to reappear more than a hundred years later." The tubby merchantman heeled slightly to a shift in the wind, and Zeno took hold of a stay without noticing the change. He was a great traveler and as used to the motions of a ship as any sailor.

"These Romans never vanished," Izates said. "They just relocated. Now they have come back. There is nothing new in it. My own ancestors were sent into captivity by the Babylonians, then were returned to their homeland by Cyrus the Persian." He had been born a Jew, but had fallen in love with Greek philosophy as a boy and now could almost pass for a native Hellene.

"This is different," Zeno insisted. "The Romans were banished by Hannibal the Great, but they have returned on their own, at the bidding of their gods. Their legions poured into Italy and took the whole peninsula like the thunderbolt of Zeus. The whole nation has followed and even now the capital is being restored."

Izates made a rude noise with his lips. "What of it? Italy has been so tame for so long that there were scarcely any Carthaginian troops anywhere on the peninsula and all the nearest garrisons had been stripped for Hamilcar's war with Egypt. A few hundred Cretan bowmen could have taken Italy. Holding it may prove to be another matter entirely."

"You will see. This is something unprecedented. This is history in the making and I must be there as it unfolds."

"You would be the Herodotus of the new Rome?" He shook his shaggy, ill-kempt head. "No, Herodotus took the whole of history for his theme. You will be the new Thucydides. He was wise enough to confine his work to a single, narrow subject. I fear that your book will be a very short one."

"Is there no end to your sourness?" Still holding the stay, Zeno jumped onto a handrail as if to urge the ship shoreward with his own body.

Izates pondered the question. "If so, I've never found it."

Zeno was from Athens and he had the classic look common to the well-born men of that fabled city. His features were cameo-cut, his physique slender but athletic. In contrast to his scruffy companion, his tawny hair and short beard were neatly trimmed, his simple clothing immaculate. He yearned to be a historian of stature, but had thought that all the worthy themes had already been exhausted. Who needed yet another account of the wars of Athens and Sparta, or the career of Alexander? Of barbarian lands, the only ones worth study were Persia and Egypt and those, too, had been done to death.

He sensed in the return of Rome to the great stage of history a subject worthy of a great work, and he was determined to be first to record their deeds.

"What are these Romans, anyhow?" Izates groused. "The city was founded by a pack of bandits, by all accounts. They became farmers and dominated this obscure peninsula for a while and then lost a war to Carthage. What is so great about that?"

Zeno shaded his eyes and gazed northward along the coast. The skipper had said they would raise Brundisium by midday. "What were Odysseus and Achilles and the rest but a pack of bandits and pirates? Nobody's ancestry is very savory if you look back far enough. The Romans were distinguished above all by their republican form of government and their extraordinary concept of military duty. From what I've been able to learn, they retained these things during their exile in the north and may even have strengthened them."

It had not been easy learning about the land called Roma Noricum, where the exiles had carved an empire from a savage wilderness, subduing its Celtic and Germanic inhabitants and expanding their territory with every year. For generations, a few Greek merchant families had monopolized trade with the Romans and had kept most of their knowledge secret to protect their commerce from competition. Most Greeks were not even aware that the Romans still existed. Yet when they had poured into Italy a few months before, it had been in such numbers that they must have prospered mightily during their exile. Surely, Zeno

thought, these must be the most remarkable people in the
world. And he, Zeno of Athens, would be their chronicler.

That afternoon they rounded the mole and entered the
harbor of Brundisium. In the ancient Messapian dialect
the name meant "stag's head," and was supposed to refer to
the shape of the harbor. Zeno could detect no such resemblance and surmised that silting had altered the form of
the little bay. In any case he was far more interested in the
men who occupied the broad plaza adjoining the docks.
He saw the glitter of arms among them and knew that
these must be Romans.

"These are the legionaries?" Izates said as the merchantman worked its way up to a stone wharf. "They don't look
like much."

Indeed they were a disappointment at first sight. Their
equipment had none of the dash and beauty so esteemed by
Greek soldiers. Most wore shirts of mail: a form of armor invented by the Gauls, consisting of thousands of interlinked
iron rings. It was tough and as flexible as cloth, but made a
baggy, almost shapeless garment utterly lacking in grace.
Their helmets were simple pots of iron or bronze with wide
neck guards and pendant cheek plates, and plain crests dis-
tinguishing the officers. Their large, oval shields were
painted with simple devices. Each man wore a short sword
belted at his waist and carried a heavy javelin no taller than
the man himself.

Two men strode down the wharf to meet the ship, and
these were clearly higher ranking than the others. One wore
an old-fashioned bronze cuirass embossed with stylized
muscles, the other a shirt of shimmering scales overlaid
with a harness of colorful leather straps studded with silver
medallions. Both wore short swords in ornate scabbards.
Neither bore shield or helmet. The man in the scale shirt

carried a large wooden tablet and had a bronze stylus tucked behind his ear. The skipper stepped ashore to meet them.

"What ship?" asked the man in bronze.

"*Calypso,* out of Dyrrhachium with a cargo of copper ingots. I am Leander of Corcyra, shipmaster."

"You'll find a market here, Leander," said the bronze man as the scaled one scratched notes with his stylus on the tablet's wax-lined inner surface. "The bronze foundries of Italy are busy as never before."

"So I heard," said the shipmaster. "Everyone with metal to sell is headed this way."

"You're the first to reach Brundisium, so you'll get the best price." The man spoke passable Greek, but the dialect was so antiquated Zeno guessed that the Romans learned their Greek from the works of Homer and other ancient authors.

"I have two passengers," Leander informed the two. "Zeno, from Athens, and Izates, from Alexandria."

The Romans glanced at them. "Are you selling anything?" the bronze one asked.

Izates laughed and Zeno bristled. "We aren't merchants!" Zeno told them.

"On official business?"

"We are philosophers," said Zeno. "We want to see Rome."

The scaled one closed his tablet, replaced the stylus behind his ear and jerked a thumb backward, over his shoulder. "Take the wide avenue to the city gate and you'll find two pillars. They mark the southern end of the Via Appia. Start walking and it'll take you to Rome in a few days." His Greek was more strongly accented than the other's. "Now," he said to the skipper, "let's have a look at that cargo and we'll clear you to start unloading."

"That's all?" Zeno said, dumbfounded. "You don't want to see our letters of introduction?"

"What for?" asked the bronze one. "You want to see Rome? Go to Rome. We won't stop you."

"But we could be spies!" Zeno protested.

The two Romans looked at each other as if they had never heard of such an idea. "What if you were?" said the bronze one. "We're not hiding anything." He looked to the other one. "Are we hiding anything?"

The man shrugged his scaled shoulders. "Not that I heard. We've retaken Italy right out in the open. And we're invading Sicily, last I heard. Nothing secret about it." He turned to Zeno. "Go ahead, look all you want." They returned their attention to the ship, having lost all interest in the two Greeks.

"Astonishing!" said Zeno as the two, their bags shouldered, walked up the wharf toward the town. "They aren't concerned about spies. Any petty tyrant in the world would require that we register with the authorities, post bonds, account for our activities and that sort of thing. These Romans seem to fear nothing."

Izates snorted. "Only idiots have no fear, and those two didn't strike me as fools. They are entirely too disingenuous. They put on a show of simplicity to gull strangers. Any soldier knows the value of military intelligence, and these men are soldiers even if they are nothing else."

They came to the plaza and stood for a while watching the soldiers, many of whom were engaged in complex drill. All over the waterfront men, apparently locals, were toiling at the restoration of buildings long neglected by the Carthaginian authorities. The city had declined after the expulsion of the Romans, and the Carthaginians had established their colonial capital at Tarentum, on the southern end of the peninsula.

Zeno looked back and forth from the native Italians to the Roman soldiers. "Do you notice something odd here?"

Izates nodded. "Some of those legionaries don't have a drop of Italian blood in them. They're not Romans at all."

The first thing that had struck both men after the plainness of their equipment was how many of the legionaries were tall men with fair hair and ruddy complexions.

"I have never traveled in the north," Zeno said, "but I've seen a good many Gallic and German slaves, and that is what these men look like. But they don't seem to be foreign mercenaries. They serve in the ranks right alongside the men who are plainly of Italian ancestry." He remembered things he had read of the old Romans, how they had conquered other Italian peoples, rewarding their good behavior with partial citizenship, eventually granting them full citizenship and immunity from tribute and taxation. In this way Rome grew stronger, for only citizens could serve in the legions. He spoke of this to his friend.

"What an odd idea," Izates said. "If I moved to Athens, not only would I not be a citizen, but my descendants five hundred years from now would not be citizens, either. They would be foreigners, just like me."

Zeno nodded. "I believe our exclusivity has been a great folly. These people are worthy of study for their political institutions alone."

They walked into the city in search of accommodations. It was far too late in the day to begin their land journey, and there were still arrangements to be made. They would need a pack animal, a servant or two, some traveling supplies. As they looked for an inn, they studied the place.

The locals had the half-stunned look common to people recently conquered, although nobody seemed to be mistreating them. Whole gangs had been impressed to clean the city, rebuild walls and restore temples, paint and plaster. Clearly, the Romans intended to transform Brundisium into a major port city once more.

The legionaries were everywhere. Those off-duty still retained their swords, their military belts and boots. Zeno found the latter accoutrements worthy of note. They were stoutly made of heavy leather, their thick soles densely studded with hobnails. He drew Izates' attention to these and said they must be an innovation as important as any weapon on the battlefield.

"I see no innovation," said the Cynic. "Your own Athenian general Iphicrates issued his men similar boots almost three hundred years ago. Rather, these Romans seem to be adept at adopting things invented by other peoples. Look at them! The helmets and shirts of mail are Gallic. Those short swords, unless I am mistaken, are of Spanish origin. The boots they probably got when they fought King Pyrrhus of Epirus one hundred and seventy-odd years back. Everything they have is Greek, Celtic or plundered from some other Italian race."

"And isn't that genius of a sort?" Zeno said. "What other people have shown the discernment to adopt only the best and most useful from other cultures?"

"What sophistry! You astound even me, and I had thought myself beyond shock. Surely you cannot believe this cultural acquisitiveness to be some sort of virtue! I grant you that these days everyone wants to be Greek, and that in this passion for all things Greek they happily adopt the worst aspects of the culture while ignoring the best. But at least those people look to the very light of the world as the only culture worthy of imitation, but look at these Romans. Some of them are wearing trousers!"

Indeed it was a somewhat shocking sight. Many of the soldiers wore, instead of civilized tunics, trousers fitting tightly to the knee.

"I suppose they are practical garments in the cold north," Zeno said. "And the same with those cloaks. The Romans used to wear red battle cloaks, like the Spartans." At least half of the soldiers wore woolen cloaks of deep, forest green, crosshatched with black lines. Zeno knew this to be another Celtic item.

"They have been transforming themselves into barbarians up there," Izates asserted. "No, they were barbarians in the first place. They have become even more primitive barbarians."

"They certainly haven't become any less warlike in the process. Come on, let's find some lodgings."

Like any other port city, Brundisium had no shortage of inns. Near the old theater they located one that was newer and cleaner than the others, and here they established themselves for the evening. At dinner they quizzed the innkeeper about the town's new masters.

"They came out of nowhere," the man told them. "The legion came marching down the Via Appia before we even had word of their coming. There had been rumors that the Romans had returned to Italy and were restoring their old capital, but nobody thought they could move so fast, or in such strength."

"What did the Carthaginians do?" Zeno asked.

The man shrugged. He was a typical southern Italian, olive-skinned with black hair, pudgy in distinct contrast to the lean, soldierly Romans. "There were hardly any Carthaginians here. Just a customs agent and a couple of coast guard ships in the harbor. Even before the shofet's Egyptian war there wasn't much Carthaginian presence in the area."

"They just walked in without a fight?" Izates asked.

"What was anyone going to do?" the landlord said. "Who is going to stop six thousand armed men? The city guard?" He laughed ruefully. "They act like the lords of the earth, and just now no one is going to dispute it with them."

Later Zeno quizzed the girl who brought them their food and wine. She was a pretty creature of about sixteen and spoke the sailor's Greek common to every port town.

"The Roman soldiers are real men," she said in a low voice, glancing about to make sure she was not overheard. "Not like the males around here. All the men here complain that the Romans treat them with contempt, but why shouldn't they, is what I ask. Carthage has run this place for so long that everyone's forgotten how to fight. Hardly a man in Italy has ever picked up a sword."

She brushed her coarse hair back from her face. "I'll tell you something else: There was no looting or rape or any other sort of misbehavior, not at all like when the shofet's hired marines come to town. The Romans took over the running of the place and quartered their troops, but they don't pick up a leek that they don't pay for and they leave even the slave girls and boys strictly alone. They just visit the working girls and the lupanars and they pay for the service."

Even as the girl spoke, a group of off-duty soldiers walked in and took a table. The girl went to serve them, smiling brightly. Zeno noted that they did not swagger or speak loudly, but there was nothing diffident in their bearing. They seemed to have perfect self-assurance. They spoke to the girl in halting, broken Greek and spoke among themselves in a language Zeno supposed must be Latin. It lacked the beautiful liquidity of Greek, but he found its hard-edged sound pleasing. Like everything else about the Romans, even the language sounded soldierly.

"Those look like dangerous men," Izates said, his habitual mockery subdued for once. "They don't have to strut like bullies. They radiate menace as the sun radiates light."

"Very true," Zeno said. He had seen soldiers in many lands, but none like these, who seemed to have been whelped by the very dam of war itself. Something caused the soldiers to laugh, and the sound made both men start slightly.

If the human voice can sound like swords clashing against shields, Zeno thought, *it is in this Roman laugh.*

THE NEXT MORNING THEY SET OFF ALONG THE VIA Appia, leading a donkey laden with their belongings and provisions. The countryside was beautiful and they passed through well-cultivated fields where sheep and cattle grazed amid a landscape that seemed taken from a pastoral poem. Most impressive, though, was the road itself. Although built more than a hundred years before, it was as solid and perfect as upon the day of its completion. The pavement was of cut stone subtly sloped to drain water. It was perfectly straight and level, with bridges over gorges, viaducts over marshy ground and, every few miles, way stations where travelers could rest and messengers could get fresh mounts. These latter were in the process of restoration and remanning by the Romans.

"What a marvelous road!" Zeno said after they had been on it for most of the morning. "There is nothing like it anywhere else in the world. Everywhere else roads are just laid atop the ground if they are paved at all. This is more like the top of a buried wall."

"They learned the art from the Etruscans," Izates said.

Once they had to step off the road as a military detachment marched past, every man in step as if the army were a single animal. Each man carried his own equipment and the army seemed to have only a minimum of noncombatant slaves to manage its heavy gear and animals. Even the slaves wore uniform and marched under military discipline.

"We should have stayed at sea," Izates groused when they stopped at noon. "We could have set ashore within a few miles of Rome instead of walking half the length of Italy."

"That would have meant sailing between Italy and Sicily. Those waters are dangerous now that Rome and Carthage are fighting over the island."

"An unsafe voyage is quicker and easier than this trudging, no matter how fine the road."

Zeno grinned at him. "It is beneath a philosopher's dignity to notice such things."

Izates made another of his rude noises. "I'm a Cynic, not a Stoic."

They could see that the countryside had been arranged in the common Carthaginian style, cut into huge plantations with few farmhouses but many slave barracks. Now, though, numerous surveying teams were at work, apparently dividing the huge tracts into smaller plots.

"Do you think they intend to restore peasant cultivation?" Zeno said.

"If they do, they've a job ahead of them," Izates observed. "There will be endless squabbling over who owns what. And what about the people who own the land now? It won't just be dispossessed Carthaginians."

"We shall see if their lawyers are as formidable as their soldiers."

The road took them first to Tarentum, only two days' travel from Brundisium, a journey that would have taken them at least four on the goat-path roads of Greece. Tarentum had been the Carthaginian capital, heavily fortified, its citadel located on a spit of land jutting into the harbor. Yet the Romans had taken it bloodlessly, moving so swiftly that the lethargic authorities scarcely knew that they had arrived.

Here the Romans had shown they had craft and guile as well as iron discipline, for they had spoken mildly of trade and diplomatic relations while their legions poured through the mountain passes. They had agreed to hire out as mercenaries (they had insisted on calling themselves allies) for Hamilcar's Egyptian war and thus had insinuated their soldiers into the city. Soon they were in control of the gates and the city was theirs.

Interesting as this was, the two paused only long enough to speak with some citizens and take notes, then they proceeded north. The next major town was Venusia, then Beneventum, then splendid Capua, once capital of beautiful Campania. Here they rested for a few days and admired the graceful town. Campania had the richest farmland in Italy and it swarmed with Roman merchants and officials overseeing the change of ownership. Here they hired a freedman fluent in both Greek and Latin to teach them the rudiments of the Roman language.

Zeno found the language far easier to learn than Persian, its many cognate words proving it to be related to Greek, unlike Syrian or Egyptian or Phoenician. Predictably, Izates grumbled at learning a "barbarian" language, but he learned anyway. A man who grew up on Aramaic and Hebrew, he said, should find a simple-minded language like Latin to be child's play.

The freedman was named Gorgas, and he proved to have an adventurous past. As a boy he had served a Greek merchant who traded in Noricum. In that land he was sold to a Roman family, with whom he lived for a number of years, employed as a clerk. His master, a military tribune, had taken him along on the trek to Italy. The tribune had fallen sick of the illness common to the marshy parts of Italy and had freed Gorgas in his will.

"My legal name is now Marcus Fulvius Bambalio, same as my former master's," he had explained, "but that's for legal documents and my tombstone. I still go by Gorgas."

They engaged Gorgas to accompany them to Rome and teach them along the way. For the much-traveled former slave this was a mere outing. Along the way Zeno questioned him about Noricum, but the man could not tell him much.

"I worked on a big estate. What I heard was mostly slave gossip. The master's family were important, but not of the highest rank. They were what the Romans call equites. That means they were rich but none of them had ever held office as high as praetor."

"Equites," Zeno said. "The word means 'horseman,' doesn't it?"

"Exactly. Once, it meant someone wealthy enough to bring his own horse and serve in the cavalry when the army was called up. Now it's just a property assessment. But near as I understand it, the equites are as important as the senators in a lot of ways. My master's family served in the lower offices, what they call quaestors and other things. They aren't judges but they form the juries, and a lot of the junior officers in the legions are equites."

"Some of the Greek cities had similar arrangements," Zeno observed to Izates.

"Why does that not surprise me?" Izates said.

"Your manumission," Zeno said, "is that common among Romans?"

"Very. What happened to me is what they call a 'testamentary manumission.' That means being freed in a will. Important Romans will free hundreds of slaves in a will, just to show off how important they are. But Romans free slaves all the time. In fact, only really stupid and unskilled people stay slaves for life. And when we're freed, we have almost full citizenship rights. We just can't hold public office. But our sons can, as long as they weren't born while we were in service."

"Amazing," Zeno said.

Izates cleared his throat. "Actually, my own people have such a custom. Bond servitude is for only seven years. After that, the slave must be freed unless he chooses to remain in bondage."

"I'll bet your freed bondservants don't have full citizen rights," Gorgas said.

Izates shrugged. "Few have that anyway."

"Tell me about Roman citizenship," Zeno said.

In this way they passed their journey from Capua to Rome.

THE CITY LAY IN A BEND OF THE RIVER TIBER. IT WAS not a great river, and the city itself would not have been impressive had it not been for the frenetic level of activity to be seen everywhere. On a field northwest of the city walls troops drilled to the snarl of trumpets. The sounds of hammer, saw and chisel could be heard in all directions. Outside the walls large farmhouses were under construction. Slave gangs worked on roads, bridges and aqueducts.

From miles away the travelers could see the roofs of the temples on the hill called the Capitol. Their fresh gilding gleamed in the sunlight, and as the men drew nearer they saw that the temples had all been newly painted and their stonework restored. The road was lined with tombs, and these, too, had been carefully restored and planted all around with new trees and shrubs.

"They restored the temples and the tombs first," Zeno noted. "The Romans were a famously pious people."

"It's not much of a town," Izates said.

"Your Alexandria sets a high standard. In Athens, only the Acropolis is truly beautiful. So it is here. It looks as if they took pains to embellish their public places and let the rest of the city sprawl in all directions with no planning. But look at the walls."

"What about them?"

"They have been restored; you can see the new stonework. But they have made no effort to strengthen them further. They haven't been raised; there are no new defensive towers, no protective ditch dug, nothing."

"An odd oversight for people who can expect a Carthaginian offensive at any moment. The army Hamilcar sent to Egypt is said to be huge, and it must be on its way to Italy by now."

"I don't think it was an oversight," Zeno said. "I heard that their capital in Noricum has no wall at all. Like the Spartans, the Romans believed that a wall would breed a cautious, defensive attitude. They preferred to entrust their safety to the perfection of their legions. They've restored this wall because it is ancient and was built by one of their kings before Rome became a republic."

"Like these Romans, the old Spartans were arrogant. Where are the Spartans now? The city is nothing and the men are the hirelings of others because they know no art save soldiering."

"Gorgas," Zeno said, "did you spend much time in Rome after you came south?"

"Just a few days. They were still dredging out the Forum. It had reverted to the marsh it once was. There is a vast drain under there, the Cloaca Maxima. It was built by another old king. They were getting it unplugged when my master took me down to Tarentum. Half the city was still in ruins. Old Hannibal's men did a thorough job of wrecking the place and after that the people who moved in grazed their cattle and sheep in the public places."

"Who moved in?" Zeno asked.

"After the Romans were exiled there were still plenty of Italians who had never really reconciled themselves to Roman rule: Campanians, Lucanians, Samnites, Etruscans and so forth. They brought their livestock and cut up the old estates into small farms. The big plantations are mainly to the south of here."

"Where are those people now?" Izates wanted to know.

Gorgas shrugged. "Pushed out. Some have hired on as labor. Some will probably be tenant farmers for the big Roman landlords. The Romans don't think the descendants of the people who wouldn't go north with the exile to be worthy of citizenship. There is talk that some will be drafted into the navy Rome is going to build. That way they may in time earn at least partial citizenship."

They entered the city through a gate whose stonework was ancient, but its wooden doors were so new that the timbers still oozed sap and their ironwork was still bright. Traffic in and out was brisk, but there were no guards to accost them or demand their business.

"This is the Capena Gate," Gorgas told them.

They passed beneath two aqueducts that ran parallel to the city wall and thence into a district of low houses. Within a few minutes they came to a valley dominated by an immense structure from which came the sound of intense hammering. The end they came to was rounded and the rest of it stretched straight northwest for an unbelievable distance.

"No need to tell us what this is," Zeno said. "This has to be the Great Circus." The histories he had read all mentioned the Romans' passion for chariot races and the unprecedentedly huge structure they had erected for the purpose. It was built primarily of wood, and wagonload after wagonload of lumber stretched in a chain from the nearby river wharfs. Slaves were busily painting away with brushes the size of brooms.

"The Romans have a taste for the gaudy and garish," Izates said. "When this monstrosity is finished, it will serve as a new standard for tastelessness."

"Considering the many oversized monuments of Alexandria," Zeno said, "that seems unwarranted."

"I confess that my native city is addicted to grotesque grandiosity. The successors of Alexander sought to cover their backwoods origins with a surfeit of marble and gilding. But at least they had the decency to employ Greek artists and architects who possessed a modicum of restraint."

Zeno had visited Alexandria more than once and had been able to detect no sense of restraint in the place, but he let it pass. He was more impressed by the Romans' energy than by their taste, anyway.

The city was built upon a series of low, rolling hills so that it was difficult to get much sense of it. No sight line extended more than a few hundred yards, and even that was rare. It did not help that the streets were for the most part twisting and narrow. Apparently, the plan for rebuilding

Rome did not include improving its layout. The Romans seemed determined to restore their city precisely to its state before Hannibal destroyed it.

The travelers made their way up one of the better streets, stepping aside for wagons of building material and tool-bearing slave gangs the whole way, until they entered a long, broad public space full of monuments and surrounded by buildings of considerable dignity. Its northern extremity ended at the base of the highest hill, which was topped by the splendid Temple of Jupiter Best and Greatest.

"This is their agora, obviously," Izates said, looking the place over for signs of vulgarity. "It's rather dignified, really," he said, disappointed.

"This is the Forum," Gorgas said. "I see they've cleared away the last of the swamp and cleaned the pavement. Those biggest buildings are what the Romans call basilicas. They're law courts, mainly. The little round temple is sacred to Vesta, goddess of the hearth. That one partway up the hill is Saturn's. The big one to Jupiter you already know and that other big one on the lower peak of the hill is Juno's. The little temples surrounding them I'm not sure about. The Romans have more gods and more temples than you can imagine. They even build temples and altars to the virtues: discipline, concord, peace—"

"Peace?" Izates said dryly. "The Romans esteem peace so highly that they have erected an altar to it?"

"I think we can assume that it's peace on Roman terms," Zeno said. "This seems to be the center of government and communal activity. Let's find an inn close by. It will be convenient since this will be where we will be spending most of our time."

They learned that, except for public areas like the Forum, Rome had no sort of districting. Houses, shops, temples, slums, parks, gardens and the town houses of the rich were jumbled together, often so closely that only one-way foot traffic was possible between them. Thus they had no trouble finding an inn no more than a few steps from the Forum, and nearby a stable to take care of their donkey.

"One thing to be said for a rebuilt city like this," Izates said, surveying the room they had engaged. "Even the inns are too new to have gotten shabby and acquire vermin."

The room was spacious, freshly painted and even featured a small balcony with potted plants, overlooking the Via Nova, one of the few streets in Rome wide enough for two-way wheeled traffic.

Zeno walked out onto the balcony, leaned on the handrail and surveyed the street below. "Do you know what is missing?" he said.

"What?" Izates asked. "I mean, what besides culture, beauty and learning?"

"Everywhere we've gone since we arrived in Italy there have been soldiers. I've seen none since we entered Rome."

"Armed soldiers are forbidden to enter the city," Gorgas informed them. "Even a general in command of troops has to stay outside the city walls. When the Senate must confer with the military, they have to meet in one of the temples outside the walls."

"That is a wise policy," Izates conceded. "I suppose that even the Romans must have good ideas upon occasion."

"I noticed some fairly grand temples standing just without the city walls," Zeno said. "Most cities have their finest temples in prominent places."

"It's another Roman thing," Gorgas said. "Certain of their gods are what the Romans call 'extramural.' That means they have all their temples and shrines outside the walls. Mars is one of them. He's their war god, sort of like

Ares, except he's also an agricultural deity. His great festival is called the *Martialis* and it's actually a harvest festival, having nothing to do with battle."

"I can see that Roman religion must be a study that will require its own volume," Zeno said.

"Why bother?" Izates asked.

After a leisurely meal they walked out to see the sights. Just off the northernmost corner of the Forum they came to a rather modest brick building. The only thing fine about it was a handsome marble stair and portico with pillars in the severe Doric style. They might have passed it by without another glance, but Gorgas informed them that this was one of the most important landmarks in Rome.

"It's the Curia, where the Senate meets."

"There!" Zeno said, gesturing toward the unassuming façade. "Does that satisfy you? This is where the Romans have held their most important, most solemn debates. This is where their consuls have been entrusted with the powers of war, where policies of diplomacy and foreign relations have been fashioned, yet it is as plain as a Spartan barracks."

"Not what one would have expected," Izates admitted. "Let's take a closer look."

They walked toward the Curia and as they did Zeno declaimed, "A visitor once described the Roman Senate as an 'assembly of kings.' Their dignity and assurance was famed the world over. It is the quality the Romans called *gravitas,* meaning a great and profound seriousness. I will—" As they drew nearer, his words tapered off.

"That's more like it," Izates said, grinning at the sounds coming from within the Curia. They carried no impression of the solemn debate of an assembly of kings.

It sounded like there was a street brawl going on inside.

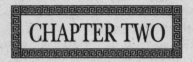

CHAPTER TWO

"SCIPIO IS A TRAITOR!" SHOUTED A RED-FACED SEN-ator. "He directed the defense of Alexandria when a Roman force was a part of the army besieging the city! He must be recalled and tried for treason!"

Another senator rushed over and shook a fist in the man's face. "That besieging army was led by the king of *Carthage*! Is a Roman a traitor for fighting Carthage? That alliance was never anything but a sham, anyway! It was done only to get intelligence of Hamilcar's army and tactics."

"Scipio was never given permission to open relations with Egypt, much less to frolic with the Egyptian queen and take charge of her army!" yelled a senator whose blond hair proclaimed his northern ancestry. "He wants to be a king in his own right!"

The uproar threatened to break into open violence until the presiding consul ordered the lictors to separate all the belligerents and restore order. When matters had settled a bit, he stood. The consul was a soldierly, fierce-faced man named Quintus Cornelius Scipio and the person being charged with treason was his son.

"Conscript fathers," he began, "this bickering is unseemly and advances our cause not at all. I remind you that my son was given a far-ranging commission with wide powers of discretion. If his methods have been unorthodox, does any man here deny that the reports he has sent to us have been invaluable? Has he not given us the city of Carthage as if we had built it ourselves?" He gestured toward the detailed model of the city that occupied a corner of the curia, constructed according to the reports and drawings of the expedition young Scipio had led. "Furthermore," here he glared around him at the assembled senators, "does any man here dare say that a Scipio has ever betrayed Rome? If so, I stand ready to lay down my imperium and meet that man, or those men, on the Field of Mars, on horseback or afoot, with sword, spear and dagger."

Amid the uneasy silence an older man stood. He was Publius Gabinius, the princeps senatus, empowered to speak first on all matters. "Gentlemen," he said calmly, "are we primitive tribesmen, to resort to arms over matters of personal honor? The gods forbid it! We are the Senate of Rome and we have raised ourselves to mastery over other nations because we prize reasoned debate, intelligent planning, compromise and discipline above brute ferocity. Rome is now embarked upon a campaign of unprecedented magnitude. Now is not the time for such unseemliness. Moderate your tone or I may be forced to expel some of you." He gazed around him, waiting for the proper moment. "And let me remind you that the Princess Selene is not queen of Egypt but merely the sister of the boy-king Ptolemy. Egypt is a nation with which Rome has no cause for hostility. In fact, as the implacable enemy of Carthage, we should seek alliance with that country."

Another senator stood. "Nonetheless, Honored Princeps, the fact remains that four of our legions are now lost somewhere in Egypt, and we can ill afford such a loss at this time."

"They are not lost, just missing," Gabinius said, hiding his own misgivings. "That force is led by the son of our other consul. Let us hear his thoughts on this matter."

"I yield the floor to my colleague," the Consul Scipio said, resuming his seat on his curule chair.

The Consul Titus Norbanus, elder of that name, stood. "That my son is in command of the missing expedition is of no consequence. A Roman soldier serves his country, without regard to parentage or family affiliation, and the highest officer is no more sacred than the commonest legionary."

There were many shouts of approval for this patriotic sentiment, and the Princeps Gabinius smiled and nodded cynically, thinking: *He neatly sidesteps the fact that his boy got the command without ever having held a higher office, as the constitution requires.*

"And while I cannot approve of young Scipio's actions in Alexandria," Norbanus went on, "the fact remains that those legions were stranded in Egypt when we, the Senate, meeting in this very chamber, voted to invade Sicily, thus declaring war upon Carthage."

As if in answer to a plea for an omen, the sound of clattering hoofbeats from without silenced even the low murmur in the room. A horse galloping across the Forum could mean only one thing: an army messenger with important dispatches.

"Clear the doorway, there!" called the princeps. Immediately, lictors made a pathway from the door to the consuls' podium. The hoofbeats ceased, and moments later a man in military belt, tunic and boots, travel-stained and exhausted, strode in. Looking neither right nor left, he went to the consuls' podium and held out a bronze tube.

"Dispatches for the honored Senate from the Proconsul Norbanus."

The presiding consul waved it away. "My colleague should read this first."

Norbanus took the message tube, forcing his hands to be steady. He examined the seal, then broke it and twisted the cap off the tube. He withdrew some sheets of Egyptian papyrus, unrolled them and began to read.

"From the Proconsul Titus Norbanus to the Senate of Rome, greeting." There were grumbles from those who thought it unfit for young Norbanus to style himself thus without having held the office of consul or even praetor first, but the father silenced them with a glare. He resumed reading.

"Our legions were in the process of subduing the cities along the Nile when word arrived from Alexandria that Hamilcar had withdrawn from Egypt and that the glorious reconquest of Italy and Sicily had begun. At a council of commanders our options were examined and discussed. We are eager to join the offensive, but a return through Carthaginian territory is unfeasible. The attitude of Egypt is uncertain, since we took part in Hamilcar's invasion. The Egyptian army is laughable and no threat to four Roman legions, but the Senate has not indicated a desire for war with Egypt, so we shall be careful not to provoke one.

"Marcus Scipio has tried to order us to Alexandria, but his commission from the Senate was merely to carry out a reconnaissance of Italy and Carthage, so none of us feel constrained to obey him, lacking orders from the Senate. There are those among us who doubt his loyalty.

"South of us lies a primitive wilderness, desert on both sides. Our only course is to march north to the Delta, then eastward, into territory unseen by Romans for more than a century. By the time the Senate receives this missive, we should be in a place called Sinai, said to be desert, but passable since the days of the pharaohs. The land beyond seems to be under some dispute. There is a sometimes-independent state ruled by a king of the Jews, and north of that lies Seleucid Syria, although both of these states are said to be under great pressure from the expanding Parthian Empire. Whatever our fate, we shall continue our reconnaissance and report faithfully to the Senate, in order that Rome's knowledge of the East may be expanded.

"Our plan is to march up the coast until we come to a port where sufficient ships are available to embark for Italy, Sicily or wherever the noble Senate shall order us. Should no such fleet present itself, then we shall march through Cilicia, Pamphilia, Lycia, Asia, Greece, Macedonia and Dalmatia until we reach Italy. We shall show the world that nothing is beyond the capabilities of the legions of Rome.

"I shall send further dispatches at every opportunity. Long live the noble Senate. Long live Rome." Norbanus the elder rolled the papyri and replaced them in the tube, his face glowing with triumph.

A senator leapt to his feat. "He proposes a feat worthy of Xenophon!" Shouts and cheers erupted.

Gabinius stood and gestured for quiet. "Let's cheer the feat when it is accomplished, shall we? Commander Norbanus proposes an extreme course, but anyone can see that his situation calls for such measures. I wish him well, as do we all. Now, we have been concentrating on Sicily, Carthage and the South to the neglect of the great world of the East. I propose we appoint a committee to study the situation there. We have assumed that the Seleucids are still supreme there, as they were when we went into exile. What sort of people are these Parthians who seem to be causing such trouble there? Will we be facing them once we have settled with Carthage? We must know."

With some routine government work under proposal, the excitement subsided and the Senate got serious. While names for the study board were submitted, everyone talked of the latest news. First war in Sicily, now this! After generations of grinding warfare against the savages of the North, Rome was engaged with the old world once more.

Satisfied that the danger of open violence was past, the princeps joined the two consuls for some serious talk.

"Your son seems to be acquitting himself well," Gabinius said to Norbanus.

"I notice that you gave him the title 'commander,' not 'proconsul,'" Norbanus said.

"I believe it will set a bad example if we let men who have never served in the offices that rightfully confer imperium to hold so lofty a title officially. This situation is unprecedented in our experience and of course certain expedients were called for. Let's not make a practice of it."

"Your boy is not being cheated of anything," the Consul Scipio said. "What any of us would have given for such an opportunity at so young an age, eh? The gods love young Norbanus; that much is clear. If he pulls this off, he'll return to Rome covered with so much glory that the highest offices will fall into his hands like ripe olives. But the princeps is right. Let's not let our young officers think they can bypass the *cursus honorum* through military glory. Men with successful wars behind them are nothing but a danger to the Republic if they don't know how to govern."

Norbanus waved a hand impatiently. "Let it pass for the moment. What concerns us now is: What's to be done? We can't leave a Roman army out wandering about with no guidance from the Senate, no matter who is in charge."

"Exactly," said his colleague. "We need a means of communication, as we have with our army in Sicily. Granted, the distances between your son's force and us are far greater than with the Sicilian expedition, but it should not be insurmountable. We need fast ships and men to sail them and a knowledge of the ports along the coast between Egypt and Greece."

"We have maps," Gabinius said, "but they are old ones. The ports will be there, but who knows who owns them now? I will take personal charge of the study board. In the meantime, we must all be thinking about how to use our reserve force. Six new legions are due from Noricum any day. Will we send them west, south or east?"

"Too soon to speculate," Norbanus said. "First they must get used to the climate. They can move into the camps down south that the Sicilian expedition left behind. From there they can move in any direction the Senate orders with minimum waste of time."

"Excellent," said the princeps. "An Italian summer is very different from one in Noricum, and it will prepare them for Africa."

The others nodded. An African campaign would be the next step, once Sicily was secured. Carthage had to be destroyed. The gods had ordained that grim task.

With the major questions settled, the Senate meeting broke up and they left the curia, in strict order of precedence: first, the consuls preceded by their lictors, then the princeps senatus, then the senior magistrates, the lower office holders, finally the mass of senators holding no particular office that year.

Gabinius stepped onto the porch of the Curia, feeling once again the exhilaration of serving Rome in the very building erected by the King Tullus Hostilius, from which every great consul and all the senators of old had made laws and sent forth the legions. Brutus and Camillus, and Appius Claudius, the builder of roads and aqueducts, had presided in this sacred building. Now he, Publius Gabinius, carried on their tradition. As he looked over the city with great satisfaction, he noticed two unusual men standing at the bottom of the steps, gazing up at him. They had the unmistakable aspect of Greeks. One of them was a handsome man of excellent bearing and immaculate dress, the other a scruffy, unkempt fellow dressed no better than a slave but with an arrogant stance and eyes that blazed with intelligence. As Gabinius descended the steps, these two climbed toward him, as if they wished to speak.

ZENO AND IZATES LISTENED TO THE NOISE FROM within the curia rise and fall. They heard individual speakers shout or project their voices in the manner approved by the teachers of rhetoric, and spoken thus they could understand that the Latin tongue had great force and dignity. Then they jumped aside as a messenger thundered up on horseback, leapt from his mount and ran into the building. Then there were a few minutes of silence followed by cheering.

"Good news, apparently," Izates said.

"Are Senate meetings usually this uproarious?" Zeno asked Gorgas.

"I've heard that they can get noisy. The Senate's divided into a lot of cliques, and they're all at each other's throat over high office and military command. They're only united against the rest of the world."

They waited a while longer, then Izates said: "I think there is nothing more to be learned here. Let's go get something to eat."

They were about to do just that when men began to emerge from the curia. First came a line of men who each carried a bundle of rods tied around an axe. These Gorgas identified as lictors: attendants to the higher magistrates. A man who wore a toga bordered with a broad purple stripe followed the lictors. Then came another line of lictors and another such magistrate. A third man emerged, unaccompanied by lictors, then more lictors preceding purple-striped magistrates and finally a crowd of senators, some of them wearing purple-bordered togas, most dressed in plain garments.

These men were different from those they had seen heretofore. Their faces were stern to the point of ferocity and their bearing was nothing short of regal. They trod like the masters of the earth. The third man to emerge after the two that Gorgas identified as consuls stood a little aside as if he were admiring the view. Then he gazed down at the two Greeks.

"I want to talk to that one," Zeno said. He began to ascend the steps.

"Why that one?" Izates asked, following him.

"He looks more intelligent than the rest. Gorgas, you wait here." They climbed to the top and stood before the white-haired man, whose austere face expressed polite interest.

"Rejoice, sir," Zeno said, hoping the man understood Greek. "We are travelers from Greece. I am Zeno of Athens and this is my friend Izates of Alexandria. We would ask the indulgence of the Roman Senate, of which august body I perceive you to be a member of high standing."

The man inclined his head slightly. "Rejoice, Greek. I am Publius Gabinius and I am a senator. How may I be of service to a distinguished visitor? I perceive that you are both men of good birth. Are you officials of Athens?" His Greek was nearly flawless, but old-fashioned in the manner they had heard their native tongue spoken by other Romans.

"Alas, we are not officials, although we bear letters of introduction from the Athenian Council. We are philosophers. Most particularly, I am a historian, and when I heard that the Romans had returned to Italy, I understood that history is now taking a momentous new turn. It is my desire to be the historian of the Roman resurgence, and I would very much like to have the approval of the Senate in carrying out my researches."

A very slight smile softened Gabinius's granite features. He liked this young man. Though handsome, he seemed to have none of the effeminacy that Romans associated with Greeks, and his words, while flattering, bore no taint of obsequiousness.

"A historian? Like Herodotus?"

Zeno sighed. It seemed he was never to escape that comparison. "I can claim nothing so grand, although my friend here thinks I might make a second-rate Thucydides."

Gabinius looked Izates over. "We haven't had much opportunity to study Greek philosophy up north, but some of us have read a bit. We tend to favor the Stoics. Are you of that school?"

"Izates is a Cynic," Zeno told him.

"Aren't the Cynics the ones who growl and snap like dogs?"

"Some people's toes need to be bitten," Izates said.

Again they heard that swords-on-shields laugh. "So they do! Come, my friends. Join me at my house for some dinner. I don't know how I may be of service to you, but what little I can do is yours to command."

This, Zeno thought, was amazing luck. If it *was* luck. They fell in beside the Roman as he went down the steps and turned up a narrow street. His stride was that of a much younger man, and something occurred to Zeno.

"I notice that most Roman men walk in exactly the same way, with paces of the same length."

"It's the legionary pace," Gabinius told him, "one thousand paces to the mile. It's drilled into us from boyhood. Short men have to hurry and tall men amble, but every man walks at the same pace." He turned up a yet narrower street. "So you are a historian. I take it that this entails much travel?"

"I've traveled more widely than most," Zeno assured him.

"And my new friend Izates is from Alexandria. I take it that you both have visited the lands to the eastern end of the sea? Our knowledge of those parts is very out of date and wasn't vast when it was current. Perhaps you could tell me something about that part of the world?"

"Gladly," Zeno said, sensing that this was why the Roman had accepted them so readily. He wanted to know about the East. Perhaps the whole Senate was eager to learn about those lands. It was hardly a matter for wonder. This hardheaded people would understand that knowledge was power, and if the Romans understood nothing else, they understood power.

As they walked, ordinary people greeted Gabinius as a personal friend and he returned their greetings, pausing to exchange words with many of them. Common citizens, it seemed, had great respect for their rulers but held them in little awe. This Zeno approved. It reminded him of the Athenian democracy in the days of Pericles. He remarked upon this to Gabinius.

"Oh, yes. The highest offices are open to all citizens save freedmen recently manumitted, and even they may hold the lower, municipal posts. Among my colleagues in the Senate are men whose ancestry stretches back to Romulus, and others whose grandfathers were barbarian warriors who fought us along the Rhine and the Danube two generations ago."

"We lack your flexible concept of citizenship," Zeno said, "but something of the sort has happened with the spread of Greek civilization. My friend here," he nudged Izates with an elbow, "could be mistaken for a native Hellene, but he was born a Jew."

Gabinius looked at Izates with new interest. "I've heard of your nation. Is it true that you have only one god? That seems unnatural."

"It seems unnatural to everyone but us. But even Plato and other philosophers have speculated that there is only a single godhead, and that men have divided that deity into many aspects in order to explain the phenomena of nature and the universe: Zeus for thunder and lightning, Poseidon for the sea, Aphrodite for the attraction between men and women, Dionysus for the terrible forces of nature, Apollo for the enlightened thoughts of men and so forth."

"This is fascinating. I can see we shall have many enthralling discussions. Tell me, do your people still have their own kingdom, between Egypt and Seleucid Syria?"

The Romans are truly concerned about the power structure of the East, Zeno thought. *Something must be happening there.*

"Yes, the Hasmonean family clings to the kingdom of

Judea. Egypt cares nothing for that part of the world any-more, and the Seleucids are too hard-pressed by the Parthi-ans to give them much trouble."

"So your kingdom is strong and secure?"

"No longer my kingdom or my people," Izates said. "I'm more of an Alexandrian Greek, as Zeno says. But a man can't separate himself from his ancestry. The kingdom is be-set by civil war, but that's an old story. When we are not united against an outside enemy, we fall to fighting among ourselves."

"Just like Greeks," Zeno said.

"Here we are. This is my house, which you are to regard as your own."

They stood before a blank wall that stretched in both di-rections for a considerable distance. They walked through the door into a spacious entrance hall dominated by a tall wooden chest. Before the chest was a bronze statue of a god, before which smoldered a small brazier. Gabinius took a pinch of incense from a box next to the brazier and dropped it onto the coals. His guests did the same.

"Is this your household god?" Zeno asked.

"This is Quirinus. He is our founder, Romulus, in deified form. This cabinet holds the wax death masks of my ances-tors. My great-grandfather took them north on the exile and I have returned them home."

"Is this the home of your ancestors?" Zeno asked, look-ing around. Like most things in Rome, it looked and smelled new.

"There was little left but the foundations when we re-turned, but I have restored it exactly as it was. Most of us were able to locate our old homes. Our ancestors kept care-ful records of everything. Most especially of our lands and houses. This one has been in my family since Rome had kings."

They passed into a courtyard surrounding a pool in which a modest fountain played. The sides and bottom of the pool were lined with blue tiles lacking any design or ornament. The surrounding colonnade shaded the entrances to a number of rooms, but it held no sculptures. Instead, climbing plants were placed at intervals in large, earthenware pots. The vines had only begun to ascend the columns.

"We could use the triclinium," Gabinius said, "but the weather is so fine I suggest we eat out here. Does that suit you?"

"Admirably," Zeno assured him. "I can think of no lovelier setting."

"It is in excellent taste," Izates said grudgingly.

Gabinius smiled. "You mean it lacks any ornament? I know that you Greeks are fond of restraint. Actually, this place is just new, or rather newly restored. We could cart away little with us on the exile, and Hannibal's men took everything else. We Romans are rather fond of display and gaudy decoration. Come back in a few years and see whether you approve then."

Slaves brought out a table and chairs. "We recline only at banquets," Gabinius explained. "For ordinary meals we prefer to sit."

"Better for the digestion anyway," Izates said. "People shouldn't lie around like beached fish at a meal. Food was not meant to pass through the body horizontally."

They took chairs, and slaves brought ewers and basins to wash their hands. Cups were filled, and each splashed a bit onto the courtyard before drinking. The first course was hard-boiled eggs, and Gabinius explained that nearly every

Roman meal began with eggs. They spoke of inconsequential matters through the simple dinner. The eggs were followed by grilled fish, then stewed lamb and, finally, fresh apples and pears. Throughout, platters of bread and cheese and bowls of oil and of a pungent fish sauce stood filled for the diner's use. When the plates were cleared away and the wine cups refilled, serious talk began.

"Why do you find Rome a fit subject for study?" Gabinius asked.

"Because the state seemed poised to take an important place on the world's stage when Hannibal eliminated it so abruptly. From obscure origins, Rome had thrust forth into importance in an incredibly short time. Its inhabitants and constitution showed every sign of destiny. Then all was cut short by Carthage. That much would rate a historical footnote.

"But over the years we received cryptic word of a new Rome in the North, busily subduing the barbarians. This was more interesting yet. Nations that have been crushed usually disappear. Now you have returned, seemingly stronger and more warlike than ever. This is most remarkable of all, an unprecedented thing. I want to know how it happened and, more importantly, I want to chronicle what happens next."

Gabinius nodded. "A laudable project. In my library are several histories of Rome, both pre- and post-exile. Please feel free to use them in your researches."

"You are more than generous," Zeno said.

"I wish to enlighten you about Rome. At the same time, I and other Romans have much to learn about this world we have reentered. Perhaps you can help me there."

"Gladly."

Zeno had no compunctions about supplying the Roman

with information that might well be put to military use. Greece was a tributary of Macedonia and he regarded the Macedonians as no better than barbarians. Rome was the implacable enemy of Carthage, and Carthage had resisted the spread of Greek interests in the western Mediterranean. The Romans were brutal, but Carthage had become a byword for cruelty.

Gabinius told them of the great northward march; when the Romans took their household gods and sacred objects, their arms and whatever tools they could carry and sought a new home beyond the Alps. He told them of the hungry early years, of the resistance by native peoples, and of the Romans' ultimate victory. He told of Roman expansion year by year, and of how certain native nobles saw in the newcomers an opportunity for themselves.

"Since that time," Gabinius said, "we have spoken of the old families and the new families. Old families like my own date from the exile. New families are of northern origin."

"And they are full citizens?" Zeno asked, intrigued as always by this unique concept of citizenship.

"Certainly. Our Consul Norbanus, whom you saw leaving the Curia today, belongs to the most prestigious of the new families. They have been consulars for more than fifty years. His father and grandfather were consuls and a great-grandfather was praetor shortly after the exile. He was a chieftain who understood that supporting Rome would make him far more than lord over a few hundred obstreperous savages."

It sounded too cozy and friendly for Zeno. No Greek could truly believe in political harmony on any profound level, and he remembered the shouting from inside the Curia. He sensed that there must be tension, jealousy and resentment between these new and old families.

In response to the Roman's questions, Zeno spoke of the situation in Greece, of the great coastal cities of Antioch, Sidon and Tyre, of the islands Cyprus and Rhodes. Gabinius asked Izates about Judea and its capital, Jerusalem. Zeno noticed that his friend was not asked about his native city, Alexandria, even though the capital of Egypt was perhaps the most important city on the sea.

He remembered reports he had heard that a Roman delegation had already visited that city. *They've been sending reports to the Senate,* he thought. *This Roman already knows all he needs to know about Alexandria.* The scope of Roman preparations was something far beyond his experience. *They have just retaken Italy and already they are laying plans for world conquest. They will know exactly what they are doing and whom they will face when they start. Even Alexander made no such plans. He just bulled his way through with luck, charisma and a confidence in his enemy's weakness.*

"Perhaps you can answer something for me," Zeno said hesitantly.

"You have but to ask," Gabinius told him.

"The world knows that you Romans are in the process of taking Sicily."

"We are taking it *back,*" Gabinius corrected. "It was ours after the first war with Carthage, when we fought Hannibal's father there."

"To be sure. Yet, travelers hear many things and there is a story on the ships and in the taverns all around the sea that a Roman force, a rather large one, accompanied the Shofet Hamilcar's expedition to Egypt. Yet now you are at war with Carthage. What has happened to that Roman army, last heard of some distance down the Nile from Alexandria?"

Gabinius leaned back in his chair and seemed to consider

this for a while. He gestured with his cup and a slave refilled it, then the others.

"Ah. This very question is getting to be something of a sore point in the Senate lately. You see, our two consuls for the year are Titus Norbanus and Quintus Scipio; one old family, one new. Each has a son. If you would understand the new Rome that has arisen here, then I must tell you about these two remarkable young men."

And so he began to speak to them of the younger Marcus Scipio, and of the younger Titus Norbanus.

CHAPTER THREE

THE PLACE WAS CALLED SINAI. IT MIGHT AS WELL have been the realm of Dis or Pluto. To the Romans, accustomed to the verdant North, to beautiful Italy, it seemed like a place cursed by the gods. Their march from Carthage to Egypt, then down the Nile, had taken them only through cultivated land. The Nile Valley had been bordered by desert, but few of them had ridden out to see it. Now they had to cross this.

From horseback, Titus Norbanus surveyed the prospect. Despite the heat, he wore his lion-mask helmet. Beneath the fanged upper jaw his face was fair, straight-lined and handsome. His eyes were intensely blue. The desert was daunting, but Alexander and his soldiers had faced worse. He felt that he and Alexander had much in common.

"Fighting is one thing," Lentulus Niger said, "but this? Roman soldiers expect to fight. It's what they're best at. Not marching across sand and rock where the lizards have to take shelter from the sun."

"We've never faced anything like this," Cato agreed.

"Roman soldiers can do anything," Norbanus assured his subordinates. "Barbarians have lived here for generations. Can Romans not do anything barbarians can do?"

"Little bands of wretched nomads scurrying from waterhole to waterhole with a few goats may be able to live here, after a fashion," Cato allowed. "But we have more than forty thousand men, plus all their animals. How are we going to make it through to the cultivated lands?"

"We should have gone by sea," Niger said. "We could have commandeered the ships at Pelusium."

"Carthage controls the sea," Norbanus said patiently. "Even preoccupied with Sicily, there are enough Carthaginian warships prowling about to deal with some wallowing transports full of Roman soldiers. We would have to trust Greeks to handle the ships, and who can trust Greeks?"

"Still," Niger said, "to undertake a march like this without ships screening us and providing us with supplies as we go up the coast"—he made a gesture of futility—"it's courting disaster."

"Had we been able to march westward," Norbanus pointed out, "we would have done so. We discussed all this at our councils. Did you miss those discussions, Lentulus?"

Niger fumed. "That was before we had a look at this place."

Norbanus leaned on his saddle pommels. His subordinates lacked vision. That was why some men led and others followed. Men who would lead must have vision. Men who would be truly great must have great vision. That was what separated men like Alexander and him from the common run of men.

"For many centuries," he explained, "armies have crossed this desert to make war. Greeks, Syrians, Persians—they have all come this way to invade Egypt. The pharaohs crossed it the other way to take war to their enemies. None of them found this desert impassable."

"Maybe it rained more then," Cato said.

"And they went along the coast, supported by their ships," Niger maintained.

"We are no one's inferior when it comes to planning and preparation," Norbanus said. "Before we begin, we will gather all the forage we can cut and bring it along on wagons and on the backs of those smelly camels. We will bring water the same way, in bags. The men can carry all the rations they will require on their own backs. We can do this, and we will reach the other side in excellent shape. And we will march inland, away from the coast. I do not want to be observed by ships or seen from the coastal towns. I don't want anyone reporting to the shofet or to Queen Selene where we are."

"Why the secrecy?" Niger wanted to know.

"I like surprises," Norbanus said, smiling.

MARCUS SCIPIO STUDIED THE MODEL WITH A CRITICAL eye. It looked like nothing he had ever seen before. He doubted that anyone had ever seen such a thing. If it resembled anything else, it would have to be a bat, he decided. Its long, slender body was a framework of reeds thinner than arrow shafts, covered with a skin of parchment. Stretching from both sides were wings made of even thinner reeds, also covered with a skin of thinnest parchment. At its rear was a tail somewhat like a bird's.

"Where are the feathers?" Marcus asked.

"I tried attaching feathers," the young man said, "fancying that these somehow made birds lighter and facilitated their flight. But they did not improve things. But we know that bats have no feathers, yet they fly admirably. Insects have no feathers, yet many have wings, and some of these, particularly the dragonfly, are more agile in the air than even birds or bats." His name was Timonides and he spoke of his passion with single-minded intensity.

"I determined that the structure of the wings gave the power of flight. Wings take many forms, but those of birds and bats, whether made of feathers or skin and bone, share a common cross-section: semi-lenticular with a very fine, thin trailing edge. I experimented with this shape until I had a structure that would provide flight, but learned that it could not be controlled without a tail." He pointed at the triangular structure at the rear.

"This stabilized flight somewhat in the vertical plane, but flight was still very irregular in the horizontal. Finally I added this." He indicated a vertical fin protruding above the tail. "Birds do not have this structure, but it is very common in fish."

"You looked to fish for lessons in flight?" Marcus said, astonished.

"When you think of it, the swimming of fish shares many things in common with the flight of birds. Fish move through water instead of air, but propulsion and steering are much the same. This vertical fin also acts rather as a rudder does on a watercraft."

"I know how the underwater boats use those little wings to dive and surface," Marcus told him. "But when I heard you had plans for making men fly, I confess I pictured something like Icarus, with great, feathered wings that they could flap."

The young man shook his head. "That is a silly myth. Men are not built for such effort. Most of the strength of our bodies is below the waist, which is why men can run better than most animals, and soldiers can march bearing heavy burdens. By contrast, our upper bodies are weak. Look at how a bird is built. Its legs are scrawny, puny things. Even its wings have very little muscle. But the greater part of its body is composed of pectoral muscle, what we call the breast." For emphasis he rapped his knuckles on Marcus's breastplate, upon which the muscles in question had been sculpted in great detail and somewhat exaggerated size.

"Picture a man whose body is three-quarters pectoral muscle. Then you would have a human fit to fly like a bird."

"So how do the wings of this thing flap?" Marcus asked. "I see no mechanism for the purpose."

"They don't," Timonides admitted. "It will not fly in that way. It will glide and soar, as gulls and eagles do."

"Oh," Marcus said, disappointed. "I believe that will limit its usefulness. I'd had visions of winged soldiers descending upon the enemy like a great swarm of hawks swooping upon helpless chickens."

"Disappointed?" Timonides cried, outraged. "But this is marvelous! For the first time, a man will fly in the air without falling. It is something no one save a god has been able to do before!" He looked about apprehensively, then crossed the room to touch a statue of Hephaestus, god of inventors. "Not," he amended hastily, "that I in any way compare myself to the immortal gods."

"Of course, of course," Marcus said. "I did not mean to denigrate your research. It is indeed wonderful. But spectacle and novelty are the things of peacetime. These times call for warlike applications." Peacetime was something he knew only in theory. War had been his whole life.

Timonides, in the fashion of Greeks, assumed a cunning look. "No military application? My dear General Scipio, do you consider an aerial view of your enemy's dispositions, his route of march, the approach of his fleet, to be useless? Consider that, with such devices, widely separated elements of your forces can stay in contact and the enemy cannot intercept your messengers."

"Hadn't thought of that," Marcus admitted. "Of course you're right. Fighting is only one aspect of warfare. Intelligence and communication are also crucial. Will your device be capable of such things?"

"Eminently," Timonides assured him. "Once I have a prototype machine built to full scale and have worked out the minutiae of maneuvering, you can have a fleet of them."

"You speak as if this maneuvering business will be simple to perfect."

The Greek shrugged eloquently. "We shall see. But I believe the principles must be quite simple. After all, who would have believed that vessels could travel underwater under human guidance? Yet the philosophers of this school proved that it could be done and you put them to work defending the city, which they did to great effect."

"Quite true. Very well, I shall tell the queen that your project merits full support. Make up your request for funding, supplies and personnel and I shall present it to Her Majesty at the next planning conference."

Timonides went to a table and took a scroll from a chest. "Already done," he said, handing over the scroll with a smile. "Among other things, I shall need some intelligent slaves to test the first full-sized prototypes. At least a dozen. Attrition may be high at first."

"That should be no problem. We have plenty of prisoners taken in the recent fighting. They should be brave enough for the task and they needn't be purchased."

Marcus left the young Greek and continued with his inspection. From all directions he could hear the sounds of new construction. This part of the Museum was his personal project and he was expanding it enormously. He had moved out many of the philosophical schools to temporary housing around Alexandria in order to make room for the expanding School of Archimedes.

Philosophers throughout the Greek world were scandalized. The Archimedeans had been held in lowest esteem, scarcely to be considered philosophers at all, because they *did* things. They took matter and, often with their own hands, transformed it into articles of utility. This, to orthodox philosophers, lowered them to the status of mere workmen. Philosophers were not supposed to *do* anything. They were supposed only to think.

Marcus had no patience with such sophistry. Rome had arrived, and Rome had no use for men who did nothing. Romans were not philosophers but they were engineers. Archimedes, the mathematician of Syracuse, was nearly a god in the pantheon of engineers. Marcus had set the despised school to designing war machines, and they had delivered handsomely.

At first he had wanted them to devise improved war machines of the sort Archimedes had invented for the defense of Syracuse against the Carthaginians more than a hundred years before: catapults and ship-killing cranes and so forth. Instead, they had come up with machines he had never dreamed of, yet which had proven invaluable in the war with Hamilcar. They had made boats that could travel beneath the surface of the water and sink enemy ships in the harbor. There was a device of mirrors that could see around corners and over walls. There were chemicals that generated dense smoke or choking fumes and one compound that burned with such furious violence that the inventor insisted it must have some military application, if only it could be harnessed.

And now: a flying machine. It made his head whirl.

He walked down a broad corridor where artisans were still busy painting the walls and inlaying the mosaic floor with scenes from the life of Alexander and the early Ptolemies. He was still uncomfortable in the spectacular parade uniform Selene had had made for him and insisted that he wear, even when not engaged in military duties. The muscle-sculpted cuirass was overlaid with gold and silver leaf, its leatherwork studded with amber and coral. His helmet was embossed on the temples with curling ram's horns, the significance of which he could not guess. He knew he'd be laughed out of Rome should he ever show up there in such a rig, but the Alexandrians lacked all restraint when it came to display.

Thought of Rome darkened his mood. He knew that he had many enemies there. His family protected him, but to some his actions of late smacked of treason. If only he could make them understand that he held the key to Rome's future greatness! Romans were for the most part conservatives and traditionalists. The scions of the great old families like his own wanted only to reestablish Rome as it had been in the time of their ancestors. He knew this to be folly. The world was very different than it had been in the day of Fabius Cunctator.

Besides, he thought, their vaunted traditions and system hadn't done them much good when it came to dealing with Hannibal, had it? This new world would call for new methods and new ideas, as much as that might pain the ancestor worshippers of the Senate.

He went into a huge courtyard where men were erecting, employing or tearing down structures of wood and metal.

Some were catapults, some scaling devices and some objects of no function he could guess at. Once in a while a timber or rope would break under too much stress and there were shouts or laughter or the screams of injured men. Never before had Marcus seen men so frantically employed, yet seeming exhilarated at the task, strenuous, frustrating and dangerous though it might be. These "active philosophers," as someone had dubbed them, were a new breed of men.

He went to an especially strange structure that consisted of a platform between uprights, the platform suspended by a complicated armature of ropes, pulleys, gears and what appeared to be large boxes full of metal bars. "What might this be?" he asked the sweating supervisor.

"We aren't sure yet what to call it," said Chilo. He was the head of the Archimedean school, but he was as dusty and ill kempt as the slaves who assisted with the work. "The new falling-weight catapults got us thinking about the possibilities of falling weights. It seems such a simple thing, something we all tend to take for granted, yet there is a whole unknown field of study here: the dynamics of falling weights."

" 'Dynamics'?" Marcus said.

"It's an old word we've revived. It means the study of how matter moves. Remember when you first came here and I told you that we seek out fundamental principles? Well, this is one of them. Matter does not move about at random and free from obedience to natural law. There are rules, and we intend to discover them. Watch this."

At Chilo's direction, a dozen slaves crowded onto the platform. A single slave seized a rope and began to haul back on it. There was a clacking of gear wheels and the platform began to rise, a few inches with each pull. At the same time, the boxes of metal bars descended at the same rate.

"You see?" Chilo said. "The strength of a single man is sufficient to raise many men. This can be used to raise soldiers above an enemy rampart, but more important to us is the demonstration of the properties of the counterweight." He looked around and indicated a man who sat on the edge of a fountain, staring at the machine. "You see that sour-faced fellow observing over there?"

Marcus looked at him. "Isn't that the mathematician who just arrived from Crete? Nikolaus, is it?"

"The very one. He seeks to penetrate to the very essence of this question: the principle of *why* objects fall as they do."

"Why?" Marcus said. "Self-evident, isn't it? Things have always fallen."

"That's just it. It isn't self-evident at all. We just take it for granted. Why doesn't smoke fall? What holds clouds up? They may not have much mass, but they have some. Some of us think that Archimedes' principle of buoyancy is involved, but Nikolaus thinks that there is a fundamental, universal force involved and he wants to understand it."

"Too deep for me," Marcus admitted. "But I like this machine. It could have all sorts of uses. Can you make one high enough to take people all the way to the top of the lighthouse?" The lighthouse of Pharos, tallest structure in the world, stood only about a mile from them.

"It would require a lot of rope and wood," Chilo said, "but the principle will work no matter how tall the machine might be."

Marcus left him pondering.

An hour later he found Queen Selene in her council chamber. Technically she was not a true queen, merely the consort of the boy-king, her brother Ptolemy. In reality she was unquestioned queen and this position she owed to Marcus. Her immature husband now sulked in a wing of the palace, enduring education from formidable teachers instead of his previous indulgent and scheming eunuchs, courtiers and advisors.

The queen was seated at a delicate table and she looked up as he entered. "Your friends have disappeared," she said in her usual, abrupt fashion. She favored the Stoic philosophers and had little use for court formality or artificial manners.

"Which friends?" he asked, tossing his helmet to a nearby slave. The adroit functionary caught it without damaging the delicate plumes.

"Norbanus, of course. And his four legions." She was studying a map, and a weathered man stood behind her, pointing out something with an ivory wand.

"Rather a large body of men to simply disappear," Marcus answered, knowing where this was leading.

"This is Achates, an officer of the Sinai Scouts," she said, indicating the man behind her. His features were a mixture of Macedonian and Bedouin, not an uncommon combination in that part of the world. He spread the fingers of one hand upon his breast and bowed in the Eastern fashion. "He says that, instead of hugging the coast as expected, they plunged straight off into the desert, more or less in the direction of Judea."

"Are your men following them?" he asked the desert soldier.

"They will shadow the army as closely as possible," Achates said, "but you must understand the special difficulties posed by the great desert. There will be very little food or water in front of that army. There will be none at all left where it passes. My scouts may have to turn back."

"Norbanus continues to amaze me," Marcus said. "I always thought he was a smooth-tongued Forum politician and no soldier at all. But he takes to the life as if he was born to it. Men follow him willingly, too. The gods have touched him somehow."

"Will his men continue to follow him as they turn to dried meat in that awful desert?" Selene asked.

The question had been sarcastic, but he treated it seriously. "That's to be seen. Soldiers are an odd lot. They'll turn on one officer for assigning an extra watch, and worship another who treats them like dogs. Alexander's men endured unbelievable hardships for him. Norbanus may have that touch with men."

"Or they may all die out there," she said, shrugging. "They certainly made extensive preparations. They denuded a whole district of forage to take along and they must have commandeered every water bag to be had. Still, it is a ruthless desert, and with so many men and animals to feed and water, they may leave their bones out there."

"They'll make it," Marcus asserted. "I won't bore you yet again with a description of my people's excellence, but rest assured that they will make it where they are going. The question is: Where is Norbanus leading them? I wouldn't put it past him to have a go at conquering India."

She smiled wryly. "He'd have to pass through a few nations before reaching there. I think he's headed for Judea, thence up the coast. He's going to Greece. From there it's just a short passage to Italy."

"That's the most likely course," Marcus agreed. "Is there anything in his path likely to stop him?"

"Judea is in a constant state of civil war," she said. "For some time the land has been ruled by the Hasmonean family, but they have split up into factions, so there are usually rival claimants. Religious differences come into it as well."

"Religious differences?" Marcus said. "I thought those were the people with only a single god."

"They differ on how that god should be worshipped," she said. "I cannot claim to understand the details."

"Norbanus will do well there," he murmured. Norbanus, he was certain, would select the weaker party, offer his services and put that claimant on the throne, and Rome would acquire a new client state. It was an old story.

"What did you say?"

"Nothing. Don't the Seleucids of Syria claim Judea?"

"They claim a great deal of territory they no longer control. Until a few months ago they were planning a campaign to retake everything east of the Delta, hoping we would be too distracted with Hamilcar's aggression to do anything about it. Now it looks as if they are facing a new assault from Parthia."

"The Parthians sound like an interesting people," Marcus said.

"Too interesting for my liking," she agreed. She turned to Achates. "Leave us now. Come to me immediately when you know something of importance." Then, back to Marcus: "They are a soldierly people, very like you Romans. A very—how shall I put it? A very *masculine* people. But also very different."

"Different how?" Marcus asked, intrigued. He was always interested in warlike people, especially those Rome was likely to have to face someday.

"You are an agricultural people, tied to the soil. They are pastoralists, or were until a few generations ago. The ruling caste are descended from the Scythians. They are horsemen and archers of great repute. The common rabble are Medes. For foot soldiers they buy slaves or levy young men as tribute from their subjects."

"Slaves as soldiers? That makes no sense. Slaves don't fight. They have nothing worth fighting for."

"Perhaps the Roman system isn't the only one that works," she commented. "The Parthians seem to have done well with theirs. Apparently they take the boys when they are very young and train them hard in special camps. They know no other life and by all accounts are as brave and loyal as other soldiers."

"I find it hard to believe. Besides, we've made little use of cavalry or archers. We like to get close and settle matters with javelin and sword."

"In those northern forests of yours that is hardly surprising. You'll find the eastern plains a different matter entirely. The horse and the bow are supreme there."

"And how did these centaurs come to be so powerful?" he asked.

"The usual. They took advantage of their enemies' weaknesses. When the successors of Alexander fell out and warred on each other, Parthia attacked whoever was most weakened by the fighting."

Marcus nodded. "We Romans are old hands at that game. Norbanus may have his hands full if he runs afoul of them. People who are both warlike and astute may be difficult to deal with. The Germans and Gauls we've done so much fighting with are just warlike."

"Welcome to civilization," she said.

Marcus gave her a report on the progress made by the Archimedean school, then retrieved his helmet and took his leave, pleading a multitude of duties. He strode out amid a swirl of Roman *virtus*.

Selene sighed. Dealing with Marcus was like wrestling with one of those absurd machines he was so fond of. He was ever full of plans and schemes, pumping for information, drafting and dispatching his everlasting reports to the Senate, inspecting and correcting and, above all, taking charge.

He had no gift for relaxing, for sitting back and enjoying the fruits of victory. She owed him much, including her life, but she found him exasperating.

The Romans were a disturbing lot and she harbored no illusions about them. They were bent upon reconquering the territory taken from them by Carthage, and they took a decided interest in the rest of the world. She was the descendant of many kings and she knew how power worked in the world. The Romans dreamed of revenge upon Carthage, but that was only the beginning. With Carthage destroyed, they would control all the territory now owned by Carthage. That meant everything west of Egypt, everything west of Italy, to the Pillars of Hercules. They would control half the world, and they were not the sort of people who would be content with half of anything.

She liked Marcus. She was grateful to him and she had conceived a genuine affection for him. Still, she gave occasional thought to having him done away with. Personal affection was one thing, politics another. When he had arrived, she had been an insecure princess, constantly threatened by her brother and his conniving courtiers. Now she was a queen. She owed it to Marcus, but now her first concern was Egypt and Egypt's security, not her Roman companion.

She had some decisions to make soon, but her situation was very precarious. She wanted the support of Rome, needed it, really, for without the Romans as allies she would soon be under siege again by the Carthaginians, or else the desperate Seleucids would have a try at Egypt, or the Parthians might take it into their heads to add the Nile to their expanding empire, as had the Persians in their day. As had Alexander.

It was wonderful being queen of the richest nation in the world. It was also perilous, owning the one thing coveted by all the grasping, rapacious powers on earth.

CHAPTER FOUR

THE COLD OF THE DESERT NIGHTS CAME AS A SUR-
prise to everyone. Roman soldiers were inured to cold
after so many years campaigning north of the Alps, but it
seemed strange to encounter it here. The sentries stood muffled in their woolen cloaks, and the men not asleep gathered
close to fires built with the skimpy brushwood that consti-
tuted the only available fuel.

The ground was hard and stony, but each day at the
end of their march the legionaries got out their pickaxes
and spades, their baskets for moving earth, and they dug
their rectangular ditch, heaping the soil into a low rampart that they topped with the long, pointed stakes carried
by each man. Only after they had accomplished this did
they go within to erect their tents. Each fortified camp was
exactly as it would have been on the Rhenus or Danubius
or on some other nameless river in the northland. In all
probability there was no enemy for many days' march in
any direction, but that made no difference. Everywhere a

Roman army stopped for the night, it erected just such a camp.

"Here we are," Cato said sourly, "fortified against jackals and foxes, when we could be camped in Sicily." He sat in a folding chair before one of the brushwood fires, a cup of watered date wine in his hand. Their wine was already souring from the heat of the days on the march, but it made the even fouler water drinkable.

"I don't care," said Lentulus Niger. "Sicily will take a year or two. As long as we're in on the finish, when we besiege Carthage, I'll be satisfied. The tale of this march will make our names, even if it doesn't bring us riches."

"You sound like a man trying to convince himself," Cato said.

"What's this?" The voice came from beyond the firelight. "Do I hear grumbling in the ranks?" Norbanus came into the firelight and held his hands out close to the flames.

"This isn't the ranks," Niger said. "It's the praetorium." He and Cato had both plodded their way up the ladder of office. Each had been military tribune, quaestor and aedile, each had put in years on the staff of a higher-ranking man and was ready to stand for the praetorship. It still rankled that Norbanus had what amounted to a proconsular command without having done any of that.

Besides, his was one of the new families, while theirs dated from before the Exile. In fact, their ancestors had been praetors and consuls when his were illiterate savages painting their backsides blue. The only thing that made him tolerable was the deadly enmity between Norbanus and Marcus Scipio, whom they detested even more. Scipio was more aristocratic than either of them and they resented that, too.

Norbanus smiled. He knew how little he was loved and

was not at all disturbed by it. The envy of lesser men was a part of greatness. Men like Lentulus Niger and Cato were destined to be used by him and to be sacrificed for his advantage, at necessity. A great man needed supporters and followers. He needed few friends.

"We face only a few more days of this," he told them. "I've just interrogated those locals from the caravan. They say that their people call this place the Wilderness of Zin."

"It's a fitting name," Cato granted. "I couldn't have come up with a better. So where are we?"

"About two days' march west of a town called Kadesh. It's a caravan stop and like all of them has its own spring. We can restore our water there and graze the animals. After that, we swing north."

"Out of this desert?" Niger said hopefully.

He grinned at them. "Any direction we go takes us out of the desert, if we just go far enough."

Their march had taken them through the blighted landscape from oasis to oasis, each of them yielding scarcely enough water and forage to keep the army moving. They had passed by incredibly ancient turquoise mines, watched over by statues of the cow-eared goddess Hathor, who for some reason was the deity of such places. Herders of goats had fled before them, and they had seen few humans other than these herdsmen. The desert was crossed by a network of caravan routes, but these were little traveled and the caravan they had met that afternoon was the first they had seen in several days.

"What's north of Kadesh?" Cato wanted to know.

"Another five or six days of marching should bring us into a cultivated district," Norbanus told them. "Its principle town is called Beersheba. It's a small place, but from there on we will be in civilized country."

"Who runs it?" Niger asked.

Norbanus grinned again. "We do."

ELIYAHU THE WATCHMAN CLIMBED TO HIS POST ATOP
the town wall, above the main gate, scratching in his beard,
grumbling. He was getting old and his knees protested at
the climb, though the mud wall stood barely twenty feet
higher than the ground surrounding. He stood on the little
platform just beside the gate and gazed out over the peace-
ful fields beyond. Not that he could see much, for there was
a heavy ground mist, as there was many mornings. Just beyond the wall, in the midst of a small pasture, there was a
little lake fed by an underground spring, and it was from
this that the fog arose.

From below came the patient exhalings of asses and the
ill-tempered snorts and groans of camels. These were the
beasts of caravan traders waiting for the south gate to open.
Eliyahu looked about and saw no sign of robbers. "Open the
gate," he said to the boys below. They were his youngest son
and a few grandsons, for charge of this gate had been in his
family since Moses. Not that there was much to watch for,
save for bandits in unsettled times, desert raiders and such.

He was about to sit in his chair and rest his bones when
he thought he heard a sound from out there in the mist. It
was not a clopping of hooves, but rather a great rustling
noise, with many clinkings and scraping sounds. Then he
heard a rhythmic tramping. What could this portend?

The mist began to disperse in the morning sun and from
it stepped a vision from a nightmare: a hundred men, then a
thousand, then many more, all marching in step, all dressed
in glinting metal, bearing shields, spears sloped over their

shoulders, all marching in perfect lockstep, as if the host were a single animal.

"Close the gate!" Eliyahu said, trying to shout but producing a strangled gasp. Then, more forcefully: "Close the gate!"

"What?" called his son, the slow-witted one.

"Close the gate, then run and bring the headmen! An army marches on Beersheba!"

Stunned, he watched as the host before him began to split up, rectangles of them swerving off to right and left, some to secure the lake, others to occupy the fields where the caravans picketed their beasts. Mounted contingents went right and left as well, riding around the walls out of sight. He guessed that these rode to prevent anyone from escaping town by the north gate. Beersheba was to be surrounded.

He hobbled to the old alarm gong by the gate, used to warn of bandit attack and not heard for many years. He seized the stubby bar and began beating vigorously on the brazen plate. At least it was something to do. Beersheba had perhaps three thousand inhabitants of all ages, and how they could defend the town from such an army he had no idea. They kept materializing from the mist like Pharaoh's army emerging from the Red Sea.

The headmen came running, eyes wide, scrambling up the stair to see what was wrong. They were the town elders, mainly merchants, and a couple of priests. "Eliyahu," gasped Simon, the elder of the council, "what is the meaning of this? If you are drunk I'll have your—"

Wordlessly, the watchman pointed south. The others crowded onto the platform and there was a great silence. "Are they Egyptians?" someone said at last.

"No army comes through the desert," Simon said quietly. "They may be from Arabia. From India, even."

After a while a little knot of men rode forward. Their faces were as fierce as any desert bandit's and their bearing was that of kings. One rode right up to the gate and looked up at them with amazing blue eyes. He wore a splendid cloak and had a helmet in the form of a lion's mask. "Does anyone up there speak Greek?" he asked. One of the priests assented and translated.

"Who are you?" Simon asked.

"We are soldiers of Rome."

"What's Rome?" Simon asked the others, quietly. Nobody knew. Then, to the man below: "What do you want?"

"We've been in the desert for a long time and we want to make use of your town, on your terms or ours."

The soldiers kept arriving in blocks of a hundred or more. The mist was almost gone now and they stretched almost out of sight on the land beyond. They were hard-looking men, burned dark, gaunt and ragged, but with their weapons and gear in perfect order. They maintained an incredible silence as they went about their evolutions, wheeling and maneuvering to the muffled tones of trumpets.

Simon smiled so broadly that his face looked fair to split. He threw his arms wide. "Welcome, my friends!"

NORBANUS AND HIS OFFICERS TOOK THEIR EASE IN the town's bathhouse. Apparently it was devoted to some sort of ritual bathing, but as far as they were concerned it was a bathhouse and they hadn't seen such a thing in a long time. They soaked and sluiced and rubbed down with olive oil and scraped it off with strigils.

"Here is what I've been able to learn," Titus Norbanus said, relaxing in the steaming water. "This country is claimed by the Seleucid ruler of Syria, but their presence is very weak. A family called the Hasmoneans have been in charge as subject-kings, but at the moment two princes are contending for power, one in the South and one in the North. I'm told that this is the usual state of affairs here. The major city is called Jerusalem and it's said to be rich."

An officer snorted. "These people think a man with two cows is rich. I've burned German villages richer than this place. The capital isn't likely to be much."

"That's yet to be seen," Norbanus told them. "Our primary objective is to get back to Italy, not to plunder."

"You're the one who brought up the supposed wealth of this Jerusalem," Cato said.

"If a little gold falls our way," Norbanus said, "so much the better."

Niger and Cato looked at each other. Just moving such an army through someone's country was cause for offense. If Norbanus turned this march into a giant bandit-raid, they would impeach him before the Senate for provoking war without the Senate's approval.

Norbanus caught the look. He knew perfectly well what they were thinking and he knew how to avoid the trap they foresaw. He had brought his army across the desert with a minimum of hardship and few losses, most of those to heat stroke and serpent bites. He had the esteem of the legionaries and was giving them a few days to rest and recuperate. They had confidence in their leader now. They would follow him anywhere.

He sat back and scooped water over his head with the greatest satisfaction. There was a great, rich world ahead of him and he intended to return to Rome having subdued much of it.

"From here," he said, "we march fast."

"THEIR RELIGION IS INCOMPREHENSIBLE," AULUS Fimbria said. He was a member of the college of pontifexes and served as augur to the expedition. "But they display great piety in matters of ritual law. In this they are as observant as any people we have ever encountered. They have a great many laws and taboos, which they honor faithfully. Unlike most people, who have many gods and a correct procedure for worshipping each of them, these have a single god but they differ bitterly over how his worship is to be conducted."

"What a peculiar people," Norbanus said. He rode at the head of his legions, but he dismounted from time to time to march along with them so they would not think him soft. They were in cultivated land now, and water was readily available if not exactly abundant. The people here cultivated the arts of irrigation, since rainfall was so infrequent. They were first-class farmers and squeezed fine crops from their acreage. Grapes grew abundantly and they made excellent wine.

Everywhere the Romans went, the people gaped at this unwonted apparition. Some fled, but more came to the camps in the evenings to trade. They brought provisions of all sorts and the soldiers had plentiful Egyptian coin to pay. Norbanus strictly forbade any mistreatment of the natives. He could not afford ill will at this stage.

"I cannot say that I understand their religious differences," Fimbria went on. "But some seem to think that sacrifices should be carried out one way, others say another. A few like to ape Greek culture and give their god only the most cursory observance. There is a sect that live in all-male communities in the desert and devote their whole lives to ritual. Their god interferes in and regulates the people's lives in ways that civilized gods do not."

Norbanus shrugged. "A man is born with his gods; he doesn't pick them. I suppose this odd deity suits these people. I am more concerned with their political situation, in any case."

They were nearing the major city. It would have been enjoyable, Norbanus thought, to appear before the walls of Jerusalem as a complete surprise, as they had appeared at Beersheba, but this was not to be. They had been spied, and fast-riding horsemen had pounded toward the capital to give warning. Even a Roman army could not outpace a galloping horse. Even so, he was sure that they would arrive before expected. Whoever was in charge would assume that the approaching army would be moving at the pace common to most armies.

He had learned that southern Judea, the district locally called Judah, was under the control of a prince named Jonathan. The northern region, called Israel, was under Jonathan's cousin, named Manasseh. The northern kingdom was larger, its men more numerous and its religious practice more fanatical. The southern was more sophisticated and its king, while militarily weaker, had possession of the holy city.

The Romans had questioned informed men in Beersheba and along their route of march and knew that this north-south split greatly predated the current dynastic dispute. In fact, it dated from before the unification of the country nearly a thousand years earlier, when a king named Saul had forged a nation out of a collection of tribes.

This nation, they were told, had flourished under a succession of brilliant kings, but for barely three generations. Then it had split once more under rival claimants, and that had been the situation for much of the time since. The land had fallen to a succession of conquerors, with Egypt dominating briefly, then Babylon, then Persia. Like everyone else, they had been conquered by Alexander, and then his Seleucid successor had taken over. One of the Seleucids had tried to suppress the local religion and institute the worship of Greek gods, and the whole region had erupted in furious rebellion, led by a family called the Maccabees. The two contending for rule at the moment were descendants of the Maccabees.

"Why so much fighting over this little place?" Lentulus Niger wondered. "It's decent farmland but I've seen better. The natives are sullen and have an outlandish religion. I doubt they'd even make good slaves."

"It must be the location," Cato said. They rode just behind Norbanus, ahead of the standard bearers. "To the east is just more of that desert. They live on this narrow coastal strip. That means that any army that wants to get to Egypt and Libya and northern Africa has to pass through here. Likewise, Egyptian or Carthaginian armies headed for Syria have to pass through here. There's no place else to go, except by sea."

"It must make life interesting here every few years," Niger said.

Late that day they came within sight of the city. Once it would have impressed them, but after the splendors of Carthage and Alexandria, it looked small and shabby. The acropolis pointed out to them as Temple Mount was the only feature that seemed comparable to the greater cities.

An army was drawn up between them and the city.

"Battle order, Commander?" Niger said.

"I estimate their numbers at less than six thousand," Norbanus said. "This is no more than a gesture—all that the local king could scrape together on short notice." He looked around at the countryside. Most of it was open fields, well cultivated. Like most towns in this part of the world, it owed its location to a reliable and abundant water source. "Find the nearest spring and pitch camp. I'll parley with the locals."

"You're not going to leave the army and put yourself in the hands of foreigners, are you?" Niger said.

"I'm not a fool. I'll take the cavalry with me and halt a good distance from them. Then they can come to me." He gestured to his mounted trumpeter and the man blew a succession of notes on his *lituus:* a straight horn with its funnel bent back sharply. It was so named for its resemblance to the crook-topped augur's staff, and it was used only by the cavalry. At the signal, the small cavalry force detached from its flanking duties and rode forward to attend the general.

Norbanus looked them over before proceeding. Romans were notoriously poor cavalrymen. These were mostly well-born young men, mainly of Gallic descent and some of them sons of allied chieftains who lacked Roman citizenship. Their equipment was more ornate than that of the legionaries but resembled it in most details except for their flat, oval shields, their longer swords and the short mail capes reinforcing the shoulders of their armor. They carried lances instead of javelins.

"Dust yourselves off and mount your plumes," Norbanus ordered. "We're going to call on a foreign king."

The men did as ordered, chasing the road grime from their armor and taking the fragile feathers and the horsehair crests from the boxes tied behind their saddles. They were too delicate and valuable for everyday wear and were reserved for parade and battle, where the display was esteemed as intimidating to the enemy. When the commander deemed their glitter to be sufficient, they rode forward, toward the native force before the city.

They halted well out of bowshot and waited. After a few minutes, a small delegation rode out from the army opposite. They were well turned out, their equipment mostly of Greek design, which was fashionable everywhere, it seemed. They reined up a hundred paces away and a man in splendid armor rode forward alone.

"Who are you?" he said in Greek, "and what are your intentions? You trespass outrageously on the domain of King Jonathan of Judea. I demand to speak with your commander." His accent was very different from that of the local people when they spoke Greek. This one spoke like Greek was his native tongue. Norbanus read him for a Greek mercenary. He had encountered many such since arriving in the Mediterranean world.

"I am Proconsul Titus Norbanus of Rome, and I am the commander of the army you see before you. We intend harm to no one here and wish only to pass through this land. However, as Proconsul of Rome, I must deal directly with your king."

"You are commander and you come to parley in person? Most irregular."

"Romans do things differently from most people. Kindly let your king know that I would speak with him. As you see," he waved an arm behind him without looking, "my men are not preparing for battle. They are encamping." The man could not know how incredibly swift the legions were at going from encampment to battle order, and Norbanus had no intention of informing him. Best to lull people into confidence until it was too late.

The man eyed the Roman army. Men had stacked their shields against their spears, hung their helmets from the shafts. They had their spades and pickaxes out and were digging. Some hauled baskets of earth. They looked more like armored farmers than soldiers.

"I will go speak to His Majesty. He may summon you to a conference."

"Roman proconsuls are not summoned by anyone. He can ride out here to speak with me and he will. I will erect a tent on this spot for our meeting."

The mercenary snorted. "A king does not come from his palace to meet with a foreign general."

"Your king will. He'll have heard of Rome by now. He'll be eager to meet with me. Go tell him I await him here."

The Greek rode off. Norbanus sent orders for his praetorium to be brought out and erected. His commanders grumbled that the traditional location for the praetorium was inside the camp, but their general was adamant. They set up the fine tent and before it erected a raised dais and upon it set his curule chair, draped with animal pelts. To either side of the chair were the shrines of his four legions and behind him stood the standard bearers of those legions, their heads and shoulders draped with skins of lion, wolf and bear, the aquilifers holding the four eagles, the signifers of the lesser formations with their animal standards. The approach to the praetorium was flanked on both sides by an honor guard of cavalry, now polished up to their full brilliance.

On the dais to both sides of him stood his senior commanders and the tribunes and legati in charge of the individual legions and the auxilia. There had been objections to this. Many had pointed out that it was folly to separate the entire senior staff from the legions, leaving them vulnerable to treachery by unknown foreigners. Norbanus had asserted that the cavalry would be adequate to extricate them from any situation likely to arise and that he anticipated not hostility, but a proposal of alliance. His subordinates were unconvinced, but they were Romans and they obeyed.

When a mounted party approached from the small host opposite them, all but Norbanus assumed that it was but another officer sent to make arrangements for the king's arrival. In the lead was a man on a splendid white horse and behind him rode a half dozen elders and an honor guard of no more than twenty horsemen in Greek gear, one of them bearing a standard tipped by a six-pointed star.

"How long are they going to keep us waiting?" Cato said. "We are prepared to receive royalty, not some flunky."

"I think this is the king," Norbanus said. "And I must say that I like his style."

"It's effective," Niger said grudgingly. "He can't hope to overawe us with a display of military might, so he rides in looking casual and confident." Others nodded and agreed. Every officer there was not only a military professional but a seasoned politician and veteran of the law courts and the voting enclosures. They had been drilled in the rhetorical arts as rigorously as with the sword, and they appreciated a clever, impressive display.

Head high, as if without a care in the world, the man rode between the guardsmen, who dipped their lances in unison. He nodded graciously to either side in acknowledgment of the salute. Drawing rein before the dais, he dismounted immediately, not waiting for an equerry. A Roman slave stepped forward to take charge of his horse and the man strode to the dais.

His robe was white, girded by a golden sash. His long coat was white as well and he wore soft, red boots with up-turned, pointed toes. He was a handsome man of about thirty years, with aquiline features. His hair was cut in the fashionable Greek style but his short beard was dressed in small, tight ringlets in the Eastern fashion. His only weapon was a long dagger thrust through his sash. He halted before the steps and touched a hand to his breast, inclining his head very slightly.

"Judah greets Rome," the king said.

Norbanus rose and descended the steps. He took the king by the hand. "Rome greets Jonathan, king of the Jews." Behind him, he knew that his subordinates were stricken as by the lightning of Jupiter. Their commander, with no authority from the Senate, was recognizing this foreigner as not only king of Judah, but of Israel as well!

Jonathan smiled. Norbanus led him up the steps to a chair beside his own. He presented his officers and proffered the compliments of the Senate and People of Rome. He apologized for not presenting his army for a royal review, informing Jonathan that regulations required every Roman legion to fortify its camp by nightfall, wherever it was. Even a proconsul could not ignore regulations. He promised a full review the next day.

"Word had reached us that the Romans had returned to Italy," Jonathan said. "I had expected to receive an embassy within the next year or so, should—"

"Should the Carthaginians not exterminate us swiftly?" Norbanus finished for him.

"Forgive me, but the whole tale of your return seemed so outlandish and unlikely, and the great might of Carthage so well known, that I thought it unlikely that I would ever see a Roman. I certainly did not expect four legions on my doorstep!" He laughed richly and Norbanus joined him. "And now I may say that I am not at all displeased. As long as you do not abuse my subjects, you have full freedom of my country. I anticipate no difficulty, for I am already assured of your fine discipline."

"My men will not take a grain of wheat that is not paid for, nor will they molest your women. They will not be quartered upon your civilians but will stay housed in their camps, and they will enter your towns only in small groups of no more than ten. My quaestors," he gestured toward four young officers, "are the bankers for their legions and will confer with your merchants and supply officers for all goods we need in bulk."

Jonathan nodded gravely. "It is good to arrange these necessary mundanities early, before there can be a chance for friction and unfortunate incidents. I find all your proposals more than reasonable. Now, the last word we had was that a large Roman contingent was with the army of Hamilcar besieging Alexandria. Is this that force? I can think of no other so near that might have come from so unexpected a direction."

"It is," Norbanus confirmed.

"I see. Please allow me to congratulate you on a tactical masterstroke. Nobody had the slightest notion that you were coming this way. Taking to the desert instead of the safe coastal route. Nobody had guessed your location or route. I suppose that this has also given you a certain—ah— shall we say, freedom of action which you might not otherwise have enjoyed." There was a rustling of shifting feet on the dais. The subtleties of his excellent Greek packed the words with a meaning clear even to the Romans: Jonathan knew that by avoiding the coastal ports Norbanus had freed himself from oversight and control by the Senate.

Norbanus shifted the subject. "I take it you have learned of our reconquest of Sicily?"

"Every ship from the West brings word of new Roman successes."

"They shall continue to do so. This detour of ours was unexpected and we are eager to return to Italy and reinforce Rome's might. Your aid in our return to our ancestral homeland will be remembered with utmost gratitude by the Senate and People of Rome."

Jonathan nodded. "I will of course do my utmost to help. Sadly, Judah is not a maritime nation. The distance to Italy is great and Carthage, at least for the moment, rules the sea. I fear that your return must entail a very long march, all the way to Greece."

Norbanus sighed theatrically. "Alas, it is as I feared. This means we must march through the land claimed by your usurping cousin, does it not?"

"It can scarcely be avoided," the king agreed.

"Might we expect the usurper to be hostile?"

"Doubtless his spies are already flogging their horses northward to tell him of your arrival. Whatever his decision, he will have ample time to prepare. He will learn that we are now friends, and he may take this amiss."

"Rome, of course, desires no conflict with the rulers of the East. However, since this—his name is Manasseh, I believe?—is clearly not the legitimate ruler, and you have proclaimed yourself to be a friend of Rome, I foresee no objection from the Senate."

The king leaned back and stroked his beard. "Things are moving very quickly."

Norbanus laid a hand upon his shoulder. "Events can never transpire too quickly for men of vision and destiny. Such men seize them and bend them to their own will."

"Very true," Jonathan said. "There is Syria to consider. The House of Seleucus is no longer what it was, but it is still formidable. As recently as this summer, Antiochus contemplated an assault upon Egypt. Parthia presses him now, but if he can make his peace with them, he may turn his attention south once more."

"My friend Jonathan," Norbanus said, now not quite so jovial, "your land is a fine one, and I do not doubt that your men are doughty warriors, but if Antiochus decides to march south in full force he will crush you. Your only course will be to kiss the ground before his feet and hope that he will allow you to keep your throne, if only as his puppet."

He paused a few moments, allowing this vision to sink in. "With the friendship of Rome, however, you have nothing to fear. Rome will not only confirm you in your throne and your titles, but will increase them. Rome always rewards her friends lavishly." He was glad that the stony faces of his subordinates yielded nothing.

"Please do not think me rude if I observe that these are vaunting words from a people who were thought extinct until last year, and who have yet to display an unshakable grip upon the peninsula of Italy."

Norbanus smiled. "Tomorrow I'll assemble my legions and put them through their paces for your entertainment. Once you have seen them, tell me whether you think Rome cannot deliver on her promises."

CHAPTER FIVE

THE SCENE WAS BIZARRE, IN SOME WAYS COMICAL. The beach was lined with frameworks where men sat on staggered benches, pulling at oars under the direction of rowing masters, while hortators set the time with trilling flutes. There was cursing and yelps of pain and bursts of laughter as men fouled one another's oar or fell from their benches.

Other frameworks held the skeletons of ships in the building process. The sound of hammering competed with the voices and the flutes, and over all hung the smell of pitch boiling in pots.

"What energy these people have!" Zeno marveled. "And what audacity! They are going to challenge the greatest naval power in the world, and they haven't so much as an hour's experience at sea."

"Until a year ago," Izates said, "no Roman had even *seen* the sea."

"Exactly. They think they can do anything."

"Such confidence is unwise. It smacks of hubris. The ancient tragedies are full of stories of men who thought thus highly of themselves. The gods put them in their place."

The rowers were men contributed by the municipalities of Italy, now eager to gain favor with the new masters.

"It looks," Izates said, "like all the madmen in the world assembled on one beach."

"And yet there are at least five other such beaches in Italy," Zeno observed, "with at least an equal number of madmen upon each."

"Thousands of hayseed landsmen," Izates mused, "sitting on shore, rowing phantom galleys. It is a scene worthy of Aristophanes."

"They did this once before, in their first war with Carthage. They were successful that time."

"According to my reading," Izates countered, "they also met with several naval disasters during those years. It does little good to defeat your enemy in a sea battle, only to lose your entire fleet to a storm any fisherman could have seen coming."

"They couldn't become competent seamen all at once."

A line of four-wheeled wagons rumbled past them. The beds held Rostra: ships' rams cast in bronze by Campanian foundries. No two were alike: The heads of real or mythical beasts were most favored, but they saw one cast as Jove's thunderbolt, another that was a godlike fist. Men trudged by dragging carts heaped with coils of rope, and lines of workmen shouldered long masts and yards.

"Between restoring the cities and building this fleet," Izates said, "Italy will be denuded of timber."

Amazing as the work itself was, Zeno found the organization the Romans brought to the process no less remarkable. A senator aided by a staff of distinguished equites oversaw each shipyard. These men directed a staff of ship-builders hired from Greece, Rhodes, Cyprus and other parts of the eastern sea. The rowing masters were likewise Greeks skilled in this demanding craft, for rowing a three-banked ship of war was not a matter of simply tugging upon an oar. Rather, it was a highly skilled trade and rowers were usually free men, rarely slaves or prisoners.

So painstaking were the organizers that they had already established a guild for the rowers to join, complete with its own tutelary deities and special festivals. Rowers were to have quasimilitary status, half legionary pay and limited citizenship upon discharge, to be upgraded to full citizenship depending upon how valuable their service should prove. Nothing was overlooked.

"The schedule calls for maneuvers to begin in the harbor by the next full moon," Zeno said. "Naval operations to commence on the full moon following."

"They're dreaming," Izates said. "They can't attain competence in so short a time, and Carthage may not allow them the leisure in any case. Hamilcar's fleet could show up in the harbor tomorrow."

"He won't try operations in Italy until he's taken Sicily back. No Carthaginian general since Hannibal has shown any real boldness or originality. It's always a slow, predictable process by regular stages."

"Maybe so," Izates allowed, "but Carthage is immensely rich and has tremendous resources. These Romans have accomplished what they have through sheer audacity. That is not a quality that prevails in the long run. Carthage can afford to lose possessions. She can even afford to lose a string of battles. With so much wealth to hire foreign mercenaries, Carthage will scarcely feel the casualties. They'll crucify a few generals and raise another army, build another navy."

"It's served them well in the past," Zeno agreed. "But I don't think it will this time. Not against this enemy."

The Princeps Gabinius had supplied them with letters and documents providing them with full permission to explore the Roman bases and see the preparations being made for the upcoming war against Carthage. "We're getting ready to fight Hamilcar and his allies, if he has any," Gabinius had explained. "We'll probably be doing little else for a number of years to come, so there's little point in hiding our intentions."

The Romans were well informed about the military capabilities of Carthage and Egypt. Gabinius wanted to know about Seleucid Syria (weak and remote, Zeno informed him), Parthia (powerful but remote) and Macedonia (formidable and very close). This last bit of information was of some concern. Ever since Hannibal, the idea of a Carthage-Macedonia alliance had been troubling. War against two powerful, professional armies at once was a daunting prospect even for people as confident as the Romans.

"Who is king of Macedonia now?" Gabinius had asked him.

"Philip the Seventh, and he is said to be a Macedonian chieftain of the old school—very martial and adventurous."

"A conqueror?"

"A mercenary, although no doubt he would like very much to revive the conquering ways of his ancestors. He hires his phalanxes out to neighboring kings and has campaigned in Illyria and Thrace, to my knowledge."

"Does he command personally?"

"He has done so."

"We know that Ptolemy depended heavily on Macedonians in his first battle against Hamilcar. They did him little good."

"From what I heard," Zeno said, "it was your legions who won that battle for Hamilcar, and that the boy-king Ptolemy's forces were ill-led."

Gabinius nodded. "It's hard to judge the quality of an army if its leadership is poor. The Macedonians accomplished little that day, but we heard that they fell back upon Alexandria in good order. On another field, with a better leader, they might be a formidable foe."

The Romans' near-obsessive fixation on military matters was stupefying, and Izates insisted that this defined them as a severely limited people, but Zeno demurred. He felt that their accomplishments in other areas were even more remarkable. Their shortcomings in the more refined intellectual strata were undeniable: They showed little cultivation of the arts and few were learned in philosophy. To Greeks these lapses set the Romans on a level little above the more primitive barbarians. But their attention to the minutiae of government and law was a thing of marvel.

From the beginning of their stay in Rome, Zeno had made a point of attending the law courts and hearing the speeches of orators. Senate meetings were forbidden to anyone not of the senatorial order, but the results of their debates were quickly relayed to the Forum crowds by way of the Rostra: the speaker's platform at the western end of the Forum.

Like most foreigners, Zeno had believed that Rome was actually ruled by the Senate, but he learned quickly that this belief was oversimplified. The Senate formed a landed aristocracy of great prestige and its powers in foreign affairs and war making were nearly absolute, but there were other assemblies of comparable power.

The Concilium Plebis, for instance, consisted only of the plebeian class and elected the tribunes of the people, en-

acted laws and conducted certain trials. The Comitia Trib-
uta consisted of all citizens assembled in their tribes and
elected, the plebeian aediles, the tribunes of the soldiers and
the quaestors. The Comitia Centuriata consisted of the entire citizenry assembled in centuries and ranked by property
assessment. They elected the highest magistrates: praetors,
consuls and censors. They also heard trials for treason.

Roman political life was a constant struggle for power
and influence among these interlocking assemblies, their
memberships and their leaders. A man of great power in one
assembly might be just another vote in another, and individual votes counted for very little. Election to office led to
a seat in the Senate and it was the senators who provided the
officer corps. Glory in war led to election to higher office, so
competition for office was both intense and complex. Zeno
knew he could devote his whole life to unraveling the com-
plexities and ramifications of it all.

Despite the multiplicity of legislative and judicial bodies, the Roman system seemed to function with great efficiency. Zeno was especially impressed with the courts. Trials
were for the most part speedy and fair, the judges impartial
and the lawyers well versed in all the intricacies of the law.
He remarked upon this to Gabinius.

"We've built up our system to be the best in the world,"
he said, "but don't be deceived. Wait until you see two important, powerful men at odds in court. Then things are not
so equitable, as when some small businessman is being tried
for fraud, or a border dispute between minor landholders is
settled. It's difficult to impanel an impartial jury when
everyone is a client to someone of greater importance, and
really wealthy men are seldom above a little bribery when
their interests are at stake."

This concept of clientage was new to the Greeks. It

turned out that, like so many Roman practices, it dated back to the primitive days of chieftains and warriors, when small peasants put themselves under the protection of a greater landowner and followed him in war. This simple relationship had grown into a complex system of interlocking obligations that included monetary and legal aid, support in the Forum, whether in trials or elections, even the obligations of death and funerals. Slaves upon manumission became clients of their former masters, and clientage was hereditary. Among Romans, no relationship was more important than that of client and patron.

Gabinius had insisted that the two Greeks move into his new house and had given each a token—a small medallion embossed with a shield of Mars—symbolizing yet another status: *hospes*. It was a word that translated as "guest-friend." It meant that, when visiting each other's city, each was obligated to provide the other with hospitality, with support in court should such prove necessary, with medical care when ill, even with proper funeral rites should a *hospes* die while visiting. This relationship was also hereditary. Should a descendant of Zeno or Izates visit Rome, he could present the token to any descendant of Gabinius and claim hospitality.

"The Romans have to have everything spelled out," Izates groused when he and Zeno were alone. "Everything involves mutual obligations and everything is hereditary."

"Maybe this is one reason for the Romans' success," Zeno remarked. "It is the great stability of all their institutions. They leave little to the whims of individual men."

"Such institutions are probably necessary because the Romans have little natural, innate sense of dignity and civility. They must have these long-established guidelines to keep them civilized."

Zeno laughed. "You always find some way to denigrate the Romans. Nothing they do ever impresses you."

Izates considered this. "That is true. I am equally skeptical of the apparent virtues of Greeks and Jews. It is part of being a Cynic. Men are full of themselves, blown up with self-importance. It takes only a little thought to find the secret inadequacy behind their vauntings. Men have feet of clay."

"Feet of what?" Zeno asked. Izates explained that the saying was from an ancient tale of his own people, about a brazen idol that rested upon feet of clay and how its weakness was exposed. Zeno protested that Izates' ancestors misunderstood the nature of the gods and their images, and Izates told him that he was missing the point. Their discussions frequently ended this way.

Now, as they inspected the impromptu shipyard and training facility, Roman method, discipline and thoroughness were once again on full display.

A small forest of masts had grown up along the shore, and men were engaged in hauling on ropes that erected these masts in artificial keels, then hauling long yards up the masts and unfurling the big, rectangular sails. Sailing masters shouted orders to the sweating sailors-in-training, making them swing the yards about so as to catch quartering winds. Experienced sailors conducted classes in how to tie the many knots required by seagoing craft.

"These are skills ordinarily learned by every sailor when he goes to sea as a boy," Zeno said. "Here grown men are trained in vast numbers, just as newly recruited soldiers learn their trade in training camps. But, there is a difference." Here Zeno paused dramatically.

"What might that be?" Izates wanted to know.

"In training camps the Romans teach skills in which they

are already expert. Here," he waved an arm, taking in the huge facility, "they are teaching a multitude of skills that they do not even possess themselves!"

Izates looked at him blankly, then he turned slowly to scan the madmen's naval base. "This exceeds even a philosopher's tolerance for the absurd."

"You need a capacity for wonder. And this is not their most improbable accomplishment of late. That rogue general of theirs has the Museum accomplishing marvels, if half the tales we've heard are true."

Izates shuddered. "Philosophers behaving like mechanics! Disgusting! Speculations about the *nature* of matter and the properties of movement are quite proper. But this Roman has them actually *building* things! They should be stripped of the status of philosophers and degraded to that of mere workmen." He turned aside and spat.

"But how can their ideas be verified without creating the machines and actually testing them?"

"It is unworthy," Izates insisted. "They should content themselves with simply thinking about such things. To sully the purity of thought with the manipulation of gross matter is a desecration!"

"Romans like to accomplish things, not just think about them. For a Cynic, you are notably respectful toward philosophical pretension."

"A true Cynic respects only purity and virtue. All else is vanity."

"And the supposed purity of philosophers is nothing but snobbery," Zeno said.

"Snobbery?" Izates said in a quiet voice. "How does reverence for the purity of thought and logic translate into snobbery?"

"It isn't purity to which most philosophers aspire," Zeno

explained. "It's respectability. Most of them are impoverished men of less than noble background, and they want desperately to be accepted as peers of the aristocracy. That's why they can't stand the thought of philosophers getting their hands dirty."

Izates peered narrowly at him. "Now it's you that sound like a Cynic."

Zeno grinned. "I was born one. You had to study. Besides," he turned serious again, "think of it! They've built a boat that can take men beneath the water and back to the surface safely!"

"And what have they accomplished thereby? They can see nothing because the boat is entirely sealed. They can stay underwater only a short time and merely risk drowning for nothing."

"But it has never before been done by mortal men," Zeno protested.

"Then it is novelty for the sake of novelty and therefore just a vulgar show, meant to impress the credulous mob."

"No, it is meant to sink enemy ships and seems to have performed the task well."

"Nonsense!" Izates performed one of the more common Greek rude noises. "Men have been sinking ships since before the time of Odysseus. The process is always much the same. Do the sailors drown more thoroughly because their ship was destroyed by an unseen craft? Does the ship sink more precipitately for being rammed by a submarine vessel?"

"As I understand it, the sinkings were accomplished more by a sawing action than by ramming. Apparently, ramming is unadvisable in one of these ships. It makes even the usual galleys leak, and this might be disastrous when you are submerged already."

"That is rank sophistry and unworthy of you. Military

toys!" Izates grumped. "As if the old-fashioned methods of mutual extermination were not lethal enough already. Demetrius Poliorcetes loved to play with such grotesque machines and whatever became of him?"

"Not all the new inventions of the Archimedean school are military in nature," Zeno said. "There are men experimenting with mirrors and lenses who say they can vastly improve our study of the stars and heavenly bodies."

"Well, I suppose that is proper," Izates admitted grudgingly. He was keenly interested in astronomy. "As long as they leave the manufacture of these new instruments to craftsmen, and confine themselves to making observations and speculating upon them. I am skeptical of how much help these instruments shall prove, anyway. Our ancestors did well enough with only their own two eyes. How much does making a star seem bigger tell us? Their courses will remain the same. Their place in the heavens will be unchanged. The rising and setting of the major constellations will occur with the same regularity as was observed by the astronomers of Babylon and Egypt thousands of years ago."

"But look at this!" Zeno said with a note of triumph that Izates recognized. His friend had been leading up to this all along.

"You've set an ambush for me," he grumbled.

Zeno drew a folded papyrus from the pouch at his waist. "This came from our friend Gabinius. It was among the most recent reports from Marcus Scipio to the Senate. Gabinius says that it is a mystery to him, but that we might find it amusing." He unfolded it portentously and began to read.

"Among the intriguing new developments are those of the Cypriote, Agathocles. I have written of him before: He is the experimenter with mirrors, who invented the device for observing around corners and over walls. This device proved very useful on the underwater boats.

"His newest creations involve parabolic mirrors and lenses of finely ground glass, which by some seemingly magical property cause distant objects to appear closer. He has used some of these devices to study the stars and the moon, and the astronomers who have looked through these things have been astonished. They say that, not only do the stars appear nearer, but they can actually see more stars than are visible to our eyes alone. Agathocles says that he is frustrated by the impurities and other imperfections in his lenses, and works feverishly with his Babylonian glass workers to create clearer, more refined glass and finer grinding and polishing agents to perfect his lenses.

"I am sure that these things must have some sort of military application. Reconnaissance, both at sea and on land, comes to mind. I shall set Agathocles to work devising small, portable viewing devices."

Zeno refolded the parchment. "What do you think of that?"

Izates looked stunned. "Can this be possible?" he said, the sneer for once gone from his voice. "Not the device— we've all seen how reflective surfaces distort, so why not control the distortion to magnify? No, I mean, can it be true that there are more stars in Heaven than we can see?"

"No sense pondering on an empty stomach," Zeno said, pleased at having stunned his friend for once.

Numerous hawkers had set up booths around the military facility, and they went to one such and purchased bread, cheese, fruit and large cups of wine. They took these to a stone jetty and sat on its rim, their feet dangling over the water, while they munched, drank and talked over the implications of this unprecedented news.

"From the earliest days of rational thought," Izates said, "it has been believed that we could understand the world by looking at it and analyzing what we see. But if this man Agathocles is correct, if his magnifying devices show what is truly there, then it means that there are things in the cosmos that we cannot see!"

"That seems clear," Izates agreed.

"And if this is true of the visible world, what of the world as perceived by our other senses? Are there sounds we cannot hear? Are there objects all around us that we cannot feel?"

"I see no reason why this may not be the case," Izates said. "Consider: A man with only slightly defective vision cannot see many things that those of us with clear vision can. That does not mean those things are not there, merely that he can't see them. We cannot see the wind, but we can feel it and we can hear it. We know that dogs can detect scents our own noses are not keen enough for, and they often seem to hear sounds when we hear nothing at all."

Izates nodded. "Quite so, quite so. There may be a whole invisible cosmos out there, previously unsuspected. Perhaps you are right, and we philosophers in our vanity have assumed upon an imperfect base of knowledge."

"This is a rather sudden shift of view," Zeno noted.

"A Cynic only needs his bottom kicked once to know that he has been kicked. One learns to understand the world as it is presented, not as an ideal dreamed up by a poet." He took a long drink, draining his cup, then he set it down. "Well. It is time for us to be going."

"Going? Where?"

"To Alexandria, of course! That is where the new world of philosophy is taking shape. Why should we want to be anywhere else?"

"But we came here to study the resurgence of Rome!" Zeno protested.

"Part of that resurgence is taking place right now, in Alexandria. And it may well prove to be the most important part. Think of Alexander. His empire did not outlast his final breath, but he spread Greek culture throughout the world. These soldierly oafs may soon be forgotten, but it may be that they have, all unwitting, changed the nature of philosophy, which is a far greater wonder than any conquest. Come along. Gabinius will give us letters of introduction to this Scipio fellow. I know plenty of people in the Museum. You want to be a great historian? We'll be at the center of history!"

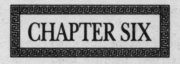

CHAPTER SIX

"A WALKING SHIP?" SELENE LOOKED FROM ONE RO-man to the other. Their expressions seemed earnest. "I can see that I have stayed away from the Museum too long. Does a ship that walks have some advantage over the more familiar sort that sails or is rowed?" She hoped for some equally ironic response, but they seemed to consider her question seriously. Irony, she had learned, was a subtlety beyond the ken of the Romans. And as for humor—she almost shuddered—what struck the Romans as funny struck most people with horror.

"It doesn't exactly walk," Marcus Scipio said. "In fact, it is more of a rotary motion, rather hard to describe, really—"

"Perhaps," Flaccus said, "a demonstration is in order." Like Scipio, Flaccus was a senator, one with a more literary bent than his friend. The other Romans considered Flaccus lazy and lacking in martial vigor. Only a Roman would have considered him so. With her own eyes Selene had on one occasion seen him kill four enemies with six swift strokes of his short sword. Marcus had upbraided him for the two wasted strokes.

"Yes," she sighed, "a demonstration." The philosophers of the Archimedean school, who had risen from obscurity to preeminence with the arrival of the Romans, dearly loved to show off their new toys.

They trooped from the palace and entered the huge royal litter, which carried them the short distance down to the royal harbor. Since her last visit, a new ship had arrived. It certainly looked strange, with the bizarre addition of wheels to its sides, but how such a thing could walk escaped her. She saw also that it was equipped with the new, single steering oar mounted at the extreme end of the stern, instead of the pair pivoted at its sides in the familiar fashion.

At the wharf they descended from the litter and boarded the ship by way of its extra-long gangplank. The addition of the huge side wheels meant that the ship itself could not directly abut the stone wharf. The main deck of the vessel was as unconventional as the rest. It was very narrow, in order to make room for immense, inboard wheels that corresponded to those on the outside of the ship. These wheels were hollow frameworks, and they contained men.

"I confess," Selene said, "to utter mystification."

A man in a philosopher's ragged tunic came forward, his face wreathed in that self-satisfied smile she had come to know so well. He bowed and waited to be addressed.

"Good afternoon, Chilo," said the queen. "What new miracle have you to show me today?"

"As so often, my queen," he said, "there is little new about it. It is a novel application for the common water-raising wheel used in irrigation operations."

"I had noticed the resemblance," she said. "Why one needs irrigation wheels on a ship is not obvious."

"It has to do with our researches into the properties of energy," he said earnestly. "There is a relationship between force exerted in one direction and another force, or perhaps the same force, in another direction. We feel that there is a principle—"

"Quite fascinating, I am sure," the queen interrupted. "You must be sure to tell me all about it when you have it all figured out. In the meantime, if you could just show me how wheels benefit a ship?"

"Of course, Majesty, of course. Well, the outer structure is not precisely a wheel. I have termed it a 'rotary oar.' You see the boards protruding from its perimeter? These are paddles, and they perform the same function as a conventional oar, except that they work in a vertical plane, instead of the horizontal, or, rather the elliptical-horizontal plane of an oar."

"Chilo," Scipio said, "why not just get it moving? The principle of the thing will be instantly appreciable to Her Majesty then."

"I suppose so," Chilo said, disappointed.

"Now he'll sulk," Selene said when the philosopher went off to give his orders to the crew. "There is nothing sadder than a philosopher cheated of a chance to lecture."

Among the ship's petty officers there was a barking of orders and a popping of whips, and a piper began to play a rhythmic tune on his double flute. Within the inboard wheels, men began climbing rungs as if ascending a ladder. The outboard wheels started to turn, churning the water. The ship commenced a slow movement. It drew away from the wharf and moved out into the harbor amid a great creaking of machinery.

"You see," Chilo explained, "the vertical motion of the slaves climbing is transformed into the rotary motion of the inboard wheel turning. This is in turn transmitted to the outboard wheel, causing the paddles to push against the water, propelling the ship forward. By turning around and climbing the rear of the wheel, the slaves can cause the ship to move backward. Direction can be controlled by causing one wheel to move more slowly than the other, and the steering oar can be used for minor corrections. By working the wheels in opposite directions, the ship can spin quickly on its axis."

"Very ingenious," the queen allowed. "But oared ships can do all these things, and have for centuries. What is the advantage of these wheels?"

"There are several," Marcus Scipio informed her. "In the first place, you need far fewer slaves to turn these wheels than to man oars. A ship this size would require at least three hundred, with plenty of relief rowers. Thirty or forty slaves are all you need to man these wheels. They eat far less and that makes for longer voyages."

"And," said Flaccus, "rowers must be highly skilled. They are expensive and are not replaced easily. Totally unskilled slaves and convicts can turn these wheels. Nothing is required except for a sound pair of legs."

"They can't be deaf," Marcus pointed out. "They have to be able to hear the flute."

Flaccus nodded. "That is true."

"If a wheel is damaged in battle," Selene pointed out, "it wouldn't be easy to replace, not like a damaged oar."

"This vessel is a prototype built to test the design," Chilo said. "For a warship, the wheels will have armored cowlings. Only the part that actually touches the water need be exposed." He looked at her expectantly.

"Very well," she said at last, "you may proceed with this project. What is the next phase?"

"Trials on the open sea, Your Majesty," Chilo told her. "These can proceed immediately, with this experimental vessel. Upon successful conclusion, a full-sized armed and manned warship will be built and tested. If all goes well, as I am sure it will, a flotilla will be constructed and deployed."

"The ultimate test will be battle," Scipio said. "If the wheeled ships prove to be more effective in battle, as well as cheaper and less wasteful of manpower, then we will convert entirely to the new system."

"Your Senate may be displeased to hear of it," she said, smiling. "I hear that they are even now building a fleet on the old model, and taking a great deal of trouble to train rowers."

"They'll adapt," he said. "We are an adaptable people."

That evening the two Romans dined with the queen on a palace terrace overlooking the beautiful little royal harbor with its jewel-like artificial island. Just to the west, they could see the huge double harbor of Alexandria, divided by the immense Heptastadion Bridge connecting the Pharos to the mainland. On the eastern end of Pharos towered the incomparable lighthouse.

All this, Selene thought, was hers. Alexandria, the most glorious city in the world. And this city was only the crowning gem among her possessions. She owned all of Egypt, from the Delta, which contained the richest farmlands in the world, all the way down the immense river and beyond the quarries near the First Cataract, where the market of the Elephantine Island received all the exotic goods of the continent to the south, such as the ivory that gave the island its name, wonderful feathers and the pelts of beautiful animals, and the animals themselves: lions, cheetahs, apes, birds. There were woods for tree-poor Egypt, dyestuffs, spices and endless coffles of black slaves from the interior to work the farms and quarries of Egypt and to be sold abroad, where they commanded high prices for their exotic looks, so different from common, pale-skinned slaves.

She was the richest as well as the most powerful woman in the world. *But,* she thought, *it means nothing, because I owe it all to these Romans.* They had saved her from political impotence as sister-wife to a reigning boy, and probable death at the hands of his corrupt ministers, once she had fulfilled her duty by delivering a royal heir. These Romans, by their arrogant intervention and surprising political sophistication, had eliminated those ministers by manipulating the Alexandrian mob. Their nation's reoccupation of Italy and invasion of Sicily had forced Hasdrubal to break off the Carthaginian assault on Alexandria, and now she sat on the throne of Egypt, her brother banished to an obscure wing of the palace.

She knew better than to be grateful. The Romans did nothing out of disinterested goodwill. Everything they did was calculated to advance the cause of Rome. First came their almost obsessive need to conquer, humiliate and destroy Carthage, as Carthage had once all but obliterated Rome. And after that?

This required careful thought. It was by no means certain that Rome could even win a single battle with Carthage, once Hamilcar mobilized his full might against them. Should Rome be defeated, or even suffer a setback, her position would prove far more secure than it now was. She would have leverage to use, positioning herself in a place of power as the most desirable ally for either nation. Should the present war be long and costly and end in an uneasy peace, she would be safe. Neither contender could afford to allow the other to have the matchless wealth of Egypt at its disposal.

But should Carthage prove victorious? That, too, might be to her advantage. The Romans would be certain to make the war costly. Even in victory, Carthage would be exhausted and close to ruin. Reoccupation and restoration of its possessions in Sicily and Italy would distract and drain Carthage for many years to come, while she consolidated her position and made new alliances. Parthia was the growing power to the east, and Syria might well see the advantage of an alliance with Egypt. If Antiochus was too stubborn to reverse his policy, there were time-honored methods for putting a more suitable heir on the throne without resorting to war.

But what if, against all expectation, Rome should win? They had the martial energy of her own Macedonian ancestors, those unbeatable warriors who in the reigns of only two kings had gone from control of an impoverished near-barbarian nation to lords of the old Persian Empire, masters of the world from Greece to India. If the Romans lacked any single leader with the tactical brilliance of Alexander, they seemed to have a great many commanders with widely differing methods, from the conventional, by-the-book generals who were reducing Sicily so methodically, to her own Marcus Scipio with his love of military machines and his preference for using foreign troops and sparing Roman legionaries for better things, to the dashing Titus Norbanus who now bid fair to become the glorious new Xenophon of his generation. The Senate would decide which general to send to take care of which situation, and this was a military advantage no other nation had ever had.

Rome, she thought, might well conquer the world, as Alexander had once almost conquered the world. Alexander's empire had not outlived the conqueror himself, immediately splitting into minor empires controlled by his generals, who swiftly fell to battling among themselves.

Her own ancestor, Ptolemy, had seized Egypt as his share. Rome, she was certain, would not allow such a thing. Its outlandish republican government seemed chaotic, but it worked and it had staying power. Their unbelievable rise from beggar nation to northern empire was proof enough of that.

So what to do in the event of Roman victory? Selene was of Greek-Macedonian descent, without a drop of native blood in her veins. But after more than two hundred years the Ptolemies had Nile water in their veins and their flesh was the soil of Egypt. They combined the qualities of the Two Lands with those of Greece. Domination by Rome would simply call for patience, and patience was an ancient Egyptian specialty.

"Your Majesty," Scipio said, breaking into her thoughts, "I have to address a disturbing report I've received."

"You are being uncommonly formal," she observed. "You don't normally address me by title except in public."

"We Romans," Flaccus said with a mischievous smile, "consider capital punishment worthy of formality."

"Capital punishment?" she said, mystified. "Who is being executed?"

"My fellow senator here," Flaccus said, jerking a thumb toward Scipio.

"What? You know I don't understand Roman humor. Please explain."

"Nothing humorous about it," Marcus said. "I understand you are having statues of me erected in towns all up the Nile."

"Naturally. You are a great man now, and Egyptians are accustomed to seeing their great men in the form of statues. They won't take them seriously otherwise."

"I am flattered, but my fellow senators will take them as

a sign of dangerous ambition and the fact will be used against me in the Forum."

"Furthermore," Flaccus pointed out, "some of them have been placed in temples, particularly those devoted to the cult of Alexander. Marcus's enemies in the Senate will say that he aspires to become king of Egypt and receive not only royal but divine honors. Among us 'king' is a foul word, and only a triumphing general receives semi-divine honors, and that for only a day. To aspire to such things warrants a gruesome death by Roman law."

"How silly," she said. "Why risk everything for power if you can't be king? And there is great precedent for living monarchs to be deified."

"We have different customs, Your Majesty," Scipio said.

"You hardly need to tell me that. Besides, I merely honor your services by ancient custom."

"Nonetheless, the mere appearance of such ambition will be quite sufficient for the Senate to demand my head. As proof of friendship with Rome, you might be asked to deliver it personally."

"In some ways you are a most unreasonable people. Oh, very well, I'll have the statues removed."

"Not removed—destroyed," Marcus specified.

"If the Egyptian people need a visible demonstration," Flaccus suggested, "why not erect tablets inscribed with words of your esteem for Rome and pledging the friendship of our two nations? If the populace truly require statues, make them statues to the *genius* of the Roman people."

"Genius?" Selene said.

"Every Roman male," Flaccus explained, "is born with a *genius:* a guardian spirit who protects him and advises him to right behavior. Girls are born with an equivalent spirit called a *juno.* Places have *genii* as well: The *genius loci* is the spirit of that place. There is a collective *genius* for the people as a whole. This will be a way for you to render divine honors to your new allies without attracting the wrath of either the Senate or the gods."

"I see. Be so good as to give my director of works instructions on how these statues should be designed. I will see that they are placed in every town in Egypt."

"Very good of you, Your Majesty," Flaccus said. "The Senate and People of Rome will be pleased."

Later the Romans took their leave and Selene sat brooding. The men had a way of undermining her most careful, foresightful plans and somehow turning them to their own advantage. Who would have imagined that they would detect the subtle implications of those statues? Most men, especially the military sort, never saw beyond their own aggrandizement. These seemingly blunt, practical men were uncannily attuned to the attitudes of their peers, and they considered no one, not even a queen of Egypt, to be higher than their own peerage.

This called for further planning.

IN THEIR QUARTERS IN WHAT WAS NOW ACKNOWL-edged as the Roman wing of the Palace, Marcus Scipio and Aulus Flaccus compared notes. They drank the Lesbian wine they had come to love, Flaccus taking three swallows for Scipio's one, in a large room filled with models of machines from the Archimedean school of the Museum.

"I found out about the horns," Flaccus said.

"What horns?" Marcus said, examining a bewildering contraption its designer insisted would lift whole cohorts of soldiers above the walls of an enemy city and set them down inside without having to storm the battlements.

"These," Flaccus said, lifting Marcus's elaborate helmet from the table. "They are ram's horns."

"That much I figured out for myself."

"You haven't done enough sightseeing around here."

"I've been busy," Marcus said.

"If you'd paid attention, you would have learned that the ram is sacred to the god Ammon. Long ago, Greek priests determined that Ammon is identical with Zeus, hence the many temples to Zeus-Ammon erected by the Ptolemies. Zeus, in these temples, is carved in the Greek fashion, but with ram's horns to identify him with the native god. I believe you've noticed that the portraits of Alexander on local coins also depict him wearing these horns."

"That much I had noticed," Marcus said, nodding. "I wondered about that."

"Well, wonder about this." Flaccus reached into his purse and withdrew something. It glittered in the lamplight as he flipped it through the air.

Marcus caught it and sucked in his breath as he saw what rested in his palm. It was a magnificent golden coin, new-minted and as broad as three of his fingers held together. On its obverse side was a beautifully carved and struck masculine profile. Its features were unmistakably his own, and a curling ram's horn sprang from the rather abundant, curling hair above his ear. He raised his eyes to meet his friend's.

"Are these in circulation?" he all but whispered.

"I visited the royal mint this morning, luckily for you. They'd only struck a few, to show to the queen for her approval; I personally watched them melted except for this one. Then I got a sledgehammer and smashed the dies. I told the master coiner that I would see him crucified if so much as a single coin or die were held back. I even found the clay model the sculptor made for the die-cutters as a guide and destroyed that."

"Thank you, old friend," Marcus said with great sincerity. Then: "What do you think the woman is up to? Is she deliberately trying to have me killed?"

"I doubt it, though I wouldn't put it past her. She's not a nasty piece of work like her brother, or like Hamilcar and his sister, but royalty have their own set of priorities. Her first order of business is to secure her own reign. Next, she has to increase or at least sustain the power and prestige of Egypt. Rome is the rising power in the world, so she sees the advantages of an alliance with Rome. You represent Rome."

"That doesn't explain giving me divine horns," Marcus pointed out.

"I haven't told you all I found in the mint."

"Do be so good," Marcus said, pouring himself a large goblet of Lesbian, all but sweating with relief at his near escape. Death was nothing, but execution by senatorial order, with its attendant disgrace to his family, was unthinkable.

"In the sculptor's shop, where I found the prototype for the coin, there was another, unfinished model. This one showed you, horns and all, paired with Selene, portrayed as an old hag in the quaint local fashion."

"What! She really has plans to make me king of Egypt?"

Flaccus shook his head. "Nothing of the sort. She has only just become virtual queen in her own right. What monarch wishes to share power by elevating someone else to equal rank? But she knows her people will feel more secure if they see a strong man by her side. No, I think she wants you for her consort: by her side and in her bed, but definitely under her authority."

"She already has a husband," Marcus said, "her brother."

"Well, he's easily disposed of, isn't he?"

Marcus shrugged. "He's nothing, I agree. But royalty only breed among themselves. I don't think she'd want a commoner like me to father her children."

"She's royal but she's also a realist. As far as she's concerned, the scion of a very ancient family holding the highest honors of a republic is good enough. After all, your ancestors were consuls long before hers were kings. She's descended from Macedonian goatherds who tied their fortunes to the local chief and hit it lucky when one of those chiefs turned out to be Alexander the Great."

"I hadn't thought of it that way," Marcus admitted.

"To give her credit, I doubt that it ever occurred to her how mortally offended the Senate and the population would be by those statues and coins. She isn't accustomed to republican institutions."

Marcus sat and pondered. "I suppose most men would find my predicament hard to comprehend. From being a minor officer and an unimportant senator I've risen to the position of the most important man in the richest nation of the world. I have the throne of Egypt almost within my grasp. Yet here I am, terrified at the implications."

Flaccus smiled. "It does seem odd. It would be a glorious thing to conquer Egypt *as a Roman general*. But to accept the rulership as the gift of Egypt's queen would be treason. Worse yet, it would make you richer than the whole Senate combined, and that could not be tolerated. And here you are, in a foreign land, all alone except for me, connected to Rome only by a few letters now and then. It's a good thing your family is so powerful and influential. You'd probably have been condemned already."

"That could change at any time," Marcus said. "If some

of my relatives are killed in Sicily, or if some of our rivals should win great glory there, the balance in the Senate could change overnight. It's happened before."

"Yes," Flaccus said, sitting at the table and pouring himself another, "our political life is always uncertain. At least it keeps things interesting. Personally, I find all this dynastic intrigue boring, compared with politics at home."

A short while later a steward appeared and summoned them to Selene's private chambers.

"What might this portend?" Marcus said, checking his appearance in the burnished silver mirror.

"Maybe she's had a change of heart," Flaccus said. "She may have decided to execute us, since we don't share her taste in statuary."

Flaccus meant it in jest, but they both knew that it could be true. Helmets beneath their arms, military cloaks swinging smartly behind them, they strode in lockstep to the queen's private quarters, where slaves opened the massive doors before them. They marched through, halted and saluted in unison before the queen, who sat at a small table.

"Nicely done," she commended. "Now, get out of that silly armor and sit down. We have some serious talking to do."

"If it's about those statues—" Marcus began as slaves rushed to free him from his dress cuirass.

"Forget about the statues. I've—" She paused and wrinkled her nose. "You've been into the wine this evening."

"We usually are, when we aren't on duty," Flaccus said, grinning. "And the best, too. Lesbian."

Selene raised a hand and a beautiful young girl ran to her side. "Go to the wine steward and tell him to send us some Lesbian. The best, not the swill these two have been drinking."

"You mean there's better?" Flaccus said as the girl dashed off.

"What's happened?" Marcus demanded, sounding cold sober.

"A ship from Tyre put in tonight. The winds have been contrary and it's the first to sail from there in almost two months. One of my agents has sent an intelligence report. It seems that your friend Titus Norbanus has reappeared, with his army intact."

"Norbanus!" Marcus all but hissed. Their scouts had lost him when he took his army into the desert, confounding their expectations. Selene's ships stood ready to shadow his progress along the coast, but Norbanus had not obliged them. Flaccus had speculated that he would march down the coast of Arabia and seize the rich frankincense ports, but Selene's Red Sea skippers had reported no sign of him.

"He showed up in southern Judea. He brought his army across that awful desert in fine form, just as you said he might," she conceded. "Now he's in Jerusalem, the capital of the southern kingdom, no doubt planning to capture the northern kingdom, Israel. It is the more populous and war-like of the two."

"And Norbanus is throwing his support behind the weaker king," Marcus said.

"You say that with a certain satisfaction," she observed.

"It's the wise thing to do. It's the Roman thing. I can't find it in me to wish a Roman army ill, though it pains me to give Titus Norbanus credit."

"Now that he's reappeared," Flaccus said, "the Senate could call him back."

"He won't report to the Senate until he's won a victory," Marcus said. "And if he's victorious, and sends home some fine loot, and has improved Rome's position in the East, the Senate won't dare call him in. My own family will vote him honors."

"You've been right about him so far," Selene said.

Marcus shook his head. "No. I was wrong about him for far too long. I thought he was nothing but a Forum politician who would be worthless at war. I don't dare underestimate him again."

"If he gets things his way in Israel," Flaccus said, "what will he do next?"

"That," said Selene, "will depend upon what Antiochus of Syria decides to do about him."

CHAPTER SEVEN

TITUS NORBANUS WATCHED HIS MEN AS THEY practiced maneuvers with Jonathan's army. The Judeans had nothing like the professionalism of the Romans, but they were spirited and had the appearance of brave men, though only the test of battle would prove that. Best of all, they had never adopted the rigid Macedonian phalanx, so he would not have to break them of the habits inherent in that obsolete combat formation.

The bulk of Jonathan's soldiers were peasants who fought as spearmen, providing both light and heavy infantry. The shepherds of the hill country fought unarmored, with small shields, javelins and curved knives. They were excellent scouts and skirmishers. Best of all, the country abounded in slingers and archers, arms in which the Romans were weak.

The well-born young men provided Jonathan's cavalry. They were excellent horsemen and their mounts were surprisingly fine. This was an added bonus, for the Romans were at best indifferent cavalrymen, despite the splendid horses of Noricum. The hilly, wooded terrain of Noricum did not favor cavalry warfare, and the Romans had never emphasized its arts.

"We can put together a finely balanced expedition force with these men as our allies," Norbanus said to his subordinates.

"At least until we've taken Manasseh's kingdom and given it to his brother," Cato said.

"Of course," said Norbanus. "Then, it will be time to renegotiate." He swept his commanders with his blue-eyed gaze and he approved of their appearance. Gone were the rags and grime of their desert crossing. Jonathan had been generous with his new allies and had given each officer rich clothing in accordance with the man's rank. Nor had the legionaries been neglected. They wore fine new tunics, and their helmets sported colorful crests and plumes.

The king had given Norbanus an extravagant purple cloak heavily embroidered with pure gold, and he now rode a horse so blindingly white that it might have been albino except for its fine black eyes. In concert with his already splendid uniform, patterned after Alexander's, he looked like a war god's statue come to life. Most men would have looked ridiculous in such a rig, but Norbanus had the swagger and presence to carry it off. His officers refrained from comment lest they appear envious.

"Lentulus Niger," Norbanus said.

"Yes, General?"

"I want as many of our men as possible to train on horseback at every opportunity. Let's not waste time trying to train them to fight from horseback, but I want them able to ride whenever necessary. That will give us a flying force in future operations. From all indications, most of the land in our immediate line of march favors mounted troops."

"Very good, sir," said Niger. "The Gallic boys are already good riders. They can help train their German and Italian friends who think horses are for pulling chariots in the Circus."

"When we've beaten Manasseh, I'll demand all his horses as part of our reward." Norbanus touched his horse's flank with a small golden spur and the animal leapt down the slope before him. His soldiers waved their heavy javelins and cheered as he rode along the front line, shouting praise or disapproval as he passed each unit.

Niger spat on the ground and snapped his fingers. The soldier detailed as his orderly ran up to his stirrup and handed him a wineskin. He took a drink and handed the skin across to Cato. "Do you think he'll demand one of the royal ladies as part of his reward, too?"

Cato grinned and raised the skin, directing a stream of rough local wine into his mouth. He passed it to the officer on his left and wiped his lips with the back of his hand. "Reward? Jonathan will demand he take them, just to get the bitches off his hands!" This raised a laugh from the knot of officers.

Their commander had proven to be a great favorite with the women of the royal household. The king's wives and daughters were kept secluded in a women's wing of the palace, but his numerous sisters and aunts had the run of the place, and court manners proved to be quite different from those of the populace. The royal family wore their religion lightly, and observed its many taboos and strictures only as suited them.

Holy men from the hinterlands, known locally as prophets, sometimes came to Jerusalem and inveighed against the loose morals of the palace. Jonathan usually found it politic to ignore them. The priests of the temple were far more accommodating.

The most aggressive of the royal women was Tamar, Jonathan's aunt. She was a great beauty and only a year or two older than the king himself. A woman of great force and passion, she might have shocked the Romans had they not already encountered Zarabel, princess and priestess of Carthage. The king's half-sisters, Glaphyra and Roxana, were twins. Their mother was Babylonian, and they were rumored to be addicted to unnatural practices. All three paid extravagant attention to the dashing Roman commander, and these were only the most notable of the palace women.

"I wonder if Manasseh's court has all the royal sons," Niger said.

"If so, I hope his luck in battle isn't as good," Cato commented.

When Norbanus had finished inspecting his troops, he rode back into Jerusalem through the Joppa gate and through the narrow, winding streets to the upper city. Above the smoky, tumbledown structures of the lower city, the wealthy had their dwellings. Finest among these was Jonathan's palace, a rambling mansion far more modest than the royal dwellings of Carthage and Alexandria.

Norbanus rode up the steps to the terrace and drew rein as servants rushed to take charge of his horse. He dismounted and surveyed the city. On higher ground stood the Temple. He still found it difficult to understand a nation that had but a single temple to house its solitary god.

The Temple was magnificently adorned, but like the palace it was of no great size. The successor kings who had followed Alexander had set the style for grandiose building projects, and like them the Jewish kings had longed to build an ostentatiously huge temple to aggrandize themselves and their city, but Jonathan had explained that ritual law thwarted them. Their holy scriptures specified the dimensions of the Temple down to the last cubit, and it could be built no larger. So the kings had contented themselves with adorning the Temple and building a vast terrace of interlocking courtyards to surround it. Much of the hilltop was surrounded by a great retaining wall to support the foundations of the spectacular terrace.

Norbanus turned from the view and strode into the palace, past the Greek mercenary guardsmen who saluted with their spears, into the cool interior. Here the walls were frescoed and the floors inset with colorful mosaics, the designs drawn from Greek mythology, in violation of the local cult's strictures against representations of living things.

The rooms of the palace were not large, for they saw little use. In this part of the world, most social life was carried on in gardens and under rooftop bowers. Even dinners and banquets were often held outdoors. He knew from Jonathan that the Judeans had once been desert wanderers and pastoralists, and they had not strayed far from their nomadic roots. They preferred a fine garden to the finest house.

He went to the great formal garden on the eastern end of the palace, where the royal family usually congregated after the sun had passed its zenith. Up the garden walls climbed ivy and along their base grew myrtle. Huge jars were planted with silphium, hyssop and other medicinal herbs. There were date palms and fig trees and grape arbors, but the greater part of the garden was in the Persian style. This meant that the many raised beds were planted with flowers, cultivated for their color and beauty alone.

In the center, near the largest of the garden's many fountains, Norbanus found the Lady Tamar, attended by her women. There were other men and women of the household lounging about the garden, but Tamar had seized this particularly attractive spot as her own and she held it against the other women. Norbanus suspected that a variety of Forum politics prevailed within the palace, with alliances, power blocs, and perhaps the occasional judicious assassination to determine rank and preeminence.

Tamar's clothing left little visible save her face and hands. Even her hair was covered by a veil. The voluminous gown that draped her body fell in graceful folds that revealed little of the shape beneath, yet she possessed the art of making even this over-modest attire subtly provocative.

"Good afternoon, General." At her gesture, servants brought a chair for Norbanus. With studied art he sat, sweeping his cloak to drape over the chair's arms in graceful folds. He opened a hand without looking and a slave placed a fine goblet in his grasp.

"Will you be marching against Manasseh soon?" she asked.

"I would prefer more time to organize and train," he told her. "Otherwise, your nephew's army and mine cannot act with cohesion."

"My nephew's army," she said, "had better cohere, and quickly, because my other nephew's army is on its way."

Norbanus cut a calculating look at her. "You've had word?"

"I have my sources." She favored him with a bland smile.

"What else have your sources told you?"

"That Manasseh has been assembling his army near Megiddo. That he has requested help from Parthia."

"Has such help arrived?" This was astounding. Unless

the woman was weaving her story from whole cloth, she had spies within Manasseh's court, and couriers to keep her in contact with them.

She smiled again. "There has hardly been time for that. Manasseh is headstrong and has already begun moving his army south. But I think you had better move rather quickly now. Parthians ride much faster than our own soldiers march, so he could have his reinforcements by the time he joins battle with you."

"Roman soldiers march faster than most ride," he assured her, but inwardly he was not so sanguine. This Manasseh was clearly a man of quick decision. "It's a risky thing, asking for Parthian assistance. Once the king has his soldiers inside Manasseh's land, he may want to keep them there."

"This is something we needn't fear from you Romans?" She smiled as she said it but he felt the sting, as was intended.

"We are most meticulous in observing our treaty obligations," he said.

"Those treaties never seem to specify a date by which allied troops should be off our territory."

"Because our allies find us so valuable. They often manage to get into another war immediately, relying upon our aid." He took a sip. "But we shall be on our way as soon as we've crushed Manasseh, and his allies, if need be. We have to get back to Rome."

"And it might be a good idea for you to move your army away from Jerusalem very soon," she said.

"Move my army away? Why?" He was instantly suspicious. It was basic sense for a general to stay close to his men. An attempt to separate him from his troops usually meant treachery on the part of an enemy or even an ally. Especially an ally.

"There are some new prophets in town. These are from the North, from Galilee. They heard of this foreign army and came to look for signs of corruption."

"Corruption?" Norbanus said, mystified.

"Exactly. The prophets make it their special duty to see that the people are not tempted to follow foreign ways. That, you see, leads to worshipping foreign gods."

"What harm does it do to honor the gods of other people?" he asked. "We are always careful not to insult the gods of others."

"It is all too easy to insult the god of the Jews without intending to. For instance, these prophets, led by one Joshua ben Joshua, are complaining about the idols your men carry before them."

"I have no idea what you are talking about."

"The eagles and bulls and scorpions and so forth that the men dressed in animal skins carry on poles before the troops."

"You mean the military standards?" he said, incredulous. "Your prophets object to our standards?"

"Yes. They are graven images, you see. Our religion forbids the making of any object that imitates a living thing."

"So I've heard. What about those lion-things with wings and human heads that flank the entrance to your temple? Or the bronze bulls that support the big water bowl in front of it?"

She smiled again. "There is of course an exception for the holy objects of the Temple. There is no exception for foreigners like you. When the Syrian Antiochus tried to introduce Greek statues and Greek rites in our holy places, there was war."

He folded his hands and leaned forward earnestly. "You do understand, don't you, that you people are quite insane?"

"If so, it's what our god requires of us. And these prophets are raising the people, haranguing them to rise against you and against Jonathan."

"And the king permits this? They are probably agents sent by Manasseh. He should have them killed."

"Prophets are sacrosanct," she said, sighing. "No matter how troublesome they may be."

"Oh. Like tribunes of the people?" He thought for a minute. "Why don't I just send some of my men to kill them? Jonathan can hold me responsible. And keep his own hands clean."

"That would be a good thing, but there would be a riot anyway."

"Then we could just massacre the rioters and peace would be restored. Jerusalem can easily spare a mob or two."

"Or you could just leave. Then they'd have nothing to complain about."

"Oh, please don't run him off so soon," said a voice behind Norbanus. He did not need to turn around. One of the twins had spoken. He knew that both would be there. He had yet to see the two of them separated by more than a few feet.

"Please join us, ladies," Tamar said, smiling without affection.

The twins drifted into Norbanus's field of vision. It was the only way he could think of to describe their motion: They *drifted*. They seemed as languid and boneless as a pair of somnolent eels, and as difficult to distinguish. Like Tamar they wore modest gowns, but their curly black hair was uncovered and they wore elaborate jewelry. Their faces were high cheekboned and full-lipped, their eyes emphasized with kohl. They looked, Norbanus thought, exactly like what they were: the final, decadent offspring of an ancient and corrupt civilization. Glorious Babylon had long disappeared, crushed beneath the boots of a succession of conquerors, but her wickedness seemed to be imperishable. Even in the rather relaxed court of Jonathan, the two were tolerated mainly for their mastery of Babylon's gift to the world: astrology. Their mother had been a star reader much valued by Jonathan and Manasseh's father.

"Are you going to tell us what the stars have to say about our guest's future?" Tamar asked warily. Norbanus knew that Tamar despised the twins, but like everyone else she was intimidated by their command of the arcane art. It surprised him that, despite their incredibly exclusive religion, almost all of these people had faith in Babylonian star augury.

The twins were attended by their own women, and as they sat, slaves slid a chair beneath each. "But of course," Glaphyra said. At least, Norbanus assumed it was Glaphyra. Her bracelets and other jewelry were studded with coral, and Glaphyra favored red stones: coral, carnelian, ruby. Roxana preferred blue: lapis lazuli, sapphire, amethyst. Of course, he realized, there was nothing to keep them from swapping jewelry to confuse people. Roxana raised her hand and a woman placed a scroll in her palm. She unrolled it with a flourish. "Our friend is a man of glorious promise, it seems," she announced. Her voice was identical to her sister's.

"What does your art tell you?" Norbanus asked, perhaps a little more eagerly than he wished. In Egypt, he had toured the splendid Temple of Hathor at Dendera and had been shown the Babylonian zodiac carved upon its ceiling in the days when the foreign art had penetrated even to the priesthood of that unthinkably ancient land. The priest had explained to him the significance of its signs and constellations.

This was an art very different from the auguries and haruspices of the Romans, and from the various divining arts of Norbanus's Celtic-Germanic ancestors. These only determined the momentary whims of the gods at a given time, and provided no long-range forecasts nor predictions of individual destiny. He was interested to hear what the twins had found.

"Titus Norbanus was most fortunate in the day and hour of his birth," Roxana said, "since it is not the custom of his people to take note of such things, being ignorant as they are in celestial matters. But he was born upon the night a certain comet appeared just above the rising crescent moon—"

"Itself a circumstance of greatest significance," Glaphyra interjected smoothly.

"—and this was noted by the Roman augurs," Roxana went on, "who usually take omens through lightning, thunder and the flight of birds, but who also note extraordinary phenomena such as comets and showers of falling stars."

"With this intelligence," Glaphyra said, "we were able to discern with great precision the stars and planets governing our guest's destiny. We think they are the most propitious to be seen since those of Alexander, almost two and one half centuries ago."

Norbanus's cup hand remained steady, but the other tightened its grip on the chair arm. This was what he wanted to hear, but he cautioned himself against credulity. These two were schemers from the womb they had shared, but the king and nobles of this court put much faith in their craft, so it could not all be trickery.

Roxana spread the scroll upon the table. The papyrus was covered with symbols and lettering that meant nothing to him. The two pointed out each, naming planets, signs, stars. They spoke of ascendancy, of declination, of precedents and fabled conjunctions, each twin taking up her sister's narration in a bewildering rhythm that kept him looking back and forth from one to the other until he was dizzy. Their presentation, he understood, was an art as polished as that of any Forum politician's.

"These are the signs of conquest, of mastery," Roxana said.

"But there is another," said Glaphyra, sweeping a gilded fingernail over a line of symbols that he thought resembled Egyptian picture writing and might as well have been, for all he could make of them.

"Another?" Norbanus said.

"Yes," Glaphyra informed him. "There is another, lesser person, born near you, with signs that are similar but not as propitious. He bears the attributes of envy and jealousy. He will be your enemy all your days."

"But you are the greater," Roxana assured him. "You will always prevail."

Scipio, he thought. It must be Marcus Scipio.

"You see," Glaphyra said, "how your sign entered the House of the Lion. Alexander's did the same. It meant that he was to take mastery of a foreign civilization and make it greater than ever before. Born in barbarous Macedon, he took up the cause of glorious Greece and spread its culture throughout the world."

And my forbears were Gauls and Germans, he thought. But it is my destiny to make Rome master of the world. It is true. It all fits. They are not frauds. How could they know this otherwise?

"What do the stars say of Manasseh?" Tamar asked. "A battle of kings is in the offing. Surely there are signs."

"The squabbling of petty monarchs are little noted in the

stars," Glaphyra said, smiling. "Not like the fortunes of one such as Titus Norbanus."

"Indeed," Tamar said through gritted teeth.

Norbanus decided that he would have to keep these two close to him from now on. He would need to consult with them frequently. No doubt he could work something out with Jonathan, along with the business of Manasseh's horses.

Never forgetting, he reminded himself, that they were still a pair of scheming bitches.

CHAPTER EIGHT

The walls of Syracuse were formidable but, Scaeva thought, they could have been a far more daunting prospect. Carthage had seized the city almost one hundred years previously in a siege of great brutality, concluded with massacres and mass crucifixions. With the city and its harbor in their hands, they had repaired the walls but had done nothing since to improve the fortifications. Rome had been eliminated as a foe several years before the siege and there was no enemy left in the western sea to threaten the primacy of Carthage. More powerful walls might only tempt what was left of the native population to rise against their masters in a future generation.

From his command tower, erected at the northern end of the island in the Great Harbor, Scaeva surveyed the works being erected against the southern wall of the city. There the bulk of the Carthaginian garrison had been concentrated in a massive fort built directly into the wall in the approved fashion developed by Carthage's military engineers.

"It's a tough one," said Fabius, his praefect of the camp. "Walls inside walls, forts inside forts, that's their style. Crack one nut, and there's another nut inside to be cracked. It's a lot of work."

"It suits me," Scaeva said. "It means that they've lost their taste for battle. They think only of defense now. It means a great deal of labor, but we're good at that. A Roman soldier is as handy with his spade and pickaxe as he is with sword and pilum."

Not that the Romans were doing all the digging and pounding. Over against the great wall, men swarmed like ants, digging trenches, erecting shelters for the workers, pounding heavy pilings into the marshy ground on the west side of the city, making an artificial island to support the great rams and catapults that soon would pound the walls. But many of these workers were locals rounded up by the Romans in the surrounding countryside. Some were mercenaries captured when the Romans took the smaller cities and forts of the island. Men working directly beneath the walls of a besieged city took awful casualties, and the Romans preferred that somebody else do the suffering.

Titus Scaeva was the proconsul sent by the Senate to reduce the island of Sicily, and he took great satisfaction in knowing that he had done a superb job of it. Against a conservative bloc of senators who had wanted to attack Syracuse at the outset of the campaign, he had insisted on a strategy of encirclement, snapping up the smaller forts and cities, seizing all the ports and fortifying them against the inevitable Carthaginian attempt to retake the island. By taking the most productive land and grabbing all the storehouses, he had made his campaign self-sustaining, so that all his shipping could be used to bring in more men and necessary military supplies instead of using precious cargo space for food, for man and beast.

He had left Syracuse till the last. True, it had given the Carthaginian commander time to improve the defenses somewhat, and concentrate his forces within, but that would work against him in the long run. More men inside would strain his resources, and Scaeva had cut him off from any hope of resupply.

"Still," Fabius said, "I wish they'd come out and fight. We'd crush them handily then."

"That's exactly why they won't opt for open battle. They think that Hamilcar will be here soon, to relieve them. If they can just hold out long enough."

The capture of Syracuse would make him the most distinguished military man in Rome, he thought with great satisfaction. He had been a famous soldier all his life, having won the Civic Crown at the age of sixteen, at the siege of Mogantum. He had risen in rank and honor up the *cursus honorem,* holding each civil office and military command in approved fashion, and had had the great good fortune to be a serving consul when the auguries had shown that the gods wanted Roma Noricum to retake Rome of the Seven Hills.

Taking the nearly demilitarized Italian peninsula had been a walkover for a few veteran Roman legions, but everyone knew that the war against Carthage itself would be another matter entirely. He had pushed for the immediate seizure of Sicily, and the command had fallen to him naturally. Already he had earned the right to petition the Senate for a triumph: the ultimate vindication for a military man. His supply ships returned to Italy with endless cargoes of loot. *Just take Syracuse,* he reminded himself, *and your name will live forever.*

This meant much to him. Like all Romans, he was ambitious for personal fame and prestige, but in his case he wanted glory for his family as well. The Scaevae were among the new families: clans of German and Gallic descent whose ancestors had helped the Roman refugees to found Roma Noricum. There was great rivalry between the old families and the new. With such a campaign to his credit, capped with the capture of Syracuse and a grand triumph in Rome of the Seven Hills, no one could claim that the new families were less patriotic, less Roman, than the old.

"Do you think they can?" Fabius asked. "Hold out long enough for Hamilcar to get here, I mean?"

"Not a chance," Scaeva said. "Those boys we sent to spy out Carthage did their job well. We know more about the capabilities of his military than Hamilcar does himself. He's under the impression that he's Hannibal come again, but we know better." Both men chuckled, but Scaeva knew well the worry that gnawed at his subordinate: Hamilcar or his designated commander would appear by sea, with an immense navy. The Roman navy was new and untried, all but untrained. The Carthaginian navy was the most powerful in the world. Scaeva had to take Syracuse before the navy could appear.

Despite their distance from the fighting, both men wore full military gear, down to belted sidearms. This was Roman military regulation, just like fortifying every camp and posting sentries even in peacetime, with no enemy within hundreds of miles. Regulations were to be obeyed, even by generals. Sunlight glittered on their polished bronze, which was collecting dust, raised by all the marching, pounding and digging. The two cut the dust in their throats by sipping at cups of *posca*: the traditional soldier's drink of vinegar diluted with water.

The soldiers working beneath the walls of Syracuse did not glitter. They toiled in full armor, again according to regulation, but their mail was dusty and dingy from the long campaign, greased against the salt sea air. Most of them wore the new iron helmets turned out by the Gallic armorers for the unprecedented expansion of legions demanded by the war of reconquest. These helmets, with their deep, flaring neckguards and broad cheekplates, completely unadorned, still looked strange and ugly to Roman eyes, but they had proved their battle-fitness repeatedly.

The battlements of Syracuse were lined with expert slingers from the Balearic Islands. They hurled lead sling-bullets the size of a boy's fist, with enough power to dent a bronze helmet deeply, often fracturing the skull beneath. The bullets merely glanced from the harder iron. Men from the older legions frequently tried to trade their beautiful old bronze helmets for the new ones, but they found few takers.

The trumpets sounded and the noise lessened for a few minutes as one legion retired to the camp on the island and another went out to take its place. By working each legion four hours at a time, the Romans were able to keep the work going day and night. The impressed labor worked in gangs for twelve hours at a stretch. Attrition among them was high, but plenty of prisoners arrived every day to replace the fallen.

"Here comes old Cyclops," Fabius said.

"He can observe, it's his duty," Scaeva said. "But don't let him try to give orders. You know he'll try. The old bugger's been giving orders all his life."

Moments later they were joined by Publius Cornelius Scipio, only living grandson of the hero of Cannae and second oldest man in the Senate. Wearing some forty-five pounds of old-fashioned armor, he climbed the steps of the command tower with the springy step of a man one-third his years. A broad eyepatch covered one side of his face.

"Proconsul," he said, nodding to Scaeva. "Praefect." Another nod, toward Fabius. "Any progress?" The old man wasted few words. He had been sent out by the Senate as special observer, with no command authority but with the right to see every aspect of operations and report in regular dispatches. He had already made forays inland to see the progress of Roman forces on the island and had been stunned by the beauty of the landscape and the richness of its farm and pasture land. The Romans were soldiers from birth, but they were agriculturalists to their bones and loved fine farmland above all else. They fought to protect their farms and they conquered to gain more land. It was that simple.

"The sappers are undermining the base of the big tower over there," Scaeva said, gesturing with his cup. "They'll have it down in a few days."

Cyclops squinted with his remaining eye at the activity opposite. "What about the rams? Are they doing any damage?"

"They're a feint," Scaeva said, "to distract the enemy from the mines. By afternoon we'll have the catapults in action; then there'll be a little relief from those damned slingers and archers. They've been the real danger in this fight, not the Carthaginians."

Cyclops nodded. "That being the case," he said, "the men will probably massacre them when the city is taken." He chose his next words carefully so that he was making a suggestion, not giving an order. "You might consider passing the word to spare them, much as it might grieve the men to let them live. We'll need every missile soldier we can get when we assault Carthage."

"Already done," Scaeva told him. "I've promised ten silver denarii a head for every archer or slinger brought in alive."

"Very well," Cyclops said, far from satisfied and showing it.

Scaeva knew what rankled the old man: Roman soldiers should obey orders. They should not be bribed. But Cyclops was an old-fashioned man, filled with antique, old family tradition. Scaeva knew that the world had changed irrevocably when the Romans crossed south of the Alps. It was a new world, a new age and a new army. The disciplines of the old legions campaigning in the savage, austere North would not prevail in the unbelievably rich and luxurious kingdoms surrounding what the Romans had gone back to calling Our Sea.

"Senator," Fabius said, wanting to change the subject and ease the tension, "has a timetable yet been set for the assault against the African mainland?"

Cyclops shook his head. "First Sicily must be secured. The new navy must be tested. We've moved so fast, accomplished so much already. There are many who want to slow down and consolidate."

"Fools!" Scaeva spat. "We've accomplished so much precisely because we've moved so fast. Because the gods have *told* us that now is our time!"

"You'll hear no argument from me," Cyclops assured him. "We must seize the favor of the gods when it is offered. The gods can always change their minds. But I am not a majority. Some want the new legions blooded gradually, not thrown into immense battles before they've even seen a skirmish. Others want to wait until young Norbanus returns with his four legions."

"They'll wait a long time, then," Scaeva said. "Where is he now, or does anyone know?"

"In Judea at last report, mixed up in a civil war between brothers."

"Judea," Scaeva mused. It was a name from old books: an obscure place, but much fought over. At least Norbanus was making progress, not least because he had cut himself loose from the authority of the Senate. Scaeva could sympathize. Senatorial meddling was the curse of commanders in the field. If the boy finished his epic march with his legions intact, he would win unprecedented glory, perhaps eclipsing that of Titus Scaeva. He pushed the thought aside as unworthy. Opportunities for winning glory would be boundless in the coming years.

"Any idea who will get the command in the African campaign?" Fabius asked.

"That depends upon who pleases the Senate and the Assemblies in the months preceding," Cyclops said.

A great shout and a roaring of masonry distracted them. A section of the wall opposite was toppling, raising a huge cloud of dust as men scrambled to get away, running for their lives, soldiers and laborers alike.

"Has it fallen?" Cyclops cried eagerly. "Are the men ready for an assault?"

Scaeva shook his head, his face worried. "This is too soon. This was not supposed to happen yet."

"There may have been a weak spot," Fabius said hopefully. "We'd better signal an assembly to take advantage instantly if there's a breach."

But already the dust was clearing and Scaeva cursed loudly. A ragged section of cut-stone facing had broken away from the wall, leaving the concrete-rubble core exposed but solid. The wall was very little weakened.

"Mars curse them!" Scaeva cried. "Now they know where

the danger lies and they'll countermine, if they haven't begun already! I'll have some heads for this."

Cyclops said nothing, but he was not greatly surprised. The Romans had read all the old military books and knew the theory, but reducing large, stone fortifications was something with which they had no practical experience. The Gauls and Germans they had been fighting for generations built earthwork and timber forts at best.

"Get the awnings up!" Scaeva called to the slaves attending the command tower. Then, to the others: "It looks like we have a long day ahead of us up here."

Beneath the battlements of Syracuse, the soldiers were already driving the work gangs back before them. Work had already resumed, repairing the shelters and now clearing away the rubble of fallen stone, all under the hot sun and the merciless pelting of missiles from above.

FROM HER LITTER ATOP THE GATE OF MELKARTH, Princess Zarabel, sister of Hamilcar, shofet of Carthage, watched as her brother inspected his army on the plain beyond the city. Since his return from the Egyptian debacle, Hamilcar had fretted and busied himself with his preparations for the coming war to take Sicily and Italy back from the upstart Romans.

It was splendid; there was no denying it. The tents of the host stretched out of sight to the east, and this was only a part of the force. The full army was too vast to encamp by one city, even so great a city as Carthage. The rest were quartered upon the subject cities.

Hamilcar, mounted on a beautiful horse, rode along the lines of a formation of Lacedaemonian spearmen: still soldiers of high repute though Sparta had ceased to be a power of military importance generations previously. Their antiquated linen cuirasses glittered with scales of bronze, their round shields were bright with new paint, their long spears held in perfect alignment as the officers, identifiable by their crests of white horsehair, saluted the shofet.

As always, the armies of Carthage were a polyglot assemblage of conscripts levied on the subject cities and mercenaries hired from every corner of the world surrounding the great Central Sea. Greeks from both Greece proper and the cities of Magna Graecia and Asia Minor formed a large part of the force. The Greek cities squabbled endlessly with one another, and between wars their soldiers hired themselves out to whoever was paying. Besides the hard core of Spartans, Hamilcar had Athenians, Corinthians, Thebans and soldiers from the Asian towns of Ionia. There were men from the Greek islands of Lesbos, Delos, Crete, Rhodes and Corcyra.

There were great pike formations from Epirus on the Ionian Sea, home of the oracle of Dodona. Their repute as professional soldiers was matchless. From the Adriatic coast came Illyrians: tough, barbarous men with tattooed bodies. Their ruler was a queen named Teuta, and this formidable woman had accompanied her soldiers, determined to extort favorable concessions from Hamilcar in return for their services. She was in a position to bargain because her land, usually of little strategic significance, lay across a narrow arm of the sea from Italy.

The bulk of Hamilcar's forces here consisted of the army he had raised to invade Egypt and had brought back with him. Further forces were being raised far from Carthage. In Spain, Hamilcar's subordinate commanders were rounding up an army from the warlike tribes of the interior and from the Greek colonies of the coast. This army would never come to Africa. Instead, it would assemble at New Carthage on the southern coast, march eastward along Hannibal's old route past the Pyrenees and into southern Gaul, picking up allies as it progressed, and enter northern Italy. This army would distract the Romans from the main thrust into Sicily and southern Italy, stripping the Romans of some of those surprisingly numerous legions that seemed to be springing up like weeds after a rainstorm.

This was the special genius of Carthage: to raise and lead armies so diverse in nation, language and custom that at any other time they would happily have massacred each other. They accomplished this by educating the most capable of the noble youth of Carthage in schools that turned out professional officers of terrible force and efficiency. Hannibal had kept such an army intact through years of campaigning, with never a murmur of mutiny, no matter how awful the hardships. His men had been ferocious on the battlefield, meek as lambs in camp.

Of course, not every Carthaginian general was a Hannibal. After the first war with Rome, the wealthy men of the city, the ruling caste at that time, had balked at paying the huge mercenary army camped immediately without the walls of Carthage. This foolishness had resulted in a rebellion and brought about a war so terrible that the rest of the world, hardened by many merciless wars, had looked on, appalled. Even Rome had offered aid.

This had been the last time that the gods of Carthage had demanded a *Tophet:* the supreme sacrifice to Baal-Hammon and the myriad of other deities who had made Carthage mistress of the world. In the ordinary, everyday sacrifices, men and women of the subject peoples supplied the victims. But, when a *Tophet* was required, Carthaginians were sacrificed. In extreme cases, the children of the greatest families, from newborns to boys and girls of ten years, were thrown into the fires that raged in the bellies of the merciless bronze idols.

The sudden reappearance of the Romans, the abortive campaign against Egypt, were clear signs of the displeasure of the gods, so said the priests. It had been too long since a great *Tophet* had been held. True, there had been a lesser such sacrifice held during a time of plague in the reign of Hamilcar's father. It had been effective and the pestilence had abated, but the priests were determined that the gods hungered for the flesh of the noble children of Carthage.

So far, Hamilcar had resisted their entreaties. He was a Hellenizing monarch and did not wish his nation to appear barbarous in the eyes of the civilized world. He also wanted to suppress the power of the priests over the minds of the people. The shofet should rule; the priests should tend to the rituals of the gods and stay out of the affairs of state.

All of these things passed through Zarabel's mind as she watched the martial display. Her brother was a competent shofet, in her estimation, but his attempts to be a great war leader like their ancestor Hannibal the Great were ludicrous. He had not been trained in the officer schools, but raised in the palace. Like so many men born to rule, he thought he was a great natural military genius and that, confronted with an enemy in the field, he would know with unerring instinct exactly what to do.

During their sojourn in Carthage, she had come to know these Romans far more intimately than her brother, who was ever surrounded by a buffer of his courtiers. She knew that they laughed at such amateurism. Not only did they insist upon absolute professionalism among military men, but also they taught that even great generals could be the victims of mere bad luck, and they planned for such eventualities. It was how they had survived defeat after devastating defeat by Hannibal, with their nation intact, though just barely. They did not intend to be defeated, but one defeat, or even several, did not demoralize them. They just analyzed what had gone wrong and took steps not to let the same thing happen again.

"When will they depart for Sicily?" she said, annoyed. "My brother could exhaust his whole army with his endless inspections."

"The winds have not been favorable, Princess," said Echaz, eunuch priest of Tanit.

"Our ships have oars. They shouldn't need to worry about winds."

"Against winds that blow untimely from the north, even the oared galleys of Carthage cannot prevail," he said. "It is further proof of the displeasure of the gods. We have neglected our duties toward the baalim for too long."

She nodded, absently running a gilded fingernail along the line of blue tears tattooed from the corner of her eye down one cheek, the ritual tears shed for Adonis. She was high priestess of Tanit and the goddess's champion in the eternal rivalry between Tanit and Baal-Hammon. She led the priestly party in its own rivalry with the secular Hellenizing court, upholding the ancient customs and religion of Carthage against the incursions of foreign philosophy.

"To the harbor!" she said to the litter slaves. Then, to Echaz: "I want to look at this inert fleet of ours."

The slaves raised the great litter to their brawny shoulders and set out at a brisk trot, their gait skillfully broken to provide a smooth ride. The litter was large enough for the princess, a dozen of her serving women and a few priests. Runners armed with staves preceded the litter, clearing away any who stood in its path. Their efforts were scarcely necessary: The moment the unique vehicle came into view, all citizens and slaves immediately went down on their faces. Only the sentries at their guard posts remained standing.

The walls of Carthage were broad enough to race chariots along the top, and tunneled through with barracks, storehouses for supplies, magazines for arms and stables for horses, oxen and elephants. It overlooked the Great Harbor from an immense height, and the circular Naval Harbor, with its artificial admiralty island, lay within the wall's protection.

Now the water and the ship sheds of the Naval Harbor were jammed with the triremes assembled for the war, and the commercial harbor was almost full with the spillover. There were warships and transports of all kinds. Some ships had been lost at Alexandria, victims of the outlandish defensive works envisioned by the School of Archimedes, and carried out under the direction of the Roman, Marcus Scipio. But these losses had been trifling. Carthage could build more ships in a day than had been lost in the Egyptian war.

But the contrary winds kept them penned here. Zarabel wrinkled her shapely nose at the stench of their refuse, dumped into the water to linger there until winds from the south should blow once again, allowing the ships to leave and the waters to refresh themselves in the accustomed fashion.

"What would happen," she wondered, "if a fire should break out on one of those ships? They are packed together like wooden tenements of the poor. A fire could sweep them all and spread to the Naval Harbor. The sea power of Carthage could be more than halved in a single hour."

"One supposes," Echaz piped dryly, "that our shofet has made all necessary sacrifices to secure us from such a disaster."

"Even so," she murmured. "Yet, as you have observed, the gods are no longer pleased with our sacrifices."

The priest lowered his gaze. "That is very true, Princess."

"Let us implore Tanit," she said, "that no such evil befall us."

"I shall pray and sacrifice daily, Princess."

"But," she amended, "the decision lies with the goddess. Should she desire to humble Baal-Hammon by striking a blow at his overweening devotee, the shofet, we can only acquiesce to her will."

"That is also true, Princess," said the priest.

The next evening, after a seasonal banquet in honor of Patechus, the god of terror and guardian of naval vessels, Zarabel spoke to her brother more sharply than was her usual custom.

"Brother," she said, speaking down a table lined with courtiers, now replete with food and wine, "you know that the people call for a *Tophet* to win back the will of our gods." Instantly the convivial hubbub quieted.

"I have heard no such thing from the people," Hamilcar said. "Only from certain priests, who would do well to hold their tongues if they wish to keep them." He wondered what his sister was up to. She had been meek for some time, itself a suspicious circumstance.

"The baalim are angry with us," she asserted.

"How so? I was forced to retire from Alexandria, but we suffered no military disaster in Egypt. These Romans have come to plague us with their outrageous aggression and their lying alliances, but that is because our ancestor Hannibal the Great neglected to destroy them when he had the opportunity. I will finish the task and will not be moved to clemency, as he was." The courtiers made sounds of agreement and tapped the table with their flywhisks in applause.

"Yet your great host stays here eating up the substance of Carthage because you cannot get a favorable wind. This alone is proof of the gods' displeasure."

"Winds favorable or unfavorable are a matter of luck at any time. They obey laws of nature that we do not understand and will blow northward when it is time for them to blow that way."

"That is Greek philosophy, not the wisdom of Carthage," she answered with the hint of a sneer in her voice.

His face darkened. "Then let us be instructed by another Greek example, one from a time before the Greeks took up philosophy. The Greek king Agamemnon assembled a great fleet, very much like mine, to sail against Troy, which had insulted him much as these Romans have insulted me. But the winds were unfavorable. To secure a good wind for Troy, the gods demanded the sacrifice of his daughter, Iphigenia. The sacrifice was duly performed and Agamemnon got his wind, but the sacrifice caused him much trouble later."

In the ensuing silence he took a sip from his jeweled cup. "Nevertheless, I might be persuaded to risk his sad fate for the good of Carthage. But, as you know, sister, I have no daughter. In fact, I have only one close kinswoman." He glared at her until she lowered her eyes.

Later, when the guests were gone and Zarabel had retired to her quarters, far from his, Hamilcar stood on his great terrace and brooded upon the evening's disturbing turn. He was tall, handsome, with the pale complexion and black hair shared by all highborn Carthaginians. His hair and beard were dressed in the Greek fashion, and his robes were Greek in design, although embroidered with gold in Carthaginian figures and befitting his lofty rank.

He wondered what his sister's outspokenness portended. She had obviously wanted to be heard by others. Why else wait until a banquet? It had not escaped his notice that she had paid more than proper attention to the Roman delegation when they visited Carthage. He was all but sure that she had been more than intimate with the one named Norbanus. Norbanus and Scipio had been the ranking men of the mission. His sister had identified Norbanus as the weaker and more corruptible of the two and had set out to exploit him. Hamilcar could only approve of her strategy, if not of her motives. Might his sister be contemplating treachery, even treason? If so, he would not be totally displeased.

For some time after returning to Carthage he had kept an eye on his sister's waistline. If she was with child by a foreigner, he could put her aside without incurring censure. But she was too clever for that and had a vast knowledge of medicines and every sort of abortifacient. Much as she provoked him, her position as royal princess, direct descendant of Hannibal and high priestess of Tanit, made her invulnerable, lacking proof of the most egregious crime.

His gaze was drawn north, past the twin lighthouses that flanked the harbor entrance. What were the Romans doing up there, to the north? The Romans he had taken to Egypt had shown themselves to be terribly effective in battle, but they were cut off from Italy, last reported somewhere in Judea. Surely, he thought, they would all die or desert long before they could reach Italy to reinforce the usurping Romans there.

But the rich and strategic island of Sicily, long a Carthaginian possession, now swarmed with Romans, more of them than he had dreamed existed. Incredibly, the sheer number of legions seemed to surpass those faced by Hannibal. Where had they all come from? Could the ragtag, beaten nation that chose exile north of the Alps have bred so many sons in a mere four or five generations? It did not seem possible, unless they had the reproductive capacity of hares.

In truth, he was not entirely displeased with his new challenge. Once, he had thought that conquering Egypt would win him undying fame. Now he knew that it would have made him merely one conqueror among many. But he would beat the Romans, annihilating them utterly, as his ancestor Hannibal had failed to do. Then he would march on and finish Egypt and, with his empire restored and the wealth of Egypt added to that of Carthage, the world was his. He would go on to swallow up the Seleucid kingdom and drive the Parthians back to their steppes, crush Macedonia and Greece, and then the sea would be his own personal lake. He would be master of the world, greater than Hannibal, greater than Alexander.

He was distracted from these pleasant musings by a glimmer far out in the darkness of the harbor. It was brighter than the oil lamps used to illuminate ships at night. The reflection of one of the beacons on polished metal? It seemed to flare brighter with each gust of wind from the north.

"Shofet?" said a feminine voice. He turned to see one of his banquet guests, Queen Teuta of Illyria.

"Please use my name," he said, smiling. "Fellow monarchs need not observe the formalities while sharing a roof. Could you not sleep? Is there anything you require? Please regard me as your personal servant." He could be as gracious and urbane as any Athenian with his peers, even this rather primitive queen of a barbarous land.

She smiled, a strange sight because it made her facial tattoos writhe. She wore a proper gown of Greek design, but it left head and neck, arms, shoulders and the upper surface of her breasts exposed. Every square inch of visible flesh was

covered with exquisitely rendered designs of twisting vege-
tation and bizarre, elongated animals in vivid colors.

"I lack for nothing, Hamilcar. In fact, I never knew the
meaning of abundance until this visit. No, the night is fair
and I am not tired and I thought that this might be an opportunity for us to speak candidly." Her accent was heavy,
but her Greek was excellent. There were a number of pros-
perous Greek colonies on the coast of her nation, and where
there were Greek cities, there were Greek teachers of language and rhetoric. It annoyed Hamilcar that the eternal rival of Carthage had such a monopoly on culture, but it was
certainly convenient that all educated people had a common
language.

"Then this is my good fortune. Will you sit?" He gestured toward the fine table and chairs in the center of the
terrace, pure Carthaginian in their drapings of precious fab-
rics and exotic animal skins.

"Thank you, but I come of a people more at home in
tents than in palaces. We are always on horseback or afoot,
surveying our herds. I think and converse better while
walking."

"Excellent. I, too, find myself pacing when I have anything serious to ponder." Idly, he wondered what this chief-
tainess might have on her mind. He knew little about her
people save that they were largely nomads, that some had
founded settlements but only in recent generations, and
that they seemed to be a mixture of Thracian, Scythian and
perhaps Gallic in blood heritage. The woman herself was
tall, strongly built and had abundant hair as white-blond as
he had ever seen. Her face was handsome, with broad cheekbones, and her brilliant blue eyes had a distinctive tilt that
hinted of Eastern ancestry. As for her complexion, he had no
idea.

She walked to the parapet and ran a palm along its polished marble. "I was struck by your exchange with the Princess Zarabel late in the banquet."

"My sister lacks tact and regards the goddess she serves as the rival of Baal-Hammon. You needn't take her words seriously."

She waved a hand dismissively. "Oh, I know all about troublesome siblings, never fear. I had to put aside a few brothers and sisters to win my throne."

"You have a refreshing directness of speech," he observed.

"'Directness' meaning I am blunt. I agree. My tutors taught me the Greek tongue. I never learned the subtleties of innuendo and indirection. Such things are alien to the customs of my people."

"All the better."

"No, what intrigued me was one of your own replies. You said that you have no close kinswomen. Have you no sons, either?"

"Nor wife," he said, striving for a Spartan terseness to match her own.

She nodded. "As I thought. Yet the survival of the Barca family must be assured, must it not? The seed of Hannibal must not be allowed to die out."

"As you can see, I am not elderly yet. There is plenty of time."

She stepped closer and held his eyes with hers. "Let me be even more blunt. If you marry a Carthaginian noblewoman, she must be of one of the other great families. With a consort and in time an heir of their own blood, that family will feel itself greater than the Barcas. Some of the great houses probably do already, is this not so?"

He nodded. "Every one of them. You studied us before making this visit, did you not?"

"I would have been a fool not to. Do I seem like a fool to you?"

"Not at all," he said, enjoying this immensely. "In fact, I wondered why a reigning queen wished to accompany what amounts to a band of mercenaries. I suspect that you have a proposal for me."

"Precisely. I have no husband and am in much the same position as you. Chieftains of other clans and their sons swarm around me, pressing their suits. If I marry one of them, he will regard himself as my master as soon as he has bred a son on me. If that happens, I will have to kill him and then there will be trouble. I am young and can breed many sons. You need a royal wife. In all the lands surrounding the sea there are only two royal women suitable for you. One is Selene of Egypt. I am the other. A match with Selene is unlikely."

"There would be obstacles to such a match," he said, stalling for time to think. "While the Barcas have never adopted the obscene Egyptian practice of brother-sister marriage, wives have always come from Carthaginian families, dating from our emigration from Phoenicia."

"And no queen of Illyria has ever wed outside the ancient clans of our people. What care the likes of you and I for such rules? They are the customs of a world as dead as that of Agamemnon and Hector. That mold was broken for good when Alexander made the world his footstool and united West with East when he wed his best men with princesses of the old Persian Empire."

It had been the right thing to say. It put him on a level with the greatest. It told him he was above the strictures of ancient custom and could dictate his own rules to the world. It was what he had suspected all his life, and it was good to hear it affirmed by a peer. Then she stared past him and pointed. "What is that?"

He turned and saw that the flickering glimmer he had noticed just before her arrival was now a discernible fire. Then a tongue of red flame shot skyward, twisting in the wind until it was a writhing, spiral pillar. All around the harbor, alarm gongs began to thunder.

Teuta stepped to the parapet and swept the jammed expanse with her gaze. "How bad is this?"

"Our firefighters are very expert. Ship fires are a common occurrence." But he was deeply alarmed.

"It is at the northern end of the harbor and the wind is strong from that direction. Have your men ever been faced with this? Has the water ever been so packed with kindling wood?"

"Never in living memory," he told her. "I'd better go and take personal charge."

"I'll come with you," she said.

"I appreciate it, but you cannot help."

"I do not intend to. I just want to view the spectacle at close hand." She said it with a hint of pleasurable anticipation. *This one will bear watching,* he thought as he shouted to his servants, demanding that swift horses be brought.

With a roar, a ship erupted like a volcano. Great amphorae flew through the air, spewing liquid fire over neighboring vessels. An oil ship, he thought. Already this was out of control.

Minutes later they were mounted and pelting down the wide, paved street that ran from the palace to the harbor. Before them rode guardsmen who cleared the street ahead, swinging huge whips to drive pedestrians from their path. The hour was late and at first there were few citizens abroad, but as they neared the harbor the crowd grew dense. The clamor of the gongs awakened sleepers and they rushed outside to see what was happening. Word of a fire in the harbor sent them down toward the water to view the flames.

Gawkers began to go down beneath the hooves of the guardsmen's mounts, and whips bit into flesh. The uproar from the harbor was so loud that few heard the royal party's approach until it was too late to get out of the way. The smell of smoke and blood and the general uproar made even the trained warhorses nervous, and the guardsmen resorted to using the weighted butts of their whips to drive them forward.

Hamilcar fretted impatiently. Already, the flames towered over the rooftops ahead. He looked to his side and saw Teuta, her horse under perfect control, her face ablaze. "I had not anticipated such excitement until we should see battle!" she told him. "This is proving a most entertaining journey!" Her Greek gown was not designed for riding and it bunched almost at her hips, baring her legs immodestly, but considering the density of her intricate tattoos, she looked fully clothed.

At last they burst from the streets onto the great plaza that separated the warehouses of the port from the water and the long, stone wharfs that ran far out into the harbor. The harbormaster stood atop a twenty-foot platform, shouting orders through a huge funnel of thin silver, one of the insignia of his office. Under his direction, firefighters ran along the wharfs carrying buckets of water and sand, some holding the axes and poles and long rakes used in their demanding profession. Hamilcar noted with approval their excellent discipline and courage. The men wore heavy fire cloaks of leather or linen and wide-brimmed helmets of painted rawhide.

Hamilcar and Teuta dismounted at the base of the platform and dashed up its steps. "How far has it spread?" Hamilcar shouted.

"The northeast quadrant is ablaze," the harbormaster said. He was a white-bearded man of many years' experience. He did not bow to his shofet or even look in his direction. At this moment his authority in the harbor was absolute. It was a law enacted before the days of Hannibal. Hamilcar stood behind him and to one side and motioned for Teuta to stay near him.

"Can the balance of the shipping be saved?" Hamilcar asked.

"We'll be lucky to save the harbor itself. If we do, you may thank your ancestors who decreed that only stone be used for construction here. We have enough firefighters to handle a fire perhaps one-tenth this size. Even that would be a large fire. This is unimaginable."

"How did it start?" Hamilcar asked grimly.

"It may have been an overturned lamp, or a cooking fire that burned after dark in violation of the law." Now he turned and looked at Hamilcar. "But if that is the case, it happened at the very worst time, and in the very worst spot, that it could have: among ships laden with oil and pitch, at the very spot where the wind would sweep the flames over the harbor."

"Then it was deliberate?"

"Either that or the gods are angry with Carthage. If it was set by an enemy, we will know in the morning. I know what to look for." Then a new battalion of firefighters arrived, their capes dripping from recent soaking, and the harbormaster turned away to shout his orders at them.

Through the night they watched as the immense flames roared across the water. A very few skippers managed to get their vessels out of the harbor before the fire cut off escape in that direction. Flames leapt from ship to ship, and in time the heat grew so intense that vessels burst into flame before they were actually touched by fire. At that point, all effort at control had to be given up. The plaza itself had to be abandoned and the shofet and the harbormaster went atop the great wall, where the population had assembled to gape at the unprecedented sight. The surviving firefighters were sent to the naval harbor to prevent the fire from spreading there. Above all, the military fleet had to be preserved.

Toward morning, the flames became a single column of fire, sucking into the center of the harbor whatever remained to burn. The fire drew a great gust of wind down the streets of Carthage, pulling leaves from the trees, scraps of papyrus, wicker furniture, domestic fowl, even a few scrawny beggars into the great central inferno. After that, the fire itself died swiftly.

The sun rose to reveal a harbor that was nothing more than an expanse of floating charcoal and ash. Charred corpses and the pale undersides of innumerable boiled fish provided variety, and for hours the stones of the wharfs were too hot to tread. In the late afternoon Hamilcar accompanied the harbormaster to the northeastern end of the harbor along the great seawall that separated the sheltered harbor from the open sea. The heat still rising from the stones was intense but bearable. The stench of burned wood, oil, pitch and bodies was bad, but no worse that the usual sacrifices. Teuta came with them, and both monarchs held sachets of perfume and spices beneath their nostrils.

"It began here," the harbormaster said. A row of bodies lay stretched upon the wharf. There were twelve of them, looking half-cooked, their arms and legs drawn up and inward in the usual fashion of burn victims. "They were the crew of an oil ship named *Dagon-Gives-Abundance,* from Tyre. It was anchored between other oil ships and pitch and bitumen carriers, here next to the seawall. The wind blew inland, so these bodies were spared the intense heat that would otherwise have reduced them to ashes.

"They did not leave the ship when they lost control of the fire," Teuta noted. "That is what sane men would ordinarily have done."

"Quite true, Your Majesty," the harbormaster said. "These men could not go overboard because they were already dead when the fire started. If you will come closer you will see how they died."

Hamilcar and Teuta bent low and examined the charred bodies without revulsion. Both of them were accustomed to far worse. Cruelty was a commonplace, and both war and religion demanded it.

"As you can see," said the harbormaster, lecturing like a schoolmaster, "the necks of some are cut deeply. Others have large wounds in the chest, probably made by sword or spear. These men were asleep on the deck. The throats of sleeping men were cut easily. Some awoke, and they were stabbed or speared. Three or four skilled men could have accomplished this efficiently, making very little noise. If any on other ships heard," he shrugged, "it would have meant nothing to them. Drunken brawls among sailors are frequent."

Hamilcar and Teuta straightened. "What do you think, Shofet?" she asked. "Was it the Egyptians or the Romans? Or have you other enemies who would profit by this?"

Hamilcar thought for a while. This woman had impressed him greatly, and she clearly was able to follow his thoughts. Whether or not she was a suitable bride for him, she was a valuable ally and possibly a sagacious counselor.

He could not be seen taking advice from a woman, not even an allied queen, but he was already thinking himself above these old customs.

"Please come aside with me, my lady," he said. They strolled to the sea side of the wall, where it was cooler and the salt-smelling breeze carried the offensive smells away from them. She waited for him to speak first.

"I am at war with Egypt and with Rome," he began, "but any king with imperial ambitions has an abundance of enemies, some of them posing as allies or as neutrals."

"That is very true," she said.

"Such a king also has enemies within his own land, within his own family and household."

"These are my own thoughts."

"The might of Carthage is based upon sea power. Our fleets, both merchant and naval, dominate the waters from the Gates of Melkarth to the Euxine Sea. Attack my fleet, and you attack my greatest power. Egypt, which is also a maritime power, has much to gain by such an act and understands this. Rome, a landlocked power until recently, likewise has a great interest in forcing me to confront them on land, where they fancy themselves unbeatable."

"So much for your open foes."

"Closer to home, the subject cities are always a threat: Utica, Sicca and others, even the colonies such as New Carthage in Spain are jealous and want more independence, more profit for themselves."

"And within Carthage itself?"

He paused, then: "Since the day of my ancestor Hannibal the Great, there has been a constant struggle for power between the shofet and the priesthoods. Every king must have a divine sponsor and mine is Baal-Hammon. His priests have grown wealthy and influential and have no stake in weakening my position. Tanit has lost power since Hannibal's day. Her priests are a wretched, weakly lot. They are mostly eunuchs who cling to power by cultivating the women of the royal household."

"Do they stand to gain by burning your support fleet?"

"Not directly. They cannot believe that giving victory to Rome or to Egypt will better their lot. But it will be much to their advantage to put it about that Baal-Hammon has abandoned me. They will cry out again that the gods are angry with me for adopting foreign ways. They will demand a *Tophet*. Zarabel will be their cat's-paw."

Her advice was simple and direct. "Kill her. Then kill the priests and suppress the cult of Tanit."

He smiled upon her. "If only it were that simple. In times of our accustomed peace and prosperity, I could take such extreme measures. But now I must have the people with me, both the commons and the wealthy. A quick war with fat, indolent Egypt was one thing. A swift victory against Selene would have made my position unassailable. But a double war that includes her new Roman allies is very different. I must take back Sicily and Italy. It will be a long, costly war, and the wealthy hate to sacrifice, while the commons adore the gods above all things. In the end, I will give Carthage the world. But for a while, they must all suffer, and the priests will take advantage of that."

She nodded. "I understand. So you think the priests of Tanit are the most likely culprits?"

"I believe so. I further believe that Zarabel put them up to it. She is far more intelligent than any of them, and she has studied the politics of world power deeply, while they understand it only as fought within the temples, the city and the court."

"But you will not take immediate action against them?"

"I cannot. That would be a mistake. I must plan against them as carefully as they have plotted against me. In the meantime, the people must be given someone to blame, and I must not allow them to think that the gods of Carthage have forsaken me."

She inclined her head toward him. "You are sagacious as well as bold. Please allow me to help in any way you think proper."

He walked back across the seawall and spoke to the harbormaster: "I find no fault with your conduct during this emergency. It was enemy action, and so I shall report it to the Assembly. The firefighters and others who died will receive all the proper rites." He gestured toward the line of bodies. "You and your men may speak freely of what you have seen here. It was a treacherous act perpetrated by Rome, seeking to weaken the sea power of Carthage."

The harbormaster bowed. "My shofet is gracious." He spoke as calmly as if the specter of the cross had never intruded upon his thoughts. "I shall see to the cleaning and repair of the harbor."

"See to it. Now go."

For a while Hamilcar and Teuta stood alone upon the seawall, save for the corpses and the guardsmen, who stood a little way off.

"What will you do when you move against your sister and the priests?" Teuta asked him.

He pondered this a while. "You come from a far place and have traveled widely. Do you know of a punishment even worse than crucifixion?"

CHAPTER NINE

THEIR SHIP WAS A CARGO VESSEL FROM CORCYRA named *Oceanus*. It was an old but trustworthy craft, veteran of more than a hundred years of voyaging to every shore touched by the Middle Sea, or so her skipper boasted. Been in his family the whole time, he said. The ship was bright with paint recently renewed, and its graceful stem, carved in the form of a swan's neck and head, was brilliantly gilt.

They saw the smoking pinnacle of the Pharos lighthouse from many miles out at sea and passed between the island and Cape Lochias at midday. Since they had letters from the Roman Senate, they would be permitted to use the exclusive Royal Harbor. A small cutter drew alongside at the entrance to the little harbor, and Zeno presented his dispatch case, sealed with a lead medallion embossed with four simple letters in the Roman script: SPQR. This was a formula signifying the Senate and people of Rome, and was placed on all official correspondence, decrees and even public monuments. It was fast becoming a familiar sight.

The glittering official, his uniform the brilliant blue and gold of the Egyptian royal house, glanced at the seal and then at the two Greeks. His golden breastplate and helmet, Zeno thought, would not have withstood the assault of an angry bird.

"You two don't look much like Romans," he noted idly.

"All the Romans are busy fighting Carthage," Zeno told him.

"So one hears. Well, your documents appear to be in order. You may proceed to the royal wharf. The palace is hard to miss. Someone will lead you to the quarters where the Romans stay."

"What is that?" Zeno cried, staring upward. The two Greeks gaped, all philosophical impassivity forgotten for the moment. Above them soared something beyond the speculations of Aristotle: a winged thing that was clearly no living creature, but rather a fabrication of wood and cloth, with batlike wings and a great, wedge-shaped tail. So bizarre was this apparition that at first they did not notice the man hanging just below it like the prey of a great, flying hunter.

"But this is marvelous!" Izates said, apparently finding nothing Cynical to say about it. "A man flies!"

"Yes," said the official, "and no good will come of it, I assure you. This is the sort of behavior that draws the wrath of the gods. Flying men, boats that travel underwater—what next? Men should not aspire to the power of the immortals."

As if to show his contempt for such cavils, the flying man swooped low, almost knocking the gilded helmet from the official's head. The official's Greek polish abandoned him and he cursed at the flyer in native Egyptian. The crowd of idlers gathered along the waterfront cheered.

Zeno and Izates proceeded to a wharf and climbed the

steps to the huge palace complex. A chamberlain examined their credentials and led them to the suite of apartments occupied by the Romans. There they found a man seated at a desk. He rose as they entered, extending his hand.

"Welcome to Alexandria, my friends. You've brought me dispatches from the Senate?" He had the Roman look, but he was a shade less martial in appearance than most others of his class they had encountered. He clearly was not as obsessed with physical fitness, being just a bit soft around the middle, his jaw and cheekbones not defined with quite the razor sharpness so noticeable in the others. "I am Aulus Flaccus, aide to Marcus Cornelius Scipio."

They introduced themselves.

"I am so pleased that the Senate has for once sent men capable of intelligent conversation and interests beyond war and conquest. Gabinius must be behind this. Only man in the Senate with more brains than ferocity. Please, sit down and I'll have some lunch brought in. You must tell me all about how Rome of the Seven Hills is progressing. It was a wasteland when Marcus and I passed through."

"It was Gabinius, indeed," Zeno told him. "He has become our patron and *hospes* in Rome. A most remarkable man." He looked around the room and saw the many models of machines being developed at the Museum. Some were clearly catapults and so forth. Others were utterly mysterious. "Remarkable as I have found the resurgence of Rome, however, developments here in Alexandria have been equally stunning. We saw a flying man when we arrived."

Flaccus smiled. "Yes, Marcus has become enthralled with military toys."

"I would think that a flying man has greater significance than the merely military," said Izates.

"I suppose so. At the moment, however, we are at war and surrounded by enemies, so military applications have pride of place. No doubt you've heard of the underwater boats. They are developing new ways to propel vessels, and people are doing amazing things with mirrors: ways to see over walls and around corners, directing light into dark mines and galleries. And now lenses."

"Lenses?" Zeno said.

"Yes, they are pieces of shaped glass with strange properties. Glass is a Babylonian invention, and the purest glass is still made by artisans from that part of the world. Actually, the Egyptians have been making glass for a thousand years or more, but they only use it for things like perfume flasks and other frivolous uses. Anyway, there is a man here named Aristobulus who has a workforce of these glassmakers who turn out lenses of varying properties. They can make small objects appear large and vice versa. He uses arrangements of these lenses to make distant objects seem closer. Other glass objects, too—prisms, he calls them. They cast a very pretty beam of many-colored light, like a flat rainbow."

"Very interesting," Izates muttered. "Not as impressive as a flying man, though."

"That is true. They seem to have the flying gadget under control now. A number of slaves got killed getting it to work, but now they have free men using them. Makes sense when you think about it. I mean, give a slave a flying machine and you've lost your slave, haven't you? The flyers have grown insufferably arrogant, though. They swagger around the city as if they're a superior breed of men."

"Well, they *do* fly," Izates said. "I suppose it could make a man conceited."

"Ah, here's our lunch," Flaccus said. Slaves carried in

trays and pitchers, and the new acquaintances confined themselves to small talk while they ate. The Greeks described the rebuilding of Rome as they had observed it; Flaccus told them of the latest Alexandrian gossip. The huge, polyglot city with its vast number of inhabitants of many nations was a bottomless well of social and political prattle, which the Roman seemed to find hugely amusing.

"The Greeks are trying to be philosophical about this sudden expansion of Roman power, but they hate to see anything eclipsing the prestige of Greek culture. The Jews are abuzz over the way our colleague, Titus Norbanus, has unified their nation under a single king. We just got the word a few days ago. They don't seem entirely pleased with the news, though. I get the impression that they *like* disunity, being a naturally fractious people. The natives are biding their time. They believe that eventually all the foreigners will be expelled and the great days of the pharaohs will return. Egyptians are patient. Their history goes back thousands of years, so the last few centuries under foreign rule don't amount to much."

"They have been conquered by foreigners before," Izates observed, "and expelled them."

"Their ancestors were more manly," said Flaccus. "Those I've met seem to be natural-born slaves."

"You Romans are born with swords in your hands," Zeno said. "I think it would take a warlike nation indeed to impress you."

Flaccus waved a dismissive hand. "Oh, the discipline and fighting skills are only a part of it. It's what everyone raves about, but I believe our political instincts are what have made us supreme. The Gauls are a brave people, skilled at arms. We've conquered them. You've never seen anyone as ferocious as the Germans, but we're conquering them, too.

We haven't really outfought them, but we've outthought them."

"This has worked well against uncivilized people," said Izates. "Clearly, tribal societies devoid of unity cannot for long prevail against a great nation with a splendid army. But now you are moving into the civilized world, and kingdoms are very different from tribes."

"Only in degree," Flaccus said. "A kingdom is one big tribe under one big chieftain. If the king is a fool, the whole nation suffers. If the royal succession is disputed, there may be civil war. We think a republic is better, and we prefer to have our disunity at the top."

"How do you mean?" Zeno asked, fascinated.

"All philosophers agree that monarchy is the wisest form of government, aristocratic oligarchy the next best, and democracy the worst," Izates said.

"I take it you've stood in the Forum and heard the Senate debate inside the curia?" Flaccus said with a sly grin. "Sounds like a big dogfight, doesn't it? That's the way we like it. Let the senators thrash it out among themselves and leave the commons and the soldiers out of it. Eventually, they'll agree on a policy and then send it out to the commanders in the field. Once policy is set, the state acts as one man."

"Yet your General Norbanus," Izates said, "is off acting like a conquering king, a new little Alexander, without guidance from the Senate."

"Just a temporary expedient," said Flaccus. "The distances are vast and we haven't yet set up a proper communication system. Sooner or later he'll return to Italy and his legions will be back under senatorial control. The whole reason for winning glory is so that he can stand for higher office, and he must lay down his command to take part in the elections. It's all part of our scheme for keeping any one man from grabbing too much power."

His words sounded confident, but both Greeks could see that this was a touchy subject, in Alexandria as at Rome. Norbanus was setting a dangerous precedent.

"Still," said Zeno, steering to a safer subject, "your government is an oligarchy. In our conversations with Gabinius, we learned that most senators came from a small group of families. The commons really have little say in their government."

"True," Flaccus admitted. "We are far from democratic and the senatorial order is a hard nut to crack, but men of outstanding merit get into the Senate, I assure you. I've known consuls whose fathers were peasant farmers and who started their careers as common legionaries. It isn't easy, but it can be done. We purposely don't make it easy. We don't want mere demagogues to rise to power, any more than we want aristocrats aspiring to royal dignity.

"Likewise, we don't allow senatorial families to produce generations of nobodies who live in idleness on inherited wealth. If they can't produce men of courage and capability, they might as well join the class of merchants and businessmen. The elections will assure that. Though not exactly democratic, they express the will of the people with a fair degree of accuracy. Cowards and bumblers do not get elected to the higher magistracies, no matter how noble their families."

"Admirable," both Greeks muttered, wondering how far reality fell short of this ideal. From what they had seen thus far, it came chillingly short.

"But I am sure you want to see what is going on here," Flaccus said, signaling for the slaves to clear away the remains of lunch.

"Aren't you going to look over the documents we've brought?" Zeno asked.

Flaccus glanced at the scrolls and tablets on the table. "Oh, I shall. Eventually."

Izates cleared his throat. "Um, if you will not think the observation too impertinent, you seem to have a rather Norbanus-like disregard for senatorial guidance."

Flaccus shrugged. "Really, there is no rush. I already know what is in there. There will be a pompous official pronouncement from the Senate. Then there will be some letters from Gabinius and other friends and allies, telling us about the real political climate in Rome and what our enemies are plotting against us. Just the usual stuff. After all, what we do here in Alexandria is merely a sideshow. The real action just now is in Sicily and Judea and parts eastward, soon to be followed by the real war against Carthage. We really don't merit much senatorial attention."

Flaccus clapped his hands and a pair of young slaves came running with his armor and weapons. "The queen insists upon these military trappings," he grumped as, with some difficulty, the boys got his old-fashioned, muscled cuirass buckled about him. "She wants everyone to be in no doubt where her support lies. The locals are frightened of Carthage, but they have learned to be truly terrified of Rome."

"We've been told of how Titus Norbanus conducted his part of the battle between Hamilcar's army and that of the deposed advisors. Also of his progress down the Nile before he set off eastward," Zeno said.

"He's shown a flair for generalship nobody expected," Flaccus admitted. "Put the fear of Jupiter's thunderbolts into the Egyptians. And if an untried boy like Norbanus can do that, what will the seasoned Roman commanders be like, eh?"

He led them from his rather lavish quarters at the now-familiar legionary pace into an adjacent courtyard that had been converted into an exercise yard for the Romans. There they found another Roman dressed in full battle armor practicing sword work against a wooden post. By now the Greeks were familiar with the legionary sword drill and were no longer astonished at the subtle use of the shield and lightning jabs of the *gladius*.

"Marcus, I've brought friends," Flaccus said.

The other man stepped back from the post and sheathed his sword. He removed his helmet, revealing a face as hard-planed as any they had ever seen. This man looked like the final refinement of the Roman soldier ideal. He was sweating abundantly, but his breathing was slow and steady and he spoke easily.

"Welcome. You look like a pair of seasoned travelers. What brings you to us?"

Flaccus made introductions and told Marcus of their mission.

"Excellent! The Senate is showing some sense for a change. You should hear the men they usually send here with dispatches. I ask them how the rebuilding of Rome is progressing and they say, 'it's going fine,' or 'slowly,' or something like that. They always resent being used as messengers and are anxious to be with the legions."

"Aren't you?" Izates asked.

"Not really. I've been fighting all my life, and there will always be plenty of campaigning to do. We're doing important work here, and it will prove crucial in the years and campaigns to come."

Zeno eyed the much-splintered post. "I confess I'm rather surprised to see a soldier of your years and experience practicing at the post like a recruit."

Marcus grinned, almost softening his harsh face. "My father put a wooden sword in my hand and a wicker shield on my arm and set me at the post when I was seven years old. I've done this drill more days than not every year since. You'd be surprised how sloppy your sword work can get if you neglect post practice. Sparring with an opponent is more enjoyable, but you lose your precision if that is all you do."

"Let him get started and he'll talk about fighting all day long," Flaccus told them. "Marcus, I've promised these two a tour of our facility. Would you care to guide them?"

"Of course! I'd like nothing better."

"You see?" Flaccus said. "This is the one thing he likes even better than fighting. The Archimedean school is his pride and joy. He'd rather test a new machine than celebrate a triumph."

"Actually," Marcus said, "there's no reason why I can't do this and celebrate a triumph as well, eventually. Come along." They set off, the two Romans unconsciously falling into lockstep.

"Archimedes has been a rather obscure figure," Izates said. "Of course, everyone knows the story of how he discovered the principles of buoyancy and displacement, and his geometric discoveries, but his school here has been practically unknown."

"That's because the heads of the Museum have been as Plato-addled as most philosophers," Marcus said. "Well, I put an end to that. Gave the school top priority and sent out word that any bright, invention-minded philosopher who wanted to actually *do* things instead of just ponder and babble could come here and accomplish wonders. More arrive every day."

"An extreme approach," Izates said, "but effective. Someone should have done this long ago."

"But you are a philosopher yourself," Flaccus said. "Aren't you shocked to see this sort of behavior?"

Izates made a rude noise. "Philosophers? A batch of Academics, Sophists, Peripatetics, Stoics and the like? I'm a Cynic and we love to see other philosophers get a boot in the rear sometimes." He cackled. "This time it's a big, hobnailed Roman boot and it must have hurt!"

They entered a newly constructed courtyard the size of a stadium, filled with a dazzling array of machines powered in every imaginable way: wind, water, falling weight, springs, twisted rope, as well as plain old muscle power, both human and animal. Scrambling slaves worked inside giant wheels or trotted on treadmills or hauled on ropes. Men turned enormous augers, pumped bellows, ran ropes through arrangements of small wheels, cranked toothed wheels and bars through various bewildering motions.

"You do things in a big way," Zeno noted.

"This facility is just one of eight we have here," Marcus said. "This one is the biggest, because here we try out the biggest machines."

"Many of these machines seem to be intended to overcome fortifications," Zeno said.

"Exactly," Marcus replied. "Now that we are back in civilization, we'll be taking a great many fortresses and walled cities. Everything I know of the subject says that besieging cities is the very worst form of warfare. It drags on and on; besiegers and besieged starve and fall to pestilence and ruin the land all around. Anything that will shorten a siege must be a good development. I want to make our sieges short."

"A laudable goal," Zeno said.

"I should think so," Marcus agreed.

"Perhaps our friends would like to see some of the subtler devices," Flaccus suggested.

They went to a smaller and far quieter courtyard where small teams of men and a few women worked in the shade of long porticoes. Here they crafted strange instruments of bronze and glass. Some peered through lenses at objects placed below and made drawings of what they observed. Marcus took his visitors to one of these, a seedy-looking little man who was filling reams of papyrus with drawings of insects, shells, feathers and other things.

"This is Myron," Marcus Scipio told them. "His is the realm of the incredibly tiny."

The man grinned at them. "I have discovered another world, and it is all around us. Look here." He gestured to the broad lens upon his table. Something incredibly tiny rested just below it, affixed to a thin straw. An arrangement of mirrors cast a bright, reflected light upon the thing. They bent close and saw the thing enormously enlarged. It was, or had been, a living creature, with a bewildering array of minute legs, feathery antennae and banded body segments.

"What is it?" Izates asked.

"A shrimp!" the man said triumphantly. "There exist whole worlds around us, invisible to our gross organs of perception! But with the instruments we develop here we may see and study them."

"And what is gained by the study of tiny shrimps and such?" Zeno asked.

"Knowledge!" Myron said, his beady eyes blazing. "By observation of even the tiniest of things, we can divine the secrets of nature! Nothing is so small as to be insignificant."

"I see," said Izates. "Knowledge for the sake of knowledge. There is something almost Platonic in the concept. The Platonists are always going on about the purity of thought. You'd think they would appreciate this, even if it means that you have to pick things up in order to look at them."

Myron made an explosively rude noise with his lips. "Those futile buggers would never dirty their hands."

"It is also possible to make fire with these lenses," Marcus said, eager as always to point out practical uses for things. This called for a demonstration, and Myron showed them how a lens of the proper shape could focus light to a tiny point, and beneath it tinder of various materials first smoked, then burst into flame before their astonished eyes.

"Dark-colored tinder takes fire more swiftly than light-colored, for some reason," Myron pointed out. "There are many properties of light and matter that we have yet to discover."

"One seldom gives light much thought," Izates mused. "Either it is there or it isn't. Bright light reveals more than dim light." He pondered a moment. "But if the light of the sun produces heat, why does that of the moon not do the same?"

Flaccus smiled. "You see? You haven't been here two hours and already you're thinking like an Archimedean philosopher."

Next they visited the yard they were most eager to see: the workplace where the flying machines were built. Marcus led them to a portico where artists studied the wings of birds and crafted wonderfully lifelike models of these wings, with every feather cleverly in place, held by bitumen.

"The eagle is the noblest of birds," Zeno said. "I would think that its wings would be the finest for flying."

"That is what I thought," Marcus said. "After all, the eagle is the sacred bird of Jupiter and therefore most suitable to fly for Rome. The Egyptians here insist that the ibis would be better. But it turns out that bird wings are not the best model for emulation. Our most successful flying devices have wings modeled after those of bats."

"The bat is a lowly creature," Izates said, "little more than a rat with wings. Surely a man should fly with something not quite so ignoble as a model."

"I'll let Timonides explain," Marcus said.

Timonides turned out to be yet another of the obsessive philosophers, his particular obsession being the properties of flight, whether those of birds, bats or insects. He showed them models built of reeds, papyrus and parchment, and explained how the unique musculature, skeletons and feathers of birds gave them their power of flight.

"This is not reproducible in a form usable by humans," he said, "although the wings of soaring birds have given me many lessons in how the wings of my gliders should be contoured. But it is the structure of bat wings that offers the greatest possibilities for imitation. A bat's wings are made up of thin struts with a membrane of skin stretched between them. This we can copy with wood and fabric. It is both light and strong."

"But they can only glide?" Zeno asked.

"Alas," Timonides said, "the propulsive, flapping actions of the wings have proven thus far impracticable. However, our fliers have discovered many unsuspected properties of the air above us that allow them to soar for extremely long times. We do not understand these properties as yet, but in time they must yield to our research. We may yet learn to fly as freely as birds."

"Gentlemen," Flaccus said quietly. Immediately all conversation stopped and the sounds of work stilled. The Greeks turned to see that a young woman had entered the courtyard. She appeared to be pure Hellene and she wore a simple, modest gown of Greek design. Her only adornment was a thin fillet of plaited silver bound about her brows. All bowed, the native Egyptians among them going to hands and knees and touching their foreheads to the ground.

The young woman walked straight up to Marcus Scipio and was about to speak when she caught sight of the Greeks and paused. Marcus introduced them to Princess Selene, consort of young King Ptolemy.

"Welcome to Alexandria, my friends," she said.

"My lady is too kind," Zeno said. "However, it is clear that you have business with our host. Please do not let us detain you. We will withdraw."

She nodded appreciation of his tact. "We will speak at dinner this evening."

They stood aside a few paces while the princess and Scipio spoke in low but urgent tones.

Izates inclined his head toward the two. "Bad news, do you think?"

"The queen perceives her situation as precarious and sometimes allows small matters to upset her. It is probably nothing."

Zeno gave the pronouncement no more respect than it deserved. These Romans would tell him nothing of real importance. He did, however, notice that Flaccus had used the word "queen," which Selene did not rate by any recognized standards. The Romans wanted her to be sovereign of Egypt for their own purposes, so as far as they were concerned she was queen.

He noted another thing: Selene and Scipio spoke with

their heads close together, and from time to time she touched his arm lightly. The gesture was trifling, yet performed thus in public, by a de facto sovereign to her supposedly subordinate ally, it spoke volumes. Zeno wondered what Marcus Scipio's enemies in Rome would pay to hear about this.

CHAPTER TEN

NORBANUS HADN'T ANTICIPATED THE EFFECTS OF dust. The shuffling feet of thousands of men, the churning hooves of thousands of horses raised a pall of dust so thick that he had trouble observing the course of the battle. He thought of the lessons drilled into him in military school: the handling of troops; the hazards of illness, unfavorable terrain, mud, cold—all of them potentially as devastating as a well-led enemy of superior numbers. Even plain bad luck had been taken into account. Somehow, though, the lessons had never mentioned dust.

"Maybe I was out with a fever the day they covered that," he mused.

"Eh?" King Jonathan said. "Covered what?" His face was drawn and concerned. His future, his very life were the issues being contested on the field before them.

"Dust. I don't recall that our instructors ever mentioned it."

"You don't have dust where you come from?" Jonathan said, astonished.

"I suppose it rains too much."

The two stood atop Norbanus's command tower, overseeing the combat. The battle had been joined about an hour earlier, beginning with an exchange of arrows, javelins and sling-stones. These preliminaries had caused casualties only among the light-armed native troops. Roman shields and armor were proof against all such trifles.

They had found Manasseh and his army toward the southern edge of the plain called Megiddo: a natural battle-field where countless engagements had been fought. Besides the Jews, it had seen the armies of Egypt, the Hittites, Persians and Greeks clash and fall. Manasseh's army was larger, but it held no Romans. Most important, his Parthian allies had not arrived yet. When he deemed the time propitious, Norbanus had committed his legions, and the cohorts strode forth to hurl their murderous pila and draw their short, razor-edged swords. The cavalry of both sides were quickly engaged on the flanks and the dust rose.

"How can we control an army we can't see?" Jonathan asked plaintively.

"We can't. In a fight like this, the general's task is done in making his dispositions and giving his commands. Now it is a soldier's battle. The junior officers and the centurions will handle their own individual parts of the fight. This is where Roman training and drill pay off. Our legionaries can win a battle with all their commanders dead."

"I see," Jonathan said without conviction.

From the cloud before them, above the sounds of clashing metal and wood and the meaty smack of weapons against unprotected flesh, they could hear the blare and snarl of Roman trumpets. Unable to see, Norbanus could follow the progress of the fight as officers closer to the action directed their trumpeters, calling some cohorts back, sending others forward, closing up lines or putting them in extended order to take advantage of momentary weaknesses in the enemy formations.

"That's a bit risky," Norbanus noted.

"What?"

"Niger just wheeled his second cohort to catch the left flanking corner of Manasseh's formation. He must see an opportunity there. I hope he knows what he's doing. It wasn't in the battle plan."

"You can tell all that from the tooting of a trumpet?"

"It's as plain as speech once your ear is accustomed to it."

"You allow your subordinates such license?"

"Of course. Rigid adherence to a battle plan in spite of changing conditions is folly. He may have won the battle for us, in which case I'll decorate him. If it's a blunder, I'll have his hide for a shield cover."

Jonathan sweated. "This is maddening. We can do nothing, know nothing."

"We still have them," Norbanus said, jerking a thumb back over his shoulder. Behind the command tower an entire legion sat on the ground, resting, ready for battle at an instant's notice.

"Why do you keep so many out of the fight when we are outnumbered to begin with?"

Norbanus hid his impatience. He hated dealing with amateurs. "They are my reserve. At any given time, only the front-line soldiers do any actual fighting. To commit everyone at once merely tires them out without accomplishing anything. They might as well stay to the rear and husband their strength. Should I see an opportunity or a great danger, I have them ready to meet the situation without having to disengage them from the battle first. It's the best way."

"Of course," Jonathan muttered. "It is just—Manasseh has so many men."

"And they are all out there, most of them able to do nothing except wave their arms and shout. They are getting very tired, I assure you." He was not as sanguine as he pretended. It was indeed wearing on the nerves to hear a battle without being able to see it clearly. He took great comfort from the presence of that legion behind him. Should the situation prove disastrous, they would extricate him and the bulk of his Romans from the fight.

He was not pessimistic, but anything could happen. He knew the story of Xenophon, who had been in a situation very much like this. His Greeks had won their part of the battle, but their Persian ally lost his part and the Greeks were forced to make their epic march to the sea. Norbanus's confidence in his legions was absolute. His confidence in Jonathan's forces was slight.

And, he thought, where were the Parthians? They could appear at any time, and there were few more disastrous occurrences than the sudden advent of enemy reinforcements after Roman forces were already committed to battle. But then, he thought further, the whole Manasseh-Parthian alliance might be nothing more than a rumor.

He shook these unproductive thoughts from his head and returned his attention to the battle before him, or as much as he could see of it. He cursed the dust once again.

GABINIUS RELAXED IN THE COURTYARD OF HIS AN-cestral home, enjoying the cool of the evening. The house was new, but it felt right. He was where he should be. He heard a small commotion from the atrium. A visitor, no doubt. A man of his importance received guests at all hours: clients in need of a favor, friends from other towns come to claim hospitality. His steward entered the courtyard.

"Princeps, a lictor has come to summon you to the curia."

"Good news or bad?"

"He would say no more than that you are summoned."

Gabinius rose. "Lictors. How they love their little secrets." He knew that it had to be something momentous for a Senate meeting to be called after sunset. Even the news of the disastrous fire in the harbor at Carthage had waited until morning. It had been by no means a decisive blow to Hamilcar, but it bought the Romans time, and time was what they needed. They were conquering too much, too fast. *How long will the gods bless us in this fashion?* he wondered.

His fellow senators milled on the curia steps, some of them looking a bit tipsy from their after-dinner drinking. At the summons of another lictor, they filed inside. The nearby forum began to fill as word spread of the extraordinary meeting.

Inside, they took their benches. The consuls were already in place. When the doors shut, the Consul Scipio stood and raised over his head a broad wooden tablet of traditional design, the letters SPQR blazoned on it in large, gilt letters. A laurel wreath encircled the tablet. A hiss of satisfaction went up from the assembly. Laureled dispatches meant victory.

"Syracuse has fallen!" Scipio announced, producing a general uproar. "Sicily is ours!"

When the cacophony died down, Scipio read the terse message. "The Proconsul Titus Scaeva sends greetings to the noble Senate. On this day, the nineteenth of Quinctilis, the city of Syracuse passed into the possession of Rome. About the middle of the second hour the undermining operations I had pursued bore fruit and a large section of the northern city wall collapsed. I immediately ordered my legions into the breach. The Carthaginians and their citizen allies fought with desperation, but they were lost when they had to face Roman soldiers at close quarters. The fighting was street-by-street and ended in the square surrounding the great temple of Zeus. Resistance ended by the seventh hour, and the inhabitants were put to the sword to let all foreigners know the price of resistance to Rome. At sundown I signaled a halt to the slaughter. In coming days I will render the noble Senate an accounting of the plunder of this very rich city. Death to Carthage. Long live Rome."

The Consul Norbanus stood. "I propose, pending a full report from both the Proconsul Scaeva and the Senate's observers in Sicily, that Titus Scaeva be voted the right to celebrate a triumph. I further propose that he be awarded the title 'Siculus' in honor of his conquest of Sicily."

Amid further cheering Gabinius made his way to the consuls' dais. Norbanus noticed him first. "I see from the princeps's sour look that even this wonderful news fails to elate him."

"Oh, I am quite elated," Gabinius assured him. "I'd always rather hear of victory than defeat. But has anyone given thought to what we are going to do with Sicily?"

"Do?" Norbanus said. "We are going to divide it up, naturally. That's what you do with conquered territory."

"And who's to get it, eh?" Gabinius asked. "You've read Cyclops's reports: The land is unbelievably rich and fertile, better than Campania. Are we to have the whole Senate at each other's throat over who gets what piece of this prize?"

"There is danger there," said the Consul Scipio. "What are your thoughts, Princeps?"

"Right now we are all a bit drunk with success and with favorable omens. A good drunk is always followed by a bad hangover. Even if we are fully successful in every campaign we undertake, there may be serious consequences. Foreigners are not the only enemy. We've expanded our legions to unprecedented numbers. What will we do with them when Carthage is destroyed and the fighting is over? Has anyone considered that?"

"They will go back home," Norbanus said uneasily.

"They will not," Gabinius assured him. "They came to Italy as farm lads and tribesmen of Noricum. Now they have seen the riches of the civilized world. Before this is over, they will have campaigned not just in Italy and Sicily, but in Africa, Egypt, Syria and the whole East. A common trooper will win more loot in a day than his father and grandfather saw in their lifetimes of toil.

"And these wars," he went on pitilessly, "will not be over soon. These early victories have come easily because nobody expected our arrival and they underestimated our strength. That will not last. Soon there will be alliances against us. Already we are looking at danger from Spain. Young Norbanus is stirring up a hornet's nest in Judea. Macedonia is watching us with alarm. We'll never be safe until we've conquered all the lands that border the sea, and that will be the work of many years. We are raising a generation of men who have no trade save war. In time they will be a great danger to the state."

"I take it you have some sort of suggestion," Norbanus grumbled.

"Exactly. Senatorial families already claimed most of Italy and there has been no little strife over conflicting claims. The new lands we are taking have no ancestral claims on them. Let's set aside some of them right now as reward for the soldiers when they are demobilized. Otherwise, the soldiers will not want to leave the profession of arms, since it will be their only source of livelihood. But with the prospects of rich farms and slaves to work their land, they'll be eager to trade the rigors of continuous campaigning for the life of gentlemen planters."

"That won't be easy," Scipio said. "Look at them." He gestured to the ebullient house. "Some of them are already in ecstasies of greed at the prospect of these Sicilian lands. They won't want to see them pass into the hands of common soldiers." He rapped his knuckles on the armrest of his curule chair. "I'll speak with the tribunes of the people. They can start groundwork for passing a new agrarian law. Maybe at first it will be best to declare the new conquests public land to keep it out of the hands of the major aristocrats. Later they can agitate for its distribution to veterans."

"That will do for a start," Gabinius said.

"You enjoy croaking of doom in the midst of celebration, don't you?" Norbanus said.

Gabinius gave them a lipless smile. "Ironic, isn't it? All this success may yet prove to be the ruin of us."

THE HUGE LEGIONARY CAMP STOOD UPON THE PLAIN of Megiddo, site of the recent battle. It was greatly expanded, for the Romans had acquired many horses and no small accumulation of loot. Near the Romans, King Jonathan's men were encamped in less orderly fashion. They had the task of guarding the prisoners.

Near the center of the Roman camp stood the praetorium. It had been the royal tent of the late King Manasseh, but Norbanus had appropriated it for his own use. Far more sumptuous than his previous campaigning tent, it had room for the twin princesses who had become a part of his following. For three successive nights since the battle, it had been the scene of a victory banquet.

Manasseh had been defeated rather handily, the Roman discipline and superiority of small unit commanders being crucial in conditions that discouraged close overall command. After long and brave resistance, Manasseh's men had finally cracked, dismayed by the iron fortitude of the Romans. Once their lines lost cohesion and men began to break away and run in panic, the slaughter was fearful. Those not caught by the legionaries or the light-armed pursuers were ridden down and lanced by Jonathan's cavalry.

Manasseh was killed trying to rally his soldiers, and with their king dead, his whole cavalry force had surrendered en masse and pledged themselves to Jonathan, before the Romans could reach them. As these were all wellborn young men, Jonathan had accepted their oath and put them under his protection, unlike the common foot soldiers of Manasseh's army, who died in droves.

At the first night's banquet, the king of the newly united kingdom of Judea and Israel had been ebullient, flushed with success. The general hilarity and good fellowship was only marred when Norbanus had Manasseh's head delivered to him on a platter between courses. This violated some rule of local decorum, and Jonathan had insisted that his defeated rival be buried with the proper rites. He explained that he could incur divine displeasure by neglecting this duty. Norbanus complied cheerfully. It cost him nothing. Manasseh's was not the head he longed to see on a platter before him.

The second night, the king had been cheerful. Now, on the third night of banqueting, he was thoughtful, even apprehensive.

"Titus, my friend," he said, "I am sole king now, and for this I shall always be grateful for your invaluable assistance. However, it is time that I see to the ordering of my country."

"And so you shall," Norbanus assured him. "I think what is in order first is a progress through your newly acquired northern province of Israel. Your people must see you and grow used to the idea that you are now their sole king. Since we must march northward as well, it is fitting that you accompany us, so that anyone of a seditious disposition can see just what they face should they ever have subversive thoughts."

"And this way we can make a proper leave-taking when we pass from your kingdom," said Lentulus Niger.

Jonathan forced a smile. "Excellent." He understood now. For all practical purposes he was a prisoner until the Romans marched away, an event he was beginning to anticipate with some pleasure. What suspicious people, he thought. They were not at all the unsophisticated brutes he had thought them at first.

"Cheer up," Cato said, grinning. "You are a Friend and Ally of Rome now. From now on, you and your descendants can petition the Senate for assistance anytime you are threatened by enemies. And Rome will come to your aid, every time. We are the best allies in the world. We never leave a friend in the lurch."

"I shall prize the friendship of Rome always." He knew that this was true. As long as he stayed faithful to Rome, he would have those incredible legions at his call. He realized something else: He had surrendered control of his own foreign policy. From now on, his policy had to be in accord with Rome's. This was the bargain he had made to become sole king.

Two days later they were traveling north when the Parthians arrived.

The legions, accompanied by their allies and a horde of camp followers, moved briskly along the road that led to the Syrian border. At least, the Romans marched at their usual pace. Many of the legionaries were now mounted, but they restrained their horses to the speed of the footmen. The allies hurried to keep up and the camp followers straggled along for miles.

They did not at first see the approaching Parthians. What they saw instead was an immense column of dust ascending skyward miles before them. Norbanus called a halt and summoned his commanders. Together with Jonathan and his principal officers they studied the alarming prodigy.

"How many horses does it take to raise such a cloud?" Lentulus Niger wanted to know.

"It isn't the number of horses," said Lemuel, commander of Jonathan's cavalry. "It's how they are ridden. There are at least as many horsemen over there as we have here, but they are not ambling along. They are coming at a fast canter. They will be here soon."

"Signal battle formation," Norbanus said. "In close order, then sound 'prepare to receive cavalry.' Be ready to order a testudo. These Parthians are said to favor the bow."

"What about all these horses?" Cato asked.

"We can't use them effectively yet. Take them all to the rear, except for the cavalry. Jonathan, I want your horsemen on our flanks. You stay close by me. They may ask for parley and you are king here."

Jonathan nodded. "They approach boldly. Are they eager for battle, or just anxious to meet up with Manasseh's army before battle is joined?" The Parthians could not know of the disaster Manasseh had met. Jonathan's riders had pursued and killed every horseman who tried to escape the debacle.

"They shall find a situation very different from that which they anticipated," Norbanus said. "I think they will wish to consider their options before committing themselves to action." Behind them the trumpets sounded and the legions went from marching order to battle formation with their usual efficiency.

An hour later the dust cloud was very near, and they began to see the glitter of metal in the dimness. The lead elements appeared: a great double file that wheeled right and left as the Parthians came in sight of the legions. Other formations behind them split likewise, and the dust began to settle as the horses slowed to a trot.

"Watch how far they extend their line," Jonathan cautioned. "If they form a great mass in front of us, they will want to talk. If they keep extending around our flanks, they are going for a surround and we can expect arrows momentarily."

Norbanus nodded, approving of both Jonathan's advice and his calm. He was not nervous, as at the earlier battle. He had confidence in his new allies. For his own part, Norbanus had little apprehension. Romans did not fear arrows, and cavalry could not break disciplined infantry. Still, he was ready for anything. These Parthians were something new, and they might know tricks and stratagems the Romans had never encountered.

Some of the horsemen before them were heavily armored and carried long lances, but most were archers, with light armor or none at all. All rode like men born on horseback. Only the very best Roman riders looked so natural in the saddle. In short order, the Parthians formed a mass perhaps five hundred yards in length, many lines deep. A small group rode forward, halting halfway between the two armies.

"It's talk," Norbanus said. "Are they likely to attempt treachery?"

Jonathan answered. "Everything I've heard of them says the Parthians are most punctilious and honorable in these matters."

"Then we talk," Norbanus said. "Now, how shall we go about this? A king should not ride out to parley unless there is a king leading those men."

"I doubt the king himself came to support Manasseh," said Jonathan, "but the leader will be a close relative. If you ride out without me, they will try to outmatch you in arrogance. Not, I admit, that that is very easy to do. If I go, my condescension will give us an edge in negotiations."

"Royal punctilio is your realm of expertise," Norbanus said. "Let's go."

With Jonathan in the lead, Norbanus riding to his right and half a horse length to his rear, a few senior officers behind them, the party rode out to confer with the strangers. Oozing confidence, Jonathan drew up within easy conversation distance of the Parthian spokesmen.

To the Romans, these riders were truly alien, far more so than the Jews, who had been exposed to Greek influence for many centuries. They wore long trousers and long-sleeved jackets stitched with colorful designs in gold thread. They were long-haired and bearded, their heads covered by tall caps with long lappets hanging before their ears. Each man wore a cased bow and arrows at his belt, and some of them wore a strange sort of armor made of small metal splints tightly laced in rows and lacquered in vivid colors. Most astonishingly, they wore facial cosmetics, with rouged cheeks and lips, and the eyebrows darkened with kohl, drawn to a point above the nose and extended into long wings at the sides. The Romans would have laughed at such a display, but the ferocity of the faces opposite removed any hint of effeminacy.

Jonathan spoke first. "I am Jonathan ben Isaac, king of all the Jews. I demand to know what brings the soldiers of King Phraates within my borders."

One of the Parthians guided his horse a few steps forward. He looked much the same as the others but his light armor was gilded. "I am Surenas, royal cousin of King Phraates. We are here at the invitation of our friend, King Manasseh. Where may we find him?" His Greek was heavily accented but clear. While he spoke, his eyes were fixed upon the Roman party, and the legions standing a bowshot beyond.

"Alas, my brother is no more, and his rebellious province is once more returned to its rightful sovereign. I take very seriously this unwarranted incursion into my kingdom." The Parthians bristled but held their tongues for the moment. Jonathan relaxed his provocative tone a few notches. "However, since you came here under the mistaken belief that you had the invitation of a sovereign, I shall not regard this as an invasion, so long as you refrain from all belligerent acts henceforth."

Surenas nodded. "I can see that things have changed here. My king must hear of the new order of things." He made a gesture of his hand, and the army behind him, until that moment tense and poised for battle, became a great crowd of relaxing horsemen. Many men dismounted and began to curry their mounts, examine hooves and dig rations from there saddlebags.

Norbanus found this an excellent show, one calculated to give an impression of safety. He also noticed that not a single man unstrung his bow. These men could be in the saddle, charging and shooting in moments. Those bows bothered him. They were great, multiple-curved weapons and looked far more powerful than any bows he had ever seen.

"I see that something else has changed," Surenas went on, still eyeing the Romans. "Who are these men whose soldierly bearing is so formidable? I can see how you value them as allies, since they hold the center of your battle line."

"These are the soldiers of my new ally, Rome."

The accented eyebrows rose fractionally. "Rome? I have never heard of this place."

"I assure you, you will be hearing a great deal more of us. I am the Proconsul Titus Norbanus, commander of the legions you see before you, envoy of the Senate of the Republic of Rome." He rode a little forward. "My republic wishes only the friendliest relations with the other nations of the world."

"The late King Manasseh seems to have learned differently," Surenas noted.

"The usurper was in rebellion against our ally, King Jonathan. Alliances are a sacred matter to us Romans. We never leave an ally without support."

"Admirable. I shall report all this to King Phraates." He was perplexed, but clearly knew that he was in no position to take action. Then, to Jonathan: "I must confer with my officers. The day advances and we would like to pitch camp here and make our preparations for departure."

Now Jonathan allowed himself to unbend. The foreigners had asked his permission to camp. Hostilities were off, for the moment. "Of course. As long as you offer no violence to my people, you are welcome to my grass, wood and water."

"With King Jonathan's permission," Norbanus said, "I would like to send some of my officers to your camp this evening. Now would be an excellent time for us to make preparations for an exchange of envoys to open diplomatic relations between our nations."

Surenas nodded curtly. "Very well. I am empowered to arrange such negotiations, pending my lord's approval."

Jonathan smiled. He knew these Romans now. Those officers would spy out every detail of the Parthian camp.

The Parthians rode back to their lines and Norbanus turned to Jonathan. "Will there be an exchange of gifts?"

"It's customary. I will give them cloaks and jewelry, that sort of thing. They will probably give me horses, saddles and so forth. Why?"

"See if you can get a few of their bows."

"Why do you want bows?" Jonathan asked.

"I've never seen their like. I want to send them to the Senate for study. It's our usual practice."

The other Roman officers nodded. They had noticed the bows, as well.

That night Norbanus took his ease beneath the awning of his new praetorium. He knew that some of his officers thought the royal tent far too luxurious for a Roman officer, and he did not care. He had been watching his fellow Romans from the time they had departed the austere northlands, and the signs of change were unmistakable.

Before crossing the Alps, Roman soldiers could make Spartans look decadent. Now, after many months in the South, having seen the rich farmlands of Italy, having experienced the incredible luxury of Carthage, the vast wealth of Egypt, they were changing. Troopers and officers often wore gold now. When they eyed a foreign city, they did not just apprehend danger, they assessed its potential in terms of loot.

They hadn't softened, and he would see to it that they didn't, but they had changed. From now on, they would fight not just for the glory and safety of Rome, but for their own enrichment. A man who would command legions henceforth could not depend upon his men's patriotism and discipline to assure their loyalty. He would have to appeal to their greed.

Titus Norbanus foresaw no problem with that.

He smelled the approaching women before he saw them. Their fragrance was wonderful. In the North, he had never understood the allure of perfume. It was what drew bees to flowers, no more. The closest Romans had come to an appreciation of scent was in the form of incense, imported at great cost to burn before the altars of the gods. Even women never anointed their bodies with fragrance. In the South and East, though, perfume was as important as color and jewels and fine food and wine. These people studied the sensual arts as Romans studied those of war. Norbanus had discovered that war would win you those luxuries, and the women and slaves to go with them. It was a simple equation.

"You see?" said Glaphyra or Roxana, he was not sure which. "All is falling into your hands, just as we foretold. The stars are never wrong."

"Do their seeresses ever make mistakes?" he asked, taking a hand and drawing her before him. It was Roxana, but he knew her twin was nearby.

"Not about the stars," she said, smiling as she slid into his lap. Immediately, he felt another pair of hands on his shoulders, another cloud of perfume.

He ran a hard palm up and down Roxana's spine. She arched, bringing her breasts closer to his face. "It would be best that you never make a mistake about me."

She stiffened slightly. "What do you mean, my lord?"

His hand went to the back of her neck and tightened. He grasped one of her sister's wrists and drew that one before

him. He slid Roxana off his lap and forced both women to
their knees before him. With a slender neck in each hand he
drew both faces close to his own. His face was set in the
mask of ferocity that was as much a part of a highborn Roman as skill with weapons. Their doelike eyes went wide
with terror and an acrid odor drifted from beneath their
clothing, overwhelming the perfume. This was a smell he
truly savored.

"I mean that you two bitches are now part of my inner
circle, closer to me than my soldiers and my officers. You
will be with me in intimate moments. Never think that I am
vulnerable. Never try to manipulate me or take advantage of
me. Never speak a word of what I have said to other people,
or of anything you have seen or heard in my company."

"Never, my lord!" both bleated.

"I have a short way with traitors. The princess of
Carthage taught me ways to make people suffer that we Romans never dreamed of. Give me reason to suspect you, and
your death will not be swift." Through his palms he felt
them shudder, felt the thunder of their hearts. In a hard
world, Carthage was a byword for extreme cruelty. Torture
was an art form in that land, and execution was never swift.

He loosened his grip and let them rise. The point had
been made. "Undress," he said. As their clothing fell away
layer by layer, their fear receded and their confidence returned. This was an area where they still had power. Naked
except for their jewelry, they were as alike as matched
pearls.

"Now," he said, "show me some of your Babylonian de-
pravities."

The twins smiled and did as they were bidden.

CHAPTER ELEVEN

QUEEN TEUTA'S FACE TWISTED, MAKING THE TAT-toos writhe. Her breath wheezed between teeth clenched in a rictus of near-grotesque intensity. Her unbound hair flew wildly, her breasts swung, her hips churned and every part of her body was in abandoned motion. Then she shuddered, stopped as if suddenly stunned and cried out hoarsely as her fingers dug into his shoulders, before she collapsed upon Hamilcar in a sweaty heap.

The shofet, drained by his own, less demonstrative release, stroked her back as his thundering heartbeat slowly returned to normal. He knew that this passionate woman might well be the death of him, but no one else had ever made him feel more kingly. She seemed perfectly unconcerned about possible impregnation, and he gathered that she believed the two of them were above such petty considerations. That, too, gave him satisfaction.

Of course, she had some annoying peculiarities. For instance, she insisted on riding him, holding that as a queen of matchless horsemen, this was her right. He longed to mount her as a lion mounts a lioness, but this she had so far refused to permit. He resolved to enjoy her this way before consenting to a royal marriage. The woman would have to learn to make concessions.

At last she arose from the bed and called for her serving women. As they attended to their mistress with damp cloths and warm towels, he admired her superb body with its covering of tattoos. He had learned that, indeed, not a square inch of her flesh had been spared the needle save her eyelids and lips. A lifetime in Carthage made one a connoisseur of the bizarre, and this was as outré as anything he had ever seen. What made it even more stirring was that the woman was a queen.

Later, dressed and seated on a terrace in the light of a full moon, they spoke of their plans. From the distance they could hear the constant work of hammers and saws. The building of new ships went on day and night now, as Carthage sought to make up the losses from the tremendous fire. The work went swiftly, but harder to replace were the cargoes that had turned to ashes and smoke. The shofet had sent out to his provinces and to neighbor kings for the supplies his armies would need so desperately. He had called in favors going back many years, spending royal capital with abandon. No matter. With the success of this war he would be master of them all.

"Syracuse has fallen," Teuta said in her customarily blunt fashion. "When do we begin?"

"Begin? You mean counterattack?"

"What else could I mean?" she said impatiently. "So far, Rome has had all the advantage in aggression. Let them win any more, and they will think themselves invincible."

"They already think themselves invincible," he pointed out.

"So did the Spartans. Then came the battle of Leuctra. Epimanondas and the Thebans smashed the Spartans and never again did the Spartans or anyone else believe that they were invincible. Once a myth is broken it is never again recovered." She took a generous swallow of unwatered Chian wine.

The woman was a constant amazement. She ate and drank like a Gallic mercenary and could be as crude as a clay pot, but she displayed a fine knowledge of history and was an astute judge of men as individuals and in their masses and nations. But she was trying to rush him and he could not allow her to think she was in charge.

"When the time is right, I shall destroy Rome and its myth together. But one should never go to war without the fullest preparation. Grain and oil, nails, tents, lumber and a thousand other things are as important to a campaign as fighting men, horses and weapons."

"It is possible to be too cautious. Sometimes it is better to hit hard and fast with what you have, than to wait until you have everything you think you must have. Many campaigns have failed because a king has always needed just one more allied contingent, one more wing of cavalry, one more ship. They are usually struck by someone more aggressive and less concerned with preparation. I am not saying that you should go off foolishly unprepared, just that these Romans don't seem to hesitate to attack and you must hit back quickly. Deal them a major setback and they will stop to figure out what went wrong. Then you will have leisure to assemble your fullest force down to the last tent peg in order to fight a war of annihilation."

This was tempting. "I see. You are not, then, suggesting that I send my main army?"

"No."

Hamilcar clapped his hands and a slave stepped forward from the shadows. "Bring my war map and more lamps."

In the light of the new lamps they studied the large parchment. Upon it were drawn all the lands bordering the Middle Sea. Carthaginian possessions were gilt, and fortifications marked, with their garrisons enumerated. Ports and their naval facilities and fleets were likewise depicted. Hamilcar stabbed a finger at a spur jutting from the southern coast of Spain.

"New Carthage. I've assembled an army there, mostly Iberian allies and mercenaries. I had intended to send them into northern Italy as a feint, to distract the Romans and draw away some of their power while I launched the main blow at Sicily and southern Italy."

"Very good," Teuta said. "But why wait until the main invasion? The Romans will know enough to concentrate on the main thrust and leave your Spanish army for a later action. Launch them now. The main Roman force is now engaged in Sicily and they've lost the four legions they left in Egypt. They'll send a minor force northward, thinking they are dealing with a minor incursion. Smash that Roman army and the effect will be demoralizing."

"Just what I was thinking," Hamilcar said, believing indeed that it had been his idea. "They will pass through the southern edge of Gaul, where we have old allies. And they can pick up the garrison of Massilia as they pass."

"Excellent! And why not send some of the mercenaries you have lying around here eating up your substance while doing no fighting? The naval fleet is untouched. Some of your warships can transport the mercenaries and then support the Spanish army on its campaign, and be back in plenty of time to take part in the real invasion."

Hamilcar smiled. "I like this. If they take fearful losses,

what of that? I can always hire more mercenaries and levy more troops from the subject cities. But I won't try to emulate my ancestor's feat and send them across the Alps. It's already been done, so there is no glory in it, and it isn't necessary, anyway. Roman power is weak in the North; they have no allies there to give my army any trouble. They can simply march along the coast, gathering strength as they go and supported by the fleet, which will leave them and return home as soon as they reach Italy." He sighed. "This is so attractive that I'm tempted to take personal command."

"No!" she said. "You must command only the main thrust, not a sideshow like this. But do entrust it to a capable general."

"I'll send Mastanabal with the reinforcements."

"Wonderful!" She poured wine for both of them and they drank to the new project. "Now that you are committed to real action," she went on, "it is time you took some action at home. Your sister is a traitor. If you don't want to kill her, let me."

But this time Hamilcar refused to be pushed. "If only it were so easy."

"YOU MUST KILL HER, MY PRINCESS," ECHAZ SAID.

"The foreign queen? That overdecorated Illyrian?"

"The same. She has become our shofet's closest advisor. More than close—intimate. She has his ear in bed."

"As well as other parts. What of it? He may have every woman in Carthage save me, for all I care. It is his right."

"Highness," he went on patiently, "he is listening to her, though she is a woman and a foreigner."

"So you think she misleads him with bad advice?"

"Worse. She may be giving him good advice."

The princess lay on a huge cushion stuffed with rare, aromatic herbs. She was exhausted after a lengthy, demanding ritual in the Temple of Tanit, and now she rolled over onto her stomach, propping her weary head on her fists. "This could be bad. I knew my brother wanted the woman for a plaything. She certainly is colorful. It did not occur to me that she might be intelligent."

"A mistake many of us make," Echaz said, sighing. "Those Romans seemed comically uncouth, yet they proved to be shrewd."

"She won't be easy to kill," Zarabel said. "She has her own men, who are very savage, and then there are my brother's own guards. It would be easier for me to kill him, but I dare not do that."

Zarabel hated and feared her brother, but she had little to gain by his death. A woman could not inherit the throne and she had no son to elevate and then manipulate. If Hamilcar died, the head of one of the great families would assume the crown and, most probably, put her away and give the high priesthood to a female relative. She wanted Hamilcar weak, not dead.

"We will find a way," Echaz assured her.

MASTANABAL WAS A TALL, LEAN MAN WITH THE CLASsic Carthaginian looks: swarthy complexion, dark brows beetling above a beaklike nose, curly black hair and beard. His deep-lined, weathered face showed every day of his twenty years of hard campaigning. Even when Carthage was not at war, there had always been bandits and pirates to suppress and insurrections to put down.

Ten days before he had arrived by ship and taken over command of the army gathered for the incursion into northern Italy. "The Divine Shofet Hamilcar, descendant of Hannibal the Great, has ordered that the invasion of Italy is to commence forthwith," he had announced. "I want every man I am to command assembled for my inspection immediately. We shall perform the sacrifices and take the omens and we shall march upon the first day pleasing to the gods of Carthage."

He did not tell them that this would not be a part of the main attack on Rome, which would not come for a few months, at least. There was no need for them to know such things. Their task was to obey the shofet's commands. Nor was he dismayed by the task before him. He had seen the Romans in action in Egypt, and he had been impressed. But for all their skill and professionalism, they were but men, and men could be beaten and killed.

He knew further that the four legions of the Egyptian campaign were lost somewhere in the East, and the Romans were massively committed to the conquest of Sicily and must even now be massing that army for an attack on Africa, on Carthage itself. He had an excellent chance of meeting an inferior force of green troops in northern Italy, and smashing them. The Romans were raising legions so fast that surely they could not all be trained and equipped to the highest standards.

Now he rode along the massed ranks of his army, and as he passed each unit, the men raised their arms and cheered. The hand of Carthage lay lightly upon Spain, for it was an invaluable resource far beyond its value as a source of horses, cattle and metal ore. For centuries, Spain had provided Carthage with mercenaries. Its many tribes produced a profusion of warriors, their skills honed by constant intertribal warfare. Many of them had no trade save that of war. Most were a mixture of Celt and native Iberian, now merged.

They were a dark people for the most part, their black hair dressed in long plaits hanging from the temples, the hair at back flowing free or gathered into a net.

Most wore white tunics with colorful borders, but the Callaici, Astures, Cantabri and Vascones wore black. From the northeast and the central plateau came the Arevaci, the Pelendones, the Berones, the Caretani and others. From the west came Lusitani and Turdetani. From the foot of the Pyrenees came the Ilergetes and Auretani. Some were horsemen, wonderfully skilled with lance and javelin.

Most were light infantry. Many carried a small, round buckler called a *caetra,* though some retained the long, oval shield of their Celtic ancestors. Their favored weapon was the *falcata:* a peculiar sword with a downcurving blade, sharpened along its inner edge, its spine thick to add weight to the blow. It was a slashing weapon and could sever a man's leg with ease. Many also carried the short, straight sword the Romans called the *gladius hispaniensis,* which they had adopted for their own legions. Each Spanish swordsman carried a number of javelins, and these slender weapons were often forged entirely of steel. Some wore helmets but few bothered with armor.

From the Greek colonies of the coast came hoplites: men with large, old-fashioned round shields; helmets, cuirasses and greaves of polished bronze; armed with long spears and short swords. They would be his heavy infantry and hold the center of the battle line. Greece had long fallen from its military preeminence, but Greek soldiers fought all over the lands of the Middle Sea. Unlike the brave but disorganized tribal peoples, the Greeks understood discipline and the importance of maintaining formation.

The rest were a rabble of Libyans, Gauls, islanders and others; slingers from the Belearics, Cretan archers, even a few hundred black spearmen, barbarously painted, their hair plastered with mud and bearing shields of zebra hide. Sadly, Hamilcar had allowed him no elephants.

At the head of the formation Hasdrubal's command staff awaited him: Carthaginian nobles, Greek professionals and some Spanish chieftains. They watched him expectantly, their eyes bright, eager for the war to come.

"Let's go to Italy," said Mastanabal.

Off they set, an army massive by the standards of most kings, but a trifling force by Carthaginian standards. And as it progressed, it grew larger. Their trek along the coast, shadowed by the Carthaginian fleet, took them through territory occupied by Carthaginian tributaries, and from each they levied troops. From Spain they passed into southern Gaul, and here many Gallic warriors, eager for action and loot, joined them. At Massilia, the principal port, they collected more Greek troops and the Carthaginian garrison. A few days march past Massilia they entered Cisalpine Gaul, the Gallic territory of northern Italy. They were now in the area called Liguria, once owned by Rome. They had as yet seen no trace of Roman occupation. This was as Mastanabal had anticipated. The Romans were not worried about attack from the north, despite their disastrous experience with Hannibal. He would teach them their error.

Near Genua the coast turned southward and they entered the peninsula of Italy proper. At each town Mastanabal's officers questioned locals. Yes, the Romans had come through, surveying and taking a census, but they had seen no Romans for months. There was said to be a garrison at Pisae, on the Arnus River.

The coastal road was wretched, little more than a goat track, so progress was not swift. His light cavalry rode ahead of the army, intercepting and killing any mounted man they saw, to prevent word of the advancing army from preceding it. Thus they arrived unannounced upon the plain east of the delta of the Arnus, near the minor town of Pisae, where a Roman army lay encamped.

DECIMUS AEMILIUS, PROPRAETOR FOR NORTHWEST-ern Italy, awoke to a pleasant morning in one of the most pleasant parts of the peninsula. The land was wonderfully fertile and occupied by diligent peasants. He had decided that, when the present war concluded, he would petition the Senate for lands here. He belonged to a minor branch of the great Aemilian gens, and the ancestral Aemilian lands to the south had already been reclaimed by the more prestigious members of the family. No matter, he thought. From what he had seen, he liked this district better than the central and southern peninsula.

He was not flawlessly happy. It grated that he had not been given a more important army and a part in the Sicilian campaign. *Not much chance of that*, he thought. *Not with the great consular families fighting tooth and nail for every commission*. Still, he knew he had little cause to complain. There would be campaigning for the rest of his lifetime, and glittering opportunities would fall his way. Even as he had the thought, something fell his way.

He became aware of a growing clamor outside his praetorium and was about to investigate when his legate, Servius Aelius Buteo, burst in. "There's a Carthaginian army on the field to the north!"

"What! How did they get here?"

"At a guess I'd say they walked," Buteo told him. "And they didn't come alone. A scout just rode in and reported a fleet off Pisae."

Aemilius shouted for his orderly and scrambled into his field armor. With his helmet beneath his arm, he strode from the tent, Buteo walking beside him. His orderly, his trumpeter and his secretary followed behind.

"Hamilcar couldn't counterattack so fast. And why here?" Aemilius said.

"Maybe the report of the fire at Carthage was exaggerated," Buteo said. "Maybe he's invading anyway, on two fronts."

"Not that it matters," Aemilius said. "If they're out there, we have to stop them. If they get through us, they'll go all the way to Rome, and except for what we have here, all our legions are down in the South. Rome is unprotected."

They came to the camp wall and ascended the tower flanking the gate called the *porta praetoria*. From its top platform they surveyed the spectacle to the north, aghast. A huge host stood there, arranged in three great blocks, with flanking cavalry. They were ominously silent. Roman soldiers along the wall were jabbering at one another, some of them forgetting their Latin and speaking their native Celtic and German dialects.

"Professionals or at least well-drilled militia in the center," Aemilius said, his voiced schooled to calm despite the sick feeling in his stomach. "Those great mobs on the flanks are barbarians. How many do you make them?"

Buteo spat over the front rail. "Thirty thousand if there's a buggering one of them. And they've ten times our strength in cavalry."

And what do I have? Aemilius thought. *Two legions plus auxiliaries, and not full strength at that, not even fifteen thousand total strength.* The odds would not have dismayed him had the legions been veteran, but they were newly raised troops just down from Noricum, only their senior centurions men of long experience. They had been drilled long and hard, but even the best training was not combat. Roman commanders considered soldiers fully reliable only after they had ten campaigns behind them.

"Well," Aemilius said. "Here's where we find out if we're really as good as we say we are." He turned to his trumpeter. "Sound battle formation." As the call rang out, he turned to his secretary, who stood by with a wooden tablet open in one hand, a pointed bronze stylus in the other, ready to inscribe his general's message on the wax that lined the inner surface of the tablet.

"Date and hour," Aemilius said. "To the noble Senate. Greeting from Decimus Aemilius, propraetor for northwestern Italy. This hour a Carthaginian army of some thirty thousand men appeared two miles north of the Arnus River near the town of Pisae, accompanied by a fleet of unknown strength. I go now to engage the land force. Long live Rome."

Amid a rustling of armor and a shuffling of hobnailed caligae, the legionaries exited the fortified camp and formed up their cohorts between the camp and the approaching enemy. They formed into their cohorts, with the two legions of heavy infantry in the center, the auxilia on the flanks and the tiny cavalry force, too small to be divided, concentrated on the left flank. The forming up was done with commendable swiftness and efficiency. Drill was a Roman specialty.

"It's not good," Buteo said, "fighting this near the camp, with our backs to a river."

Aemilius knew what he meant. Outnumbered as they were, should the Romans be hard-pressed, with nowhere else to flee except the river, the fortified camp would be a temptation. Men whose nerve failed under the strain of battle would break formation and run for the camp. It could quickly turn into a rout. Had there been time, Aemilius would have demolished the camp before offering battle. That was standard procedure. Romans were realists about warfare, and recognized that to ensure steadfastness in battle, it was best to remove all possibility of safety in flight.

"Speaking of which," Aemilius said, "we'd best get out there ourselves. Can't have the men thinking we're lurking back here in safety."

Buteo snorted. "Safety!"

They went below and mounted their horses. Just behind the legions, in the center, carpenters were assembling the command tower. It was not high, just a platform about twelve feet above the ground, from which the commander could survey his army and the battlefield. Aemilius ordered all his mounted messengers to assemble by the tower, for he intended to send continuous reports to the Senate as the battle progressed.

With his staff officers, he rode through the gaps between the cohorts and emerged before the center of the battle line. A hundred paces before the center of the first rank, they drew up and awaited the Carthaginian negotiators. Every battle began with a parley: demands, refusals, conditions, agreements and so forth. It was expected. In due time, a party of horsemen rode out from the Carthaginian lines. Their harness was ornate, their arms shining or colorfully painted. Their standard, the triangle-and-crescent of Tanit, was draped with white ribbons in token of truce. In the forefront was a hard-faced Greek. Aemilius read him for a Spartan mercenary. That state had long since fallen from any claim to power, but it still produced professional soldiers who were in demand wherever there was fighting.

"Romans!" the Greek said without preamble. "My general, Mastanabal, servant of the Shofet Hamilcar, bids you surrender your arms and your persons to him. Lay down your arms, pass beneath his yoke and you will live. The alternative is extermination."

The Roman party laughed, though without much amusement. The Carthaginian party stared. There was something extremely unsettling about that Roman laugh.

"Well, that's blunt enough," Aemilius said when he had breath. "Why did your general not come to deliver his ultimatum? Why is he lurking behind his army?"

"A nobleman of Carthage does not treat with foreign peasants!" the Greek said scornfully.

"Is that so?" Aemilius said. "Tell your general that before this day is over, this peasant will flay his princely hide from his body and make saddlebags from it. I need a new set."

The Greek seemed not to understand. "That is all you have to say? No counterterms? No offers?"

"If your general wishes to surrender to us, he may," Aemilius said. "Same terms: Lay down your arms and pass beneath our yoke. Or if he wishes to go back to Spain, where I presume this expedition originated, he may. We shall not molest him. But tell him that he has come as close to Rome as he is going to get."

"You are mad!" the Greek said. "None of you will live to see the sun go down."

"Are we keeping you here, hireling?" Aemilius asked. "Don't you have pressing business elsewhere?"

"Your blood is on your own heads!" the Greek said. He wheeled his horse and pelted back to the Carthaginian lines, followed by the rest of his party.

"Fine, arrogant words," Buteo commented. "Think we can live up to them?"

Aemilius shrugged. "In a situation like this, you might as well speak arrogantly. It doesn't cost anything and may give them something to think about. While I speak to the men, the rest of you join your units or go to the command tower. Send your horses to the rear. From here on, only the cavalry and the messengers are to be mounted."

As customary as the parley was the harangue. Every army expected to be given a rousing, inspirational speech by its general. But how to inspire on an occasion like this, when the odds were worse than two to one and most of the soldiers had never seen battle before? Aemilius prayed to Mars and the Muses to gild his tongue and inspire him to say the right thing. He reined up before his men and used the Forum speaker's voice that could be heard from one end of the line to the other.

"Soldiers of Rome! Until today, we have been stationed here, complaining that the other legions were winning all the glory and wealth in Sicily, and in the East. But now, today, it falls to you to win glory far beyond the lot of any other legions. Today, you must save Rome of the Seven Hills! Except for us, Rome lies defenseless, all her temples and tombs naked to the desecration of the barbarians! Over there," he swept an arm around, pointing to the host opposite, "are those who would destroy Rome. But they are barbarians, and barbarians cannot outfight Roman soldiers. Crush them, and the names of your legions will live forever, and you will have undying glory for yourselves and for your descendants. As long as Romans speak of the glories of their ancestors, they will speak of the men who stopped the barbarians here, on the River Arnus!"

The men raised a deafening shout, beating the insides of their shields with spear butts. Aemilius rode back to his command tower, dismounted and slapped his horse on the rump before climbing to his post.

"No time for the sacrifices," he commented.

"Pretty soon," Buteo said, "there'll be all the blood spilled that any god could want."

"Still," Aemilius said, "it's always best to make the sacrifices and take the omens. Oh, well, I suppose Jupiter will understand."

"Is there any reason to wait?" Buteo asked.

"None at all. Sound the advance."

The *cornus* brayed and the standard-bearers, draped with wolfskins, stepped out toward the enemy. There would be no maneuver, no subtle play of tactical advantage and deception. There was no time for planning and preparation. This would be a simple clash of two armies in an open field, a test of strength and courage. Aemilius knew all too well that in such a fight, numbers could be decisive. It was too late to worry about it.

As the trumpets conveyed their general's orders, the cohorts transformed from a series of blocks in checkered formation to a solid battle line, with four cohorts of each legion in reserve, keeping open order so that they were free to maneuver to defend a flank or strengthen a weak spot in the line should there be danger of a breakthrough.

"I think we should extend the line," Buteo said.

"I'll send the reserves to the flanks if it looks like they're going to outflank us," Aemilius said.

The Carthaginian army advanced at a slow, deliberate pace. Officers advanced along the whole front, but walking backward, facing their own men. They barked orders to speed up or slow down, close right or left, as they saw disorder in their lines. The watching Romans could only approve. This was the sort of professionalism they understood.

"This is going to be different from fighting a pack of howling Germans, isn't it?" Aemilius commented. Buteo didn't bother to answer. On the field across from them, a large number of lightly armed men ran out past the flanks and arranged themselves in double lines.

"Here come the arrows," Aemilius said. The trumpets sounded, and all along the Roman lines shields were lifted. Except for the front line, each man raised his shield and held it over the head of the man in front of him. In seconds, the whole army looked as if it had grown a tile roof. The Carthaginian flankers drew their bows and soon arrows came down like rain on the Roman force. Very few got through, but here and there a shaft slipped beneath an unsteadily held shield and the Romans took the first casualties of the battle.

"First blood to the enemy," Buteo said.

Aemilius's look was bleak, but he was a Roman. "It's last blood that counts."

When the Carthaginian front line was within fifty paces of the legions, the arrow storm let up. Aemilius spoke to his trumpeter, and the signal to advance and close with the enemy brayed out, to be echoed by the trumpeters who accompanied the individual standards. As one man, the first two lines stepped out toward the Carthaginian center.

Soon the Carthaginian light troops began to pelt the Romans with light javelins. Since the light infantry was concentrated on the flanks, the center of the Roman lines took no casualties. When the opposing lines were fifty feet apart, a trumpet barked and the Roman advance stopped abruptly. As if controlled by a single nervous system, the right arms of the Romans rocked back, poised a moment, then shot forward. The heavy, murderous javelin called the pilum was a mainstay of the Roman arsenal. The front line hurled theirs directly at the men a few paces before them. The second line launched theirs over the heads of the men in front. These fell into the ranks of the enemy behind the battle line.

Instantly, hundreds of men went down, their shields and bodies pierced by the deadliest close-quarters missile ever invented. Hundreds more found their shields rendered useless by the massive spears impaling them. The small, barbed heads could not be easily withdrawn, nor the long, iron necks and thick, wooden shafts easily cut through.

With a move as precise as the spear hurling, the Romans drew their short, razor-edged swords. They advanced at the double, striking the Carthaginian center along its length. Behind the protection of their large, body-covering shields, they brushed the enemy's long spears aside or lifted them overhead. Where a pilum protruded from an enemy shield, it was kicked aside or trodden down, exposing the man behind the shield for execution. These front-rankers wore excellent armor, so the short swords lanced into throats, into the lower abdomen below the rim of the breastplate, directly into the face between the cheekplates of the helmet. While it was intended primarily for thrusting, the broad, heavy blade of the *gladius* also cut extremely well, and wielded in short, vicious chops it exposed the user no more than did a swift thrust. An exposed arm could be severed completely, and an incautiously advanced thigh could be laid open to the bone on its inner side, severing the great artery and dumping out all of a man's blood in a few seconds.

In this stage of the battle the Romans took very few casualties, though the footing grew treacherous with bodies, blood and fallen weapons. This was the sort of fighting at which Romans excelled above all others. The legion thus employed was a vast killing machine. After a few minutes, before the men could tire too much, Aemilius gave another order and the trumpets roared out. The fighting men disengaged and stepped back as the next two ranks of the legions marched forward. The men who had been fighting fell back through gaps between the advancing soldiers. The enemy, surprised at this maneuver, were still reeling when the second volley of heavy javelins fell among them and the killing recommenced.

The Romans who had been fighting went to the rear to get new pila and have their wounds dressed. Long ago, the Romans had realized that only a small part of the army could be fighting at any one time, so they devised this system to keep fresh men at the front at all times. In the army opposite, the rear ranks were in a close-packed mass, shouting, waving their arms in excitement and getting tired without contributing at all to the fighting strength.

In the center, this battle belonged to the Romans. The flanks were another matter. The great masses of Mastanabal's light-armed troops were pressing against the Roman flanks and their cavalry rushed in, hurling light javelins with great accuracy, riding back before the Romans could come to grips with them. The Iberians, insanely brave and aggressive, charged against the iron-clad Romans with great ferocity. In this sort of fighting, the *falcata* was as effective as the *gladius*. The down-curved, wide-bladed sword was not versatile; it was a pure slasher, but swung down by the arm of a strong man, it could shear through helmet and armor, and only quick shield work could save the target. If the unarmored Spaniard missed his blow, he was dead, dispatched by the lightning thrust of the *gladius*.

The Roman right flank suffered especially, for these attacks fell upon their unshielded sides. If they were to defend themselves, they had to face right, disordering the Roman lines. Seeing this, Aemilius sent his reserve cohorts to reinforce the flanks. This left him with nothing to commit in case of an emergency or an opportunity, but he had no choice, not when he was this badly outnumbered.

The sun rose higher, and the battle wore on. The Carthaginian cavalry made several attempts to encircle the Romans, but the rear ranks faced about and drove them off with volleys of pila, killing some riders and many horses. Mastanabal called his horsemen back. They would be better employed in pursuing the enemy when they broke ranks and fled, speared in their backs as they ran. In most battles, the great bulk of the killing took place in the rout, when helpless, terrified men were slaughtered by the thousands.

One of the Greek professionals who sat his horse next to the Carthaginian general remarked, "These Romans are taking their time about panicking."

"Well, we've heard they were tough," said a man with a Spartan accent.

"They cannot last much longer," the Carthaginian commander said. "They are better than I anticipated; they fight well and hold their ranks. But these men are not the equal of the legions I saw fighting in Egypt. Their commander is not inspired, like Titus Norbanus." In truth, Mastanabal had no doubt that he would be victorious, but at what cost? His army was taking fearful casualties. He cared nothing for the men, who were just foreigners and many of them savages, but every man who fell would mean a weaker army to proceed against Rome.

In another campaign, he would levy troops from the subject cities he passed, but Carthage had demilitarized Italy after Hannibal's conquest. There were no soldiers on the whole peninsula, except for the Romans. If he lost too many, he would have to fall back into Gaul to rebuild his strength. When he returned, he knew he would find far more than two green legions in his way. He had to bring this battle to a successful conclusion, and soon.

His center was being chewed away by the Roman swords

and spears, but he resisted the temptation to reinforce it. The center would not collapse any time soon. Both his long schooling and his many years of experience in war told Mastanabal not to waste his resources in attacking the enemy's greatest strength. Concentrate instead on his weakest spots.

"I want all the archers and slingers on the Roman right flank," he ordered. "I want them to pour missiles into that flank until they run out of ammunition."

His officers rode off to do his bidding. Soon the lightly armed troops were on that flank, standing just beyond range of the Roman javelins. The arrows and sling-bullets began to rain into the legion's flank, and this time the disorder in their lines did not allow an effective shield roof to form. Arrows found their marks and the sling-bullets—egg-shaped slugs of lead the size of a boy's fist—wrought terrible damage, smashing exposed faces and necks, sometimes denting a helmet deeply enough to crack the skull beneath. Romans began to fall by the score, then by the hundred.

Aemilius turned to his secretary. "To the noble Senate of Rome. We will need more and better and cavalry. Also, we must find great numbers of missile troops. The enemy is very strong in these arms, and they are very annoying. Our men cannot close with them without breaking ranks, and their effects wear us down." This was the fifth such message he had dictated since the outset of the battle. "Append my seal and send it off."

The messenger galloped off toward the bridge across the Avernus. Aemilius had one tablet and one messenger left. This he would hold until the last minute, to announce either his victory or his defeat. He heard renewed shouting and looked to see its source. The missile troops, emboldened by their success, were creeping forward, raising their trajectories to rain arrows and bullets almost into the center of the

Roman lines. A few were transfixed by javelins, but the Romans were running out of spears to throw.

"Buteo," he said, "before our center gets totally disordered, we have to do something about those archers and slingers. I want the rear lines to about-face as they did when the cavalry tried to encircle us. Then I want them to step out, pivoting on their left flank like a big door swinging shut. If they carry it out briskly, they can encircle and kill all those half-naked foreigners."

"That's a parade-ground maneuver," Buteo said, sounding like his throat was very dry. "Do you think these boys are up to it?"

"If you have any better ideas, I'll listen."

Buteo turned to the trumpeter and spoke very urgently, at length. The man nodded and began to sound a very complex series of calls, which were picked up and echoed throughout the now badly depleted Roman army. The rear ranks turned about and began the maneuver. The pivot man at what was now their left flank marched in place while those nearer the center walked and those on the right flank trotted, to keep the wheeling line straight.

From his command prominence, Mastanabal watched with wonder, understanding instantly what his opposite intended. It was a marvel to behold, but it further weakened the Roman forces and he saw exactly how to take advantage of it.

"They are out of those damned spears," he said to his officers. "I want the entire cavalry to go around their left flank and charge into the back of that pivoting line, then turn inward against the Roman rear. Now!"

Moments later the horsemen thundered toward the Romans as if they were attacking the center, then they wheeled right and swept around the Roman flank. Moments later they crashed into the line advancing against the missile troops, spearing them from behind, annihilating them before turning against the Roman rear. As before, the rear ranks faced about, but this time they had no pila to hurl, only short swords with which to face mounted men, and they were tired, slow to get their shields up as the lancers thrust and the Libyans threw their own short javelins with deadly accuracy. The Romans did not die easily, but they died anyway.

Aemilius turned to his secretary for the last time. "To the noble Senate. The battle of the River Arnus is lost. I die here on the field with my legions. Long live Rome." He watched as the messenger pelted away, saw him almost overtaken by enemy horsemen; then he was clear and riding for the bridge.

Then he and Buteo watched, helpless, as his proud legions broke up into isolated groups, fighting shield-to-shield, and then there were just pairs of men back-to-back, all of them struggling until they fell.

"Not one of them fled for the camp or the bridge," Aemilius said.

"They're Romans," Buteo said, "even if some of their fathers came from Germania. Will you fall on your sword?"

"No, I'll make some of those bastards fall on mine. Will you join me?"

"Might as well," Buteo said. The little group of men on the platform drew their swords and descended to the bloody field below. Only the secretary stayed. He was a slave and noncombatant.

Within an hour the field was a vast expanse of fallen men and horses, shattered shields, weapons and standards. Of the fallen, many were still alive but maimed. Soldiers went among the wounded Romans, killing them with swift stabs of sword or spear. Already, ravens hopped among the dead, pecking at eyes and spilled viscera.

"So they aren't unbeatable," said the Spartan officer.

"No, they are not," Mastanabal concurred. But his satisfaction was severely tempered. The dead of his own army far outnumbered the Roman dead. His clerks had brought him a preliminary casualty list: more than twenty thousand dead and many others severely wounded. The Romans had sold their lives dearly. And this had not been a first-rate Roman army. What would it be like to face the cream of the legions?

A man rode up holding in his hand something that dripped blood. He halted before his general and raised his trophy. It was a human head. "This is the Roman commander, general. A captive slave identified him."

Mastanabal looked into the rolled-back eyes of his late adversary. This had been a second-rate commander of inexperienced soldiers and he had almost ruined a splendid Carthaginian army almost twice the size of his own. Mastanabal reached out, bloodied his fingers on the severed neck and drew three red lines across his forehead to protect himself from the vengeful spirits of the dead.

"Do we march on Rome, General?" asked the Spartan.

Mastanabal surveyed the field once more. "With this cut-up remnant?" he snarled. "No! We return to Gaul. We have to rebuild our strength before we engage these people again." He wondered how he was going to explain this to the shofet.

CHAPTER TWELVE

FOR ONCE, THE SENATE OF ROME WAS NOT BOIS-
terous. The senators stood in their ranks downcast and
grim. All day the messengers had been coming in from the
battlefield to the north. The first report had sounded ominous, and subsequent reports had done nothing to lighten
the sense of foreboding. Now the princeps stood with
Aemilius's final report in his hand, and it required an effort
to keep that hand from trembling.

"There you have it," Gabinius said. "Two legions destroyed, and Rome now open to attack from the north." He
closed the tablet, lowered his head, then looked up at his
peers. "We have been too confident. We have had everything
our own way for too long. We have been too contemptuous
of our enemy. I point no fingers, for I have been as foolish as
anyone here. We should have seen it coming. This
Carthaginian used Hannibal's old route, only he bypassed
the Alps."

An elderly senator stepped forward. He was an old family

conservative, and notoriously reactionary. "They were inferior legions. They were made up of half-Gauls and Germans! We should never have entrusted our safety to such men!" This raised shouts of agreement and of protest.

The senior consul stood. "Let's have none of that! Those men were Roman citizens. They were guilty of no worse than being green troops. This is an inevitable consequence of raising so many new legions, so quickly. We sent them north precisely because it seemed like a quiet theater of the war, a place where they could be trained and blooded without demanding their utmost. We thought there might be a weak feint from the north, accompanying the thrust of the main Carthaginian army and navy from the south. As the princeps has pointed out, we were wrong. The blame lies with this body assembled here, not with men who stood between Rome and her enemies, and died on their feet, sword in hand, to repel the barbarian! I will hear no word spoken against them!" This raised a fierce roar of agreement.

"Senators!" shouted Gabinius, whose duty as princeps it was to set the order of debate. "We must now decide upon a course of action, and do it quickly. Above all, we must know the Carthaginian's intentions. Is he still in sufficient strength to march upon Rome? We have sent scouts north to report upon the Carthaginian's movement, but we dare not wait for them to return. I suggest that we summon some of the legions garrisoned in Campania. If it should prove that this Mastanabal and his hirelings have been so bloodied that they dare not advance, our legions can always be sent back, or else posted to the north against a renewed offensive. Let's have a show of hands." His suggestion was carried unanimously.

"Secondly," he continued, "I urge that we take every measure to get the younger Titus Norbanus and his four legions back to Italy."

Norbanus the elder stood from his curule seat. "My son is already striving to return. Have you not read his reports?"

"I have," Gabinius said, dryly. "He's not striving hard enough. He's getting involved with Eastern politics and building his own foreign policy over there."

"Building his own power base, you mean!" shouted the same old senator.

"Quiet, if you please," said Gabinius. "I submit that young Norbanus now commands our four most hardened, most experienced legions, and that they are legions that we require here in Italy. Time enough later for adventures in the East. First, we must make Italy and Sicily absolutely secure, and that is going to take every man we have. We must smash Carthage utterly! Only then will we be free to bring the rest of the world beneath the Roman yoke."

"And how are we to go about this?" asked the Consul Scipio. "Young Norbanus is as far away as ever, and we can only send messages, which he is inclined to ignore."

"Perhaps," Gabinius said, "this might be a model training exercise for that new navy we've built. A voyage around southern Greece and across to the coast of Asia might just be the thing to accustom our new sailors to voyaging. If Norbanus finds transport home awaiting him at some convenient port, he will have no excuse to avoid returning."

The possibilities were thrashed out over the rest of the afternoon. Outside, word of the defeat had spread through the city and the mood was bleak. People began to speculate that the gods had withdrawn their favor. Gabinius was concerned that panic might set in, should word come that the victors of the Arnus were marching upon undefended Rome. He summoned a meeting of all the augurs still in Rome. Since the members of the college were all senators, all were present in the curia and he took them into a side room.

"I want no unfavorable omens spread about," he told them tersely. "If you see any, keep them to yourselves. People here are on edge as it is. Until our legions arrive from the south, or else we know that the Carthaginians are not on the march toward us, let's see nothing but approval from the gods." The rest nodded. Augurs were not priests, but elected officials co-opted into the college of augurs. They read the omens according to an ancient list and did not believe themselves to be divinely inspired.

"How could this have happened without a single unfavorable omen?" asked one of them. "Since leaving Noricum, we have had an unbroken series of favorable omens. What has happened?"

A thought struck the princeps. "The gods gave us no sign because this is not a serious defeat. Jupiter and Juno would have given us warning had this been a true disaster, threatening the city. The gods do not consider the deaths of a few thousand mortals to be of great account. Only had it signaled the fall of a great nation would they have considered it worthy of their notice."

"That is very true," said the head of the college, one of the elders of the great clan of Brutus. "I'll wager our scouts return with word of the Carthaginians in full retreat, or if they come here and invest the city, our legions will come up from the south and crush them against the walls like bugs."

Gabinius nodded eagerly. "That's the way to talk! Let the citizens hear that and all will be well. They're Romans, after all. It's just that, as Romans, they have never known news of a defeat in generations."

That evening, the princeps and consuls convoked a special meeting for further military planning. As always, Gabinius spoke first.

"Conscript fathers," he began, "I need hardly point out that the reconquest of our old empire has proven an even more formidable task than we had anticipated. It is clear that our legions will not be sufficient to the task unaided. At the moment, we have no allies. We have drained the manpower pool of Noricum to build all these new legions. We need many cohorts of auxilia and where are we to find the men?" He paused for rhetorical effect, then went on. "Here in Italy, that is where!"

The Consul Scipio stood. "Princeps, Italy lost its manhood when our ancestors went north in the Exile! Those who stayed bent their necks to the Carthaginian yoke. They are little more than slaves! Early on it was proposed that they earn their way back into our good graces and limited citizenship by serving as rowers in our new navy. But to give them arms and place them in the battle line with our citizen legions? That is to give them too much honor." Applause greeted this.

"Honor can be earned," Gabinius answered, "and let us not fool ourselves. We have no alternative. We know from the battle of the Arnus that we were defeated not through the weakness of our legions, green though they were, but for lack of sufficient auxilia to support their flanks. We need light infantry, archers, slingers and, above all, cavalry!" He held their attention with his intensity and went on.

"North of the River Arnus is what used to be Cisalpine Gaul. The people there were our allies in the old days. By all accounts, they suffered little from Carthage, and most of them never even saw a Carthaginian. I'll wager they have not lost all of their warrior heritage. Let's start there. Then we can scour old Latium and central Italy, paying special attention to the mountainous regions; the places where living is rough and the Carthaginians never went. Let's call in those bandits who infest this peninsula. Yes, I know what you'll all say: 'What! Bandits in Roman service?' And to that I say: 'Yes!' These are men of spirit; men who refused to till the soil for absentee landlords, who found more honor in taking arms and raiding. Were Romulus, Remus and their followers any different? Offer them amnesty with no demand that they lay down their arms. Offer them limited citizenship in exchange for service in our auxilia. I promise you we will quickly raise a sizable force of first-rate skirmishers and foragers!"

There were howls of protest but Gabinius smiled grimly. He knew he could bring them around. There was no question about it, because he and they knew that there was no choice. They were registering their protests for the sake of form. They knew now that Roman legions could lose a battle. He would get his way.

For a few days the city remained tense, until the scouts came pounding back down the Via Clodia with word that the Carthaginian force had, indeed, returned from whence it came. There was no jubilation, but a general sense of relief settled over the city. Sacrifices and omen taking resumed, and further scouts were dispatched to shadow Mastanabal's army and report upon its every movement.

When two legions arrived from Campania, they were sent north to the Arnus, there to undertake construction of extensive fortifications. It was defensive warfare, the sort Romans hated the most, but unavoidable since the main Roman forces had to be concentrated in the South. The legions in the North were also to raise, arm and train as many auxilia as they possibly could.

One question plagued the consuls, the princeps and the Senate: Where were Titus Norbanus and those four veteran legions?

THE LEGIONS LANDED ON THE LITTLE PIRATE COVE like a thunderbolt from heaven. By their thousands, the armored men poured over the narrow pass in the inland hills during the hours before dawn, moving with their now-accustomed quiet. By the time the village was awake, the soldiers were upon it, killing wherever they met resistance, taking prisoners where there was none. The pirates were sturdy men and tough fighters, but they had neither the numbers, the equipment nor the discipline of their pitiless conquerors. A few minutes of vicious fighting saw the utter destruction of the pirates; then came the sack of the town. The prisoners, mostly women and children, were herded into a compound and kept under guard.

Titus Norbanus rode in and inspected his latest acquisition. First, he assured himself that not a single pirate had escaped by sea. It would not do to let anyone spread the word of his coming to the many other pirate towns along the coast. Satisfied, he rode into the little town square and dismounted. His men had already secured the town's finest house for his use, and he seated himself upon its spacious, covered porch, sipping wine while his men piled the loot before him.

Norbanus was outrageously pleased with this stage of his march. It was proving incredibly profitable. The march north through Syria had been tense but uneventful. They had been shadowed the whole way by native soldiers, not a real threat but in enough strength to discourage any attempts upon the cities of the coast. Norbanus had sent word to the Seleucid governor that he meant no hostility, that he and his soldiers just wanted to get home. The governor had made no offer of help, but neither did he make any aggressive move. They passed within sight of the walls of splendid Antioch, and Norbanus was greatly tempted to sack the place, but that might have been more than the Senate could stomach, so he merely used its crossing of the River Orontes, paying the ferry companies meticulously and paying also for all the necessities they needed.

Then they turned westward, along the south-facing coast of Cilicia, and the Syrian troops had halted at the border. This rugged country was claimed by the Seleucids, but they had never occupied the place in any meaningful fashion. The only major city was Tarsus, which regarded itself as independent and was mainly Greek rather than native. Norbanus was diplomatic with the fathers of Tarsus and his army availed itself of the excellent water there.

Most of Cilicia was too mountainous and primitive for any kind of rule save the tribal sort. Its towns were virtually independent, and on the coast the only trade practiced was piracy. This was what made the Cilician stage of the march so lucrative.

Nearly every day's march brought them to a range of hills, and on the other side of those hills there was nearly always a little cove, with its own village and its own pirate fleet. There were never more than a few hundred to a few thousand men in each town. Except for the practice of piracy, these would have been nothing but squalid fishing villages. With it, they were fine little towns, their warehouses stuffed with the loot of the sea, taken in raids on coastal towns and from captured ships, and their treasuries filled with gold and silver, most of it ransom money, for the most profitable enterprise of the pirates was the capture of wealthy persons. All over the Inner Sea, there were factors that arranged for the ransom of captives on a fixed scale.

When all the loot had been counted, a group of about twenty men and women were brought before him. They wore clothing of good quality, although some of their garments were very much the worse for wear. They stared about them apprehensively, clearly alarmed by these outlandish soldiers who had appeared from nowhere and displayed such ferocity.

"You are the captives of this little band of pirates, are you not?" Norbanus asked them in Greek.

"We are," said one of them, a tall, distinguished man who appeared to be Greek.

"Are you the spokesman of this group?"

The man looked at the others, who looked back at him blankly. "It would appear so."

"Excellent. I am Titus Norbanus, proconsul of Rome. You have heard of us?"

The man inclined his head. "We have heard reports of your return to Italy, Proconsul. We scarcely expected to see you in Cilicia. Might I inquire of our fate?"

"You may well rejoice in our advent among you. Rome is mighty, and Rome is orderly. I am offended by the disorder of this pirate business. Rome will correct this evil, in time. In the meanwhile, like the other captives in the other pirate towns we have liberated, you will be returned to your homelands by the first available transportation. Rome is just, and Rome wants only friendly relations with the people of the Middle Sea." He paused a moment. "Except, of course, for Carthage. We will destroy Carthage."

The tall man bowed, as did the rest. "Rome is merciful, indeed."

"I said just, not merciful," Norbanus corrected. "Mercy is

an attribute of weakness. Justice and clemency are attributes of the strong. Nothing is stronger than Rome."

A woman stepped forward. "Proconsul, I am Atalanta, from Herakleion, on Crete. My ransom of two thousand Athenian drachmas has already been delivered. I was waiting on the next ship bound for Crete."

"Your ransom will be returned to you," Norbanus said grandly. "If any others among you have already been ransomed, report the sum to my quaestor and you will be repaid. Of course, I will want to see receipts. These pirates seem to be meticulous in their accounts, so there should be no problem." No sense letting them take him for a fool, he thought.

The liberated captives were led away, thanking him profusely, some of them coming forward to kiss the hem of his cloak.

"Nice bit of diplomacy, that," Lentulus Niger commented.

"It costs us nothing," Norbanus said, "and it spreads goodwill. These people we liberate will spread word throughout the eastern half of the Middle Sea that Rome has arrived and Rome is their friend, if they are wise. Without conquering a foot of ground, we've put much of the East in Rome's debt and made the rest terrified of us. When Roman armies show up for the real conquest, our enemies will already be half-defeated by their own fears."

By afternoon, Norbanus had sold all the captives to the Syrian slave traders who followed the army like vultures. He made arrangements for the liberated prisoners to be taken to the nearest port city, where they could take a ship for home, and as always reminded the escort what a terrible fate awaited them should their charges not reach their destination safely. Norbanus found it a wise policy always to assume the worst of foreigners and took precautions accordingly.

Preparations for dinner were well under way when look-
outs stationed on a headland jutting into the sea signaled
that a ship approached. Shortly thereafter the vessel appeared and they saw at once that it was not a pirate ship returning to its base. It was a small galley under sail in a
favorable wind, and upon its square sail was painted
Jupiter's eagle, clutching thunderbolts in its talons.

Cato set down his cup. "The Roman navy appears at
last!" Previously, they had seen only Greek ships commandeered by Rome, usually carrying orders from the Senate
which Norbanus always found excuses to ignore.

"Whatever does the noble Senate want now?" Norbanus
grumped. "Does anyone want to wager that it's something
other than 'come home right this minute'? As if I weren't
hurrying there as fast as I can!"

The others maintained detached expressions. Norbanus
had had plenty of opportunity to arrange for sea transportation to Italy. He just had no intention of doing so. He was
embarked upon his own personal epic and wanted no inter-
ference with it.

An hour later the ship was made fast to the town's wharf
and a Roman official strode into the square and up to the
house where Norbanus and his staff sat at dinner. He wore a
silvered cuirass and helmet and his tunic and cloak were
blue. Romans had not used blue as a military color since
giving up their navy more than a century previously.

"Servius Papirius Caldus," the man announced. "Naval
quaestor of the Brundisium fleet. Which of you is Titus
Norbanus?" Of course there was no question which was
Norbanus, but no Roman would admit to recognizing another purely because of his splendor.

"I'm Norbanus. Have a seat, Papirius, you look hungry.
I never heard of a naval quaestor or a Brundisium fleet,

but times are changing fast, it seems. Is your ship truly all Roman?"

Papirius took a seat and accepted a cup of wine. "We have a Greek sailing master and a few experienced Greek crewmen, but the rest are Italian. We'll depend on the Greeks for a while, until we've more experience at sea. I'm carrying messages from the Senate, plus a sealed letter from your father, the consul." He looked around at the officers seated at the table, all hard-faced men wearing an unusual amount of gold. He looked at the great heap of loot before the steps, then he turned back.

"We sailed too far east at first and learned in Tarsus that you'd already passed. Then we turned around and just followed the smoke of burning towns until we caught up with you. You certainly seem to have made your mark on this part of the world."

"We have made the presence of Rome felt," Norbanus said modestly.

"It looks like it's been fun," Papirius said. "But I think your adventure is about to come to an end. These are excellent figs, by the way."

Norbanus's eyes narrowed. "End? What do you mean?"

Papirius spat out an olive pit. "There's a big fleet of transports just been built and undergoing sea trials when I left Brundisium. They'll be coming this way to pick you all up and fetch you back to Italy. They could be sailing this way already."

Everyone looked at Norbanus, whose face had turned to stone. "Excellent," he grated at last. "We shall be home sooner than anticipated."

"Unless," said Lentulus Niger, "the omens prove unfavorable to a sea voyage." He eyed his plate innocently as he said it.

"And," Cato commented, "we are well into fall. The good sailing days are numbered." He eyed Norbanus above his cup.

Titus Norbanus suppressed a smile. These two had been loyal in the field, but they had been his adversaries in all else. But he had enriched them beyond their wildest dreams, giving them leading parts in the greatest adventure in the history of Rome. Now they were his, their fortunes committed to his.

"Of course," he said, "anything could happen."

Papirius nodded. "I suppose." He dipped a piece of bread into a pot of olive oil in which fragrant herbs steeped. "You got word about the defeat on the Arnus?"

"We heard," Niger said grimly. "The report that came with the last ship from Rome didn't give us much in the way of details."

Papirius launched into a colorful description of the debacle. As always happened, a few survivors had made it across the river and back to Rome in the days after the battle, so the people had a fairly clear account of the fighting to supplement Aemilius's bare-bones dispatches to the Senate. While Papirius spoke, Norbanus turned over the possibilities in his mind. It was not in his nature simply to defy the Senate. He was far more inclined to turn this annoyance somehow to his own advantage.

He was certain that there was no real rush about getting back to Italy. The defeat on the Arnus was a setback from which Rome would need time to recover. Hamilcar was not going to attack soon. He had several months yet to continue his march, and by the time he returned to Rome there would have been new elections, new consuls presiding over the Senate. He did not have to please men who would be out of office soon. Thinking of this, he opened the letter from his father.

My son: I hope this finds you well and victorious.

Our enemies in the Senate, most of them old family diehards, wish you ill. They are jealous of your magnificent accomplishments in the East. Stay your course and pay them no heed. You will return in glory to Rome and you will be the idol of the people. I have been working all year to see that you will have a sympathetic new family consul in office when you return. I have called in all my political debts to win support for Gaius Hermanicus. He is not militarily ambitious, so he is quite content to spend the next year sitting in a curule chair instead of in the field. More importantly, he is a firm supporter of our family.

I am all but assured of a proconsular command of one of the armies being readied for the African campaign. My colleague, Scipio the elder, will have another. I foresee trouble with so many proconsuls in the field at once, but there is little help for it with a war this vast. Speaking of which, many here resent your using the title "proconsul." It is true that you have what amounts to a proconsular command, but since you have not held the requisite offices, there are those who whisper that you have dictatorial ambitions. When you return, I urge you to make a show of modesty and say that you assumed the title only to encourage the proper awe in foreigners.

Do not hurry at the behest of our rivals, but do not delay too long, either. Return covered with honors and take your place in the Senate. Long Live Rome and the family Norbanus.

Nothing much of interest there, he thought. Just what he already knew. Dictatorial ambitions, eh? He decided he liked the sound of that.

He went back to pondering what to do about this fleet that wanted to whisk him away to Italy before he completed his planned journey. As he thought, the first animals of the baggage train entered the town. It had grown so vast that it followed his legions at some distance. The bulk of it would have to encamp outside the small town. He would have to scour the countryside for more pack beasts and wagons to transport his takings.

He had been wondering how he was going to get all of this loot to Italy, but now it seemed that he had sea transport on the way. This presented him with a new possibility. He had greatly enjoyed commanding his own army. Now it might be just as pleasurable to have his own navy.

A MONTH LATER THEY WERE ON THE COAST OF Lycia, having made a profitable march along the coast of Pamphylia. The Pamphylians were a half-Asiatic, barbarous people who had much finer cities than the Cilicians, but had the same penchant for piracy. To make the situation even better, they had the temerity to try to stop the legions from crossing their territory. They mounted aggressive attacks against the marching columns, and this gave Norbanus the perfect excuse to acquire those cities for his own. In most places he installed petty chieftains as the new rulers and they pledged themselves as his personal clients.

From Pamphylia they passed into Lycia. This proved to be an extremely rugged land, composed of the many spurs of Mount Taurus that fanned out to the sea, where many of them formed high, wave-splashed promontories. It was impossible to hug the coast, so they had to make their way through one mountain pass after another, and progress was slow. They were further slowed by the immense baggage train, but the soldiers never complained when a wagon broke down and they had to put their shoulders to the wheels. They knew it was their own wealth they were transporting.

At the mouth of the Xanthus near the Lycian town of Myra, they found the Roman fleet in the harbor.

"That's quite a sight," Lentulus Niger said with some understatement as they crested a pass in the hills to the east of the little bay. The harbor was full of galleys and transports, all of them bright with new paint, their prows, masts and sails sporting Roman eagles. On the narrow, rocky beach spare sails had been employed to make marquees. Most of the ships' crews appeared to be ashore, relaxing, tending fires or dickering with locals for livestock and produce.

"Let's go down and have a few words with them," Norbanus said. They nudged their horses into a walk and descended the hillside. Behind them came the standard bearers, and then the rest of the army. Down below someone shouted and pointed upward. A huge cheer rang out from the men below when they saw the standards and the dusty men coming down toward them.

Norbanus and his party rode into the shore camp amid the cheers and congratulations. They saw a sprinkling of Greeks, but most of the men in blue tunics were clearly native Italians. There were marines among them, wearing bronze helmets and armed with sword and spear, but without body armor. Norbanus rode up to the largest marquee and a man emerged dressed in splendid armor and grinning broadly.

"Greetings, Titus Norbanus!" he called. "Your feat is the talk of all Italy."

Norbanus took the man's hand. "Decimus Arrunteius, isn't it? Haven't seen you since Noricum. In the Senate now, eh?" He dismounted, as did his officers. He remembered the family as soldierly but poor. They could rarely afford to have more than one man in the Senate in any generation. That could work well for him.

"Enrolled last year. Now I'm *duumvir* of the Brundisium fleet. Come inside out of this sun."*Duumvir* was the old Roman title for "admiral," revived for the new era.

They followed him into the shade of the spread sail. Long tables had been erected and they sat on benches. Arrunteius told them of the latest doings in Italy, and the much-traveled officers told him and the other Roman naval commanders of their adventures in the East.

When the wine had flowed sufficiently, Norbanus said: "*Duumvir*, eh? Of course, I'm sure it's an honor to have so much responsibility so young, but with your family's long military reputation, I'd have thought you'd be given an army command." In the old days, the navy had always been considered an inferior service, no matter how crucial it might be.

"Oh, you know how it is," Arrunteius said. "The good commands always go to the old families, no matter how distinguished anyone else might be. With everybody clamoring for officer's commissions these days, you're lucky to get any kind of appointment. I have friends qualified to lead cohorts who've taken appointments as centurions just to get in on the fighting. And I can't complain that it isn't interesting, whipping a fleet into shape. You've never had fun until you've tried to bludgeon a pack of Italians into being sailors. Especially if you've never been to sea yourself."

Under the bluff words Norbanus heard the edge of resentment. This was something with which he was familiar. It was something he could use.

"So you've been given the task of ferrying me and my men back to Italy, eh?" he said, reminding Arrunteius that he had not been given the task of battle with the Carthaginian fleet.

"Well, yes. I believe we've carrying capacity enough for your whole force. There'll be crowding, of course, but that can't be helped."

"I have more than men to transport. Come outside with me for a moment."

Puzzled, Arrunteius took his cup and walked outside. The other officers went with them, Norbanus's looking amused, Arrunteius's puzzled. Outside, they studied the legionaries, now encamping on a field off the beach. They were lean, burned dark, and wild-looking. Their arms were perfectly kept, but their tunics were of every color and design, scavenged along their route. Clothing wore out quickly on a long campaign, and the fine tunics Jonathan had given them had long since been reduced to rags. Most oddly, many now wore their swords on belts studded with plaques of gold and silver. Their hands and arms wore rings, bracelets and armlets that winked gold and jewels.

"Well, they seem to have done well in your service," Arrunteius said. "I think we'll have no trouble getting them all aboard."

"Look up there," Norbanus said, nodding toward the pass. Arrunteius followed his gaze and gasped. An endless line of pack animals and wagons still poured over the pass to join a huge compound next to the legionary camp.

"Is that your baggage train? I'm sorry, Titus, but you'll have to leave most of it here. We can't get a tenth of it into our transports along with your men. How much more is there?"

"I'd say about half has come through the pass now." He enjoyed his friend's gape-mouthed expression, then said, "It's not exactly baggage, Decimus. Come have a look."

They walked to the compound where the animals were being unloaded and the wagons parked in long rows. "Pick something at random."

Mystified, Arrunteius walked to a wagon and pointed to a chest. "Open it." Norbanus ordered the wagoneer. With a small prybar the man pried the lid from the chest. Arrunteius and his officers gasped. The box was packed with a miscellaneous heap of gold coins, bars of the same metal, gemstones in the raw or carved and set in jewelry, pearls in endless ropes, chains of every sort of precious metal. Their eyes dazzled.

"Is it all like this?" Arrunteius said when he could get his breath. He looked out over the fast-growing compound, up at the train still coming through the pass.

"Oh, it's not all gold and jewels, by any means, but other things equally valuable and portable: spices, incense, fine weapons, ivory, works of art, wonderful cloth—I've even got a few bolts of silk."

"Silk! I've heard of the stuff, but I've never seen it." Silk was to the Romans no more than a rumor—the magical cloth from somewhere far east that was so valuable that when it reached the West it was unwoven thread by thread and rewoven together with common thread. Even thus adulterated, it sold for many times its weight in gold and was owned mainly by oriental monarchs.

"It's real," Norbanus assured him. "Near Antioch we encountered some bandits who'd waylaid a caravan from far inland. We relieved them of it. It's the pure cloth, too."

He watched their stunned expressions for a while, then said, "Now, Decimus, you really don't expect me to leave all this here on the beach, do you?"

"What are we going to do, Titus?" Arrunteius said in a strangled voice. "My orders from the Senate are to bring you and your legions home at once."

"Some of this goes into the state treasury. The Senate will not thank you for impoverishing Rome at the outset of what must be a very costly war."

"Just *some* of it?" said one of the naval officers.

"By ancient tradition," Norbanus said, "the general in charge is free to determine the division of the spoils. Some must go to the treasury, of course. The rest he may divide among his officers and men and, of course, keep a substantial share for himself. It's been that way since the beginning of the republic."

Arrunteius shook his head. "That's in wartime, and you haven't been given a war to fight."

"The situation is unique, I'll grant you that," Norbanus said easily. "But let me work things out with the Senate when we get back. I'm sure that I can appeal to their good sense. In the meantime, this is what I propose: My men and I will continue our march along the coast. You will accompany us offshore, carrying our, ah, baggage. We can move much faster with it loaded on ships. It really has been slowing us down. We'll proceed up the coast of Asia. At one of the major cities—Miletus or Smyrna or Ephesus—we can arrange for transport to take the legions across to Greece. We can make a march there, just to let the Greeks know firsthand that Rome is back in earnest, then do the same thing there. It's a short hop across the strait from Greece to Brundisium." He saw the tormented look on the *duumvir's* face as he considered his duty, then looked at the huge heaps of loot now assembling before his eyes.

"Elections are coming up," Norbanus reminded him. "This year's magistrates will be out of office when we get back, and they'll be thinking about nothing but the commands they'll be taking up. This is Roman history in the making, Decimus, and you," he nodded to the other naval officers, "and your subordinates, can be a part of it. Think of the glory when we return. And you'll have a part when it comes to the shareout, of course."

After a long while Arrunteius turned to his officers. "Start loading all this baggage onto our ships." They jumped to do his bidding.

Titus Norbanus, de facto proconsul and now, it seemed, de facto admiral, smiled.

CHAPTER THIRTEEN

"SURELY THIS THING CAN NEVER FLOAT," ZENO said, shouting over the clangor.

"Yet they assure us it can," Izates said. "They quoted all sorts of Archimedean arcana about weights and volumes and displacement and buoyancy. They insisted that the substance itself was immaterial."

"But ships should be made of wood!" Zeno said.

The thing that drew their incredulous attention was a ship such as no one had ever seen or envisioned. The underwater craft had been mind-boggling enough, but this was even more unnatural. It was a ship made entirely of bronze. Its long keel and arching ribs were made of the ruddy metal, and even now long planks of the same material were being affixed to the ribs with rivets. The din was like all the armories in the world working full blast in one place.

They walked around the thing, which seemed to be at least three times as long as a conventional galley. The insane-looking designer of this prodigy had explained that wooden ships were limited in length by the size of trees available to make their keels. There was no practical limit to the size of a ship with a metal keel.

"It can't be rammed, can't be set afire and it won't rot," cried the designer. "No galley can stand against it. Once in motion, it will plow right through a wooden ship without even slowing down!"

Upon its prow, instead of the conventional ram, it had a huge, concave saw-toothed beak. Its lower, forward-thrusting end would be far beneath the water when it was at sea, and the upper end would tower twenty feet above the surface. It was indeed designed to cut enemy galleys clean in two instead of merely punching holes in them.

"Maybe it will float," Zeno conceded, "but will it move or merely wallow there?"

The radical vessel had no provision for oars. Instead, it had a pair of the huge paddle wheels on its sides, also made of bronze. These would be worked by hundreds of slaves scrambling on treadmills and hollow wheels within the hull.

"Well," Izates said, "if it won't move, someone even crazier will find a way to do it. That madman from Corinth, maybe." The Corinthian had an apparatus of tubs and pipes in which he boiled water and experimented with the steam that resulted. He was not discouraged, even though more than once a boiler had exploded, killing a number of slaves each time. He said it just proved that steam was powerful and swore that he would harness that power. What he would do with it was a mystery.

"Does it occur to you," Zeno asked his friend, "that these Archimedeans tend to overdo things?"

"I suppose that is the way to test the limits," said Izates. "Kings and nations overdo things. Look at the Colossus of

Rhodes, or the Pyramids, or that great huge lighthouse out there in the harbor. At least these men are learning something by their overambitious mistakes. It's not all just to glorify some inconsequential king."

"Still," Zeno said, scratching his head, "wood floats. Metal doesn't. It just seems unnatural."

"We are learning that many things we thought we knew about nature were unwarranted assumptions." Izates was already speaking in the jargon of the Archimedean school with its terms such as "evidence," "observation," "experimentation" and "proof." At one time he would have thought these concepts unworthy of a philosopher. Seeing a man fly was enough to unsettle one's old beliefs about such things.

In the palace, Marcus Scipio found that he could no longer take his customary delight in the work of the Museum. For more than two years it had consumed his days and he was fascinated by every new discovery, every new invention. He had taken endless pleasure in finding new applications, most of them warlike, for the outlandish devices the philosophers of the Archimedean school dreamed up.

But now it was different. Now Rome had suffered a defeat.

Flaccus tried to jolly him out of it. "A trifling defeat!" he insisted. "Rome suffered far worse defeats in the past. How about Cannae and Trebbia and Lake Trasimene? How about the Caudine Forks? Entire consular armies were lost in those disasters. You knew Aemilius as well as I did: a plodding, uninspired commander. That's why they gave him green legions and sent him north where they never expected him to tangle with a first-rate Carthaginian general with an army twice the size of his. As it turned out, he was the first Roman commander to have that experience. It was just bad luck."

"We've been sitting here amid incredible luxury, playing with our toys, while real Roman soldiers have been dying by the thousands," Marcus said glumly.

"You don't sound like yourself. You've told everyone else that it's going to be a long war and everyone will have a chance at winning glory. Why all of a sudden do you not believe it yourself?"

"Glory? I don't care about glory!" He shrugged. "Not much, anyway. No more than most Romans. But I've been a soldier all my life, from a long line of soldiers, and it galls me to be sitting here in Alexandria wearing gilded armor and a helmet with ram's horns while Roman armies are being defeated and Sicily is being overrun and Hamilcar is preparing to strike back. And Norbanus!" He threw a handful of papyri toward the ceiling and watched them drift back down.

This was more like it. "Ah, our old friend and colleague Titus Norbanus, now bruited about as the greatest thing since Alexander. That bothers you, does it?"

"Do you think I'm jealous of the likes of Titus Norbanus?" He slammed a hard palm onto his desk. "Did you hear that they're thinking of allowing him to stand for consul? At his age and without having held an aedileship, much less a praetorship?"

"I heard. I read the same dispatches that you do. In order to do that he has to get back to Rome first. Last we heard he was preparing to cross over from Ephesus to Greece."

Marcus made a rude noise. "Greeks! What are they going to do about someone like Norbanus and his four legions? Can you imagine what those soldiers must be like by now? They were first-rate when they were here in Egypt. Now they've made a march like something from an ancient hero tale, fighting much of the way. Those have to be the toughest, saltiest legionaries Rome has ever fielded by now, and they clearly worship Norbanus."

"Envy ill becomes you, Marcus. But up to now they've faced only the disorganized Judeans and the tottering, decadent Seleucids and primitive pirates and tribesmen, the sort of trash a Roman legion brushes from its path. Forget the Greeks. When he enters Greece, he's in Macedonian territory, and they're a different proposition entirely, as you well know."

"I don't mean that I want to see another Roman army defeated!" Marcus protested.

"But it would be nice to see Titus Norbanus humbled just a little, wouldn't it?"

"He needs some taking down. A proconsular command, a whole army and now even a navy! Plus he's making his own foreign policy in the East, building up a clientage among foreign kings; it's outrageous!"

"Marcus, Marcus," Flaccus said crooningly, "there are people back in Rome who say exactly the same thing about you, and you know it. They say you are making yourself de facto king of Egypt, that Selene never makes a move that you don't direct, that you have imperial ambitions."

"I wish Selene was that biddable. The woman has been getting damned independent lately. She forgets who put her shapely backside on that throne." He glowered at the gaudy helmet on its stand upon his desk. "She's the one who manipulates me, if truth were known. Dressing me up like one of her strutting guardsmen, making me a centerpiece at her endless banquets."

"And you are complaining? Oh, come now, Marcus. She's making everyone grant you divine honors, and your presence at her banquets tells all those foreign dignitaries where her power lies." He spread his hands expansively. "You are the greatest man in Egypt, and here you are feeling sorry for yourself because you've missed a couple of brawls."

"Brawls! Aulus, you are not a military man!"

Flaccus grinned. "I admit it freely."

Scipio leaned back in his chair, musing. "Hamilcar must have his fleet restored and reprovisioned by now. Why is he waiting?"

Flaccus nodded. This was better. His friend was thinking strategically again. "Does it occur to you, as it does to me, that perhaps Hamilcar has a new advisor?"

"Selene's spies in Carthage say that the shofet spends a lot of time with a foreign queen, an Illyrian named Teuta. Is it conceivable that Hamilcar is actually listening to a woman? When we saw him, he would scarcely listen to any of his own generals. He was not a man inclined to taking advice."

"Since we last saw him, he has been defeated before the walls of Alexandria, forced to retreat, had Italy and Sicily taken from beneath his nose, and had much of his fleet and most of his invasion materiel destroyed by fire. It's enough to make most men change their ways." He paused. "And this Teuta may be an extraordinary woman. What do we know about her?"

"Nothing. Illyria is just across the Adriatic from Italy, but we know more about Spain. It's as remote as Britannia and Hibernia."

"How can we find out about the woman and her country?" Marcus asked.

Flaccus's eyebrows went up. "Find out? The Museum and Library contain all the knowledge in the world."

"That will take too long and involve talking with a lot of dusty old scholars who have no grasp of military matters or politics. I have a better idea." He seized his helmet from its stand.

Flaccus got up. "Where are we going?"

Minutes later they were at the queen's apartments. Selene, as usual, was closeted with her scholars and ministers. At the Romans' entrance, all but Selene rose and bowed.

"We are discussing the Nile floods," Selene told the Romans. "Will you join us?"

"When Your Majesty has a moment, there is a matter we would like to discuss with you," Marcus said.

"Gentlemen, give us leave," she said. The men rose, made their obeisances and left.

"You are gracious to set aside business of state to give us an audience," Flaccus said.

She gave them a crooked smile. "Do you think I relish listening to accounts of water level and mud deposit? What is it?"

They told her of their concerns.

"Queen Teuta? Yes, I met her a few years ago. She accompanied an embassy here after she'd secured her power in her homeland. An extraordinary creature: half-savage, more tattoos than a Sarmatian slave. It made her difficult to take seriously. But I spoke with her at some length, and she proved to have wit and intelligence. She also possessed what you Romans would consider an inappropriately masculine force: strength, courage, dominance, aggressiveness, that sort of thing."

"*Virtus,*" Marcus said. "Those qualities becoming a man. So this woman is an Amazon?"

"Of sorts. She is also quite adept at using her feminine allure. I noticed that many men here found her bizarre aspect stimulating, and she took advantage of that."

"Do you think she's capable of manipulating Hamilcar?" Flaccus asked.

"I don't know Hamilcar," she said. "But from what I've

heard of him, from you and from others, he sounds like a weak man masquerading as a strong one. He surrounds himself with forceful men, but can't bring himself to dispose of his troublesome sister. I think he is secretly in awe of women. He is easily bored and has a taste for the outlandish. Yes, I think he is exactly the type that a woman like Teuta could bend to her will. He will tell himself that it is fitting that he listen to her, because she is a reigning queen."

"He is vain," Flaccus said. "How can this sit well with his vanity?"

"She is both clever and subtle," she said. "By the time her ideas have lodged in his head, he will think that they were his ideas originally."

"I see," Marcus murmured, wondering if this was exactly what Selene had been doing with him.

They were distracted by a series of unearthly shrieks coming from the direction of the Museum. The sound was so hideous as to make the hair stand and teeth grind together.

"What is that?" Flaccus gasped.

"Someone at the Museum," Selene said through tight-clenched teeth, "has succeeded in drilling a path to the underworld and has let all the tormenting demons out."

They hurried from the royal apartments and across the courtyard that separated them from the Museum. They were not alone in doing so. A knot of philosophers from the respectable schools stormed toward the source of the noise, hands over their ears.

"Majesty, this is intolerable!" shouted Bacchylides the mathematician. "The incessant hammering and clanging is bad enough! How are philosophers to go calmly about their work with this cacophony?"

Now the noise began to vary. Instead of a single, eerie,

wailing note, other notes, just as loud, joined in an almost musical progression, rising and falling, until it was making a recognizable tune.

Following the noise, they entered one of the smaller courtyards. In its center towered an arrangement of vertical pipes of varying length, like the pipes of Pan upended, made of metal and of a godlike size. From the pipes shot streamers of white steam. Marcus recognized the thing. It was the great water organ from the Hippodrome. Ordinarily, teams of men worked pumps to maintain the pressure of the water in its reservoir. When the organist pushed its keys, water pressure forced air through the pipes. In the Hippodrome, its music was clear and mellow. Here it bellowed like an ox in a mud hole, only a hundred times louder.

Now there were no men working pumps. Instead, the thing was connected to one of the bronze boilers by a long pipe. A slave shoveled wood chips into the furnace beneath the boiler, watching the color of the coals closely, all too aware of the fate of his predecessors. The inventor himself danced excitedly before his creation, punching his fists in the air, hair and beard swirling like some ecstatic priest of a mysterious Eastern god. The organist—a woman, as was the custom—was just as enthusiastic, swaying her bottom from side to side as she smashed down upon the keys with hammered fists and sang along with her incredibly amplified instrument.

"Stop this!" Selene shouted, but no one could hear her. The philosophers were waving their arms, wailing in protest. Guards and slaves were gathering from all over the Museum, Library and palace to find out what the noise portended. Some caught the organist's enthusiasm, and impromptu dances broke out over the courtyard.

Selene pointed at the man shoveling wood under the

boiler. "Marcus, you have your sword, don't you? Go kill that man. Maybe that will make it stop."

Instead, Scipio went and spoke to the slave, who nodded and began to shovel hot coals out of the furnace. Gradually, the hooting of the pipes grew less intense, then faded quickly. When she could be heard, Selene shouted to the crowd.

"This is not a festival day! All of you return to your duties!" Disappointed, the soldiers and servants filtered back into the buildings, leaving the philosophers, the Romans and, she now saw, those itinerant Greeks, Zeno and Izates.

Half-dazed, the inventor turned around to see who was spoiling his fun. He seemed amazed to find that he had attracted a crowd that included Queen Selene. "Er, Majesty," he said. "What brings you here?"

She stared at him, astonished. "What brings me here? The most hellish racket ever heard in Alexandria, that's what! What's your name?"

The man gathered his wits together and bowed. "Euphenes of Caria, Majesty. And today I stand before you as the discoverer of the most important principle ever known to mankind!" He drew himself up, eyes blazing with a demented light.

"And what have you discovered?" Selene demanded. "A new way to make people go deaf?"

"Steam!" he shouted. "I have learned to harness steam!"

"Majesty," Flaccus said, leaning close to her, "we have so many philosophers here. I think we can hang this one without suffering any great loss. It might encourage the rest to keep the noise level down."

"No, let's hear what he has to say first," Scipio cautioned.

"Steam," Euphenes began, "is simply water in another form. Raise its temperature high enough and water, which is matter in a liquid state, is transformed into a gaseous state."

"Every housewife knows that water will boil away," Selene said impatiently.

"Yes, but since this occurs in open vessels, those housewives, and everyone else prior to my own researches, did not realize that a given volume of water, once heated sufficiently, is transformed to a much *larger* volume of steam!" Blank looks greeted this ringing pronouncement. He waved his hands, seeking the right words to get his concept across to these clearly nonphilosophical people. "It is like harnessing the wind! Wind is powerful, is it not? Wind drives ships. In great tempests, it uproots trees, tears the roofs from temples, drives the sea up onto dry land. What I have done is to confine the power of Boreas and Zephyrus within closed vessels, from which I may direct it in any direction I desire by means of pipes and valves."

"What can you do with it?" Marcus asked.

"Do with it? I shall develop innumerable uses for this power, of course. I have only just now proved the truth of my theory."

"You had better come up with something better than a loud noise," Selene said ominously.

"Majesty," said Zeno. "Might I speak?"

She looked at him. "Zeno, isn't it? Of course you may. You struck me as a man of good sense, and I could use some just now."

"Majesty, this great instrument makes an intolerable noise here in this small courtyard that is almost adjacent to your palace. But it strikes me that, in the immense space of the Hippodrome, its volume will match the scale of the greatest building in the world. Huge as it is, when it employs conventional water power it can barely be heard by distant spectators. I think if you let it be played there with the new steam power, it could prove a great hit with the crowds."

"What?" said Euphenes indignantly. "I did not do this to produce some trivial toy to please the mob! I simply found it an elegant way to prove my theory of the ratio between the volumes of water and steam—ow!"

The organist had joined them and now she trod on the philosopher's toes to shut him up. She bowed almost double. "Majesty, I am Chrysis, chief organist of the Hippodrome. If you will permit me to play my organ at the next games with the new steam power, I can promise that it will be a sensation! The crowds will adore you as never before. Nothing like it has ever been heard before."

"That is certainly true," Selene allowed.

"And you could use a bit of popularity just now," Flaccus said, practical as always. "The enthusiasm over turning back Hamilcar's invasion has worn off. The Alexandrian mob is famously fickle, and now they grumble about high prices for corn and the new taxes to pay for renewed hostilities. This might be just the thing to put them back in a good mood."

"But this trivializes my momentous discoveries!" Euphenes cried.

Selene turned on him with a basilisk gaze. "Sir, I am still displeased with you for disturbing the peace of my morning. I grant permission to install your steam-tooter in the Hippodrome. The first races of the season begin in ten days. As always, I will be there for opening day. If, as Chrysis predicts, the crowd reacts favorably and I benefit from this, then I will fund your further researches. But you must find a place away from the palace and Museum to carry out your work—somewhere where the noise will not offend my ears, and where your exploding boilers will only endanger yourself and your slaves."

Euphenes bowed low. "Your Majesty is too generous. My steam organ will be the hit of the games."

The queen and the Romans swept out of the courtyard, leaving Euphenes, the organist and the wandering Greeks alone.

"Euphenes," Izates asked, "I believe I grasp the principle you propose: that water transformed by heat into steam creates great pressure that may be intelligently directed."

"Succinctly put," Euphenes said, nodding.

"But," Izates went on, "how do you propose to harness it to useful work?"

With an audience of like-minded persons, Euphenes lost much of his impatient demeanor and explained patiently: "The applications must be limitless. What can one not do with the power of the very wind harnessed to the human will? This great toy merely proved my thesis. I believe it to be the greatest discovery since the principle of the lever was first articulated. Look at how much has resulted from that!"

"But you have no specific applications with which to please Her Majesty and the Romans?" Zeno asked.

"Ah—no, not really," Euphenes admitted. "I deal more in the realm of pure theory. The water organ occurred to me immediately, because the common flute is nothing but a pipe through which one blows breath, which is a form of wind. It seemed natural to apply the matchless power of steam to the biggest set of flutes in the world."

"Very sagacious," Zeno commended. "Might I suggest, now that you have proven your theory, that you speak with Chilo and convene a meeting of all the natural philosophers and mechanics of the Museum. If you explain to them the principles you have discovered, it may be that some of them will find applications for your work within their own disciplines."

Euphenes combed his fingers through his scruffy beard. "That is a possibility. Of course, it must be understood that discovery of the principle belongs to me."

"The glory will be all yours, Euphenes," Izates assured him. "You will lecture and publish your theories. After all, it is Archimedes everyone remembers, not the generations of mechanics who have made use of his principles of leverage, of buoyancy and displacement."

Euphenes nodded his grizzled head. "Yes, yes, that is true. This bears thinking about, my friends. But first, I must make a favorable impression upon the queen and the Hippodrome crowds." Now the head shook. "Imagine! I, a philosopher, reduced to pleasing a silly woman and an ignorant mob. Oh, the things we must do for the advancement of philosophy!" He turned to the organist and they discussed moving the huge organ back to its accustomed location.

Zeno and Izates stepped aside. "What kind of Cynic are you, Izates?" Zeno asked, grinning. "I've never known you to flatter a man's vanity like that."

Izates shrugged. "Of late, I find myself becoming less of a Cynic and more—what shall I call it? A utilitarian? It's the atmosphere of this place. It encourages a less rigid, more flexible frame of mind. One does what is necessary to produce a desirable result."

"And this place was once your very model of hidebound, inflexible conservatism," Zeno noted.

"We live in a new age, my friend," Izates said. "Come on, let's go find some lunch. That is a necessity as well."

CHAPTER FOURTEEN

HAMILCAR, SHOFET OF CARTHAGE, FOUND TO HIS surprise that he was pleased with the world. The failure of his Egyptian expedition was no more than a temporary setback, the usurpation of Carthaginian territory by resurgent Rome nothing more than a worthy challenge whereby he could prove to the world his greatness, that he was no mere inheritor, but a conqueror in his own right.

The news from the River Arnus had filled him with satisfaction. Two whole Roman legions utterly annihilated! The myth of Roman superiority destroyed! And he was not at all displeased that Mastanabal had been forced by his losses to retreat. For the general to have continued to march against Rome, even to capture the city, would have given him more honor than he should have. Then Mastanabal would have been the hero of this war, not his shofet. That would have been unfitting, and would have resulted in the general's immediate execution, lest he march against Hamilcar and seize the throne for himself. With Mastanabal safely in Gaul, raising troops for a renewed assault upon Rome from the north, he served his purpose perfectly. The Romans would strip badly needed legions from the South to guard against that renewed attack, which would not come until Hamilcar was ready.

True, the great delay in his war plans caused by the fire rankled, but it might have been a blessing sent by the gods of Carthage, restraining him from moving too fast. There was no doubt that he was now in a far better position than he had been. Perhaps they had also sent him Queen Teuta, who had so stimulated his mind, bringing out his true genius and helping him to recognize his destiny.

As a bonus, news of the victory had deflated Zarabel's pretensions. The priests of Tanit did not call quite so loudly for a *Tophet*. They could not claim that the gods of Carthage had deserted her. Possibly, it was time to do something about Zarabel, as Queen Teuta urged constantly.

"PRINCESS, THIS IS NO MORE THAN A SETBACK," Echaz said, wringing his hands. "Who could have foretold that General Mastanabal would prove so capable, or that all the Roman legions are not as formidable as those we saw here?"

"How, indeed," she said bitterly, glaring at the eunuch. "Or that Hamilcar would strike from the north before even setting sail with his main army? Has my brother suddenly grown crafty? I doubt it." With a hiss, she threw herself upon her couch. Slaves rushed to fan her.

She shook her head. The priest was useless in this crisis. He could think only in terms of the temples and the city of Carthage itself. He was incapable of thinking on a world scale. This very thought set her mind along another course.

She had let herself be distracted too long by the ancient struggle for power between priest and shofet, between Tanit and Baal-Hammon, between herself and her brother.

New powers were at work now. Rome was back. Parthia threatened to engulf the East. Even Ptolemaic Egypt, sunk in decadence and torpor, was waking under the influence of the strange Roman soldier-savant Scipio and the bizarre Archimedean school of the Museum. It was time for her to take action on a world scale. She must bend some of these powers to her own purposes or go under along with Carthage. Courses of action began to come together in her mind, and it was like waking from a long sleep. She sat up and waved her slaves aside. She leapt from the bed and began pacing back and forth.

"Echaz, call in my scribes. Then send out servants to summon my confidential sea agents. I have letters to deliver over a wide area of the sea, and I want this done quickly."

"At once, Princess!" the priest chirped, overjoyed to see his sovereign and high priestess taking decisive action.

The faces of important men appeared in her mind's eye, and she ticked them off one by one: Hamilcar, her brother, was the enemy. Marcus Scipio was lost to her, now involved with Selene of Egypt. Titus Norbanus, the would-be new Alexander, was both capable and malleable. And General Mastanabal, victor of the Avernus, was an ambitious man.

Swiftly, her lethargy now gone, she put them in order and made her plans for what to do with each of them.

"WHAT ARE WE TO DO WITH THEM?" AGATHOCLES asked. He was the head of the Athenian Council, a board of the glorious city's richest men.

"Do with them?" said Herophilus, his eyes twinkling maliciously. "You mean, they are ours to do with as we please? The question is: What are they going to do with us?"

"They look awful and smell worse," Laches said, "but they are not all that numerous and they are in our territory."

The council had been in emergency session since word had come of the arrival of the Romans. It did not come as a total surprise, since Greek skippers had been reporting regularly of the amazing progress of the Roman legions from Egypt through Judea and the Seleucid territories and along the coastline of Ionia. The speed of the march was phenomenal, and the Roman commander's almost offhanded acquisition of a naval arm was stupefying. Still, when they woke up to find that the Romans occupied Piraeus, just a quick march down the Long Walls from Athens, the effect was stunning.

"What advantage is it that they are in our territory?" Herophilus demanded. "Can we just call up an army of veterans to repel them? Half the fighting men of Greece have turned mercenary and are signing on with Hamilcar of Carthage. Many of our best naval officers are helping the Romans build and officer a fleet."

"There have been no threats of hostility so far," cautioned Libon, the greatest banker in Athens. "Let's not talk as if war was in the offing. These Romans seem to be eminently practical men, except for their somewhat obsessive need to humble Carthage. The Roman ambassador has already requested that we render every assistance to their wandering army, and that we will incur the gratitude of the Senate thereby."

"And the undying enmity of Carthage," Agathocles said.

"When have we ever known anything but hostility from Carthage?" Laches asked. "I don't like this resurgence of

Rome, but they have put a check to Hamilcar's ambitions, and for this we owe them something."

Agathocles was about to say something when the doorman entered and informed them that a Roman spokesman had arrived from Piraeus.

"Well, let's have a look at this prodigy," Agathocles said. Moments later a man in gilded armor strode into the room, trailing a brilliant scarlet cloak. Under his arm he cradled a plumed helmet. His handsome face was craggy and fierce, as they had come to expect from Romans. Agathocles introduced himself and the other members of the council. "I take it I address the glorious Titus Norbanus?"

"I am Decimus Arrunteius, admiral of the Roman fleet. My general sends his compliments to the noble Council of Athens, and regrets that he cannot come to you personally, but must attend to his duties in Piraeus."

"It is most irregular to send a subordinate, when only eight miles separate Piraeus from Athens," Agathocles said.

"Yes," concurred Herophilus, "I'd think that your commander would be anxious to tour the Long Walls and scout for weak spots." The others chuckled uncomfortably.

"No need," Arrunteius said. "I can describe every stone myself. There's a shocking bulge in the wall two miles from Piraeus. I suspect it dates from the rebuilding after Lysander of Sparta tore the walls down. A little battering at that spot will bring down a section twenty paces wide, and it wouldn't take a whole morning's work." He enjoyed their stupefied expressions for a moment. "But, enough of military matters. My general is most anxious to establish friendly relations with the noble Council."

"We have already established cordial relations with your Senate," Agathocles said with great dignity.

"Yes, I'm sure," said the very young and impossibly arrogant Roman. "But General Norbanus wishes to put his esteem on a more personal footing, something to proclaim his own friendship with this august body." He clapped his hands. His palms were so hardened by a lifetime of drill with sword, spear and shield that it was like two slabs of hardwood striking together. Slaves entered, bearing on their shoulders poles from which hung bronze-strapped chests. These they set down, and soon there were some fifty of the boxes nearly covering the floor. Arrunteius began flinging back the lids.

"Thus does General Norbanus declare his esteem, with gifts for the noble Council of Athens."

The Council gazed upon the boxes with bedazzled eyes. Each was full of gold in the form of bars or coins. They were rich men, but the wealth of Greece was trifling compared with that of the East.

"I think," said Libon the banker, "that your general will find that he has many, many friends in Athens."

TITUS NORBANUS WATCHED THE BUILDING OF HIS fleet and fretted at the slowness of the work, although he knew perfectly well that it was proceeding with unprecedented speed. The ship works of Piraeus and the neighboring ports had been put at his disposal, and he was constructing transports for all his men, all his treasure and even his animals. It would have been feasible simply to use the hulls he arrived with to ferry men and materiel to Italy, each vessel making several crossings. But for his own reasons, he wanted everything to arrive at once.

Besides, he had much more than a short crossing in mind for his fleet. These ships were destined for a very long voyage, indeed.

"When do we sail, Master?" asked Glaphyra, drifting into his line of vision from the right. Roxana appeared from the left. As usual, he had heard neither of them.

"We long to see Italy," Roxana said. "Will we have a great villa there? We hear it is so much more beautiful than Judea, or Greece."

"I will give you luxury beyond your expectations, never fear," he assured them. "And we sail before the next turning of the moon. I've already sacrificed at the great temple of Poseidon for a safe voyage."

"We have calculated the best days for sailing," Glaphyra said, unrolling a scroll. "It must be on the waxing of the moon, so that your fortunes will increase proportionately."

"And your father's birth sign indicates that his destiny and yours will intersect momentously," Roxana added.

"What are my immediate prospects?" Norbanus wanted to know.

"Limitless," said both sisters together.

"Leave me," he said. "I have work to do." The sisters drifted away and he went over the election results. They had arrived by courier that morning, the news only a few days old. Courier routes were now established throughout Italy, and swift cutters plied the waters to Rome's ever-growing establishment of overseas bases.

True to his father's promise, one of the year's consuls was Hermanicus, the new family adherent of the Norbani. The other was a Gracchus, old family but not a man of great distinction. This was only to be expected with most of the best soldiers on active service with the legions. The old and the unfit would be presiding in Rome for some time to come, and that would be bad in the future. Bad for the republic at large, anyway. Norbanus planned to use the fact to his advantage.

The rest of the list of winners was even more satisfying. The key office was the tribunate of the plebs, and this year's slate included no fewer than five whose influence could be counted upon. This was enough to ensure almost any favorable legislation he might need. The Senate was powerful in assigning military commands, but the Plebeian Assembly could override Senate appointments. A tribune could veto an act of the Senate. A tribune could enact a bill to give command to a favorite of the plebs.

The old families had the prestige of long tenure in the Senate, but the new families were supreme in the popular assemblies where most of the work of Rome got done. And greatest of the new families were the Norbani.

He went into the great warehouse he had commandeered as his headquarters. Here his secretaries copied out his orders, his quaestors kept accounts, his officers rendered their reports. At one end of the huge room a crew of draftsmen worked at a crucial task. Norbanus had ordered maps drawn: maps of the whole littoral touched by the great Middle Sea. He wanted careful depictions of every port, every town, every river, with distances noted and resources listed. He knew how frustrating it was for a general to be lost, and how much easier it was to make plans if he knew what lay before him.

Greek skippers knew every foot of that coastline intimately, and he paid them well to yield their secrets. Titus Norbanus plundered mercilessly, but he did not value wealth for its own sake. Gold was just something with which to buy the important things. With gold he subverted foreign rulers. With gold he enriched his men and secured their loyalty to himself. He could buy the secrets of Greek traders and the services of spies. He could afford to spend lavishly because with these things at his disposal he could seize all the wealth in the world. Gold was good. Power was better.

He went to the table and called for a particular map. It depicted the coast of southern Gaul and Spain all the way to the Pillars of Hercules. This was where the Carthaginian, Mastanabal, had advanced and then retreated. Another showed the North African coast from the southern pillar all the way to Carthage. He had been studying these maps with intensity for some time, memorizing their every feature. He had plans for those particular stretches of coast.

Back outside, he listened to the sound of hammering from the shipyards and fretted once again, trying by sheer will to hurry the process. His expanded fleet had to be ready to sail by the next waxing moon. Then he would ride the sea to his destiny.

QUEEN TEUTA SAT BENEATH THE SHADE OF THE awning stretched before her great tent. She had permanent quarters in the enormous palace of the shofet, but she could not abide stone walls and solid ceilings for long. After a few days they seemed to press in upon her and she had to go back to her tent. Always, she felt most at home beneath the limitless sky, where dwelt the spirits of her nomad ancestors.

She was bored and eager for action. The army was strong enough, the transport fleet almost completely rebuilt. There was nothing to be gained by further waiting. She wanted to urge Hamilcar to action, but she knew better. She had planted the seeds of her own plans, and now they had to reach fruition in his mind as if they had been his own. Too much pressure from her would ruin it.

"My queen, the shofet comes," said one of her guards.

"I hope he's made up his mind," she muttered.

Hamilcar arrived amid a suite of officers and an honor guard of a hundred Spanish horsemen. Teuta rose to greet him and he dismounted and took her hands.

"Queen Teuta," he said, "I have given orders. The army will begin its march on the morning after tomorrow. I will want you in the vanguard with me when we move west."

"West?" she said, marveling as if it were not her own plan to begin with. "We go to the Pillars and across the strait to Spain? It is a bold plan. I know it is one of several we discussed, but I considered it the most unlikely."

"I know," he said, "but for that very reason it is the last one the Romans will suspect. They think to lure me to Sicily. That island is a fought-over carcass now, and all its strong points are already in their hands. My army would starve while theirs rested behind strong walls. No, better to take Hannibal's old route, but with my navy accompanying us just offshore as we march."

She pretended doubt. "But the Romans are bold as well. They may cross from Sicily and lay siege to Carthage itself."

He shrugged. "The walls of Carthage are the strongest in the world. Only the subject people would suffer, and it's time they repaid Carthage for all they have gained from us. If the Romans come, they will pull back to Italy as soon as they know their precious seven hills are menaced."

"Then let us go to Spain, Your Majesty," she said, her tattooed face twisting into a smile.

"CONSULS AND SENATORS OF ROME," GABINIUS ANnounced, "our wandering general is back, with his army and a baggage train that sounds as if it is the size of a small nation."

The news had come from Brundisium days ago that Norbanus had landed and that he had with him a huge fleet. Just unloading it all had taken several days, and only then had the army made its way toward the Seven Hills.

Now, from outside the curia, the Senate could hear the wild cheering of the citizenry as they flocked to the walls to see this prodigy.

The Consul Hermanicus stood. "I propose that we vote days of thanksgiving to the gods for this happy event."

"Why?" demanded his colleague. "Because the boy managed to get home alive and didn't lose most of his army doing it?"

A senator stood. "You are just jealous that a new family general has so gloriously won a name for himself!" The house erupted into the customary squabble, which lasted until Gabinius managed to calm them.

"Senators, we have a greater question before us: Are we to go out and meet Norbanus as he desires, or do we demand that he report here to us?"

Things subsided into a low mutter, for this was a thorny question. Norbanus did not want to cross the *pomerium*, the ancient boundary of the city marked out by Romulus with his plow. By custom, to do so would mean laying down his imperium, becoming an ordinary citizen. Many argued that he had never been properly invested with imperium in the first place. He was not an official general, could not petition the Senate for a triumph and was duty-bound as an ordinary Roman officer to come to the Senate on foot and render his report. The debate had raged since word of his arrival in Italy.

.   The Consul Hermanicus stood. "Senators, we may plead to Jupiter himself for a decision, but in the end we must face reality. There is no precedent for the things that have happened since we left Noricum to retake our homeland. The extraordinary command that we gave to the younger Titus Norbanus is one of those things. We allowed him proconsular power, and now we must render him proconsular honors. He is at the head of a large army made up of men who by now adore him. He has made them rich and has gotten very few of them killed in the process. It would be ill-advised of us to alienate such men."

Gabinius stood. "I agree with our consul. It pains me to see the Senate of Rome humble itself before a young man who has yet to win a major battle or add a foot of territory to Rome's empire, yet it is expedient. If there has been a miscalculation, it was made here when we bestowed upon him a command without his having first held the requisite offices. We will make many more such decisions in the future, and then as now we will have to live with the consequences. He has done something extraordinary, so let's go out and greet this young Alexander."

There was some protest, but in the end the Senate of Rome, at least what was available of it with so many members away with the legions, set out for the encampment upon the Field of Mars, the traditional drill and exercise ground northwest of the city. Here the legions of Norbanus had set up their tents, and the place swarmed with citizens, slaves and foreigners who had poured from the city to greet the returning heroes. It was a short walk from the Senate house out the Fontinalis Gate and along the Clivus Argentarius to the great field.

At the Senate's approach, the trumpets sounded and the legions drew up as if for inspection. As the senators passed the soldiers, they examined them. Some senators were amused, others appalled.

"Did you ever see such a pack of bandits?" asked one.

"They look—*successful*," hazarded another.

The legionaries wore tunics of every conceivable color. Most had managed to retain their Roman armor, but some wore Greek, Syrian or Judean gear, and there were some peculiar helmets. Many wore helmet crests made from the feathers of birds previously unseen by Romans. They sported splendid cloaks and wore a great deal of gold and silver. Even amid all this finery, they were burned dark and splendidly fit.

"They look dangerous," commented Gabinius.

"To Rome's enemies or to Rome?" asked a companion in a low voice.

"To any who displease them," Gabinius answered.

They found Titus Norbanus the younger awaiting them in front of the biggest tent any of them had ever seen. Its colors were extravagant, and on the ground before it were spread carpets of fabulous weave. Around the tent were set huge braziers of worked bronze, in which burned a fortune in incense, perfuming the air.

"Is that a tent or has he raised a temple to himself?" quipped a senator.

"Do try not to look too impressed, gentlemen," Gabinius sighed. "The boy seems to think quite enough of himself as it is."

Only when the lictors who preceded the consuls stepped onto the carpeted ground did Norbanus make his appearance, striding from within the tent, smiling. At the sight of him, jaws dropped and eyes bugged. He wore his golden armor, patterned on Alexander's, and he carried his lion-mask helmet. The hilt of his sword was of ivory carved with an eagle's head. His belt was made of plates of solid gold. Instead of soldiers' hobnailed caligae, he wore Greek hunting boots that laced to the knee and were topped with lynx skin.

What raised their outrage, though, was his cloak. It was voluminous and trailed behind him in graceful folds. It was also dyed with Tyrian purple. Someone made a strangled sound, but the consuls made calming gestures.

"Welcome to Rome, Titus Norbanus," said the Consul Hermanicus.

"I greet the noble Senate," Norbanus said.

"We can hardly help noting," said the other consul, "that you are wearing a *triumphator's* robe. By what right do you assume this?"

Norbanus stroked the incredible garment. "This was a gift from King Jonathan of Judea. It was not voted by the Senate."

"Take it off!" shouted several senators.

"One day I will enter Rome in triumph, and then I shall wear it as part of my regalia. In the meantime, I am outside the walls and can wear anything I want." He savored the fuming for a few moments, then: "But let's not bicker, honored senators. Please come into my tent. I have something within that you will wish to see."

Baffled by such presumption, they went within. Light of many colors shone through the cloth of the roof, revealing that spectacular hangings encircled the walls. A set of bleachers had been erected within, shaped like a horseshoe and rising to five tiers of seats, but no wood could be seen. All was covered with carpeting, rich cloth and animal skins. At one end stood a dais for the consuls, with twin curule chairs made of carved ivory, the seats draped with the striped skins of Indian tigers.

But what drew the amazed eyes of the senators was not the tent, or the incredible seating arrangements, but what lay within the horseshoe of seats. Upon the carpeted ground was a map, but such a map as none of them had ever seen. It was not drawn, but modeled in three dimensions. It showed the western half of the Middle Sea, from Italy in the north and Carthage in the south, westward all the way to the Pillars of Hercules. The mainland and islands were subtly carved from fragrant woods; the cities modeled in gold and silver and carved amber inlaid with jewels. The principal roads were inlaid in silver, as was the lettering that identified every feature. Most intriguing of all was the sea itself: It was made of some shiny, rippling blue cloth.

"Pollux!" someone croaked at last. "That sea is made of silk!" It was the most precious substance on earth, and here were hundreds of yards of it used to make a map!

"Gentlemen," Norbanus said, "if you will take your seats, I will make a proposal that I believe you will all find to be of greatest interest."

Silently, the senators filed into the bleachers as the consuls took their curule chairs and the lictors ranged themselves before the serving magistrates. Gabinius took his own place without comment. He knew the boy had them now, as surely as a man who has thoroughly seduced a woman—not by the glory of his arms, or the greatness of his accomplishments. No, he had won them more subtly, using a great national weakness: the Romans' childlike love of spectacle. He was putting on a presentation worthy of the funeral games for a great leader.

Now young Norbanus was joined by the previous year's consul, his father. The elder Norbanus wore military uniform, ready to take up a proconsular command voted by the Senate. He looked upon his son and beamed with pride. At precisely the right moment, young Norbanus stepped out onto the sea and walked across it as if he were able to stride upon water. The spectators gasped. A man dared to walk on silk!

"Noble senators, revered consuls," young Norbanus began, "I return to you with a vast treasure, more wealth than Rome ever saw in her most glorious days before Hannibal. Even now, my slaves prepare to carry the bulk of it to the Temple of Saturn." From ancient times, the crypts beneath that temple had served as Rome's principal treasury.

"I bring four legions, experienced as no legions have ever before been, accompanied by auxilia who have volunteered themselves to Rome's service. All these fighting men, the finest in the world, await the orders of the noble Senate." He paused and looked over his map, half turning to take it all in, like Jupiter himself surveying his kingdom. "And yet this treasure is not safe. Rome is not safe. Because, senators and consuls, Carthage still stands!" On the last three words his voice rose to a thrilling shout. He held them spellbound, experienced orators though they were.

"Senators, I stand before you as Rome's most loyal servant. Outside stand Rome's most capable soldiers. Use us! I did not just lead the greatest march in Roman history so that I could stay here and build a villa and bask in the admiration of my peers. Senators, my march is not yet half-completed!"

The senators muttered and looked at one another. What could he mean?

"Senators, for more than a hundred years we let our minds be fixated upon one thought: Destroy Carthage! Like a man tracking a lion to its den, we thought only of going south, taking Sicily, and jumping off from there to attack the great city itself. We thought about this so single-mindedly that we left a back door open to the Carthaginians. We forgot that they could attack us from the north, despite the fact that Hannibal did that very thing! Only by luck and the favor of the gods did we survive this blunder. The soldiers fought like Romans always do, and the

Carthaginian general, while better than ours, was no Hannibal. Look!"

He pointed a beringed finger at the golden model of Rome, then drew an imaginary line along the Italian coast northward to Cisalpine Gaul, then along its southern coast and that of Spain.

"I propose that I take my army and march north. I will pick up the legions that replaced those lost at the Arnus and with them proceed through Gaul to Spain and the Pillars of Hercules. I will take every city along my route: Massilia, Narbo, Cartago Nova and the rest. I will reduce them and make them swear obedience to Rome. Any natives who resist I will crush. Any Carthaginian army I meet I will destroy, and I swear by all the gods that I will not spare a single man who takes the pay of Hamilcar. All must die."

Now he looked at Africa. "From Spain I will cross the strait to Mauretania and then march east. I will make alliance with the kings and chieftains of Numidia and Libya. Failing that, I will crush them, too. I will strike the city of Carthage from the west, while the main force strikes from Sicily. We will have Carthage in a vise and she will crack open like rotten wood."

"How will such a campaign be supported, even supposing we agree to it?" Gabinius asked.

"I have a navy now, a very large one. It will accompany my march and will deal with any Carthaginian fleet that dares show itself."

An elderly Brutus stood. "*Your* army! *Your* fleet! Have *you* become Rome, young Norbanus?"

Norbanus did not flinch. "We knew what the gods wanted when the eagles flew south from Noricum. I think the gods have now shown that they favor me. Dare their displeasure if you will."

The Senate held its collective breath, but Jupiter sent no lightning.

"And I want the main thrust, to be launched from Sicily, to be commanded by my father, Titus Norbanus the elder."

The uproar was fit to rend the roof and send it skyward in tattered ribbons. The consuls sent their lictors into the bleachers to enforce silence.

"General Norbanus," said the Consul Gracchus when order was restored, "we cannot contemplate a major campaign in which members of the same family hold the highest command. We have already apportioned military duties for the upcoming invasion of Africa. Your father, the Proconsul Norbanus, of course has a splendid command, with three legions assigned to the first thrust against Carthage. But overall command has been given to the Proconsul Scaeva, hero of Syracuse. You both deserve honor, but not this." There came a rumble of agreement.

Now the elder Norbanus stepped forward. He had nothing like his son's dash and flair, and he wore plain iron mail of Gallic make and carried a simple bronze helmet beneath his arm, but he was a man of impressive gravity. "Noble senators, there will be quibbling in this house until we all die of old age. My son's war plan is bold, but it is worthy of Rome, where only greatness is acceptable. You may call for a division of the house, you may call for ten divisions. It does not matter, because this will be determined by the Roman people."

He swept the assembled senators with his eagle gaze. "Even now, the tribunes of the plebs are calling for an assembly. The Tribune Aemilius will place before the people a new law, the *lex Aemilia,* which will assign the commands for this war exactly as has just been outlined to you. That law will pass, I assure you. You can accede gracefully and ratify the law, or you can continue in stiff-necked opposition, but then you will only earn the contempt the people always give to obstinate aristocrats."

In the low mutter that followed this statement, Gabinius sat with his eyes closed, feeling every one of his many years. Much was clear now. All year there had been rumors: that young Norbanus was sending chests of money from the East, that some decidedly odd men were standing for the office of tribune of the plebs. He had paid little attention at the time. Strange things were bound to happen when all the best men were away with the legions. Now he understood what had been happening all along. The Norbani had accomplished something very like a coup.

He looked around at his fellow senators. Had this been an ordinary session, had the younger senators not been away on military service, violence would have broken out by now. Weapons might have been drawn. These men were too old or unfit to resist strongly, and that, too, had been a part of the Norbanus plan. He rose, leaning on his walking stick, and slowly the Senate quieted.

"My colleagues, I see that a new star has risen in the Roman firmament. In the past, since we expelled the Etruscan kings, it has been our practice to see that no one family, no one man, ever held the power that we once granted only to kings. But who is to say that this did not bring upon us many disastrous defeats? Perhaps a Roman king would have crushed Hannibal in the first battle. No matter. What is absolutely clear is that these are extraordinary times. At this hour, we are as the Greek army before Troy, when the actions of Agamemnon offended Apollo. Are we to send Achilles to his tent to sulk in the hour when we need him most?" He gestured eloquently in supplication to his peers. Then he went on.

"I think not. You all know me. None has been so firm in opposing the pretensions of military adventurers. None has been so staunch in defense of our ancient liberties. Yet, all of you know me as a voice of reason. When many accused young Scipio of treason, I counseled that we give him his head. He is doing something new; let us see what he can make of it. When others said that young Norbanus was far exceeding the authority granted him, I said that we put him in a terrible position, let him extricate himself and his men as he may. And now who can say that he has not succeeded gloriously?

"Now this same youth proposes something incredible. He wants to finish a complete circumambulation of the Middle Sea by a Roman army, finishing with a siege of Carthage. Is this overweening ambition? Absolutely. But I agree with his father. This thing is *worthy*! The gods do not expect less of us. I, wholeheartedly and in advance of any decision by the *Consilium Plebis,* say that we must give Norbanus the younger what he demands." Abruptly, he sat. He hoped fervently that his colleagues would understand his implication: that by conceding, they set the incredibly ambitious boy up to fail in a spectacular manner. And if he should succeed?

Well, Gabinius thought, *perhaps this is the future and the will of the gods: that Rome be ruled henceforth by its best generals instead of its oldest families. Who is to say that this is not just?*

While the Senate debated, the two Norbani came to speak with the princeps.

"That was the sort of statesmanship that raised Rome to power over the barbarians," the elder Norbanus said.

"I did not expect this, Princeps," said the younger.

Hands folded atop his cane, Gabinius studied the glittering boy before him. "You have risen far and fast, young

Titus. Men have risen so before. Rome has a way of raising such men in times of crisis. Rome also has a way of tearing them down as swiftly."

The father smiled crookedly. "You think I haven't told him that?"

"You are making mortal enemies," Gabinius pointed out.

"The greatness of a man is judged by the number and quality of his enemies," said Norbanus the younger. "What else is the point of our lives?" It was the simple philosophy of the Senate, an intensely competitive body of men in which each strove for honor above his peers.

"Much leeway is granted the truly gifted among us," Gabinius told him. "Those touched by the gods are not always treated as ordinary men. But their actions must always be understood to be for Rome's benefit, not their own."

Young Norbanus bristled, but his father stepped in smoothly. "No one has ever accused the Norbani of disloyalty, or of striving for their own glory to the detriment of Rome's welfare. But this is our hour, and Rome will be the greater for it."

Gabinius nodded, knowing destiny when it stared him in the face. In time the senators came to an agreement and they descended from the seats, coming down onto the "sea" to congratulate the Norbani.

I have lived to see the Senate of Rome walking on silk, Gabinius thought. *What can this portend for the future?*

CHAPTER FIFTEEN

"**M**Y INSTRUCTIONS ARE QUITE UNEQUIVOCAL,"
Marcus Scipio explained. "I am to proceed against
Carthage upon orders from the Senate, which, it is implied,
will not be long in coming."

"You won't frighten the Carthaginians much," said Selene. "Just two Romans, though I've given you impressive
uniforms."

The Romans and the de facto queen of Egypt were alone
in her conference room, as Scipio had insisted.

"It is understood that I will arrive at the harbor of
Carthage with a sizable navy, including the new vessels designed by the Archimedeans."

"I believe the navy you refer to is the Egyptian navy, not
the Roman. It is mine."

"And, Your Majesty," Flaccus said smoothly, "it is for
that very reason that we speak with you today. Rome is at
war with Carthage. Egypt is at war with Carthage. An alliance only makes sense."

"Why?" she asked. "Hamilcar attacked Alexandria. Hamilcar was defeated. He has gone back to Carthage. I do not see why I should undertake an expensive, destructive war out of pique."

"Majesty," Scipio said, trying to hold his temper, "it is not enough to drive an enemy away. To be safe, you must track him to his lair and destroy both the enemy and the lair. It is the only way."

"Say you so?" She studied him coolly. "I am most grateful for your contributions to the defense of Alexandria, yet I recall that there were Roman legions with Hamilcar's army. They were instrumental in defeating my brother's force in the first battle, and then they ravaged their way down the Nile doing great harm."

"Yes," Flaccus agreed, "but there was no Rome-Carthage alliance. The agreement was purely one of convenience, and terminated when we invaded Sicily."

"I see," she said without expression. "And what if it should suit your 'convenience' to turn against Egypt as well? How am I to know that you will treat me any less treacherously than you treated Hamilcar?"

"Treachery?" Scipio shouted, his face going crimson. "There was no treachery! Hamilcar insisted on regarding the legions as mercenaries, mere hirelings. That in itself was a deadly insult! Rome owed him no friendship, no loyalty."

"If, on the other hand," Flaccus added, "Your Majesty signs a treaty of alliance with Rome, your position will be absolutely unassailable. Your enemies become ours and you may call upon the legions of Rome at any threat. This is no small thing. Rome is most scrupulous about observing the particulars of treaties."

"Let me think about this," she said. "You will have my answer tomorrow. You have my leave to go now."

The men bowed and withdrew. They left the conference room and passed through a crowd of courtiers, their faces set in the impassive Roman mask. They crossed a wide courtyard and entered their own quarters, where Scipio threw his helmet across the room against the wall. It fell to the floor, flattened on one side and its precious plumes tattered.

"Damn the woman!" he shouted. "Two years of sweet talk and cooperation—I save her city, her kingdom, her throne and her life, and this is how she treats us! How am I to face the Senate if I can't get an Egyptian alliance after all this!"

"Calm yourself, Marcus," Flaccus said, pouring them both some wine. "She is just playing with us. She wants to remind us that she is a sovereign queen—"

"She's not a sovereign queen," Scipio reminded him. "She's a princess and her brother is the king. She rules through our actions and favor."

"Nonetheless, she does not want to be seen as our puppet. Her court and the city of Alexandria must perceive her as a divine ruler and descendant of Ptolemy the Great, not a client of the Roman Senate. They've deposed other rulers who showed themselves to be under the thumb of foreigners. Believe me, she knows that her only future lies in alliance with Rome. She just has to grant it, not beg for it."

"Graciously grant this to *me,* eh?" He thumped himself on his bronze-sheathed chest. "The man to whom she owes everything?"

"Rulers don't like to be reminded of their debts," Flaccus told him. "They'd rather be praised for their greatness." He paused. "You must face it, Marcus: You have no legions. You can't impose your will on a foreign ruler, like Norbanus."

"Norbanus!" Scipio said, exasperated. Friends in Rome

had sent them word of his new march and the war plan. "The gods must love him. He will be immortal."

"He's just been lucky," Flaccus said. "He was born to an important family; he was chosen for the reconnaissance mission; he was on the spot when a commander was needed and it coincided with his father's consulship. Then he made his march just at a time when the territory he went through was disorganized and fought over by petty princelings."

"Luck like that is proof of the gods' favor."

"This is not like you, Marcus. You shouldn't allow a schoolboy rivalry to sour you. Your own accomplishments have been fabulous."

"I don't envy the reputation he's won!" He took a deep swallow from the golden cup, then set it on an ivory-inlaid table. "Not much, anyway. No, the man is a menace to the republic. He wants to make himself dictator, or king."

"Your enemies in the Senate say exactly the same of you," Flaccus pointed out.

"Yes, but my enemies are wrong, whereas I am right. His own father to command the main army! How could he make his dynastic ambitions more plain? And taking his army on a complete circuit of the Middle Sea! He's just doing it because no one else has done it before!"

Flaccus nodded somberly. "Yes, the expense in boots and hobnails alone must be staggering."

"Don't be flippant," Marcus said disgustedly.

"You know he's overreaching himself. His battle experience hasn't been great, and Carthage will be throwing its best against him. He's being set up to fail; that's the only explanation why the Senate has gone along with his harebrained scheme."

Scipio refilled his cup and stared into it gloomily. "It's

not that bad a scheme, you know, just ambitious. I might have proposed such a thing myself, only I would have waited until all these new legions were more experienced and our leadership had a better grasp of how to command and coordinate so many men. As it is, there are too many ways for things to go wrong. We'll be trying to coordinate the movements of large armies over vast distances . . ." He trailed off, his eyes going vacant.

That was more like it, Flaccus thought. Now his friend was going over the possibilities in his mind, finding applications for the new inventions of the Archimedean school.

"They say Norbanus has a pair of Eastern women to read the stars for him," Flaccus remarked. "Alexandria is full of astrologers and I have been speaking with the Egyptian and Greek priests about them. They seem about evenly divided whether the stars are of any use in foretelling the future. Norbanus seems to set great store by these two."

"It's a weakness," Scipio said. "They're just telling him what he wants to hear."

"That has long been a major part of the seer's art," Flaccus said. "That and being equivocal, making statements that could be interpreted more than one way and fitting any outcome."

"What are you getting at?" Marcus asked, knowing his friend all too well.

"As you pointed out, this reliance upon soothsayers is a weakness, and an enemy's weakness is something to be exploited."

"Subvert his astrologers? But how? They are rather far away, you know."

"True, true. But we are in the process of turning the Middle Sea into a Roman lake. The Archimedeans have designed some extremely swift vessels. Why should we not wish to keep in contact with Norbanus's army on its march? It only makes military sense."

"It does," Scipio agreed. "The Senate will resent such collusion. They would prefer to hold the reins."

"What of it?" Flaccus asked. "We now have armies spread out over vast distances. Our generals will be nearly autonomous of necessity, whatever the Senate wants. What's sitting in Rome right now is an elderly pack of old soldiers reminiscing about their younger days when Roman soldiers were real Romans. They think what we're doing is the same as fighting German tribesmen on the Northern Sea."

Marcus was silent for a while. "No, we can't do it."

"What? Keep in contact with Norbanus's army?"

"No, that's an excellent idea. I mean we can't subvert these prophetesses or whatever they are."

"Whyever not? The opportunity is there. Norbanus is your enemy. Do something to him before he does it to you. It's the sensible thing to do."

"Should I endanger Rome for the sake of a personal vendetta? My sabotage might result in a Roman defeat. It's not something I can do just to trump a man I detest."

Flaccus sighed. "Marcus, you are a splendid soldier. You are a genuine visionary. But you are a political infant. To defeat a rival, you use whatever comes to hand. These Judean woman are a gift from the gods which you spurn at your peril."

"Still, I reject them. Let the gods punish me for rejecting their favor."

At this Flaccus held his counsel.

The next morning they were at the naval shipyard, which had been all but taken over by the Archimedean school. There were vessels under construction and on the slips and in the water that were unlike anything ever seen before.

There were also many craft of foreign design brought by the queen's order from the most distant waters. Their hull and sail designs were copied, analyzed and experimented with.

"What about that madman with the steam project?" Scipio asked the ship philosopher, head of the facility. He was a Spanish Greek named Archelaus.

"Worthless," he said. "He's trying to adapt it to water wheels and screw-type water raisers using a system of metal tubes and rods and sliding cylinders, but it can't possibly work."

"Why not?" Scipio asked.

"Two reasons. One is the weight. Even if the machine can be made to work, it will require a great weight of metal. Another is the fire. The last thing you want on a ship is a big fire. And you'd have to go ashore constantly to replenish the firewood. No, it has no real advantage over rowers, who need nothing but food."

"Well, what else, then? I know we've been concentrating on coastal warships and harbor defense, but I need a cutter that can cover great distances on open water fast. It can't carry a lot of rowers. I don't want it putting in to shore every day or two. It should keep on the move every hour, even traveling at night."

"That's a challenge. What is it to carry?"

"Aside from sustenance for the crew, just information. I want the water equivalent of a horseback courier. It's to keep me in contact with an army that will be constantly on the march."

Archelaus nodded, stroking his small beard. "I see. How intriguing. And how fortuitous. Come with me."

The two Romans followed the man. He led them past a barge-like boat, its deck holding a number of the flying machines and equipped with a system of towering masts from which to launch them. Other ships were fitted with paddle wheels, with varying arrangements of cranks and treadmills to drive them. They came to a pier to which were fastened several small vessels featuring a bewildering array of masts, yards and sails.

"Here," Archelaus informed them, "we experiment with new sail plans and rigging systems."

"And how do these affect performance?" Flaccus asked.

"In many ways, we have found. We've been using a single, large, square sail spread before the mast since the Argo. With a wind astern, it moves the ship well. But only if the wind is from almost directly astern."

"That much we know from our admittedly limited seafaring experience," Flaccus said. "How may it be done otherwise?"

"Look at this." They came to a small, narrow vessel. It was no more than forty feet long and had the familiar, single mast. But its yard, instead of being set square across the length of the vessel, slanted across it. "You can't get a good idea from this; you'll have to see it sailing. It's copied from a type of ship used off the coast of India. One of our skippers brought one back this season, along with some Indian sailors to show us how it is employed."

"What is its advantage?" Marcus wanted to know.

"It can make use of a wind that is not blowing from directly astern. With skill, using both sail and steering oar, it can even make use of a wind that comes from slightly ahead."

"Sail into a headwind?" Flaccus said. "That makes no sense."

"As I said, you'll have to see it demonstrated. It takes a skilled crew, but it needs only five or six men. We built this one small, because it was to be used just for experiment with the sail. There's no cargo space and precious little for the crew. But it may be ideal for your purpose. If all you want is a courier, this is it."

"Show us," Marcus said.

And so the little vessel set out with its small crew and two Romans, first in the sheltered waters of the harbor, then past Point Lochias into the open sea. All morning and into the afternoon the shipmaster, a hard-bitten old pirate from Cilicia, and his crew of strange men from fabled India, demonstrated the bizarre sail and its seemingly unnatural capabilities. It proved to be triangular, and when set, its extremely long yard almost touched the bow rail on one side of the ship, while the opposite end towered above the stern on the opposite side. It was huge in proportion to the vessel, and the Romans remarked upon this.

"It's a lot of mast and sail for such a small ship," the master agreed. "She has to be heavily ballasted to keep her from capsizing. Her bottom's filled with lead bricks to keep her upright."

He showed them how, by a combination of slanting the sail and working the steering oar, the ship could take advantage of a less-than-favorable wind. After taking the wind from one side for a while, at the master's order the crew performed a breathtaking maneuver, collapsing the sail and slewing the long yard up and across to hang on the other side of the mast and take the same wind from that side. The ship changed direction, but its general trend was still in the direction desired.

"You see?" the skipper said. "When the wind's not right, you travel in a series of zigzags to keep moving ahead. It's not as fast as with a stern wind, but it beats sitting on shore and sacrificing rams for one."

"What about a wind from directly ahead?" Marcus asked.

"Not much you can do about that," the skipper admitted. "This sail's clever, but it's not magical. Still, if you want to get from one end of the sea to the other and you don't want to feed a lot of oarsmen doing it, this rig will beat anything else afloat."

By the time they returned to the harbor, Marcus had decided. The little vessel would be the first of his new fleet of courier craft. As soon as he set foot to the pier, he was bellowing for the master shipbuilder, the harbormaster and the ship philosopher. He said that he wanted twenty of the ships for a start, and training of the crews was to begin immediately, that very day. He named the little ship *Hermes*. There was no argument. Functionaries and workmen had grown accustomed to the peremptory ways of the Romans.

"And get some paint on that ship," Flaccus said, pointing to *Hermes*. "She's plain as a fishing boat."

"Any color in particular?" asked the master shipbuilder dryly.

The Romans considered this. "I think blue would be good," said Flaccus.

Scipio nodded. "Blue with gold trim. Paint all our courier vessels that way. And dye the sails blue as well. Can you do that?"

The master shipbuilder rolled his eyes skyward. "As long as you don't insist on Tyrian purple, I think we can manage."

"What about a device?" Marcus mused. "Our new Roman navy uses Jupiter's eagle, but the queen might resent that. What's that sea-horse thing?"

"The *hippokampus*, you mean?" Flaccus asked. "The front part of a horse and a long fish-tail behind?"

"That's it. Master shipbuilder, decorate the sails with the

hippocampus, and carve them as figureheads, above where the ram would be, if these ships had rams."

"It shall be done," promised the official.

Pleased with their day's work, the Romans returned to the palace. A steward summoned them to the queen's presence. They found her waiting in her privy chamber next to the throne room. She frowned when she saw Marcus.

"Where is the helmet I gave you?"

"It suffered some damage," he told her. "The armorer and the jeweler are working on it now."

"Must you practice at swords in your best dress uniform?" she asked, exasperated. "Well, never mind. Just make the best show you can. We are going to perform before the court. I am going out there now. You be ready to come at my summons." Amid a flurry of serving girls and fan wavers, she strode out into the vast room and took her seat next to her brother. A hundred courtiers and foreign dignitaries bowed deeply and made sounds of worshipful admiration.

"What's it to be, do you think?" Flaccus asked. "A treaty or our execution?"

Marcus gave it some thought. "I don't think she'd have inquired about my helmet if she planned to have us killed."

A few minutes later the steward summoned them and they followed him into the throne room. They passed between lines of dignitaries, many of them attended by their own retinues, most of whom watched the Romans with calculation as they made their way toward the dais that held the twin thrones.

Not quite twins, though. Selene's throne, to the right of her brother's, was slightly higher. Ptolemy, still no more than a boy, sat sullenly, watching the Romans with no favor. They had eliminated his counselors and set his sister above him. She had made him dress decently in Greek fashion, without the wigs and cosmetics with which his former handlers had adorned him.

The Romans halted before the dais and bowed in the only fashion approved by Roman etiquette: a slight inclination of the head.

"I wish it to be known to the people of Egypt," Selene began, "to the Senate and people of Rome, and to all the world, that Hamilcar of Carthage is a menace to the lives and liberties of all people who dwell around the Middle Sea. In all the world, there are only two nations capable of resisting his vicious aggression: the glorious kingdom of Egypt and the Republic of Rome with its dauntless legions. To this end, I proclaim a treaty of alliance and friendship between the nations of Egypt and Rome." She held a hand out to one side and an official placed a scroll into her upturned palm. With a hieratic gesture she brought it before her and unrolled it, with her arms at full extension. It looked impressive, made of parchment from Pergamum instead of the more common papyrus. It bore a great deal of gold leaf, lavishly applied, and carried a large waxen seal stamped with the Ptolemaic device and a somewhat smaller seal stamped with Selene's personal cartouche, with her Egyptian reign-name in hieroglyphics. The text was written in austere Attic Greek letters.

"This document," she announced, "makes official and lasting the relationship between our nations. It specifies trade relations, mutual rights to port facilities, the aid and repatriation of shipwrecked mariners and so forth. It spells out the relative values of goods and spheres of trade influence. These are very simple, because Rome is not a commercial power and there is almost no problem of competition.

"In the military sphere, our armed forces are to operate as one in the war with Hamilcar of Carthage. Rome's army is formidable, but her navy is in its infancy, small and untried against the naval might of Carthage. Egypt's navy is great, and I shall call upon the ships of our sister kingdom of Cyprus and our allies of Rhodes, Crete and the Greek cities of Asia. Together, we will prove more than a match for Hamilcar.

"Our land formations will be commanded at the unit level by our professional officer corps, under the overall direction of our good and trusted friend, Marcus Cornelius Scipio of Rome." She looked at the Romans. "Marcus Cornelius Scipio, approach."

He took the few steps forward. With an efficient gesture she rerolled the treaty and handed it to him. He accepted it with the same minuscule bow. She held her hand to one side again and a different official gave her a massive collar of gold. This she placed over Marcus's head, forcing him to bend his neck a bit more.

"Show a little humility," she whispered, "you arrogant twit!"

This ceremony accomplished, Marcus backed away a few steps. "On behalf of the Senate and People of Rome, I accept this document for the Senate's approval, which, I have no doubt, will be granted wholeheartedly. This signals a new era for Rome, for Egypt and for the world. Not for many lifetimes have two great powers sworn friendship and cooperation. Never before have two such united to resist the depredations of a would-be conqueror.

"When Egypt and Rome together have eliminated for all time the threat of Carthage, all the world that borders the Middle Sea may look forward to a golden age, for Rome and

Egypt together will protect them from any who henceforth would aspire to the crown and empire and reputation of Alexander."

To this Selene said nothing, but her look, and that of the onlookers, said it all: *And who will protect the world from you Romans?*

CHAPTER SIXTEEN

"A SHIP," THE SIGNALS OFFICER ANNOUNCED. THE massive army of Titus Norbanus the younger was encamped outside the walls of Massilia, an old Greek colony established on the southern coast of Gaul, where it had prospered mightily. Norbanus had demanded their immediate surrender, but the citizens feared Roman reprisal because they had contributed troops to Mastanabal's army.

Norbanus looked up from where he stood on his command platform. The city was not yet formally under siege, pending a decision of its council, but Norbanus liked to keep control from a position that left no one in doubt of his military preeminence.

"What sort of ship, and is it alone?" he asked.

The signals officer stood with the rest of his staff to one side of the platform. He was squinting toward a small headland to the southeast, where lights flashed from mirrors of polished silver. "A single vessel of unknown type," he reported.

"Unknown type? How many are there? Is it military or a merchant vessel?"

From where they stood the sun was at the wrong angle for mirror signaling, and there was too much wind for smoke, so the signals officer ordered certain flags raised on long poles and waved according to his direction. More flashes answered. "Says he doesn't know."

"Doesn't know, eh?" Norbanus said. "If it turns out to be some common vessel, I'll have his balls for lunch."

"My staff know their work, General," the signals officer replied stiffly.

Norbanus had lost interest. He studied the walls opposite him, assault plans running through his head. He did not want to lay siege to this place, but he would if necessary. He had several reasons for reluctance. One was delay. He was impatient to come to grips with Hamilcar before some other Roman commander, even his father, should have a chance to. Another was a certain proposal he had in mind to put before the Massiliotes; one he thought would surprise them. But barring a favorable outcome, he would massacre them all. He did not really wish to slaughter civilized Greeks, particularly the inhabitants of a city that had sided with Rome in the wars with Carthage. But if an example had to be made, he would make it here.

"There it is!" someone shouted later. Norbanus looked to see a bizarre little ship rounding the cape. Actually, he thought, the ship itself was not especially odd. But its long, triangular sail was unlike anything he had seen before. Not that his nautical experience was vast. Like most Romans, he had never laid eyes upon the sea until crossing south of the Alps less than three years previously. Only a few Romans who had traveled or soldiered as far as the Northern Sea had seen such a body of water, and seafaring was utterly new to

them. Still, all the sails Norbanus had laid eyes on before
were square.

"Go get the fleet master," he ordered, and a messenger
hurried off. Norbanus's fleet filled Massilia's splendid harbor, and while Roman officers commanded it, most of the
ships had Greek sailing masters under the direction of a
Greek fleet master. The Romans were still too new on the
water to trust their own skills. The weather-beaten Greek
climbed to the platform and saluted.

"What sort of ship is that?" Norbanus asked, pointing to
the little craft just making its way through the fleet in the
harbor.

"Never saw the like of it," the man admitted. "I've heard
of Indian ships that must look like that, but never laid eyes
on one. The hull looks Alexandrian, so I'd say what we have
here is one of the toys they've been playing with. I'd like to
get aboard her and see how that sail works."

Even as they spoke, the yard lowered and the blue sail
with its hippocampus was furled. Long sweeps, three to a
side, were run out and the ship was laboriously rowed up to
a stone pier.

"Scipio," Norbanus said, shaking his head. "Does he
think he can impress me with another of his playthings? If
so, he should have sent one of those flying men I hear he has.
Now that would impress me." His officers chuckled. Nobody knew whether they should believe the stories coming
out of Alexandria.

Norbanus studied the angle of the sun. "It's late," he announced. "There won't be any fighting today. If that boat
carries anyone of importance, send them to my tent."

Later, he was sitting at dinner with his officers when two
men were ushered in. They were Greeks with the look of
scholars, but they carried a number of document cases that

bore Roman markings. They bowed before the general and introduced themselves.

"Zeno and Izates?" Norbanus said. "I've heard of you. Some sort of philosopher-historians with a roving commission from the Senate as messengers and envoys, aren't you?"

"That is roughly the situation," said the handsomer of the two. "I can't claim that we have any official status, but we've been enjoying the duties immensely."

"Spoken like a true Greek," Norbanus said. "Have a seat and join us for dinner while I look over what you've brought us." The first document to come beneath his eye was from Marcus Scipio. This one he set aside for later, so as not to ruin his appetite. Others were from the Senate and from contacts in Rome and on Sicily. The little ship had stopped at Syracuse and Ostia on its way to him. These he perused with interest. His father was now at Lilybaeum, amassing his army. The city was the westernmost point of the island, just a short hop across the strait from Carthage—always assuming that the Carthaginian fleet would not interfere with the hop.

The elder Norbanus informed his son that there had been great anger and bitterness when he arrived to take over command. Scaeva and his principal officers were outraged that, after securing Sicily for Rome, they were to be shunted aside in favor of a proconsul just sent out from Rome with his own clique of senior officers. The old family officers, headed by the Cornelia Scipiones, were his enemies to a man. Had they not been Romans, he wrote, and sticklers for subordination to Senate orders, there would have been mutiny.

The legionaries grumbled a bit but there had been no serious insubordination. With the huge expansion of the legions, the bulk of them were new family men, most of them just a generation or two removed from their Gallic and German tribal origins. They might admire the officers who had led them to victory, but they resented the aristocratic airs of too many of them to allow a takeover by a Norbanus to upset them.

The Senate communications he scanned briefly and set aside. *A pack of fretting old women*, he thought, *afraid now because they've just realized that practically every Roman soldier is away from Italy.* They were sending him several cohorts of the newly raised auxiliary forces, mostly Italian natives and many of them freshly retired from their vocation as bandits. He looked forward to trying them out. They might prove useful and would certainly be expendable. Highly trained Roman legionaries were never expendable.

"One other thing we've brought you," said the Greek named Zeno. "It's a gift from Quee—that is, the Princess Regent Selene." He produced a beautiful wooden box inlaid with shell and ivory. It was about a cubit long. He slipped its delicate latch and opened the lid. Inside was what looked like a tube of dark wood, both ends ringed with bronze chased with a Greek key fret. From one end protruded a circle of ivory shaped like a shallow cup.

"What is it?" Norbanus asked, intrigued despite himself. The thing looked valuable.

"Another product of the Archimedean school." Zeno took the thing from the box. First he showed Norbanus and the others the end lacking the ivory finial. It was covered with a cap of thin bronze, which he removed, displaying a large piece of glass that seemed to be slightly convex. Then he reversed it and showed the ivory end. In its center was a much smaller piece of glass. He grasped the ivory circle and tugged at it. A tube of bronze slid from inside the wooden cylinder.

"This is a device for making distant objects seem nearer. You gaze through the small lens in the ivory eyepiece"—he put the thing to his own eye—"and you aim the larger lens toward the object you wish to examine." He turned and pointed the instrument toward the tent entrance, which faced the landward gate of Massilia. "If the object appears fuzzy, you adjust the length of the instrument until it becomes clear." He showed how minute adjustments could be made to the sliding tube. He handed it to Norbanus. The general put the ivory piece to his eye and aimed the thing toward the gate.

"Can't see a thing. Just a little dot of light that comes and goes away."

"It takes a bit of practice," Zeno told him. "Keep trying and you will get that little dot of light under control. It will open up and then you need merely adjust the length as I demonstrated."

Norbanus played with the thing and was about to give it up when suddenly the light filled the vision of his right eye. Slowly, he worked the tube in and out and, abruptly, the gate of Massilia leapt into stark clarity, seeming a hundred paces closer. He gasped. "It's magic!"

His other officers clamored to try it next and he handed it to Niger. "So they've come up with something useful at last. Please convey the princess my thanks, when you return."

"I shall certainly do so," Zeno said. "And allow me to say that your great feat in marching your army from Egypt all the way back to Italy, and now to Gaul, is the talk of Alexandria: of the whole world, if truth be known."

"So I am told," Norbanus said, nodding. "But I have far more to accomplish before I take my place in the Senate."

"And that is another thing much spoken of," Izates said. "It seems that most Romans receive such great trust only *after* a lengthy tenure in the Senate."

"Our general is not like most Romans," Cato said. "And times are not what they were. Rome must adapt to a new world."

Food was brought in and the wine flowed. The Romans asked for information and gossip from Sicily and Italy, and the two Greeks obliged. There was little discussion of military matters, certainly not of any future prospects for Massilia. Zeno assumed that they guarded their words in the presence of men who could relay them to rivals and enemies.

"I understand, General," said Izates, "that you have astrologers among your retinue."

"I have," Norbanus said, frowning slightly.

"If you will grant me a favor, I would like to consult with them." At Norbanus's deepening frown, he added: "I understand that they are women of your household, and I would never suggest anything improper. It is just that, in the course of my studies, I spoke with a number of astrologers in Alexandria, most of them claiming to be Chaldeans of some sort, and I found almost every one of them to be utterly fraudulent. Yet it seems that these Judean princesses of yours—they are true princesses, I understand?—give you the most reliable advice. I would very much like to speak with practitioners of the true art."

Norbanus nodded. "I think it can be arranged," he said, thinking: *Those two bitches do pretty much as they please anyway, so why not?*

"I am most grateful," Izates said.

After dinner the Greeks took their leave and Norbanus put an officer's tent at their disposal for the length of their stay. When they were gone, he picked up the message from

Marcus Scipio and read it. Once he had its gist, he read it aloud to his officers.

"Just like him," Niger grumbled. "He doesn't command a single legionary, but he wants to keep tabs on us."

"Still," said Cato, "the idea makes sense. Militarily, I mean. Close communication between the armies and navies can be important in a war as big as this one, and it looks like these new boats will do the job better than the older type. Not," he added hastily, "that I'd ever trust a traitor like Marcus Scipio."

Norbanus nodded. "My own thoughts. Well, there's an answer to this: I want my shipmasters and shipwrights to study that little vessel while it's here, learn how to sail it, then build me a flotilla of them. That way I can keep in control of my own flow of information, without everything going through Alexandria and Scipio's hands."

Everyone agreed that this was a brilliant idea.

Outside, the Greeks strolled through the legionary camp, admiring the superb discipline of the soldiers. Norbanus's veterans were easily distinguishable from the men of the new legions recently added to his army. The former were more weather-beaten, and their motley equipment gave them a raffish distinction. The newer legions were made up of mostly younger men, and their arms and clothing were turned out by the new *fabricae* to standardized patterns. It gave them a uniformity of appearance that was odd to the eyes of men accustomed to armies made up of soldiers who were expected to supply their own panoply, usually whatever they had at home or could afford to purchase.

"They're a fierce-looking lot," Izates said, nodding toward a unit of the veterans. A centurion had found some fault with a legionary and was beating him mercilessly with the *vitis:* a stick carried by all centurions for just this purpose. The man being beaten did not betray pain or distress by the slightest change of expression. His comrades, clearly the recipients of many such beatings, looked on with amusement.

"There hasn't been anything like them since the great days of Sparta," Zeno agreed. "I've seen citizen militias of the sort most Greek cities produce, and Macedonian professional phalangists, and mercenaries of the sort hired by Egypt and Carthage. But I've never before seen a nation of men who are professional soldiers from the cradle. Did you know that some Roman officers don't consider men truly reliable until they reach their forties? It's an age when most soldiers give up war for good."

"Our friend Marcus Scipio's one-eyed grandfather still serves in arms. I think old Gabinius would pick up his sword if he wasn't so arthritic."

For a while the Greeks admired the colors of the sunset, then Zeno said: "We could be playing a dangerous game, dealing with these Judean women."

"I've found that I have a taste for dangerous games," Izates said. "We were a pair of penniless, itinerant scholars, and by pure chance we were thrust into the regions of power. Perhaps the gods had a hand in it; perhaps it was blind chance. Whichever, I find that it has a powerful attraction. It's a game where one throws the knucklebones not merely for wealth, not even for life and death. The stakes are lordship and immortal fame. It gives life a flavor that scholarship lacks."

Zeno laughed. "What would Diogenes think of you? A Cynic is supposed to scorn all such things as mere vanity."

"Diogenes was never presented with such an opportunity." He brooded for a while. "I once thought philosophy held the answer to everything. Now I see that far too often it is a turning away from the world. One has no power, therefore one despises power. One has no wealth, so one scorns wealth. It is the old fable of the fox and the grapes, and if that is not vanity, what is?"

"Surely you are not giving up philosophy? It is your whole life."

"Certainly not. But I now know that philosophy as it has come to us has taken some incorrect turns. In the days of Heraclitus, philosophy took all of existence as its subject, and nothing in the cosmos was deemed unworthy of study. But then it came under the domination of Plato and the Academics. Plato was a great philosopher, but he had an aristocratic blindness and taught that the material world was unworthy of a philosopher's attention.

"Chilo and the philosophers of the Archimedean school are very different. They are engaged in the world. They *do* things! They accomplish wonders. True, they sometimes build mere toys for the vulgar mob to marvel at, and they have to please the patron of the Museum, but this enables them to do serious work. I suppose I will always be a questioning Cynic, but I now perceive the world through different eyes. And I confess that playing this game gives me a thrill that even the greatest intellectual accomplishment lacks. I think it must be akin to the exaltation of battle."

"But Marcus Scipio was against suborning these astrologers," Zeno pointed out.

"Marcus Scipio is a remarkable man," Izates said judiciously. "He is a true visionary. But still, he is too much the man of action. He wants to use the Archimedean school and the wealth of Egypt to achieve his ends, whatever those may be. Flaccus, now, he is different. He is more deep-minded, more subtle, more farsighted. He is the least Roman of any Roman we have met thus far. He could almost be a Greek.

And he wants us to undermine Norbanus through the Judean women. In this instance, far from Alexandria, we are well employed in doing his will, rather than Scipio's."

"And how do you propose to approach these women?" Zeno asked. "Bribery seems the usual method, but with what does one tempt women who have attached themselves to a man who is already outrageously wealthy and successful, and who bids fair to become master of the world?"

"A good question, and one that will require some thought. I must meet them, sound them out and find out their weaknesses and desires. We need to know what they want. Perhaps most of all, we need to know what they fear."

The next morning, a delegation of the leading men of Massilia emerged from the city. Led by a pair of white-robed heralds wearing wreaths of laurel and bearing staffs, they walked to the great awning stretched before the command tent of Titus Norbanus. The general sat enthroned upon his dais, seated in a curule chair, enfolded in his purple robe. Behind him stood his principal officers, looking stern.

"Great General Norbanus," said the senior of the heralds, "here before you stand the governors of the Assembly of Massilia." He introduced them, beginning with Socrates, elder of the council. "They come to you under the protection of Apollo, guardian of envoys. Any harm that comes to them in this place must be regarded as sacrilege, and will surely be punished by the immortals."

"Rome yields to none in observance of divine law," announced Lentulus Niger. "These dignitaries are under Rome's protection for the duration of their visit among us. What shall become of them after their return to their city shall be the subject of these negotiations."

"Socrates, son of Archilochus," Norbanus said, addressing the leader of the council, "you have heard already the terms laid down by me: surrender of your city to me, or utter extermination. How have you decided?"

It escaped no one that Norbanus laid down terms and demanded surrender in his own name, not in that of Rome.

Socrates came forward. He was a white-bearded, dignified man who had the look of one who had already accepted his own death. "Great General Norbanus, the ancient and independent city of Massilia is proud, but we Massiliotes understand overwhelming power when we see it. As once we yielded to Carthage, paying tribute and sending our young men to serve in her armies, so we must now bow our necks to Rome. Your army invests our walls and your navy occupies our harbor. Only fools could ignore this, and we are not fools. I know that it is customary for a conqueror to execute the leading men of a surrendered city and to take hostages of the wealthiest houses to ensure loyalty. We ask only that you spare our city and our people."

"You have chosen wisely," Norbanus told the old man. "And I am perfectly within my rights to kill you all, and to sack your town and leave the bulk of the population with nothing but their lives." He paused as if in deep thought. "However, it is also within my power to grant clemency, and in this case, since there has been no fighting and no Roman lives have been lost, I choose to be clement. The lives, houses and treasures of Massilia shall not be harmed. Your young men will now serve with my army and your harbor will shelter my fleet."

Socrates and the rest of the councillors looked stunned. "This is most generous."

"I am generous and just. But you must swear an oath."

"That of course is understood."

"You will swear eternal friendship with Rome. And you will swear yourselves, your city and your descendants to be my clients, and the clients of my family and descendants. You are familiar with the Roman system of clientage?"

"It is similar to that observed by many civilized peoples, is it not? As your clients we vow to support and aid you in all your endeavors. You become our protector in all our dealings with Rome. Massilia and the House of Norbanus will henceforth enjoy a special relationship, beyond that which we will have with Rome."

"That is the case. How do you choose?"

Socrates looked toward his peers, and one by one, in order of rank, they nodded. He turned to Norbanus and bowed. "Most merciful general, let the sacrifices be made. Upon our altars and upon yours, we will take your oath, to bind us everlastingly in the eyes of the gods."

THAT EVENING, WHILE A GREAT FEAST WAS PREPARED to celebrate the new relationship between Massilia, Rome and the glorious Titus Norbanus, the two Greeks met with Roxana and Glaphyra. They spoke in the open, within plain view of all, so that the proprieties should be observed. A space of ground near the general's tent had been carpeted and set with chairs and with a broad table to hold the charts and instruments of the women's craft. Slaves stood discreetly by to attend to their needs.

To the cosmopolitan eyes of the Greeks, the women were not particularly exotic. In deference to their master they had adopted Roman dress, which for women was about as modest as their native Judean. They wore far heavier cosmetics than any respectable Roman woman would, but nothing out of the ordinary by Alexandrian standards. But they were twins, always a strange circumstance, and they had a singular attitude that put both men ill at ease. They were like one creature with two bodies, and that creature was not quite human. Something about their speech and movements was not quite right, and both men wondered whether this might be the result of nature or of calculation.

The women told them of the zodiac, and of the nature of birth signs and of the calculation of fortunes therefrom. They learned of the influence of the planets and of the significance of *kometes*, those "bearded stars" that appeared in the heavens from time to time, marking the advent of momentous events, the death of kings and the coming of great conquerors. Some of this they already knew, for astrologers abounded in Egypt and in other lands as well, but these women truly seemed to possess a far deeper knowledge of the subject than others and claimed access to certain Babylonian texts long thought to be lost.

The men in their turn entertained them with tales of the lands they had visited, of the wonders they had seen, of volcanoes and whales and lands where frankincense was traded by the shipload, where feathers of the giant rukh came in bales, and chests filled with the aphrodisiac horn of the unicorn. Slowly, they steered the conversation toward their city of residence.

"You have come all the way from Alexandria," Glaphyra said. "We have heard so much of Alexandria, and have longed to see it."

"The great palace of the Ptolemys," Roxana said, "the Museum and Library, the Paneum and the Sarapeion and the tomb of Alexander! It must be a place of wonders."

"Jerusalem is such a backwater," Glaphyra said, pouring wine for all of them. "Yet to hear the priests sing of it, it is the wonder of the world."

"Is it not the holiest of your cities, and the residing place of your god?" Zeno asked.

The women shrugged in unison. "Our god is a god of the mountain and desert," Roxana said. "Cities do not seem to be of great concern to him. The prophets of old railed against the wickedness of cities."

"Our faith has a long and unfortunate tradition of unwashed holy men from the wilderness," Glaphyra added. "Thus the values of ragged desert dwellers are exalted as the shining ideal of the cosmos. Anything sophisticated or beautiful, anything pleasurable or artistic—all are condemned as ungodly."

"I quite agree," Izates told them. "I, too, was born in your faith, in the Jewish Quarter of Alexandria. In our quarter there were many reactionary rabbis who condemned the Gentile world as you destribe. Fortunately for me, there were also many enlightened, Hellenized Jews, open to the wonders of learning and philosophy. They understood that clinging to the ancient world of our ancestors is futile. At an early age I took up lectures and studies in the Museum and understood the narrowness of our old ways."

"How fortunate you were," said Roxana. "Our mother was Babylonian, and she taught us much of the wisdom of her homeland, but women, even royal women, have never been permitted a true education in Judea."

"Many women study and even teach at the Museum and the other schools in Alexandria," Izates said. "Our city does not share the prejudice of the rest of the Greek world. I have known women of Alexandria who are distinguished mathematicians, philosophers and astronomers."

"Really?" said both sisters, seeming truly astonished for the first time.

"Very much so. And with the Princess Selene as de facto queen, the position of women in Alexandrian society has seldom been higher."

"It sounds like a vision of Paradise." Glaphyra sighed. "But I fear that our lord, the great General Norbanus, would never permit us to travel there."

"He desires to keep us close always," Roxana concurred.

"You are favored far beyond the lot of common women," Zeno said. "You must be the envy of the princesses of the earth. And yet—"

"'And yet'?" said both women in their disconcerting way.

"Nothing," Zeno said, with a dismissive gesture.

"No, tell us," Glaphyra insisted. "You were about to say that our happiness is not without flaw, weren't you?"

"He was," Roxana said.

"My ladies are most acute," Izates said. "I believe that what my friend was too delicate to say—I am a Cynic, and not nearly so delicate—was that all favors of men are untrustworthy and easily withdrawn. Men are changeable, and rulers the most fickle of all. Their unreliability is literally Proverbial, for does not our own holy book advise: 'Put not thy trust in princes'?"

"And how might such a fortune befall us?" Glaphyra asked. She said it coolly, as if it were an idle remark, but Izates could tell that she had given the matter much thought.

"In many ways, Olympus forbid that any of them befall. I would never suggest that you would give him a prediction that might prove to be wrong, but a ruler may easily be displeased with one that proves to be all too accurate."

"Such things have happened to other seers," Roxana murmured.

"And, forgive me, ladies, but the philosophy of Cynics is very hard on the vanity of the world, as hard as the prophets, but even such radiant beauty as yours must fade with time.

A new mistress or wife can bring about a catastrophic downfall." He said it with great sadness.

"On the other hand," Zeno said, "wisdom and learning such as your own will last a lifetime, in the right setting."

Both women nodded. "The court of Alexandria being such a setting?" Glaphyra said.

"Nowhere else are women such as you held in so much honor," Zeno assured them. "And the learned ladies of Alexandria are free to come and go as they will, to have their own houses and schools, to found their own salons and control all their own properties. Even husbands cannot forbid this, and no woman of learning and property needs the protection of husband or master. So long as they attend at court upon the queen's pleasure, the rest of their time is entirely their own."

"It does sound more attractive than these rough soldiers' camps," Roxana admitted, "or the crude palaces of Judea, with their throngs of ignorant, uneducated women of the great families."

"You would not believe the sort of petty intrigue that prevails there should we tell you of it," said Glaphyra.

"I think we can imagine it," Izates assured her.

"We must consider what you have told us," Roxana said. "These are weighty matters, and not to be taken lightly. Will you be here for long?"

"We sail in a day or two, bearing General Norbanus's correspondence," Zeno said. "But now that the new sea-courier service is under way, the Roman establishment of Egypt and that of the peripatetic General Norbanus will keep in close touch. It may well be that we shall have occasion to call upon you ladies again, soon should that be your pleasure."

"Be sure to inform us upon your arrival," Glaphyra said.

"It may be that we shall have much to speak of." She gestured toward the table full of astrological paraphernalia. "We have not begun to disclose to you our deepest knowledge."

That night the two Greeks lounged in the fine tent Norbanus had put at their disposal.

"Well, our first roll of the bones came up Venus, as the Romans would say," Zeno commented.

"Thus far, we have succeeded beyond our expectations," Izates agreed, sipping at his wine. It was very fine wine, and he found that he was growing accustomed to fine things. This was unworthy of a philosopher, he knew. He also knew that he didn't care.

"We must be very careful with those two," Zeno said.

"It goes without saying."

"You noticed how they spoke in turn?"

Izates nodded. "It's meant to baffle people; confuse them and throw them off guard."

"That's what I thought. Even after a lapse in conversation, one would speak forthrightly while the other kept silence. Never once did both try to speak at once. I wonder how they arrange that. Some secret signal, do you think?"

"Twins share a bond that others lack. Perhaps no signal is needed, so sensitive is each to the other's thoughts and will. In some ways they are uncanny, but in most ways they are just common women. Better born, more learned than most, but ordinary, mortal women for all that."

"Ordinary?" Zeno said. "But how? I found them most extraordinary."

"No matter how high they started and how much higher they have risen, they have the same fears that haunt other women. Men, too, if truth were known. They fear loss of all they have. They fear old age and mortality."

"They fear being supplanted by other women," Zeno

said, nodding. "And now we know what they want that Norbanus cannot give them: a secure future."

"And that is the weakness we will exploit," Izates said. "We have come a long way from our studies, my friend. We have gone from contemplation of the ideal and the ineffable to the manipulation of human beings for our own purposes."

"Then it behooves us to do this well. Power is more dangerous than wisdom."

IN HIS OWN TENT, NORBANUS WAS CONTEMPLATING his own future. The acquisition of Massilia was a great coup. It would cause outrage in the Senate, but so what? Every great Roman sought to increase his *clientela*. If he used his army to do it, he would not be the first. Others before him had placed tribes and nations in clientage to their families. He had merely done it better. Jonathan of Judea and the city of Massilia were now his. More would be his soon. Always assuming, of course, that he remained victorious.

Now he looked at the scroll before him. It held his future in a way that the predictions of the Judean women could not. Another boat had put in that day, this one from far west. It had sailed from Cartago Nova, and it carried a messenger: a taciturn man who had refused to speak to anyone but the general. The man had shown him a seal, and it had given Norbanus a little thrill that told him the gods had something exceptional in store for him. It was the seal of Princess Zarabel of Carthage.

Great Proconsul Norbanus, the message began. *The time has come for us to make common cause, as we did while you were my guest in Carthage. Your countryman Scipio and his Egyptian queen are preparing to make the Middle Sea their own, while my foolish brother tries to emulate Alexander. With what I send you, you can make yourself master of the world. Make good use of this, and you and I can rule that world together.*

This was bald enough, he thought, though why she thought he would need her, having destroyed Hamilcar, he could not guess. Desperation, he supposed. But what she had sent him was invaluable. It was nothing less than Hamilcar's campaign route and schedule and his order of battle, complete with numbers and units.

Hamilcar had departed Carthage with his army and was marching west. That meant he was heading for the Pillars of Hercules and Spain. Then he would turn east and march for Rome. But first he would meet Titus Norbanus.

He, Norbanus, would be first to crush Hamilcar. Not his father, not Scipio or any other Roman. The glory would go to Titus Norbanus the younger. He might have to share the glory of taking Carthage itself, but this would be his alone. It was destiny. It was the will of the gods.

He began to pore feverishly over his maps. Hamilcar would be moving slowly. Norbanus had seen the army of Carthage on the march, and it could not move at anything like the speed of the Roman legions. Hamilcar would plan to link with Mastanabal, to add that victorious general's army to his own.

But he could not do that if Norbanus found Mastanabal first. It was always good to destroy the enemy's forces in detail, before they had a chance to mass against the Romans. It was one of the oldest dicta taught in Roman military schools: Bring your greatest strength against the enemy's weakness. This was far better than challenging strength with strength. He studied his maps.

Where was Mastanabal?

CHAPTER SEVENTEEN

THE MARCH WAS PROCEEDING ALTOGETHER GLORI-
ously. The massive Carthaginian Army trailed out behind him so far that should he halt, the last elements would
not arrive in his camp for two or three days. Size alone did
not dictate this attenuation. So vast a host would devastate
any country through which it passed. Friendly territory
would suffer nearly as sorely as that of the enemy. Not that
Hamilcar worried overmuch for the welfare and happiness of
his subjects, but his Libyan and Numidian allies could
quickly become enemies and their raids might slow and distract his troops. He needed his allied cavalry and dared not
offend even their flea-bitten, barbarous chieftains.

Thinking of cavalry, he admired the horsemen who rode
as his escort. They were Queen Teuta's Illyrians, and they
provided not only his immediate guard, but rode as flankers
and forward scouts as well. Their bizarre appearance had the
locals gaping wherever they rode. The tattooed men were as
fair as Gauls, but they wore tight-fitting trousers and soft

boots with pointed, upturned toes. They had long-sleeved jackets and tall, pointed caps with dangling ear-flaps, and every bit of their clothing was stitched with colorful embroidery in fanciful designs: flowers and twining vines and elongated animals writhing into poses of knotted complexity. In their hands were long lances from which streamed banners, and at their belts they carried cased bows and quivers of arrows. Across their backs they carried short sabers in sheaths of figured leather and tucked into their sashes were curved daggers. They did not wear armor and regarded it as unmanly.

Their queen rode beside him, and she looked as fearsome as her men. Her clothing was similar to theirs, but made of gold-embroidered silk, her trousers voluminous, her jacket fitting like a second skin. Instead of the native cap, a light-weight crown of thin gold encircled her brow. The jeweled dagger at her waist was not an ornamental weapon, and at her saddlebow was slung on one side a circular buckler of thick hide faced with bronze, and on the other an axe with a long, slender handle, its head bearing a crescent blade on one side and a cruel, down-curving spike on the other. Once, Hamilcar had asked if she could actually use this odd weapon, and she had only smiled. Later, a hare started from beneath her horse's hooves. She had given chase, then unlimbered the axe, leaned from her saddle and beheaded the creature in mid-leap, her own horse at a full gallop.

Hamilcar reminded himself to ask her no more idle questions.

The weather was splendid, clearly a gift from the gods of Carthage to their favorite. The days were sunny but cool, the evenings just slightly rainy, so that the marching feet and hooves raised little dust.

Their route was along the coastal road. Sometimes it

passed behind ranges of hills, and there were days when they were out of sight of the sea, but each time the water came into view again, so did Hamilcar's fleet, keeping easy pace with the army. As they approached prearranged harbors, the ships would speed ahead, so that when Hamilcar and his army reached that spot, the supplies he needed would already have been unloaded, supplies levied from the allies, subjects readied to be carried aboard and new rowers drafted from the locals. All was orderly and in the well-organized fashion that had given Carthage dominion over sea and land for so many years.

"I never knew that so great an enterprise could be run so smoothly," Queen Teuta said when they came in sight of the Pillars. "My chieftains would be hopeless at such a thing, and even the Greeks were not so well ordered in their glory days."

Hamilcar nodded with smug satisfaction. "It is our special gift from the gods. We are not truly a race of warriors, despite our military supremacy. We are sailors and merchants and explorers. These are activities that cannot prosper without close cooperation, discipline and careful planning. Alexander accomplished wonders, but his army marched hungry and thirsty much of the time. It did not occur to that glory-hungry boy to find out whether there was forage, or water, along his route of march. He depended instead upon inspiration, and the love of the gods, and the fanatical loyalty of his men.

"We know that such things are not to be depended upon. The favor of the gods must be purchased with continuous sacrifice. Men must be paid well and regularly. The supplies required by a marching army and a sailing navy must be arranged for down to the last detail before the first trumpet is sounded. Only thus does one gain an empire, and sustain it through generations."

"I shall remember that," she said.

At the Pillars, the fleet was waiting to ferry the army across. Triremes, cargo vessels and great, wallowing barges, many of them built since the fire in the harbor, were ready to take them across the narrow waters. The operation took more than ten days, with ships plying back and forth, carrying men and animals and supplies. Hamilcar found his confidence waning, his nerves assailing him.

"What troubles you?" Teuta asked. They watched the crossing from the tower erected on his personal warship: a huge vessel made of two ordinary triremes with a single deck spanning both.

"We are vulnerable here," he told her, an admission he would have made to no man. "If the Romans arrive, they could catch me with half my army on one side of the strait, half on the other. Even their contemptible navy could give us great trouble, with most of my fleet overloaded and dedicated to transport."

"Still, your might is sufficient to deal with them."

"True, though it would be a great bother. But what I truly dread is a change in the weather. At this time of year great storms can appear on the horizon and be upon us before we can seek shelter. Entire fleets have been lost to such storms, and there would be no way to rebuild here. I would have to march such of my army as I could salvage back to Carthage, and then I could not resume the war for at least a year, perhaps two. And that would mean waiting for a Roman army to cross from Sicily and besiege us."

"Worry does no good," she assured him. "You must trust your destiny."

Somehow, her words did not inspire him as usual. It was not her empire in the balance here, imperiled by every puff of wind and the whim of the gods. What if Zarabel was right and the gods were angry because he had not dedicated them a *Tophet*?

NORBANUS FOUND THE ARMY OF MASTANABAL IN A valley south of the Pyrenees. His outriding Gallic cavalry located a foraging party and returned with prisoners to confirm what lay ahead. These men were local Gauls, of a breed heavily interbred with the old Spanish natives, impressed into the Carthaginian forces to make up for the heavy losses inflicted by Rome. They said that Mastanabal was drilling his new army just miles away, near the confluence of the rivers Iberis and Secoris.

Immediately, Norbanus gave two orders. First, the land forces were to redouble their marching speed. Second, his warships were to speed westward and catch any naval force supporting Mastanabal's army. Not a single craft was to be allowed to escape.

He wanted to achieve complete surprise, but knew that this was unlikely with an army the size of the one he led. Sooner or later a patrol of Mastanabal's cavalry must detect them and speed back with warning. No help for that. But he could be assured that the Carthaginian would have as little time as possible to prepare.

The land was hilly and wooded, very different from the lands of the East his men had seen on the long march. But the Romans felt at home here. It was not greatly different from the country where they had been fighting for generations, since the Exile.

He was tense but exultant. At last, he would be tested in a real battle, against a formidable army led by a general of proven experience and skill. Not that he had any doubt of the outcome. Clearly, Mastanabal could not be accounted a general of the first rank. He had allowed himself to be badly mauled by an inferior Roman army, indifferently led. This was no Hannibal. The situation was ideal. Norbanus's army could be blooded here, at no great risk. Victorious, they would believe themselves to be invincible always. And he knew that true victory lay not just in arms and skill, but in the minds of men.

With a small band of his officers, he rode ahead of his army. They rode cloaked to cover the gleam of their armor, keeping away from the skyline. It was risky, but Norbanus wanted to examine the ground personally before committing his troops. Reconnaissance was an art that a commander neglected at his greatest peril.

The smoke from hundreds of campfires told them they were near the main army, and from this point they proceeded with caution. Eventually they found a spot of high ground and rode just short of the crest. Then they dismounted and went on foot to peer over the ridge at the huge camp below. It spread along the river for a great distance, behind an earthen rampart set with stakes and patrolled by sentries.

"It's a pretty well-ordered camp, for barbarians," noted Niger.

Norbanus had Selene's gift out and was using it to scan the camp, counting standards. "He has his Greek troops on the south end. You can tell by the way their tents are lined up. The rest must be Gauls and Iberians and other savages. They have no idea how to encamp. I'm amazed he got them to stay behind the wall." He passed the instrument to Cato.

Cato looked over the camp and passed the thing to Niger. "The important thing is: He hasn't linked up with

Hamilcar yet." Word had come to them that Hamilcar had crossed the strait and that meant they would meet him in Spain.

"Close to our numbers," Niger said. "I'd say we have a slight superiority, unless he has some sizable elements out foraging." That was a matter for concern. The sudden return of a large party after a battle was joined could be disastrous.

"We'll chance it," Norbanus said. "We'll never have a better chance. I want our men in battle order on that field at first light tomorrow, even if it means moving them around all night to get them in position."

What he proposed was risky and difficult, but his subordinates made no protest. They had confidence in their leader now.

JUST BEFORE SUNDOWN A PARTY OF SCOUTS RODE IN and informed Mastanabal that they had seen elements of an approaching Roman army. The scouts were Edetani, black-haired warriors with legs formed to the barrel of a horse.

"What were these Romans doing?" the general asked.

"They behaved very strangely," the head scout said. "Almost as soon as we saw them, they halted at a piece of flat ground. Some men took odd instruments from their shoulders and stuck them into the ground. They looked along the tops of these instruments and waved their arms and shouted to the others. Then many men ran about the field and stuck colored flags into the ground. We think it was some sort of religious rite, although we saw no sacrifices."

Mastanabal and his senior officers chuckled. They had seen the elaborate Roman system of encampment many times during the Alexandrian campaign. These Spaniards were too primitive even to post sentries, much less recognize the nature of such a proceeding. The general made sure that he had the exact distance and location of the Roman force and dismissed the scouts.

"Excellent!" Mastanabal said. "They will break that camp before first light and will be here by late afternoon tomorrow to find us blocking their way."

"So, will we give battle the morning after?" asked a subordinate.

"Why wait? If there is as much as an hour's light left when they arrive, I intend to give battle immediately! These Romans rely heavily upon their formations and battle order. We will strike before they can deploy fully."

IN THE BLACKNESS BEFORE DAWN MASTANABAL WAS awakened by the sound of trumpets. His eyes snapped open and he knew something had to be wrong. His groom held his horse ready and he mounted. As he pelted through the camp, men were tumbling from their tents, demanding from one another what was happening. Roman soldiers would already be armed and on their way to their positions on the rampart, Mastanabal thought enviously. He had seen the Romans' night drills, how every man tented in exactly the same spot in every camp and manned the same spot on the wall, so that no matter where they were, the Romans were in the same fort as always.

Not for the first time, Mastanabal wished he had an army made up solely of Carthaginians, instead of this polyglot rabble. But that would not be the Carthaginian way, he thought resignedly. He came to the tower over the main gate and ran up its wooden stair. "What is it?" he barked. "If this is a false alarm, I'll have you all crucified!" The soldiers looked fearful, knowing this was no idle threat. Their officer seemed unimpressed.

"Movement out there, General," he said. "They're being quiet, but it's no scouting probe." He gestured to a rope ladder that lay coiled at his feet. "I went down the wall and walked out a way to be sure. Couldn't see anything, but there's a sizable force gathering on the field to the east of us." The officer, a Spartan professional, knew his business. Mastanabal began to have a very bad feeling.

His senior officers gathered behind him on the platform. No one spoke while their general held his silence. He was not about to speak until he knew exactly what he faced. The coming dawn would tell him all he needed to know. Dawn was not long in coming.

Shouts of wonder ran up and down the rampart; men babbled in a score of tongues and called upon a hundred gods as growing light revealed what had appeared upon the field before them. A huge army stood there, drawn up in great rectangles, standard-bearers to the fore. The most terrifying thing about them was not their numbers, which were no greater than those of the Carthaginian army, or their perfect order, for the Greeks and Macedonians were as disciplined. What struck Mastanabal's men with fear was their eerie, utter silence. It was like beholding an army of ghosts.

The Roman encampment had been a ruse. Mastanabal cursed himself for falling for such a trick. They had marched all night to get here. Such a night march was in itself a considerable feat. But to get out onto that field and form up from marching order to battle order in darkness, completely undetected save for a keen-eared Spartan soldier? Who was capable of such a thing? Certainly not a Roman general like the one he had already beaten. Then he knew.

"It's Norbanus," he said quietly.

"Can it be he, my General?" said a subordinate. "The spies said he was back in Italy, but to come all the way here—"

"It can be no other. I came to know him on the Egyptian campaign. He is wily and imaginative. Only he could have done this."

"I knew him, too," said a Libyan commander. "He can make men march, but he has little reputation as a fighting general. His part in the battle outside Alexandria was well done, but it was just a field maneuver that gave us the advantage. His men did little fighting."

That was true, and the words put heart in the Carthaginian leader. "Counting standards, I make his strength at eight legions. We still have superior numbers, and we are far stronger in cavalry. And the gods of Carthage are stronger than the gods of Rome. He's taken the best ground, naturally, but we won't fight him there. He can come here and fight us, where we have the fortified camp at our backs and the river on our flanks. The advantage is all ours here."

"What if he refuses to give battle, My General?" asked the Libyan.

Mastanabal smiled wolfishly, showing sharp teeth. "Then we will take our ease right here. Soon the shofet will join us, with an army twice our size. Norbanus can fight us then, if it pleases him." His commanders chuckled. That was better. The unexpected shock to their nerves was receding. "Order the men to breakfast. We'll send out a delegation to parley, then make our battle dispositions when the sun is high—"

"My General," said the phlegmatic Spartan, "you had better look over there."

The sun had risen behind the Romans, casting its glitter from standards and spear points and polished armor. At first, nothing seemed to have changed. Then he saw the rhythmic flashing along the line. It came from the polished greaves worn by the centurions. They were walking. With the same incredible precision, without the sound of so much as a single trumpet, the Roman army was *advancing*.

"My General," said someone, "I don't think they want to parley."

They had given him no time! No time to plan, no time to feed his men, no time for a harangue, no time to make the customary sacrifices. Were he to rush through the ceremonies now, he would look like a half-beaten man, no longer in control of his and his army's fate.

"Do we meet them here or on the field?" demanded the Libyan. "We must know now."

"There is no time to deploy properly. They would catch us with half our men outside the camp, half in. We will meet them here on the walls. It will just take longer to kill them all this way. They must be exhausted after marching all night, and our men are well rested. This is just like Norbanus. What he is doing is bold, but it is foolish. He wastes his men needlessly." It galled him but he had little choice. It was safe enough, but from here he could not concentrate his strength as he pleased. He could not take advantage if he saw a weakness in the Roman formation. There was no scope for generalship in such a fight. On the walls, the ferocity of his Gauls and his Spaniards would be wasted. His splendid cavalry would remain penned up like sheep, completely useless.

Remorselessly, the legionaries came on. He scanned to their flanks and rear. They seemed to have no siege-train. That was excellent. With no heavy missile hurlers or specialized assault equipment, they must attack the rampart with infantry alone. That would prove very costly to them. It was the worst possible way to assault a fortification, simply hurling human flesh against steel.

He looked along his own wall. It was only earth and tim-ber, but the earth was heaped eight feet high and topped with sharpened stakes. He had not entrenched. He had not dug a ditch lined with traps and foot stakes. But he had never expected to have to defend this place. It was merely a temporary camp for amassing a force to renew the attack on Rome.

It was no matter. He had beaten Romans before. He would beat this army as well. Already, his men were over their first astonishment. All up and down the western wall, tribal war chants boomed out. Spaniards waved their vicious *falcatas* and Gauls whirled their long swords. Slingers were taking their positions, their pouches full of lead slugs. Archers arranged their arrows tidily. At the southern end of the wall the Greeks stood silent and ready, superbly ar-mored and holding their long spears.

Mastanabal was satisfied. There were few recruits in his army. Most were men with long experience of war. The Ro-mans were raising legions too fast. They had too many un-tried boys, not enough veterans. It had led them to disaster before, in Hannibal's time and now in his own. He squinted toward the approaching Romans and tried to make out their dispositions. The rising sun at their backs made this diffi-cult. They had chosen the right direction from which to make their assault.

This one leaves little to chance, Mastanabal thought.

NORBANUS WATCHED THE ADVANCE WITH GREATEST satisfaction. All had worked out perfectly. The ruse with the false camp had paid off handsomely. His greatest worry had been that the scouts would leave some men behind to make a count of the arriving legions. They would have seen that the army did not halt at the camp and would have known the truth. His own horsemen might not have caught them. But the scouts had been satisfied with what they had seen and they had been too lacking in initiative to wait to see more.

And, as always, the gods of Rome were watching over their favorite, Titus Norbanus.

His men made a splendid show as they marched in perfect silence. They had stripped the covers from their shields, displaying bright new paint, the colors and devices identifying the various units. Those who had crests and plumes had mounted them on their helmets, the bright feathers and horsehair nodding to their steps. Armor and weapons were polished bright. Brightest of all were the standards. His four old legions, veterans of the long march, had turned in their old standards and been given the new, standardized eagles of silver and gold. The men who carried them were draped with the skins of lions. The bearers of the lesser standards wore pelts of wolf and bear.

And, he reflected with some satisfaction, the ruse and the night march had not been his only inspired decisions. The silent advance had been his idea as well. He had instructed his men carefully that there would be no trumpets, but all orders must be given with the voice, in words quietly but clearly spoken. Here the oratorical training of the officers had paid off, for they knew how to make themselves heard without shouting. He knew that to the enemy on the wall opposite, the sight would be awesome and frightening.

The crowning achievement was his decision to attack at first light without negotiation. It looked foolish, but he knew that it made the best possible use of his strength while crippling his enemy. Mastanabal could not know that his fortified camp was, to the Romans, nothing but a big Gallic oppidum, and they had taken hundreds of such by storm. It was one of the most basic tasks given to legionary trainees.

They had marched all night, but he had given them two days of rest before beginning it. This had been risky, since they might have been reported by locals anxious to curry favor with Carthage, and it gave Hamilcar more time to link up with Mastanabal's army, but he had deemed the risk acceptable.

No doubt about it, he thought, his planning and execution had been without flaw and without peer. The name of Titus Norbanus would live forever. And this was only the beginning.

First, though, to reduce this fortification and exterminate this army that had the impudence to exist upon what was, by right and the will of the gods, Roman territory. His battle plan was fully formulated and was even now being implemented. It was unique and, of course, it was risky. But a man proved his greatness only by pressing his luck relentlessly.

And, did the Carthaginian but know it, this was just one part of a two-part battle. The other phase was even now being fought. It galled Norbanus that he could not be in control of that battle as well.

DECIMUS ARRUNTEIUS, *DUUMVIR* OF THE FLEET AL-ready called the Norbanian, paced the long deck of his flag-ship, *Avenging Mars*. The deck itself was a new innovation. The traditional warship had a mere catwalk stretching its length between the benches of the upper banks of rowers. Romans liked room for soldiers to maneuver, so they had raised the catwalk above the rowers' heads and widened it into a true deck. The Greek shipwrights had protested that this would destroy the ships' stability and make them prone to capsizing. The Romans' answer had been swift and impatient: Build the ships wider. The Greeks had said that this would make the ships slow and unwieldy. The Romans answered that men were cheap: Add more rowers.

The result Arrunteius surveyed all around him: a fleet of ships larger and more powerful than the traditional Greek trireme that had been supreme on the Middle Sea for centuries. The ships might not be quite as quick or maneuverable as the Greek ships, but he had confidence that their superior qualities would more than make up for this.

And confidence was needed. He knew that a Carthaginian fleet lay ahead of him, not far away. That nation had reigned supreme on the sea since the expulsion of Rome from Italy. The Carthaginians and their many seagoing allies were long experienced and tested in sailing, in rowing, and in battle upon the waters. The Romans were none of these things. But once before Rome had bested Carthage at sea, and they counted on Carthaginian arrogance, that Carthage would have forgotten the lessons learned at such cost.

Arrunteius walked forward and mounted the "castle," a strong tower erected near the prow of *Avenging Mars.* Similar towers adorned the foredecks of the larger warships. Behind each tower stood a long bridge, one end hinged to a circular pivot on the deck, the other featuring a three-foot spike of iron. In battle it would be swung outboard and dropped so that the spike sank into an enemy deck, forming a boarding bridge for the marines manning every Roman ship. It was called a *corvus:* "crow."

In addition, every ship was built atop an extra-massive keel, its fore end tipped with a heavy ram of cast bronze.

The Romans had little confidence in their ability to maneuver in action and to ram, but they wanted both to be decisive when accomplished.

In all, the new, Italian-built fleet had nothing like the wildly imaginative innovations of the Alexandrian fleet, but its improvements had been well thought out, and some, like the tower and the *corvus,* had proven successful nearly two centuries before, in the first war against Carthage.

About the men, Arrunteius was not so certain. The sailors were mainly Greek, each with an Italian understudy learning the craft. The rowers were Italians, working their way into Roman favor in the most arduous way imaginable. They had mastered the skills of the oar and now took pride in their work. They had formed their own guild with its special gods, rituals and sacrifices. Their loyalty they would prove in action.

The marines, likewise, were mostly Italians, with a leavening of legionaries for stiffening. They had been drilled with great intensity in the arts of Roman close combat. Every man was armed with heavy and light javelins, a short, razor-edged gladius and a dagger. They wore iron helmets and shirts of Gallic mail. These last were shorter than the legionary type, extending only to the waist, and they lacked the distinctive shoulder doublings of legionary armor. Their shields, likewise, were somewhat smaller and far lighter than those used on land. These changes had been deemed expedient for warfare at sea. The shields were painted blue for sea service, and adorned with pictures of tritons, Nereids, *hippokampi,* the trident of Neptune and other nautical designs.

"Admiral!" called the sailing master, a Greek like most of them. "Around that point," he jabbed a finger at a cape of land that jutted into the sea to the southwest, "lies a cove near the mouth of the Iberis. If the Carthaginian army is anywhere nearby inland, it is a natural place for their fleet to put in."

"Then we will go around the cape in battle order. If there are no hostile forces in sight, resume cruising as usual." The requisite orders were passed by flag, and the fleet prepared for action, as it had numerous times before: Yards and sails were lowered and stored away, but the masts were left standing, for the *corvi* were slung from them. Arms were prepared; the sky was scanned for omens. The ships took up position abreast with the heavy triremes in the first line, the smaller, swifter biremes in the second and the smallest vessels and the transports well astern. In a slow and stately maneuver, like a legion changing front on the parade ground, the great line of ships swept around the cape. On the other side they found the Carthaginians.

Despite himself, Arrunteius gaped at the sight, his hands gripping the rail of the castle's waist-high bulwark. Drill and training was one thing. This was the first time Romans had beheld an enemy fleet since before the days of their grandfathers. "How many?" he demanded of the sailing master.

"Forty triremes at least. Not the main fleet by at least a hundred warships."

Arrunteius felt the sweat of relief spring from beneath his helmet. His greatest fear had been that his untested fleet would be thrown against the far larger combined battle fleet of Carthage. He needed a smaller fight to get his men blooded first, and it looked like that fight would be big enough. He had thirty-four triremes in his command, and twenty of the smaller biremes. He was outnumbered and the enemy was more experienced at this sort of fighting, but his ships were already arrayed for battle and had caught the other fleet by surprise. That advantage, plus the heaviness and power of his capital ships, should be enough.

"Advance and take them all," he called. "I want none to escape." His signals officer barked orders and the flagmen transferred the admiral's commands. The triremes swept forward in a broad crescent, pivoting on the right, landward ship, swinging around like a huge door to close off the little harbor. A large detachment of the biremes broke away from the main formation and rowed southwestward along the coast. They would take up a position in line abreast to trap any vessel that tried to escape and carry warning to Hamilcar's fleet.

All this was one of several prearranged battle plans. The Romans, consulting with their Greek sailing masters, had concocted a number of these, each with its own signals, each precise but allowing for flexibility for individual initiative and contingencies. History had taught them the folly of rigid adherence to a battle plan.

Inshore, the enemy was wasting no time. From the moment the Roman fleet heaved in sight, battle preparations commenced. Even with the before-action tension twisting his stomach, Arrunteius found himself admiring the efficiency with which his opposite number was coping with the unexpected danger. Ships in the water were prepared for battle with amazing speed. Masts were lowered, sails and yards stowed away or merely pitched overboard to clear the decks. All inessential gear was disposed of in this manner. Even slaves working on the ships were thrown into the water to swim or drown.

Ships that had been drawn up on shore were dragged into the water, their crews scrambling aboard, running out oars before the hulls were fully afloat. Transports and cargo vessels were pulled close inshore, leaving the war fleet as much maneuvering room as possible. All, clearly, was according to a long-established naval practice.

In an amazingly short time the Carthaginian fleet was in the water, in battle order and heading for the Roman line, before the Romans had even completed their encircling sweep to shut off the harbor. The first elements were heading straight for the Roman center. Straight for *Avenging Mars.*

The first Carthaginian trireme seemed on top of him more quickly than Arrunteius could have imagined. He felt cooler now, because his task as admiral was substantially done. Now the battle devolved upon the individual ships' captains and their crews. The ship bearing down upon him was like something out of Hades: a lean, low dragon shape from which trails of smoke arched toward him—fire arrows, he realized. Above the ship's fanged ram squatted the hideous little god Patechus, the Punic terror demon. The archers around Arrunteius on the castle began to send shafts toward the enemy, and from the deck below him came the thudding of the ballistae as they fired their heavy iron javelins.

The enemy ship swerved to one side, an old naval maneuver intended to send the galley plowing through the oars on one side of Arrunteius's ship, their flailing handles reducing the rowers inside to dog meat, crippling his ship so that the Carthaginian could ram at leisure. But his sailing master turned into the other's bow, an unexpected maneuver devised to take advantage of the Roman galley's greater mass.

Going ram-to-ram was the one thing the Carthaginians were not prepared for. The bronze-sheathed ram of *Avenging Mars* struck just below and to one side of the crouching god, crunching through the wood with the awful momentum of both ships. Seconds before the impact, the Roman rowers drew in their oars. Arrunteius grabbed the railing before him as his ship lurched, then rose. Amazed, he realized that his own vessel was riding up over the keel of the lighter craft, splitting its deck like a huge saw splitting a plank. Boards and timbers flew; splinters showered the men on the tower as the heavy Roman galley plowed through the Carthaginian. Below, men screamed, flailed, dived into the water or were pulped.

Arrunteius saw one side of the enemy ship open up and the oar benches, along with the rowers, topple into the sea. Armored men waved their weapons in perfect futility as their ship broke up beneath them. A man he took to be the captain stood for a moment beside the steering oar, his face a mask of incomprehension. Then the stern was swamped and the whole ship, now in many pieces, settled into the water.

Arrunteius stood, astounded. In moments, a magnificent ship was reduced to bits of floating debris. And *he* had done it! He, Decimus Arrunteius, in his invincible ship! He waved his fists aloft. "Mars is victorious!" he shouted. All over the ship, men regained use of their tongues and took up the cry. "Mars is victorious! Mars is victorious!"

Now he remembered that he was an admiral and there was still a battle to win. He looked around him and saw a score of ship fights in progress. Some ships were locked together by the *corvi*, soldiers swarming across to fight hand-to-hand. Others lay grappled, and men scrambled over the rails. He could see the results of other rammings, some of them with the same devastating result his own had accomplished. Here and there, Carthaginians had managed to ram Roman vessels, and some of these were sinking, though the heavier timbers of the Roman ships usually gave their men time to board the enemy. Roman boarding inevitably led to the Carthaginians' capture, for the mercenaries manning their decks were no match for Roman swordsmen, even those who had been mere Italian villagers or bandits the year before. Their *gladii* quickly turned the enemy deck to a bloody shambles.

"How are our oarsmen?" Arrunteius demanded. "Can we maneuver?"

"Haven't lost many," the sailing master answered. "They shipped oars in time."

"Then find us another to ram!" He looked around, and saw a Carthaginian galley backing away from the hole it had punched in the side of a Roman vessel. Arrunteius pointed toward it. "That one!"

With the sailing master shouting down to the oar master and that officer barking the orders to his charges, *Avenging Mars* turned on its axis until its ram was pointed at the Carthaginian; then it surged forward, picking up speed as the *hortator* increased the tempo of his drumbeats. Arrunteius saw faces along the enemy rail turn, go pale. He saw fingers pointing and mouths forming shouts as they saw the doom bearing down upon them, but it was far too late.

The ram of *Avenging Mars* caught the Carthaginian galley amidships, where the timbers were thinnest and most stressed. This time the castle barely vibrated beneath Arrunteius's feet as the enemy ship broke in two, filled and sank so swiftly that it was like some sort of conjurer's trick. Again he raised the shout, "Mars is victorious!" The men aboard the rammed Roman ship cheered as loudly to see their vessel so quickly avenged, cheering as they scrambled to jam canvas and wood and dead bodies into the gaping hole in her side.

"Find me another!" Arrunteius cried, exulting. He knew

now that his ship was invincible. Rome was invincible.

Within an hour, the battle was effectively over. The wait-ing biremes pounced on the few warships that managed to get through the Roman battle line, two or three biremes at-tacking each larger Carthaginian craft, ramming and then sending boarders across to butcher the defenders. Desperate crews beached their ships, threw away their arms and took to their heels, running for the interior. They would be des-perate, hunted men, for if the Romans caught them they faced slavery, while Carthage would crucify them.

Avenging Mars rowed through the wreckage toward a wharf, and Arrunteius surveyed the scene with the greatest satisfaction. Here and there, hulks lay low in the water, smoke drifting from their timbers. Some ships were still sinking; others wallowed, abandoned, their crews all dead. The water was thick with blood, and sharks converged from all quarters, tearing excitedly at this abundance of flesh. Ar-runteius's officers were taking inventory of the captured supply ships and transports and were questioning surviving officers with great rigor.

The entire Carthaginian fleet was destroyed or captured. Arrunteius had lost seven triremes and a handful of biremes, but the crews, rowers and marines of these ships had mostly been saved. A few days of hard work would put his fleet back in order. He knew that the main Carthaginian fleet would be far larger and it would be a harder fight, but now his men had confidence in their admiral, in their ships and in themselves.

With his ship made fast to the wharf, Arrunteius went ashore and erected an altar, demolishing a Carthaginian al-tar to Baal-Hammon for the purpose. He sacrificed to Jupiter, to Mars and to Neptune in gratitude for his victory. He poured oil and wine over the altar, then the blood of the sacrificial animals; then he kindled a fire and burned the sacrifices, chanting the ancient prayers until all was thoroughly consumed. When the ritual obligations had been observed, he assembled his officers.

"I want the rams from all those Carthaginian ships," he ordered. "Send salvage divers down if you have to, but I must have every one of them. They will adorn the monument I will erect in the Forum when we return to Rome. I can't petition the Senate for a triumph—it's not allowed for a mere naval battle, especially since it hasn't concluded a successful war—but I will see to it that Rome never forgets what we did here this day. Our generals are taking back our empire from Carthage. But we are taking back our sea!"

His officers cheered lustily, and his marines and sailors took up the shout. He felt all his ancestors looking down upon him with approval. He had made the name of Arrunteius shine with glory. He was the first *duumvir* of Rome's resurgence.

MASTANABAL WATCHED THE APPROACHING ROMAN lines with wonder. What could they possibly intend? With no ladders and no towers or other machines, how did they expect to take his wall? And they were not concentrating on a single point, but advancing on a front as wide as the wall itself. Arrows began arching out from his fort, but at such range the Romans had plenty of time to see them coming and raise their shields. When the Romans were a hundred paces away, they stopped, the entire front freezing on the same step, as if the army were a single creature. The silence continued.

"Ah!" Mastanabal said. "They have made their show;

now they will send out envoys to negotiate." But the Romans surprised him again.

Abruptly, all the trumpets blared, using a technique he had never heard before—a great, feral snarl that sent a bolt of cold fear up the spine. Then, in unison, the soldiers beat the inner sides of their shields with their spear butts, chanting something incomprehensible. At last, they raised spears and shields, shaking them and roaring as if to draw the attention of the infernal gods.

Mastanabal saw that his men were already confused and terrified, and they had not yet experienced the first arrow, spear or sling-stone of battle. "It's just noise!" he shouted. "Don't let a little noise scare you!" But even his Spartans looked uneasy. He felt shaken himself. That war cry made the Greek paean sound like a whimper of surrender.

"Tanit!" someone breathed behind him. "What now?"

For the Romans were advancing again, and not at their previous, stately pace. This time they were *running*.

Carthaginian arrows began to fall among them, then sling-bullets, then javelins, but the Romans kept their shields high and took few casualties from the missiles. When they were close, closer than Mastanabal would have deemed possible, the front-line shields dropped, arms rocked back, and the men hurled their javelins. First the light javelins sailed over the wall and its defenders to land among the reinforcements behind. Then the heavy, murderous pila smashed into men and shields, sowing havoc.

Their javelins gone, the front-line men knelt at the base of the earthwork, their shields overlapped and raised overhead. The second line hurled their javelins and knelt behind the first, then the third line did the same. Another line charged in. These men jumped onto the roof of shields, threw their pila, then formed a second story to the human platform.

Mastanabal had seen these intricate formations practiced when the Roman soldiers first arrived at Carthage, but now he was seeing them under battle conditions. He saw the bright paint on the unscarred shields, the new armor worn by the men. "He's using his untried boys for a platform," he said. Now there were three layers to the platform. The shields were now at the base of the wooden palisade. Mastanabal's men threw down anything that might break the formation: first heavy spears, then stones, timbers, even wagon wheels. Nothing shook the overlapping shields.

"Bring oil and torches!" the general shouted. Then he saw the next line advancing: fierce-looking, sunburned men whose stride carried a chilling assurance. The veterans had arrived, men he had last seen half a world away, in Egypt. "Get the oil quick!" he screamed.

But already the veterans were mounting the human platform, fending off missiles with contemptuous ease, until they were standing against the palisade, thrusting with their spears at the faces that appeared there. *Why aren't they throwing the spears?* Mastanabal wondered. It was always their prelude to a hand-to-hand fight. Then the trumpets blared out again, and all along his wall, the crouching legionaries who made up the platform *stood*.

There came a great, cry from beneath the structure of overlapped shields as men made a superhuman effort and got to their feet, lifting the vast weight above them. Slowly, not quite evenly, the great formation lifted, extended, rose by inches like some gigantic, incomprehensible machine. Then the veteran legionaries of Norbanus were standing *above* the palisade that topped his camp wall. And now their arms rocked back and they threw their spears, casting them downward onto the terrified enemy, already unmanned by this seemingly inhuman method of making war.

There was a brief, shield-to-shield struggle as the Romans drew their swords and sought to force a way onto the wall. Every man was determined to win the *corona muralis*: the crown awarded to the first man atop an enemy wall. The mercenaries and allies strove as desperately to keep them out, but now the Romans had the advantage of height and gravity. The front line, first here and there, then along the whole length of the wall, began jumping from the shield platform onto the walk behind the palisade. They tore at the timbers and made gaps for easier passage. More of the veteran troops mounted the shield platform and poured across. Fighting was general all along the wall; then it spilled down the rear face of the earthwork and into the camp.

Mastanabal looked on, appalled. Once in the camp, the Romans could not use their fine teamwork and coordination, and had no time to muster a formation. But his own men were crowded together, getting in one another's way, while the Romans never let themselves get too close for a man to be able to wield his weapons. They fought as individuals as fiercely as they did in formation, and these men had the smell of blood in their nostrils. They slew relentlessly, the razor-edged *gladii* lancing out to open throats, bellies, breasts, severing arms, opening thighs to let the bright, arterial blood jet out into the befouled air. Mastanabal's men were going down in heaps, often unable to so much as raise their arms.

Below him, Romans were forcing the gate open from inside, and now the shield platform was breaking up, the young men forcing their way into the camp through the gate, or over the earthwork now that the palisade was demolished. Mastanabal's cavalry tried frantically to escape, heading for the river. In an unbelievably short time he knew that all was lost. Only his Greek and Macedonian professionals still stood firm, holding their tight, disciplined formation. There was a standoff in that part of the battle, as the Romans isolated the Greeks from the others. Now they were surrounding his tower and he saw the golden boy himself, Titus Norbanus, riding leisurely to the base.

"General Mastanabal!" Norbanus called up to him. "It's good to see you again, after so long. Will you surrender? It's only a formality, you know. You're beaten. I am willing to spare your life."

Mastanabal snorted. "I'll not surrender to an enemy I have beaten before. Today the gods love you, Titus Norbanus. Perhaps we should have performed the *Tophet* before embarking on this war. No, between your yoke and my master's cross, I will choose honor instead." So saying, he drew his sword. Balancing atop the tower wall, he saw the Romans watching with great interest as he placed the point of his sword into his mouth. Then he toppled from the wall, headfirst. His blood showered Norbanus and made his horse shy. The other Carthaginian officers followed suit until all were dead. Only the Spartan remained on the tower, and he leaned over its parapet.

"I think we should talk, Roman," the Greek officer said.

Norbanus looked toward the south end of the wall, where the Greeks still held firm. His men were probing with long spears they had picked up, some of them rushing in and hacking at shields and spear shafts with pickaxes. He sent an officer with an order to pull back for a while.

"Can you negotiate for those Greeks? They are good soldiers."

"They will listen to me," said the Spartan. "I'm Xantippus."

"Then here are my terms, offered once. If they lay down their arms, they may live. Otherwise, I will kill every one of them."

"Does surrender mean slavery, or will you let them go home?"

"They will be free to go. If they will take service with me as auxilia, they may even keep their arms."

The Spartan seemed surprised. "That is very generous. Let me speak with them."

Norbanus rode though the gate, and Xantippus descended from the tower. He walked along beside Norbanus as they passed along the wall. Norbanus watched with interest as his men mopped up the last, desperate resistance. Most of the surviving mercenaries were at the river, fighting knee-deep in the water or trying to swim to the other side. But the Roman cavalry had already crossed and cut off escape for all but a very few.

The legionaries were in no mood for merciful gestures, and enemy warriors were seldom good slave material, so most were cut down where they stood and the wounded finished off on the ground with swift thrusts of pilum and *gladius*. The women of the camp, some with children in tow, were already being rounded up, as were the slaves, who now had new masters.

Across the river, Norbanus saw detachments of Mastanabal's former cavalry force splitting up and running, some with his own horsemen in pursuit. He would have preferred to bag all the cavalry as well, but there had been no possibility of shutting off all escape.

He rode to where the Greeks stood sullenly, weapons gripped in their fists, many of them bloodied. They had taken some casualties and had inflicted some as well, but in this sort of fight the casualties were usually light until one side lost its cohesiveness and broke formation. That was when the real slaughter began. He let Xantippus go and confer with the officers; then he addressed them.

"I am Titus Norbanus. I have just destroyed Mastanabal, as you have seen. I intend to do the same to Hamilcar, and to Carthage. But that is for the future. Right here and right now, you have a choice. We can make a fight of it, and it will be a hard one, and all of you will die, and some of us will, as well. You can lay down your arms and I promise none of you will be enslaved. Or you can take my oath, keep your arms and join my army as auxilia. You'll get no share of the loot from this fight, of course, but otherwise you will have the same status as the rest of my soldiers, short of citizenship. I am generous, but I am not patient. Decide quickly."

Xantippus and the other officers conferred in low voices; then they took a quick poll of the men. The Spartan spoke first: "We accept your offer of honorable service. We will be your faithful soldiers to the end."

"Then speak with my quartermaster and he will assign you your place in camp. I will make you all rich men."

In all, Norbanus reflected as he rode away, it was turning out to be a very fine day. But it got even better. As he sat in front of the late Carthaginian general's tent while the loot was piled up and tallied, a rider came from the coast on a lathered mount. He brought news from the *duumvir* Decimus Arrunteius: victory on the sea, that very same day! Wood spread through the camp and men congratulated one another on serving so lucky a general, such a favorite of the gods.

In the evening, Norbanus performed the proper sacrifices, then assembled all the men for the award ceremony.

He gave the *corona muralis* to a young officer who had been first to stand atop the wall, and the civic crown to several men who had saved the lives of fellow citizens in the fighting. Certain centurions he singled out for honor, bestowing upon them military bracelets. He was about to dismiss the formation when the senior centurion of one of his legions strode forth and stood below his reviewing stand. The man raised an arm and extended his fist toward his general.

"Imperator!" the grizzled officer shouted. "Imperator!"

The other soldiers took up the shout: "Imperator! Imperator!!" Slowly, it turned into a chant: "Im-per-a-tor! Im-per-a-tor! Im-per-a-tor!" On and on it went and Titus Norbanus felt himself to be a god. To be honored with the title of imperator by spontaneous acclamation of his own soldiers was the highest honor to which a Roman general could aspire. In a triumph he would be honored by the citizenry as a whole, but these were the men who counted.

Hamilcar and Carthage might still await, but this would never be taken from him. He let the intoxication flow through him as the chant went on and on and he knew what it was to be worshipped.

CHAPTER EIGHTEEN

THE SENATE HELD SILENCE WHILE PUBLIUS Gabinius read out the dispatches. They had arrived that morning, two of them at once, and both wreathed in laurel. It was a thing unprecedented in Roman history. First, he read the report of the *duumvir* Decimus Arrunteius. The senators gasped and broke into spontaneous clapping as he detailed the battle, the enemy ships destroyed, the loot taken. Otherwise, they remained quiet.

The princeps came to a momentous passage: "My marines and sailors behaved with uniform valor and discipline. I cannot commend their behavior too highly. Most of them are men from the towns and countryside of Italy, with only a few citizen legionaries to act as their officers. I believe that our Italian allies have rediscovered their manhood forfeited by their ancestors when ours accepted the Exile."

Gabinius looked around him. Some of the senators looked pleased to hear this; others did not. Hostility against the Italians went deep in this body. Most had agreed that the Italians should do the dangerous but menial work of rowing in the new fleet. Many had protested their bearing arms as marines. While sea service was inferior to that of the legions, it was honorable, and many believed the Italians had forfeited all claim to honor when they knuckled under to Carthage in the days of Hannibal the Great. But there had been no choice. They were embarked upon a war of unprecedented magnitude and every citizen was needed for the legions. If they were to have a fighting navy, the Italians had to be enrolled.

Next, Gabinius brought out the dispatch from Norbanus. This time the senators could not keep quiet. The faction that supported the Norbani cheered lustily, and even the old family adherents who despised them made sounds of approval, lest they seem churlish. The totality of the victory lost nothing in the telling, as young Norbanus detailed his ruse, his night march to the battlefield, his daring direct assault upon the Carthaginian camp and his novel assault plan, culminating in the suicide of Mastanabal and his principle officers, the destruction of his army and the sack of his camp. The loot was described in great detail, along with the information that the eagles and other standards captured at the disaster of the Arnus had been recaptured and were returning to Rome with an honor guard, to be deposited in the Temple of Saturn.

Finished, Gabinius closed the wooden case with a snap. "Senators, I propose that we declare ten days of thanksgiving for these great victories. The gods must be thanked properly."

A new family senator stood. "Ten days? These victories deserve a month of thanksgiving!"

Old Scipio Cyclops stepped forward. He had just returned from a tour of inspection in the South. "I agree with our princeps. These are fine victories and I rejoice that the standards have been taken back. But the main Carthaginian fleet is still afloat. The main Carthaginian army is still intact, under the personal command of Hamilcar. Carthage itself still stands. Let us not celebrate foolishly, when so much is left to be done."

"Sour grapes, Cyclops?" jeered the same new family senator. "You are just jealous because our new family commanders are winning glory while your grandson luxuriates in Alexandria, accomplishing nothing!"

Scipio looked at the man scornfully, his single eye glaring down his long nose. "Which one are you? Oh, yes, I remember. I believe I flogged your grandfather's blue-painted backside at the battle of Five Forks."

The senator went scarlet while half the Senate growled and the other half roared with laughter.

The Consul Hermanicus stood. "Gentlemen! Let's not disgrace these proceedings with partisan bickering. The Roman people expect better from us. I propose that we declare fifteen days of thanksgiving, to commence at once and to conclude with the dedication of the recaptured standards at the Temple of Saturn. I further move that the Italian communities that sent men to serve in the fleet be awarded with the status of *socii,* with full rights of citizenship to be conferred at the successful conclusion of the war, should their actions continue to prove as valorous as they were in this instance."

There was approval and disapproval. There was more arguing. But in the end the proposals carried. Then Herennius, followed by the rest of the Senate, went out into the Forum, mounted the Rostra and read out the dispatches to the assembled citizens, concluding with the actions declared by the Senate. With so many citizens away with the legions, ratification by the Plebeian Assembly and the Centuriate Assembly was impossible, but the tribunes of the plebs carried the vote by acclamation. The mood that had oppressed the city since the defeat at the Arnus lifted, and the name of Norbanus gained yet new luster.

It gave Gabinius much to think about as they all trooped up the winding Clivus Capitolinus, past the restored Archive, up to the crest of the Capitoline Hill. First the lictors with their fasces, preceding the senior magistrates—the consuls and the praetors—followed by the lesser officials, the priests, then the rest of the Senate, and last of all the great mass of citizens.

As they stood upon the great terrace before the Temple of Jupiter Optimus Maximus, Gabinius pondered upon this new phenomenon: the Roman warlord. For that was what they were, he knew. The younger Titus Norbanus with his fanatically loyal soldiers—men loyal to Norbanus himself rather than to Rome. His father, now with the other great military command, leading the new family bloc in the Senate and the assemblies and now sure to woo the Italian communities as they gained limited citizenship rights through military service. There was justice in that, Gabinius knew. It was the bullheaded members of his own peers, the old families, who were so stubbornly prejudiced against the Italians, as if a dispute between great-grandfathers had the same immediacy as the present war with Carthage.

And then there was young Scipio, who had no Roman soldiers at his command, but who was a potent force nonetheless. Gabinius had a great fondness for young Scipio and that whole remarkable, irascible family, but the boy was making his own foreign policy in Egypt and playing some dangerous game with the Princess Selene. And that redoubtable woman was playing manipulative games of her own. Word had long come back to Rome, whispered by his many enemies, of Scipio's dalliance with the Egyptian princess. There were strange stories of statues erected in villages and cities all up and down the Nile—statues of Marcus Scipio adorned with the curling ram's horns of Zeus-Ammon. These were attributes of divine kingship. Alexander the Great had had just such statues erected to himself, to remind people of his divine and royal status.

A Roman god-king? The idea was unthinkable! What had the boy got himself into? But the position of young Norbanus was far more worrying. As he looked about him, Gabinius could see how the people's faces lit up at mention of Norbanus, how they spoke that name with near reverence. He was acquiring something close to divine regard.

Gabinius tried to puzzle it out. Perhaps there was no explaining such things. The boy had come out of nowhere and wangled himself an unearned army command. He had performed a truly remarkable march that was little more than a plundering expedition, meddling in the affairs of Eastern kings. He had fought a cleverly managed battle and turned in a victory. And now the people thought he was a son of Mars. Men who had campaigned hard all their lives, fought in many battles, won greater victories and saved the Romans from dangers far greater, simply had not won such adulation from the citizens.

Young Norbanus, he knew, had some gift. It was a thing some men had and it could not be explained. It was something that made men want to serve him loyally, made others want to worship him, made them regard him as something more than human, whatever his real deserts. Alexander had had such a gift. The Macedonian golden boy had taken the superb army forged by his father and attacked the rotten, tottering old Persian Empire, and it fell into his hands like overripe fruit. He'd fought a few battles with the incredibly inept Darius and gained half the world, then had gone on a pointless march all the way to India, taking land he hadn't a prayer of governing. He'd acted like a drunken fool and murdered close friends, and in the end his own once fanatically loyal soldiers rebelled. Now, more than two hundred years later, men still worshipped him as a god.

For generations we fought Gauls and Germans to carve for ourselves an empire in the North, Gabinius thought. *For all those generations we brooded on the insult Carthage had done us and plotted our return. All we thought about was defeating barbarians and destroying Carthage. How ironic that now, on the verge of victory against all our foreign enemies and regaining our old empire on the Middle Sea, we should discover that the real threat, the real enemy, is Roman.*

MARCUS SCIPIO STUDIED THE MAP HE HAD ORDERED made. It depicted the whole world around the Middle Sea and what was known of the lands farther east: India and the land of the Silk People and the islands rumored to lie beyond. It showed Arabia and the land mass of Africa down to coastal Punt. It even had the legendary Tin Isles to the north. He had wanted a large map, perhaps ten feet wide and covering a wall. Selene had had it made in the typically overdone Alexandrian fashion, covering a floor fifty feet by one hundred feet, everything inlaid in mosaic. It was so large that he needed a platform made so that he could take it in all at once.

Just now, though, he didn't need the whole map. He was concentrating on Spain. Spain was where the next great chapter of this epic would unfold. As soon as word of the naval battle had arrived, the artisans had torn up a section of mosaic depicting that part of the sea and created a picture of hundreds of little ships fighting, sinking and burning. The site of the land battle was also marked, with a Roman sword wrapped in laurel.

"Where is Hamilcar?" Marcus fretted. He felt frustrated and impotent while all the important events were going on so far away.

"The latest word has him dallying at Cartago Nova," Selena said, not for the first time.

"Why is he waiting so long?" Marcus muttered.

"Isn't it obvious?" Flaccus said. "He wanted Mastanabal to soften up the Roman army first, so he declined to reinforce the man. What has he lost? A handful of Carthaginian officers and a great many barbarians. It is nothing to him and he is weakened in no way."

"Flaccus is right," Selene concurred. "I don't know how you Romans go about it, but in most of the world kings regard successful generals as dangerous rivals. Mastanabal won a battle against Rome, so his days were numbered. I was fairly certain that it would turn out this way."

"But that is infamous!" Marcus said. "What sort of loyalty can men have to such a sovereign? I detest Titus Norbanus, but never would I leave him and an army of Roman soldiers without support in the face of a strong enemy! No Roman commander could ever do such a thing!"

"Perhaps the rest of us cannot contest with the Romans on points of virtue," Selene said, sighing as the barb sailed right over Marcus's head, as usual. She had never met such a combination of intelligence and obtuseness as Marcus Scipio. She also caught Flaccus's grin and returned it with a smile of her own.

"They have to meet soon," Scipio said. "Where?" He studied the map. It showed the major rivers and mountain ranges, but gave no sense of any other terrain. In the great

Library he had studied the books concerning Spain, but those were concerned mainly with the coastal cities and had few tales of the peoples of the interior. The historians and geographers had never considered Spain to be a very interesting place.

"I don't know where," Flaccus said, "but I know who will choose the time and place: Norbanus. He won't wait, Marcus. He will be on top of Hamilcar before he knows it. Hamilcar is hesitant and cautious. Titus Norbanus is not. He loves action and he believes himself to be invincible."

"I agree," Scipio said, nodding. "He's bold and he'll move before anyone else has a chance to win glory. They may have fought already." That was what galled him the most: that great things were happening and he had no way of knowing about them until many days afterward. Even the swift new courier ships could travel only so fast, and they were as vulnerable to storms and calms as other vessels.

"I wish you would stop fretting here," Selene said to him.

"What?" He seemed to drag his thoughts from far away as he turned and looked at her. "What am I to do?"

"This isn't like you, Marcus," she said. "You always have a plan of action. Very well, if you lack one, I'll suggest one: Go attack Carthage."

Both men looked at her as if they had been struck by Jupiter's thunderbolts. "What?" Scipio said. "Unless you haven't noticed, I don't have an army."

"You don't have a *Roman* army," she said, "but I have rather a large one. It sits around eating up my substance without doing me any good, so you may as well take it and put it to some use. March it to Carthage with my blessing. Take all those toys you've been playing with at the Museum as well. At least they will make the war a fine spectacle, even if you lose. You've been saying for months that your legions are about to cross from Sicily to attack Carthage. If you go immediately, you might get there before they do, with Hamilcar and his army away from the city. That will do you no end of good at the next elections."

They gaped at her. "Majesty," Flaccus said at last, "are we to understand that you desire a full military alliance with Rome?"

"Of course it's an alliance!" she yelled. "Do you think I am going to let you take my army away as your personal property?" Then she added, more quietly: "Naturally, there is something I want from Rome in return."

"The Senate is to recognize you as full sovereign of Egypt," Marcus said. "You are queen, and your brother is deposed."

"I knew you were not as stupid as you sometimes pretend."

Flaccus whirled on his heel and strode off. "I'll get the papers ready right now. They'll be on their way to the Senate under your seal with the morning's first wind."

"There goes a man who understands things and does not waste time," she said, smiling.

"Selene," Scipio said, "I am overwhelmed."

She had never expected to hear this from the incomparably arrogant Roman. "I will be honest with you. As long as you are here, I am not queen. I am just another member of the court, playing power games. I want to be queen in truth and I want to be an ally in your own legal sense of the word. I can call upon you for aid and you can call on me, but I want Rome out of Egypt. I will do nothing against your interests but I want no Roman occupation. Agree to this, and my army is yours."

"I'll need your navy, too," he said.

She closed her eyes. "You Romans make my head hurt. You shall have the navy, too. And before you ask, you shall have all the material support of Egypt, which you know to be incomparable, for your use during the campaign. What allies I have in Libya will be yours as well. I'll even send along my best beasts for your sacrifices. Is that satisfactory?"

"Eminently, Majesty."

HAMILCAR STUDIED THE HEAD OF HIS LATE GENERAL, Mastanabal. It had arrived that morning by courier, under a flag of truce, packed neatly in a cedar box and preserved in aromatic oils. It was disfigured by the general's method of suicide, but was quite recognizable.

"If we had marched faster," Queen Teuta said, "this need not have happened."

"What need not have happened?" he said, still musing upon the ruined features, the faintly reproachful expression.

"The disaster, of course!" she said impatiently. "We have lost a fine army and many capable officers because we were too slow."

Her use of the word "we" did not escape his notice. "Disaster? The man was not worthy and his army consisted of nothing but hired scum. Where is the disaster in this? The naval battle was more costly. Ships are more expensive to replace than men. But it was a small affair." His scouts had rounded up a number of the surviving sailors and marines. They had spoken of the Roman innovations: the taller ships with their heavy timbers and their castles and *corvi*. Hamilcar had attended their interrogation closely before ordering that all of them be crucified.

"Now your army will be weaker when you confront Norbanus," she insisted. "It is weaker by several thousand men." The shofet astonished her. He seemed to be absolutely impervious to his folly. She began to doubt the wisdom of allying herself with him. His previous setbacks had been the workings of chance or bad luck, but this was a disaster of his own making. From the moment they crossed the Strait of Hercules, she had urged him to march with all possible speed, so that they could link up with Mastanabal and fall upon the Romans with their combined forces. Instead, he had dawdled, making one excuse after another. Now she could see that it was deliberate. He did not want to share the glory with a possible rival. Arrogance and willfulness she could forgive in a king, but not stupidity.

"Norbanus," he mused, seeming only to half-hear her. "That man needs to be humbled."

A letter had accompanied the general's head from the Roman.

> *From Titus Norbanus, proconsul of Rome, to Hamilcar, shofet of Carthage, greeting.*
>
> *Shofet, I rejoice that you and I will meet again so soon. I have found a splendid battleground, well watered and with plenty of room for both armies to camp. The ground is level, not too stony and with plenty of grass. Personally, I cannot think of a finer spot to add you and your army to my battle honors.*
>
> *Of course, certain formalities must be honored. I am charged by the Senate of Rome to order you to turn around and march your army back to Africa. Should you choose that course, I will follow you, but not too closely. I will not hinder your crossing of the Strait of Hercules.*
>
> *However, I know that you are a soldier and a man of spirit, so I fully expect you to choose honorable battle rather than ignominious retreat. I await your pleasure, here on this excellent field near the aptly named town of Cartago Nova.*

"He actually tells you that he has picked his ground for battle. Does he seriously expect that you will comply?"

"It would keep matters simple. A fight on level ground to decide the contest in a day. And to avoid battle might be taken for cowardice."

"You cannot mean it! Your ancestor Hannibal *never* let the Romans choose their own ground for fighting. On some occasions he retreated before them for days, until he found the ground that suited him, and *then* he fought, on ground and terms of his own choosing. Did anyone ever accuse Hannibal of cowardice for this?"

"My ancestor was glorious, but he never had numerical superiority. Always, his numbers were inferior. I have here a far larger army than Norbanus commands. And doubtless he lost many men in the fight with this fool." He waved contemptuously toward the oil-gleaming head.

"I think he lost very few," she said.

"No matter. Many or few, I will crush his contemptible legions and march on, destroying any Roman force that dares to defy me. Then I will destroy Rome, and I will not be as merciful as my ancestor was. I will pulverize every last stone of the city and I will kill or enslave every Roman in Italy. Then, when I am ready, I will march north, to their capital of Noricum, and destroy that and every other vestige of those misbegotten people."

"Excellent words," she said. "I think there are better ways to put them into effect."

"That will be enough. I will not have men saying that the shofet of Carthage is following the advice of a woman, even a queen and distinguished ally."

With an effort, she restrained herself from answering. She knew now that she had done her work too well. She had set out to convince him that he was the new Alexander and greater than Hannibal, and that his destiny and hers were linked. Now it seemed that he accepted the first part, but thought that she was somehow his inferior, a mere woman rather than a queen of more than mortal status. She would have to correct this.

TITUS NORBANUS RODE OVER THE BATTLEFIELD HE had chosen, and it was not for the first time. It looked level and consistent throughout, but this was not quite so. A narrow stream ran through it, and certain pieces of ground near the stream were boglike. He had had horses graze upon these patches, to crop the longer grasses down to the length of the rest. There were stony bits of ground, too. The stream itself was deceptively deep in spots. He had had it sounded along the whole length of the field, and knew exactly where all the deep spots were. When the time came for the battle, he would know the field intimately, and his enemy would not.

He looked southward along the stream. He could just make out the fine city of Cartago Nova. He had not bothered to besiege the city, nor had he even sent envoys to demand its surrender. He had an immediate use for that city, and it was not as mere loot. His officers were mystified by his actions, and he had not enlightened them. He had ordered his admiral to stand his fleet well up the coast, out of sight of the city with its fine harbor. This, too, puzzled everyone, and that was exactly how he wanted it.

Satisfied that he knew precisely the nature of the ground, he rode back to the Roman camp. He had ordered its rampart to be raised higher than usual, and had denuded a nearby hill of trees to construct its palisade. He wanted to give the appearance of a defensive posture.

He rode through the gate and along the *via principalis* to the praetorium, where he dismounted and passed inside. A slave took his helmet and others stripped off his armor so efficiently that he did not have to pause as he strode through the huge tent. He pushed aside a leapord-skin hanging and went within his women's quarters. Within, the two Judean princesses sat at a table, poring over their everlasting astrological charts. At his entrance they knelt and pressed their foreheads to the carpeted ground, an unusual thing to see from the proud sisters. He grasped a shoulder of each and raised them to their feet.

"Little princesses, what have the stars in store for me?"

"Master, we are sorely puzzled," Glaphyra said, her eyes downcast. "Until now, all our forecasts were favorable. Now something is wrong."

"Wrong? How? Do the stars say I will be defeated?"

"Not exactly," Roxana said. "But you must not fight tomorrow. The signs say that you will not win glory tomorrow."

"Is that all? Do not trouble yourselves. I expect Hamilcar to arrive this afternoon, and I will fight him tomorrow, and all will go as I have planned."

"Master!" Glaphyra gasped. "Do you not trust in our art and our gifts? You must not fight tomorrow!"

"I believe implicitly in your predictions and your mastery of your art. But, you see, all battles are not fought to win glory."

"We do not understand, Master," Roxana said.

"That is very good. You do not understand what I intend, and neither do my officers. That means that Hamilcar will never guess what I have in store for him."

That afternoon, Norbanus stood atop the battle tower he had had erected at the edge of the field. It was higher than usual, shaded with an awning and equipped with all the signaling gear he would require. As his scouts had foretold earlier that day, the army of Hamilcar was marching onto the far side of the field, regiment after massive regiment of them. With great interest, Norbanus studied the units as they arrived, peering through Selene's unique gift. As always, he marveled at how the device made distant things seem so much nearer. With it he could make out the details of standards, the shapes and colors of shields, making it easy to identify the units as they arrived and deployed to their camping sites.

This was very important, for he knew that the camping arrangement would correspond closely with their order of battle. Old Hannibal had made it a doctrine of Carthaginian military practice that, in deployment for battle, no unit should cross another's path of march unless it be for purposes of deception.

On the extreme left of the Carthaginian camp he saw Spaniards: famed not only for their savagery but for toughness and endurance. In the middle was a huge mass of Gauls. These were ferocious in the attack, but had a reputation for faltering if the first mad rush failed to carry the day. On Hamilcar's right, the southern end, the Greek and Macedonian professionals were setting up a neat and orderly camp. These were the principal nations, but many others were there as well, most of them skirmishers, slingers, archers and horsemen. They were men of Libya and Numidia, of the desert and nameless nations of the African interior. There were light cavalry of a sort he had never seen before: men in trousers and long-sleeved jackets and pointed caps. He guessed these might be the Illyrians. Norbanus paid them little attention. Controlling Hamilcar's main battle line was the key to tomorrow's fight.

"General," said Cato, "I make their numbers to be at least twice our strength."

"No matter. We've destroyed barbarian armies many times our own numbers before." He handed the magical little device to Niger, who snatched it and scanned the enemy camp feverishly.

"What I see over there isn't a great mob of disorganized tribesmen. Those are hard-bitten professional soldiers and warriors under tight discipline."

"If their strength doesn't bother you," Cato said, "what about the news that his navy showed up in the harbor of Cartago Nova this morning?" He jabbed a finger toward the city, just visible in the distance to the south. "Why didn't we take that town when it would have been easy?"

Norbanus sighed. "Because it did not suit my purposes. I have a plan for that city."

Niger handed the device over to Cato. "Perhaps it's time for you to explain just what that plan is."

"All in good time." Norbanus leaned over the railing and called for a herald. An olive wreath encircling his brow, the man appeared on the platform minutes later, draped in a white robe, holding a staff of hazelwood. "Go to the camp of Hamilcar," Norbanus instructed. "Extend to him my invitation to confer just before sunset at the stream. Neither of us is to be accompanied by more than two companions, the armies to remain in their camps." The herald repeated the message, bowed and left to deliver it.

"Don't go, General," Niger advised. "He'll do something treacherous. Let some of us go to deal with his officers."

"But that would be unworthy," Norbanus said. "And he won't do anything to besmirch the victory he is sure he will win. Now he's seen our army, and he has every confidence in his chances."

Niger closed the optical device with a horny palm. "He buggering well has a right to be confident."

That evening, as the sun lowered in the west, Norbanus rode out, accompanied only by Niger and Cato. His spectacular armor was freshly polished to reflect the rays of the setting sun and cast them back toward the enemy. His splendid cloak, Jonathan's gift, billowed out behind him. He rode a gleaming black stallion and was perfectly aware of the picture he made. His companions, more soberly attired, frowned, but as they approached the stream their faces smoothed into the impassive Roman mask, drilled into them since youth as the only proper expression to assume when dealing with foreigners.

Hamilcar arrived at the stream at the same time as the Romans. He, too, was splendidly arrayed, in golden boots, gold-embroidered purple tunic and robe. On his brow rested a circlet of gold attesting his royal status. Behind him rode an armor bearer who held his sword and helmet, in token of his military mission. Beside him rode a woman who was bizarre even to the now well-traveled Romans: a veritable Amazon with yellow hair and blue eyes and tattooed all over. She looked more like a goddess of some savage race than a proper companion for a civilized monarch.

"Greetings in the name of the noble Senate of Rome," Norbanus said. "I have not seen you in far too long, Shofet."

"You have come up in the world, Norbanus," Hamilcar said, taking in the lion-mask helmet and the abundance of royal purple the Roman general wore. "I would remind you that I was already at the crest of the world when you were still living in some obscure German fort."

"And this must be the famous Queen Teuta of Illyria, of

whom we have heard so much." He bowed slightly. "Greetings, Your Majesty. I rejoice to meet you at last."

She glared at him with the coldest eyes he had ever seen in a female face. "You are a jumped-up peasant from the North. Perhaps you are empowered to speak on behalf of your Senate, but do not presume to address us on your own behalf."

Norbanus smiled. "I believe I am here to confer with your ally, the Shofet Hamilcar."

Hamilcar radiated boredom. "Speak, Roman. It grows late."

"Well, then. Would you like to surrender to me now?"

"Don't be absurd!"

"I had to ask. Protocol, you know. Then shall we fight tomorrow?"

"Why should I fight at a time and in a place of your choosing?"

Norbanus made a show of looking all around. "Does this field not suit you? I couldn't find a better. It's level; there are no nearby hills to hide surprise reinforcements; there's a clear field of view for miles in all directions. If you know of a better place, I am willing to listen. As for the time, it makes little sense for us to sit here with our two camps glaring at each other, our men eating up all the food in the area and the horses devouring all the grass. More convenient all around to fight it out now."

"It hardly matters, since I will crush your contemptible little army in an hour."

"Tomorrow morning, then, at first light?"

Teuta snorted. "And fight with the sun in our eyes, like Mastanabal?" She ignored Hamilcar's irritated glance.

"Noon, then," Norbanus said. "With the sun at zenith, nobody will have the advantage."

"Tomorrow, then," Hamilcar said impatiently. "Tomorrow at noon I will destroy you, and the gods of Carthage will prevail over the gods of Rome."

"We'll be looking forward to it," Norbanus said. He made a sketchy but graceful double bow toward the shofet and the queen, then wheeled his mount and trotted away.

"The arrogance of that man!" Teuta said. "Did you see that helmet? It's the one Alexander wore in his portraits. He thinks well of himself.

"I did not fail to notice that little detail," Hamilcar said. "It is degrading to speak with such an upstart. At least Alexander was a king, and the son of a king, although of an obscure country."

Teuta forbore to snap back at that, knowing that Illyria was an obscure country. That man Norbanus intrigued her. She could not quite name what it was, but the Roman had something that Hamilcar lacked: some essential quality that raised him above the level of ordinary men. *What a pity this Norbanus comes of an upstart, soon-to-be-extinct nation instead of a great empire,* she thought. *And too bad his army is so small by comparison. Otherwise, I might have done better to choose him as my companion, rather than Hamilcar.*

The Roman party rode back toward the camp and discussed matters as they went.

"We'd better keep an eye on that wild woman," Cato advised. "She strikes me as twice the man Hamilcar is."

"So I noticed," Norbanus agreed. "Remember the story of Queen Artemisia of Halicarnassus at the battle of Salamis? The warrior-queens can give you a nasty surprise."

"Are you going to tell us what you intend now?" Niger demanded.

"Tonight. And I want no surprises tomorrow, so everyone is to be out on that field, in battle order, in silence as before.

It will mean a long, hot wait until noon, but I've given them two days of rest, so they'll be up to it."

On the next morning, at first light, Norbanus was again atop his command tower. Before him was ranged his army, the legions in neat, elongated rectangles, extended to keep Hamilcar's much larger army from overwhelming its flanks. It gave them very little depth, but Norbanus was confident in the Roman legionary's ability to hold formation, no matter how heavy the pressure.

On his extreme left, the southern end, were the Gauls and Spaniards that had joined him, hearing that this Roman was extremely clever and lucky, a clear favorite of the gods who could make his friends rich. To the extreme north was the formation upon which so much of the coming battle depended: the Greek and Macedonian mercenaries he had inherited from the defeated Mastanabal. They were specialists in close-order fighting. Unlike the Romans, they hurled no javelins and placed little reliance on the sword. Instead, they fought with overlapped shields and long spears, overcoming their enemy through the weight of their formation and their own iron discipline. Those men had a crucial role to play.

It did not bother him in the least that both armies included so many Gauls, Spaniards, Greeks and Macedonians. The civilized men were professionals, and the savages just didn't care. All of them fought among themselves constantly.

His men sat on the ground, their shields propped up by their spears, while the noncombatant slaves distributed breakfast. Norbanus knew that it was folly to send men into battle on empty stomachs. He watched through his optical glass as Hamilcar's army marched from its encampment in leisurely fashion, two hours before the sun reached zenith.

They took up their positions exactly as they had encamped: Hamilcar's Greek and Macedonian units on the south, facing Norbanus's Gauls and Spaniards, Hamilcar's own Gauls facing the legions, his Spaniards fronting the northernmost legion and the massive block of the Greek-Macedonian phalanx.

"Splendid!" Norbanus said, marveling as always at how much the gods loved him. "If he'd allowed me to make his dispositions myself, I couldn't have done a better job."

"Maybe," Niger grumbled. "But it still seems a strange way to fight a battle."

Norbanus turned and addressed the officers crowding the platform behind him: all his cohort commanders and the senior centurions. "Gentlemen, you will never see me fight a battle that looks other than strange. It's the key to winning."

"But general," said a grizzled old centurion, "this business of keeping the legions purely on the defensive—the boys won't like it, sir. It goes against their training and their instincts."

"They'll like it when the battle is over," Norbanus assured them. "Believe me, soldiers love it when you don't get them killed. If anybody has any doubts when all this is over, I will deliver a speech that will let them know what this is all about." He turned and saw that Hamilcar's army was finally in full array—a terrifying sight in its great numbers. "Now go to your places. You all know what to do. Just watch and listen for my signals."

In order of rank, the officers filed from the platform. Norbanus watched them rejoin their units, saw the men stand and take up their shields and pila. He savored the moment. This was where he would lay the foundations for his future. Up until now, he had built a reputation, first as a daring commander, then as a victorious general. Here, on this field, he would establish his true greatness. And he would do it by eschewing glory for once.

BY THE TIME THE SUN WAS HIGH, HAMILCAR HAD HIS own observation and command platform erected. It was not as high as the rather Spartan Roman construction, but it was far more splendid. Its fine wood was richly carved and inlaid with ivory and shell. It was draped with beautiful cloth and adorned with bronze tripods in which burned incense to fend off the disagreeable smells of battle. His own throne, and the slightly lower throne of Queen Teuta, were covered with the skins of rare animals. At the shofet's right hand stood an altar consecrated to the gods of Carthage.

Hamilcar had performed all the prayers and sacrifices; he had seen to the final dispositions of his troops, and now he was ready to observe the battle and enjoy the pleasures of victory.

Opposite him, on the far side of the stream, the Roman army was thinly stretched, grown attenuated as Norbanus extended his line to avoid outflanking. It only thinned at the center, where his own troops would punch through by their sheer weight.

"Why," Hamilcar mused, "did this man Norbanus choose such an exposed field? I have studied the old Roman tactics, you know. In the old days, a Roman commander, faced with an enemy so much larger, would anchor his flanks with a swamp or a rocky hill or other terrain that would make it difficult for the enemy to flank him. That way he could achieve maximum depth all along his line of battle. I think Norbanus is overrated."

"I don't doubt he fancies he has a surprise for us," Teuta said, "though I can't imagine what it might be."

"No matter." Hamilcar stood, a resplendent sight in his golden armor and crown-shaped helmet. An attendant handed him a golden spear and Hamilcar held it high, then slowly lowered it until it pointed toward the center of the Roman line.

The horns brayed and the drums thundered and an enormous shout rose from the huge army. With a great surge, it began to advance toward the enemy. In front of the rest, the missile troops went forth at a run, singing tribal war songs. The Romans stayed where they were. The missile troops ran into the stream and began to flounder across.

Teuta felt the first feathery touch of apprehension along her spine. "That stream is deeper than it looks."

Hamilcar shrugged. "As long as it is fordable, that means nothing."

The missile troops halted before the Roman lines and began raining arrows, javelins and lead sling-bullets among them. The Romans replied by raising their customary shield roof. The more lightly equipped Gauls and Spaniards suffered more, but most of them obeyed Norbanus's instructions and stayed in place. A few high-spirited warriors ran out and attacked on their own, to little effect.

"This is tedious," Hamilcar complained, watching the missiles fall upon the shields. As far as he could see, not a single Roman had been harmed.

"Let them keep up their fire," Teuta advised. "Their arms have to get tired. Soon gaps will appear and the arrows will get through."

"No, I've seen them practice this formation before, outside Carthage and in the siege at Alexandria. It would take too long. I will send my army in and finish this." He nodded to an officer, who called out to the trumpeters, and the call went out from them for the missile troops and skirmishers to fall back. These men scrambled to find gaps for themselves to fade back within the advancing ranks.

Now the shield roof came down and the Roman legions began to advance, very slowly and deliberately, keeping their lines strictly dressed, in what was almost a parade-ground maneuver. The cavalry force rode to the right flank next to the Greek-Macedonian block and, strangely, halted there, keeping up with the advance at a walking pace. Hamilcar's lead regiments entered the stream and trudged across, many stumbling, some falling, thrashing briefly as the men behind trod them under.

On the eastern side of the stream they paused to dress their lines. At this point the Roman army had halted, foot and horse, barely fifty paces away. The Romans stood in utter calm, making no war cries, sounding no trumpets; neither did they wave weapons aloft. Only at their southern flank was there any uproar, for the Gauls and Spaniards had a noisy way of displaying their warrior spirit, and they did not depart from it now. Their countrymen in Hamilcar's army made similar demonstration.

Their order restored, Hamilcar's men advanced at the double-quick, and so many of them were of warrior races that soon they were half-running. When twenty paces separated the two armies, the arms of the first three Roman ranks rocked back as one, then shot forward. The terrible, heavy, viciously barbed pila arched briefly skyward, then plunged downward with awful force, sending men tumbling, skewered, pierced, bleeding, to the ground. Men had their shields nailed to their bodies, their bodies pinned to the ground. So tightly were the men packed that scarcely a Roman spear failed to kill or wound an enemy soldier. The weight of the heavy javelin at such close range carried it through armor, helmet or shield. Even when a shield was stout enough to resist the weapon, it could not be dislodged, forcing its bearer to abandon it and fight henceforth unprotected.

For crucial moments the attack faltered as men fell and others tripped over the fallen. Shaken but confident and valiant, Hamilcar's men reordered themselves and prepared another charge. But the men behind them, still crossing the stream and unaware of what was happening ahead, pressed forward. Hamilcar's army grew very dense. Men were still waiting to step into the stream, the bottom of which was being churned to a deep, clinging mud.

Maddened, the bloodied warriors charged again. But during the lull, slaves and rear-rankers had passed more pila forward. Again, the arms of the first three ranks went back, shot forward and again men tumbled like wheat before the scythe. Slowed, many hurled lighter javelins of their own, but these were easily fended off by the large, heavy Roman shields.

After a shorter pause, the massive army resumed its advance and a third volley of pila fell among them. Now the front lines were barely twenty feet apart, but so many corpses and writhing, wounded men littering the ground slowed the advance to a crawl. Still, their anger and the terrible pressure from behind drove Hamilcar's men on.

Teuta was filled with a terrible apprehension. What sort of fighting was this? The army before them, small as it was, was like some sort of terrible machine. In moments she had seen thousands of men go down before the simple but devastating Roman javelin. And then it happened again and yet again and the mad rush was stalled, and the Romans had hardly lost a man yet. Now she saw the glitter all along the Roman lines as thousands of their short swords, worn so strangely on the right hip instead of the left, were drawn in a singular, upward-and-forward motion. Instantly, distracted though she was, she knew the reason for the strange carry and draw. *The man is not hindered by his shield and his draw does not disturb the men to either side. These people think of everything.*

And still the men were crossing the stream, churning the ground on the far side to mud, crowding the ranks against one another. The army was losing cohesion and turning into a mob. She looked north and saw that Norbanus's small cavalry force was confining its activities to keeping the much larger Carthaginian force from flanking the Greek contingent.

"Hamilcar," she said, her voice sounding hoarse in her own ears. "Stop your men from crossing the water. They can do no good and the pressure over there will not let up until the Romans begin to retreat."

The shofet just looked annoyed. "They will break very soon. Look, I am already victorious on the south."

She looked that way and indeed the Gauls there were being driven back in confusion by the orderly lines of the Greeks and the Macedonians. Soon they would flank the Romans at that end and roll up the line. This looked encouraging, but a nagging thought assailed her: *He knowingly left his south end weak and vulnerable. He did not take the city and port to the south. The road south is wide open. What can this mean?*

Then she was appalled to see Hamilcar order his reserve regiments across the stream, into the center. "Shofet! You tire your men to no cause!"

"That will be enough, woman!" he snapped. "They are engaged all along the front now. Soon the weight of my army will crush them underfoot!"

Frustrated, she sat and watched. It occurred to her that Hamilcar had not studied his battles as closely as he thought. His ancestor, Hannibal, had once won a battle something like this: beating a larger army with a smaller. That was Cannae, his greatest victory. She was sure that Norbanus was using some form of the Cannae strategy, but the battles were so dissimilar that she could not understand what he intended.

. She did see, plainly, that the Romans were not distressed by the vaunted "weight" of Hamilcar's army. Only the men of the front lines could engage actively. The Romans had a well-drilled maneuver by which, every few minutes, the front-line men stepped back and those behind them stepped forward, keeping fresh, untired men at the fighting line. If the rear men of Hamilcar's army pushed, they merely drove the front-line men into the Roman swords. At intervals, more of the murderous pila would arch out above the heads of the legionaries and plunge into the struggling mass of Hamilcar's men.

She saw men detach from the rear of the Roman formation, form a neat, orderly rectangle and march to the southern end of the Roman line, there to form a thickened, south-facing line just as Hamilcar's Greeks had their flanking maneuver almost concluded. The Gauls, caught between the two forces, were slaughtered. But the Roman line held. They inflicted few casualties on the orderly Greeks, but the phalanx was stymied.

Teuta stood and paced before the glowering shofet. She saw how long her shadow had grown and turned to look at the sun. She was amazed to see how low it stood in the west. To the north she saw a new movement. The block of Norbanus's Greek-Macedonian phalanx was moving, pushing against the lightly armored Iberians, shoving them back, spearing them, striding over their bodies. Already, men were breaking away from the battle, frustrated at being unable to come to grips with the Romans, unable to take heads and win glory. Slowly, a step at a time, the Greeks were cutting themselves a strong position at Hamilcar's left flank.

"Look!" she said, grasping the shofet by the shoulder and shaking him. "You are being flanked!"

He shook off her hand. "They can accomplish nothing! There are not enough of them."

She knew now that Hamilcar was seeing only the ideal battle in his head, the battle that he wanted to see. Immediately, she determined to extricate her men from this disaster. Hamilcar did not even glance in her direction as she walked to the rear of the platform and leapt upon her horse. Her bodyguard rode behind her as she pelted northward, toward the cavalry action. Beside her rode her standard-bearer. Atop a long pole he bore a golden dragon, its long, waving tail a silken tube that filled with air as he galloped, making the queen conspicuous to her men.

She rode through thousands of wounded men, seeking to put distance between themselves and the battle. She saw that not all were wounded. Idly, she axed a few of these deserters down when they strayed too near. She did not plan to stay on this field, but neither was she deserting. She knew when it was time to withdraw an army to fight another day.

She found her men engaging the Roman cavalry. They were greatly frustrated that the smaller Roman force refused to engage them in a mass and obligingly allow themselves to be slaughtered. Teuta shouted and her trumpeter sounded his horn, and swiftly, the Illyrian horsemen rallied to their queen's banner.

"Come with me!" she yelled to them. "You are needed in the south!" Without question they obeyed, ignoring the dismayed cries and jeers of the other cavalry. They followed their queen, not some foreign king. They cared nothing for his hired lackeys and their fate.

While they assembled, she studied the progress of the battle. The Greeks at this end were now at the stream, able to spear with contemptuous ease the men still trying to cross. When their enemy gave up and ceased trying to cross, the Greeks raised their spears upright, then performed an elegant left-facing maneuver and lowered their spears once again. This time the formation, and its spears, faced south. Then the Greeks began their slow, inexorable push.

They have us boxed! she thought. *There is no way out but south.* Now she could see what Norbanus intended. *Why* he was doing it remained a mystery. With her men behind her, she made a wide half circle around the now-disintegrating army. Whole units were pulling away and retreating to the west, unwilling to cross the stream into what was now nothing more than a slaughter yard. *With just a few more men, he could have bagged this whole army,* she realized. Yet another doubt assailed her on this day full of doubts. She had a suspicion that the utter destruction of the Carthaginian army and its shofet was the last thing Norbanus wanted. But why?

She found Hamilcar pacing on his platform. His face was worried, his glance straying every few seconds to the city on the southern horizon. She dismounted and climbed to the carpeted deck. "Hamilcar," she said quietly. "It is time to go. You are doing nothing to harm them. You still have the bulk of your army. Break off and retreat. Fight this man somewhere else, some other time. You won't beat him here, today, no matter how many men you sacrifice."

"It cannot be!" he cried. "He has a paltry little army and I have a great host. He should be at my feet begging for his life!"

"That is not going to happen. If you stay here, he will grind all your men to blood sausage and then it will be your turn to beg. Get away from here, now!"

Abruptly, his face went slack. "How did this happen?" he said with little expression.

"You allowed him first to destroy the army of Mastanabal, that otherwise would have been here this day, making you truly invincible. You allowed Norbanus to choose the time and the ground for this battle, then you gave him all the time he needed to make his preparations." She saw no reason for merciful words. Now she was sure that she had chosen the wrong man. Perhaps that could be rectified. In the meantime, it was up to her to salvage what she could from this debacle.

He said nothing for a while, then: "You are wise. I should have listened to you."

She nodded. Perhaps he was beginning to show some sense.

"But that cannot be all of it," he said further. "I must have offended the gods in some fashion. When I return to Carthage, I shall order a *Tophet*. The children of the highest families of Carthage shall be sacrificed in the fires of Baal-Hammon."

She rolled her eyes. Like every other man who could not face the reality of his own failure, he was passing responsibility to the gods. "Then let us go now. Back the way we came. The Romans will pause here to loot your camp. With your men reorganized, we can make a fighting retreat."

"No," Hamilcar said. "Do you not see that the way south is unimpeded? My fleet is in the harbor of Cartago Nova. We will take ship from there."

"Notice?" she said, frustrated. "I've been noticing it all day! He left Cartago Nova untouched! He put his weakest forces on his south flank, opposite your strongest! His Macedonian phalanx is pressing your men southward! In the name of all the gods, Hamilcar, can't you see when you are being *herded*?" She all but screamed the last word.

Oddly, he took no offense at her tone. He pointed to the mass of Gauls and Iberians now trudging westward, away from the battlefield. "Those men will regain their spirit and their senses soon. It will occur to them that they can curry favor with Rome by attacking us. It will be that way all the long road to the Strait of Hercules. I can rely only on my Greek professionals, and I do not have enough of them."

She calmed herself. His words were not without sense. At least that was something. "Very well. But we don't wait and try to defend Cartago Nova. He's already thought of that and has something planned. I don't care about the rest of your army. I want my men and their horses embarked on the first transports, along with you and me. We don't wait for the rest of the army to go. We leave as soon as we're aboard. The rest can follow, if they can contrive to. You can raise another army when we get to Carthage."

A dusty, bloody man climbed the steps to the platform. It was Euximenes, the commander of the Greeks. "Shofet," he said, "we've won our part of the field, but everywhere else is chaos. My men are in good order and haven't taken many casualties. Let us get you out of here. There is no time to waste." He looked back and forth between the two, as if unsure where his orders were to come from.

"Prepare a retreat to Cartago Nova, Commander," Hamilcar said, sounding firm and decisive again.

"Then if Your Majesties will come with me, you'll be safest among my men."

The two mounted, and surrounded by Hamilcar's honor guard and Teuta's Illyrians, they crossed the stream and joined the solid, orderly mass of the Greek-Macedonian mercenaries. The officers called their orders, and the standards waved and the trumpets sounded. They turned southward and walked away from the field. Behind them, the survivors of the army followed them, some throwing away shields and stripping off armor to move more easily. Far in their rear, the other phalanx kept up its steady pressure. The Roman legions had not advanced a step from the battle line they had established at the outset of the fight.

ATOP HIS OWN HIGH TOWER, NORBANUS WATCHED them go. His highest officers stood with him. Although they understood everything that had happened, they were still amazed.

"General, we could still bag the lot and finish this," Cato said, his fingers working feverishly on his sword grip.

"Finish what?" said Norbanus. "Finish this battle? It is finished. Killing every man out there, including Hamilcar, would not finish the war. Another war, perhaps, but not this one, because we have sword to destroy Carthage utterly and Carthage still stands. That is why we will now invest Cartago Nova, but we will not hinder his escape."

"It seems a pity just to let him go," said the commander of one of the new legions, one of the younger Caesars.

"Long ago," Norbanus explained, "a defeated shofet could be crucified. But old Hannibal put an end to that. He abolished the republic and made the shofet a true king. If we kill Hamilcar now, as we easily could, who knows what might happen? He has no heir. The Council of One Hundred might choose a really capable man to lead them. They could raise up another Hannibal. But as I have arranged things, when we arrive before the walls of Carthage, who do you think will be in charge there?" He looked around at them, smiling. "Why, none other than Hamilcar Barca, the man whose fat backside we've just flogged bloody and sent running back to Africa!"

The men on the tower laughed uproariously, that swords-on-shields Roman laugh that struck terror into other nations. "General," Niger said, pointing to the natives who had abandoned Hamilcar and now fled westward, "shall we send out men to kill those fleeing savages?"

"No," Norbanus said. "I will treat with them later. They'll listen to me, because today they saw us accomplish the impossible. They will have the choice of being slaves or being allies of Rome. It will be the same choice the rest of the world will have, and I think they'll choose wisely. We can add their numbers to our army as we continue our march. There's nothing wrong with them as warriors. They were just badly led and they know it."

Now the officers looked at one another blankly with the same question in all their minds: *Continue* this already endless march?

That night, encamped outside the walls of Cartago Nova, Norbanus addressed his men, who were sorely puzzled about the events of the day—exhilarated by the victory that had cost so few of their lives, but baffled by its strange incompleteness.

"My soldiers," Norbanus began, "today you have won a great victory, one that shall shine in the annals of Roman history. Twice I have led you against the armies of Carthage. Twice I have crowned your standards with laurel!" He paused to let them cheer. "Today we could have annihilated that army whose numbers were so much greater than our own. It would have been glorious. It would have been satisfying. But it would have been foolish."

His men were silent, waiting for him to explain this enigma.

"Suppose we had wiped them out. What then? A great mass of Gauls and Iberians of all sorts would have been slaughtered. Hamilcar would have ridden away on his swiftest horse, or perhaps he would have been killed, and to what end? *Carthage* would have suffered little, and it is *Carthage* we have come so far to destroy!

"Carthage is not like Rome! Carthage does not send forth armies of its best, of its citizens. Carthage is rich in gold, and with this gold Carthage hires great masses of foreigners, and if they are wiped out, Carthage suffers little for it, because the hired soldiers are doled out only a pittance until the end of the war, when they are paid off." His men booed and jeered at the idea of such unmanly warmaking, of citizens so lacking in pride that they did not take up arms to fight their country's wars.

"So we will let this failure, this whipped dog, go back to Carthage to conduct its defense. We have nothing to fear from this man, this unworthy descendant of the great Hannibal. So, as soon as his ships have departed, to be shadowed by my own fleet, we shall resume our march. We will go west to the Pillars of Hercules and cross to Africa. And when we cross, we march on Carthage. And when we get to Carthage, we'll have done something nobody has ever done before. My veteran legions, who have been with me since the Alexandrian campaign, will have marched clear around the Middle Sea, making it Our Sea once again. How does that sound?" He gazed around at their silent, stunned faces, and he broke into a broad, orator's grin, so that his teeth reflected the torchlight to the men in the farthest ranks.

"I know. Sounds like a long, buggering walk and nothing

to show for it but the bragging rights, eh? But listen to me, and I will tell you how you will be rewarded and exalted over all other citizens. Have any of you given thought to what you will do after this war is over?" More silence, but he knew he had their full attention.

"I can tell you. We will celebrate a fine triumph in Rome. You will get a vote of thanks from the Senate and the people. And that is all. For so long have we concentrated upon destroying Carthage, that we've given no thought to what happens next. I tell you, my soldiers, that when Carthage is nothing but smoke in the skies and rock dust at our feet, the noble Senate will have no further use for most of you. You, who have given so much to the state, will have nothing!" He watched their expressions of puzzlement turn to concern, then anger.

"Yes, those who were on the first part of this march did well. There was plenty of loot to be had. But what of the rest of you, and the others who will join us in destroying Carthage? Is there land for you to retire to? Not in Italy! And why not? You know very well. When Rome crossed the Alps and retook Italy, the first thing the old families did was to lay claim to their ancestral lands, which comprised most of Italy! All the finest, most fertile lands of the peninsula went right back to those families that claimed to have owned them before the Exile! None was left for the new family men, the men those old senatorial families so desperately needed to take those lands back for them. They would cast you off like an old, broken sword as soon as they had no further use for you!" Now there were grumbles and shouts of protest. Behind Norbanus, his senior officers looked at one another uneasily. This was beginning to sound ominous. Was their commander going to propose war on the Senate?

"I will not allow this to happen!" Norbanus shouted, silencing the grumblers. "The soldiers of Rome, the very backbone of our new empire, must not go unrewarded! If you stay with me, if you swear an oath to support me against all rivals, I will force the Senate's hand. At my demand, there will be rich lands for all of you in Africa. We will not allow the old families, those senators who are already unthinkably rich, to divide up the former possessions of Carthage among them. Those of you who joined us in Italy, ask the men of my old legions what those lands are like. They marched through them from Carthage to Alexandria. They are lands as fine, as fertile and well watered as any in Italy, lands where grain and grape and olive grow in abundance. The natives are docile and industrious and will make excellent slaves to work that land for you." He watched their faces as they lit up with hope, with determination, with greed. He knew now that he had them.

"You men know how these things work. You are citizens and voters. We will make the marches and do the fighting. We will fight our way to the very gates of Carthage. We will have the war all but won. And then what will happen? Why, the Senate, that glorious body of old men, will send out one of their own to take over command. They will set me aside and put some fat-bottomed old politician over *you*, the hardest-fighting army Rome has ever seen, so that some old family time-server can be in on the kill and claim all the loot. Are you going to let this happen?" First the men grumbled, then they shouted, "No! Never!"

Niger turned to Cato and said in a low voice: "I thought he had already extorted this command from the Senate. That he and his father were to have control of the war until its conclusion."

Cato, more politically astute than his friend, answered: "These men don't understand senatorial politics. They just know that their vote doesn't count for much. He's making them co-conspirators with him. When the time comes, they will back him against the Senate itself."

"But will *we* back him then?" Niger asked, deeply disturbed.

"That will depend upon where our interests lie. This is the new age. We will never betray Rome. But this is a new Rome. Will we side with the Rome of the Senate and the old families? Or with the new Rome of Titus Norbanus? We will have to see when we stand before the gates of Carthage. In the meantime, I suggest that we take direction from those men out there. Let's agree with what they decide, if we value our lives."

Lentulus Niger nodded, but he was still unsettled. Things were changing too fast. He had begun this campaign when Rome was united in purpose, in devotion to the will of the gods and in obligation to the revered ancestors. Now it was breaking up into the squabbles of rival families, of rival voting blocs, of old and new families, of—he could think of no other term—rival *warlords*.

The soldiers made their decision plain. Once again, they chanted: "Im-per-a-tor! Im-per-a-tor! Im-per-a-tor!"

EPILOGUE

The town was called Thapsus. It was a tributary of Carthage, located on the Mare Internum south of the great city. It had been holding out for a number of days, but Marcus Scipio did not expect it to last much longer. The defense was halfhearted. These people had no reason to love Carthage—a brutal mistress to all its subjects. But the citizens were in the habit of fearing Carthage, and its terrible punishments for disloyalty.

Well, Marcus thought, *we'll just have to teach them to fear Rome instead.*

The lesson in terror was already well under way. The army encamped outside their walls had been frightening enough, if rather conventional. But the citizens had seen the ships in their harbor sunk by the weird underwater rams Scipio had brought. They were not seaworthy and had been carried on the decks of huge transport galleys.

The flying men had sown even more panic, though they

were unable to do any actual harm. Marcus had thought of giving them incendiary pots to drop on buildings of the city, but Flaccus had dissuaded him, pointing out that the damage would be slight and would actually lessen the fear felt by the citizens of Thapsus. The terror inspired by flying men was enough. So every day they swooped low over the walls of the city, filling all and sundry with awe. If these Romans could make men fly, what could they not do?

The army provided Scipio by Selene was excellent, if not quite up to legionary standards. They were solid professionals, and he spent his days drilling them in Roman-style tactics so that when the time came, they would be ready to mesh with the legions converging upon Carthage.

Of far more concern to him than the weakening resolve of Thapsus was the word that had come to him that morning by one of his swift intelligence cutters. The two eccentric Greek philosophers had come to his command tent with the story of Norbanus's remarkable battle, and of his no less ominous speech to the soldiers afterward.

"Do you think he's making a bid for the dictatorship?" he asked Flaccus.

"He'd better, if he wants to save his head. The Senate will see him as nothing but a tyrant in the making now, because he's challenged their privileges. It's brilliant, you know."

"All too well," Scipio agreed. "All the more so because he's absolutely right. He foresaw what would happen to those soldiers and he turned it to his own purposes. They don't serve Rome now. They serve him. He will be their benefactor and they will be his private army. And there's more."

"What else?" Flaccus asked. He had put on weight in Egypt, and when they set out, he had had to let out the straps of his cuirass to accommodate his expanded girth. Now, after weeks of rigorous campaigning, it almost fit again.

"He spoke to them of Africa, so as not to inflame the Senate utterly. But you and I know he was thinking of Egypt. If he can take Egypt, he'll be the richest and most powerful man in the world. We have to keep Egypt out of his hands—out of *any* Roman hands. We can't allow that sort of concentration of wealth and power in one man. From now on, Rome must support Selene and the House of Ptolemy, but from a distance."

Flaccus scratched his head, itchy from wearing his helmet all day. "We weren't thinking about this sort of thing when we crossed the Alps, were we?"

"We were not. Sometimes I wish we had stayed in Noricum and forgot about regaining our old empire. This may cost us what made us good Romans in the first place."

Flaccus shrugged. "I don't want to remain in the cold North anymore. I've gotten used to the good life on the sea. Besides, there's no help for it. This was clearly the will of the gods. The times have changed. Rome and we will just have to accommodate to the new world."

"So we must," Marcus agreed. Once more he looked at the papyrus the Greeks had given him. It was a personal letter to him from Titus Norbanus, and very brief. He read the few words again:

I will meet you at the walls of Carthage. Let the gods decide there.

John Maddox Roberts

HANNIBAL'S CHILDREN

Enter a world in which Rome fell to Carthage—then rose again.

215 B.C. The Third Punic War has left Rome defeated and in ruins. Under the leadership of the legendary Hannibal, the Carthaginian troops are prepared to slaughter their enemies. Instead, Hannibal gives his adversaries a choice: exile or extermination. But in doing so, he has made a grave miscalculation.

100 B.C. In exile for one hundred and fifteen years, the Romans are about to re-emerge—stronger and more powerful than ever—in an ultimate battle for supremacy.

"His knowledge of the period is unassailable."
—*Publishers Weekly*

"A fascinating alternate history novel... the reader is immersed in the culture of Rome."
—*Midwest Book Review*

0-441-01038-5

Available wherever books are sold or at penguin.com

THE ULTIMATE IN
SCIENCE FICTION AND FANTASY!

From magical tales of distant worlds to stories of
technological advances beyond the grasp of man, Penguin has
everything you need to stretch your imagination to its limits.
Sign up for a monthly in-box delivery of
one of three newsletters at

penguin.com

ACE
Get the latest information on favorites like
William Gibson, T.A. Barron, Brian Jacques,
Ursula Le Guin, Sharon Shinn, and Charlaine Harris,
as well as updates on the best new authors.

Roc
Escape with Harry Turtledove, Anne Bishop,
S.M. Stirling, Simon Green, Chris Bunch, and many
others—plus news on the latest and hottest in
science fiction and fantasy.

DAW
Mercedes Lackey, Kristen Britain, Tanya Huff,
Tad Williams, C.J. Cherryh, and many more—
DAW has something to satisfy the cravings of any
science fiction and fantasy lover.
Also visit dawbooks.com.

*Sign up, and have the best of science fiction
and fantasy at your fingertips!*